LETHAL SEX

A famous medical researcher suddenly falls over dead, leaving his mistress stunned . . . a superstar actor dies mysteriously after a weekend of wild lovemaking . . . a prominent U.S. Senator becomes deathly ill after a one-night stand . . . a playboy doctor meets a violent end after a fabulous fling with a sexy salesgirl. They all die hideously after a spectacular sexual experience.

Something very strange is going on. And Kris Erlanger, a beautiful investigative reporter, risks her life to expose the terrifying secret. The nightmarish truth is far more horrible than anything she could have imagined. . . .

DOUBLE-BLINDED

Medical Thrillers from SIGNET

DOUBLE-BLINDED

LESLIE ALAN HORVITZ and H. HARRIS GERHARD, M.D.

A SIGNET BOOK

NEW AMERICAN LIBRARY

NAL BOOKS ARE AVAILABLE AT QUANTITY DISCOUNTS WHEN USED TO PROMOTE PRODUCTS OR SERVICES. FOR INFORMATION PLEASE WRITE TO PREMIUM MARKETING DIVISION, NEW AMERICAN LIBRARY, 1633 BROADWAY, NEW YORK, NEW YORK 10019.

SIGNET, SIGNET CLASSIC, MENTOR, PLUME, MERIDIAN AND NAL BOOKS are published by
New American Library,
1633 Broadway,
New York, New York 10019

First Printing, September, 1984

1 2 3 4 5 6 7 8 9

PRINTED IN THE UNITED STATES OF AMERICA

She loved the games men played with death
  Where death must win . . .

—SWINBURNE

[Woman] knows that masculine morality, as it concerns her, is a vast hoax. Man pompously thunders forth his code of virtue and honor; but in secret he invites her to disobey it, and he even counts on this disobedience; without it, all that splendid facade behind which he takes cover would collapse.

—SIMONE DE BEAUVOIR

A young man about to be wed places his ring in mockery on the finger of a recently dug up bronze statue of Venus; this statue bears the inscription "*Cave Amantem*"—"Beware of the lover" or: "Fear her if she loves you." He finds to his dismay that he cannot remove the ring from the finger of the statue and proceeds to his wedding with dire forebodings. As he enters the bridal chamber, the statue is waiting for him in bed. The next morning he is found dead, the bride insane.

—WOLFGANG LEDERER, *Men's
Fear of Women* (after a story
by Prosper Merimée, cited
by O. Brachfeld)

PART ONE

AFTER A WEEK HAD PASSED Helen Voyles telephoned Rollins Hazard at his office.

His secretary informed her he wasn't in that day and could be reached at home.

Helen knew that he had a wife and that he might be angry with her if she called. But she needed to see him. After what had happened to the other two men, she could not allow rules of etiquette—whatever rules of etiquette governed brief affairs in anonymous hotel rooms—to interfere with her plans.

She decided that if she heard a woman's voice on the other end she would hang up and try again in another hour.

But Hazard answered. His voice sounded groggy, as if he'd just woken up. She identified herself, because she didn't know whether he would recognize her voice.

"I didn't expect to hear from you," he said.

"Well, here I am. How are you?"

He hesitated. "A bit under the weather, I'm afraid."

"Could we meet?"

"Meet?" The very idea seemed to amaze him. "Yes, I suppose so. Let me check my calender."

"No, I mean today. Could we meet today?" She glanced at her watch. It was just a little after two. "How about in an hour? I'm on Beach Street, but we can meet anywhere. I can even come to your place."

"No, not here. Not here."

Either his wife was there with him or would be back shortly.

"Wherever you say, then, Rollins."

He took a long time to respond. "All right, but it can't be for long." He named a restaurant on Polk Street and said he'd be there by three-thirty.

The restaurant in the middle of the afternoon was practically empty. It also had the advantage of being dark and, from what Helen could see, was favored by a predominantly homosexual clientele. A perfect setting for a couple enjoying an illicit affair; certainly this was not a place where anyone was likely to be acquainted with the chief of immunology at Coleman Memorial. And there was hardly any chance that anyone would know her, since she was only a visitor to San Francisco.

Not that it mattered. It was unimportant to her whether someone recognized her or not.

He was late, and when he entered the restaurant, he blinked several times in an effort to accustom himself to the sudden absence of light.

She noted that his gait was unsteady; he walked like someone who has had one too many. Sweat was trickling down his face and neck, staining his collar with dark blotches. He was a man of fifty, vigorous, with well-toned muscles, and his face was virtually unlined; but now, in the subdued lighting of the restaurant, he looked every bit his age. His face was slack, his eyes bulged, and when he came close to her, she noticed that they'd turned yellowish.

She didn't want to kiss him, but she was anxious not to offend him.

His breath was stale. It smelled of death.

"You're looking well," he said, taking a seat across from her.

She thought that he might be mocking her, then realized he was not.

In some way, she had never looked better. The West Coast sun had burnished her with a flattering tan which also served to emphasize her gray-green eyes. At the age of sixteen she'd resigned herself to never becoming beautiful, but she was striking, long-limbed, with sharp features that hinted at both intelligence and a wild, impulsive nature.

This afternoon, even in this restaurant, she kept her eyes from view, concealed behind expensive owl-rimmed sunglasses. She did not want anyone, least of all Rollins, to see that she'd been crying.

He ordered a double Scotch. "Think I'm coming down with a cold," he muttered.

She nodded. She knew what this meant, but would not say a word about it.

"You know," he continued, "I'm happy that you called. I didn't think I'd miss you."

"But you did."

She was not surprised. She was a doctor, a scientist, but for all of her intellectual acuity, she could never understand what drew men to her. There were women with great looks who found themselves always alone. Her problem was keeping men away. She wished that she could have fallen in love with one man and stayed with him, but it was too late for that.

She was only thirty-two, but it was already too late.

When she regarded Rollins Hazard, it was with sadness, but she realized that the sadness didn't have very much to do with him. It was a sadness for herself, for all that had happened, for all the opportunities wasted.

"How've you been spending your time here? I thought, after the conference, you'd have gone back to New York," he said.

It was at a conference on genetic engineering where they'd met, in the middle of a cocktail party at the Hyatt Regency. Helen had only come over to say hello on behalf of an old colleague of Hazard's, but it had gone much further than hello.

"I decided to take a vacation," she said.

The vacation had been spent with another man she'd met at the conference—Douglas Rosen.

Douglas Rosen was dead.

"A vacation," he said. It was as if the word were new to him. "And have you been in touch with Leo?"

Leo was Leo Heisler, Hazard's former colleague and for the last five years, Helen's boss.

She shook her head. "I told you, I was on vacation. I didn't want to talk to anyone in New York, least of all Leo."

Until they'd had a chance to speak, she had had no idea that Hazard despised Heisler as much as he did. They'd worked together at an army base called Fort Detrick. There, during the early 1970s, the two had collaborated on biochemical experiments, attempting to find cures for diseases like Lassa fever and Green-Monkey disease. There, too, they'd created diseases for the army to use in the event of all-out war.

According to Hazard, Heisler had plagiarized the work of others, even some far less brilliant than he. Hazard was among his victims.

"Leo always wins in the end. He knows how to play politics. Something I never learned," he admitted.

She didn't doubt Hazard for a moment. Heisler had done the same thing to her; she should have left him a long time ago. Perhaps it was because they'd suffered from the same plight, been exploited by the same man, that Helen had seduced Hazard.

She was never attracted to him—she just felt sorry for him. And he'd been ready to be seduced. His marriage was empty; he might not have known it, but she could tell right off. She knew all about empty marriages.

"I could kill him . . ." he mumbled.

She looked up. With the tinted lenses, Hazard looked incorporeal, a shadowy presence sitting across from her. "Who?" Then she realized he meant Heisler. "But you won't. People always want to kill Leo, and never do."

"There's no way to get to him." He groaned. It seemed

for a moment that something had broken apart inside him. "I didn't mean that literally. I couldn't kill him. But it would be a pleasure to see him destroyed."

"Are you all right?" she asked, understanding at once that he could not be.

His eyes squeezed tight in pain.

He breathed deeply, opened his eyes again. "It'll pass."

She nodded. He finished his drink and ordered another. It was possible he had the mistaken impression that the Scotch would alleviate his misery.

"Why did you want to see me?" he asked.

"I don't know. I just did. I like you. Isn't that reason enough?"

Shrugging, he said, "I have no idea. I've never met a woman like you before. On the other hand, I never had a . . . a fling before. So I don't know how one is supposed to behave in such cases."

"Like yourself." She smiled.

He ran his tongue over his lips, which had become caked with a yellowish gunk of some kind. "You'll excuse me."

When he rose from the table it was necessary for him to hold on to the back of his chair for support. "I think I drank too fast," he said.

Watching him stagger toward the men's room, she thought: He's acting just like the others.

She considered waiting for his return, out of politeness, but what would be the sense of that? She'd found out what she'd wanted to. Found out too much, actually.

Leaving enough cash to pay for both their drinks, she quickly got up from the table and strode out of the restaurant, barely eliciting a glance from the bartender on duty.

Five minutes later Rollins Hazard emerged from the men's room, peered into the dimness for Helen. His vision was blurring and he might have thought she was there but that he just couldn't make her out.

As he walked toward the table, he crashed into a chair and sent it toppling noisily to the floor. "Sir?" he heard someone say, but he couldn't see who it was.

Everything was out of focus no matter how hard he struggled to see. Where was Helen? He called out her name, but he couldn't be certain he'd made himself heard.

Overcome by a wave of nausea, he tottered forward, his hand sweeping along the top of a table. A glass fell to the floor, broke apart.

He felt a hand gripping his arm as if to steady him. The blood drained from his head, and then he collapsed to the floor. He did not get up.

Later one of the police officers accompanying the ambulance asked if he'd been alone. When told there had been a woman with him, the officer asked if anyone knew who she was.

But no one knew anything about her. She was just a woman who wore a white dress and dark glasses and hadn't wanted to stick around.

THE LATE-NIGHT OPERATOR in the midtown offices of *America Now* was accustomed to desperate callers, to people all across the country who believed that they had information of critical importance that should be revealed at once to the world. It got worse on nights when there was a full moon. Then the callers demanded immediate attention from the editor-in-chief himself, saying that they knew for certain that the government was covering up the presence of flying saucers over the Midwest or was actively conspiring to turn the United States over to the Communists.

But seldom in the time she'd been employed at the switchboard at *America Now* ("Serving All America All the Time") had she heard someone sound so hysterical as on the night of February 9. It was a woman who sounded like she was in her late twenties or thirties. She asked to speak to Kris Erlanger.

"It's urgent. Tell her that I have to talk to her now."

The operator, an even-tempered woman of fifty-four, glanced through the personnel book and calmly replied that Kris Erlanger was a free-lance contributor and consequently had no office or private extension.

"I tried her at home and all I got was her goddamn answering machine."

"I'm sorry. It's half-past twelve at night. Miss Erlanger only comes in during the days."

"Half-past twelve?" the woman said, sounding puzzled. "Oh, that's right, there's three hours' difference." She paused. "Could you tell Miss Erlanger when she comes in tomorrow that Dr. Voyles called."

Her voice had changed, turning smoother, almost cold. It might have been a different woman completely.

The operator was anxious to conclude this call as soon as she could. "Yes, of course. Is there a number where she can reach you?"

"No. No, there isn't."

"You'll call back, then?"

"I don't think so. Tell Miss Erlanger that I'm not coming home, that she'll never hear from me again. Tell her that no one will."

THE WIND ROSE OUT OF THE NORTH and drove south, bearing the storm ahead of it. Gusts of forty miles an hour caused the snow to spread with great speed, shutting down highways in Massachusetts, Connecticut, and Rhode Island, knocking out power lines and causing blackouts throughout many sections of the Northeast. Then, unexpectedly, it veered out to sea, sparing New York from the brunt of its fury. But while the snow blew into the Atlantic, the winds lashed at the coast as far south as Baltimore.

And it was the winds which woke Matthew Barrett, rattling the window of his condominium and rousing him several seconds before the phone rang. He reached over instinctively for his wife, but then remembered that she wasn't there, that he had no wife anymore. Not that he missed Miriam in particular. More that he missed the comforting presence of a woman.

Somehow the phone's ringing didn't surprise him. He was a doctor and on call; why should it surprise him? The phosphorescent digits on his bedside clock read 3:57. A bad hour.

When he answered, his voice sounded disembodied.

"Dr. Barrett?" The caller's voice, on the other hand, was high-pitched, betraying overexcitement. "This is Dr. Fromm, the resident on duty tonight. I'm calling about your patient Mr. Sandor."

After a moment he remembered that he'd admitted him the previous morning. "Yes, what about him?"

"I'm afraid his condition is deteriorating rapidly."

"What? I admitted him with a simple bread-and-butter pneumonia."

"I know, doctor, but something's happened to him." He went on to catalog a grim litany of symptoms: an elevated temperature, shallow breathing, a falling platelet count, acute respiratory failure, internal bleeding, severe liver failure.

Barrett heard all the words—petachypneic, acidotic, encephalopathic, coagulopathy, icteric—but his mind could barely register them. It was difficult to imagine that they were talking about the same Jim Sandor. The Jim Sandor he remembered was in healthy enough shape to be treated at home.

"We've decided to work him up," Fromm was saying. "Besides the blood gases, we've sent off several hematological studies. We still haven't gotten his chemistries back yet, but I'd say, just by looking at those eyes, he'd have to be in liver failure. Basically he's septic and falling apart."

Barrett had no idea what to make of all this. "See if you can get him into the ICU, will you? I'll be right over to see him."

Ordinarily Barrett did not rush out in the middle of the night; New York Westside Medical was a teaching hospital, and residents and interns were on duty to handle most problems. But this case was obviously one demanding special attention. Fromm was out of his depth.

Groaning, Barrett got himself out of bed and drew open the curtains to have a look at Manhattan across the river. For such a grim hour there were still a great many lights on in the high-rises that demarcated the landscape. He pictured people like himself—insomniacs, worriers, lovers cast adrift . . .

His apartment was like a museum. A museum of memories. A museum of women who'd passed in and out of his life. The furniture—a combination of Swedish modern and eighteenth-century resurrected American—was his ex-wife's legacy. She didn't want to take it with her when she left, perhaps because she wanted it to remain behind as a constant reminder to Barrett of what he'd lost.

The porcelain vase dating back to the middle of the Han dynasty, the Yoruba ghost mask, the Benin leopard, and the Ashanti doll with the enormous head and stunted body had all been gifts from Kris during the year and a half she'd spent with him.

He had to go further back in time, like an archaeologist of the self, to get to the origin of the oil painting that hung in the living room opposite his expensive window view of the island of Manhattan. The painting depicted another island, a deserted one, partially shrouded in an early-morning mist. The painting, like the love affair from which it originated, was nearly sixteen years old. In the corner, scrawled in such tiny letters as to be practically invisible, was the signature of the lover: Helen Voyles.

The beveled mirror in which he observed himself daily, habitually inspecting his thick head of hair for any strands of gray that might warn him of his diminishing youth, hadn't been given to him by any wife or lover; he'd had to go out and buy it for himself.

When he was fourteen he used to bundle himself into a trench coat two sizes too big for him, slap on a visored cap, don somewhat sinister-looking shades, and head into Manhattan, hoping to pass as eighteen so he could be served a drink. Sometimes he accompanied his older sister, sometimes he went on his own, slipping out of his house in Rockville Centre in the dead of night while his parents lay asleep. His disguise usually worked. He even succeeded in taking in the occasional NYU girl ready to believe his story that he was a Village artist.

And now he was as old as he wanted to get, and looked

as much in his prime as he expected to be, with no need to fool bartenders or NYU girls any longer.

Wakened in the middle of the night, however, he looked a little past his prime, like the man he'd yet to become, with his brown eyes settled into a fixed skepticism and his lips pressed into a permanent scowl. When he woke up a bit more, his features would soften, giving him back some of his youth, endowing his face with a certain openness that tended to invite confidences, not only from his patients but also from complete strangers who had stories of infinite sadness they wanted him to hear.

He didn't like exercising particularly, but he did like swimming, and his body reflected the twenty laps he swam daily in the Westwide pool, toning his muscles, keeping him lean and limber enough so that he never worried about how much he ate. His back gave him problems, though, problems that seemed to resist all solutions. It was just something that he had decided he would have to live with. Until he'd married Miriam, his back had never given him any trouble. He considered it possible that the stress of his short and unhappy marriage might have accounted for his back giving out on him. But even when Miriam left, the pain hadn't gone away.

Like the furniture, like the landscape painting, like the African sculpture, the pain had stayed around so that he wouldn't forget.

And he didn't. He might regret, but he would never forget.

Before leaving the apartment, he gave a last glance at the Ashanti doll. The doll's expression seemed unusually tragic tonight; maybe the doll knew what he was in for better than he did.

Twenty minutes later, Barrett was across the George Washington Bridge and drawing his Cutlass up into the parking lot reserved for the Westside medical staff. The complex of buildings that composed Westside seemed inspired by a walled medieval fortress. They seemed to have been built for the intention not of curing the ill but of

holding off invading armies. In the gloom, one was indistinguishable from the other; they were just massive gray
structures connected by walkways above ground and tun-
nels underneath it.

Barrett entered through a basement door, nodding to a
uniformed security guard who sat by a bank of video
monitors. His destination lay seventeen floors higher, at the
intensive-care unit.

An electronic eye noted Barrett's presence and threw
open the twin doors to the ICU to admit him.

A nurse, middle-aged and vaguely familiar, glanced up
at him from the nurses' station and smiled in a recognition
he couldn't reciprocate. "Hi, Dr. Barrett, how are you
tonight?"

"I could be worse. Is Dr. Fromm here?"

"Oh, he's just gone to see a patient on one of the floors,
but your patient is in bed six. His chart is over there with
the others."

As Barrett retrieved the chart from the rack, he became
aware of a whooshing sound, one that repeated itself every
few seconds. It was originating from bed six. He saw that
the patient was now attached to a ventilator. No one had
mentioned a ventilator to him. Another complication.

The patient was not really his, but belonged to his
partner, Jerry Perretta. Barrett was covering for him while
he was vacationing in Martinique, undoubtedly sipping
piña coladas with some lovely long-legged brunette.

Inspecting James Sandor's chart, Barrett could find nothing in his past history to explain the sudden physical
breakdown. Nor was there any clue in the admitting lab
data.

The additional two pages the resident had added to the chart
revealed nothing new. The patient's liver failure and clot-
ting problem had already been described. Nowhere could
he find anything about Sandor's being intubated, or any
mention of his respiratory problem. The decision to intu-
bate him had probably been made while he was on his way
to the hospital.

"Dr. Barrett?"

The voice was the same as the one he'd heard over the phone, slightly high-pitched, almost adolescent.

Barrett regarded Dr. Fromm and saw a man perhaps six years his junior. His face was full of sharp angular lines and his skin betrayed a pallor that came from spending too much time under the glare of fluorescent lights.

Barely glancing over at the patient under discussion, Fromm said, "He just started going down the tubes so rapidly we couldn't oxygenate him. We called you, but you'd already left."

As though in accompaniment to the cylic whooshing of the ventilator, nearby cardiac monitors were emitting a succession of beeps that seemed somehow louder, more dramatic, with all the silence around.

"It's unbelievable," mumbled Fromm when Barrett did not immediately say anything. "He had such a two-bit pneumonia. We haven't found any evidence of any drug reaction. Either there's something else going on or he just has a crazy pneumonia. I don't know, we might have a case of legionnaire's disease."

Barrett remained perplexed. "I don't know what he could have. But with his liver failure and that coagulopathy, he might bleed to death pretty soon if we can't put a stop to it. I've never heard of any pneumonia progressing so rapidly. There may be some underlying disease we're seeing. Have you got his chest X ray?"

Fromm indicated the illuminated board where the X rays were pinned. "The tube's in the right place," he said, "but the pneumonia is all over his chest."

The lungs were whitened out, Barrett observed, completely filled with fluid.

When he looked around behind him, he saw that an intern and a medical student had taken up positions in back of them. They were switching their gaze from the chest X ray to Sandor and back again, as though trying to make the connection between one and the other.

"Well, let's take a look at him."

Barrett led the party of three to his bed. Sandor was, of

course, oblivious of their intrusion; his glassy eyes were fixed and staring at the ceiling.

Barrett leaned closer to him, and the intern handed him a flashlight. Shining it into Sandor's eyes, he noted that the pupils did not respond. His blue irises were no longer surrounded by a clear white sclera; they were now yellow, more evidence of his liver failure. The telltale spots proliferating on his chest and neck and arms—petechiae—indicated just how far down his platelet count had gone.

"I forgot to tell you—he's not peeing, either," said Fromm. "Seems he's in renal failure." Another unwelcome revelation.

Barrett tried to recall how Sandor had appeared to him that morning, but the man in front of him was a stranger, devoid of personality.

"I hope we can get a post on him when he dies," the intern said with unseemly enthusiasm.

Barrett had an urge to upbraid him, but held back. He might very well have said the same thing himself if he were still an intern. It was only putting into words what was on everybody else's mind.

Picking up the chart, Barrett now began to discuss with Fromm the X rays to be taken, the lab tests to be ordered—the whole technology of medicine, in fact, that could be called into play for Sandor. But in all probability he'd be dead before any of the studies ordered could be carried out.

"I suppose," he said finally, "I have no choice but to let the man's wife know what's happening."

The telephone number was on the chart. Barrett returned to the nurse's station. The nurse who had greeted him when he walked in gave him a commiserating smile.

At the desk he picked up the phone and considered just how he would go about informing Sandor's wife—Beth, according to the chart—without actually saying so, that her husband was dying.

Finally he dialed. It was a quarter to five in the morning. The phone rang and rang. He had a habit of counting the rings even while making routine calls. This was an eight-ring call.

"Hello?"

"Is this Mrs. Sandor?"

A strange silence on the other end. Wasn't she sure? Barrett wondered.

"Yes, this is Mrs. Sandor."

"I'm Dr. Barrett. I admitted your husband this morning to Westside Medical?"

There was another pause before Beth Sandor said, "Yes."

Her voice was low and flat. Under the circumstances, Barrett would have expected to hear a tinge of panic, certainly of apprehension, in her voice. Obviously at nearly five in the morning he was not making a casual phone call.

"I'm sorry to have gotten you out of bed, Mrs. Sandor, but something has happened that I think you should know about."

'Yes?"

She sounded puzzled, but in no way concerned. She might even be a bit irritated at being awakened.

"Mrs. Sandor, I'm afraid that your husband's taken a turn for the worse."

He saw Dr. Fromm signaling to him. He couldn't make out what he was trying to communicate. He gestured for another moment so that he could complete the phone call. "We've had to transfer him to the intensive-care unit. I didn't want you coming to his room and not finding him there tomorrow."

"What's the matter with him?"

Fromm was still trying to get his attention.

"We don't know, Mrs. Sandor. We're doing some tests now and hope to have a clearer idea of what's wrong very shortly. Would you hold on a moment, please?"

He looked up at Fromm. "What is it?"

"He's dead. Sandor just checked out."

Over the speaker he heard a code nine. Medical personnel were hurrying toward the bed, but Barrett knew that Sandor was long past helping.

"Mrs. Sandor?" He spoke into the phone again.

But there was no one on the other end. She'd hung up.

Dialing the number again, all he got was a busy signal. She must have left the phone off the hook. Probably she'd heard all the bad news she wanted for the night. Either that or she just didn't give a damn.

4

BARRETT WAS IN A SOUR MOOD when he entered his office, situated two blocks distant from the main Westside Medical Center complex. The lack of sleep hadn't helped his disposition, nor had the heavy traffic coming into Manhattan that morning. And because he'd been so singularly unsuccessful in locating Beth Sandor, his irritability threatened to persist through the day.

His secretary, Mrs. Preston, a silver-haired woman, ageless in appearance, with smooth unblemished skin and penetrating eyes that seemed to read too deeply into her employer's thoughts, agreed to see if she could locate the woman, but her efforts were no more successful than his had been.

Maybe Beth Sandor didn't care that her husband had died. But even so, he needed to contact her, if only to obtain her permission for an autopsy. Having no idea what had caused an unexceptional pneumonia to turn so catastrophic, he was looking forward to a pathologist's observations.

Consulting Sandor's records, he discovered that he worked for a company called Stargel Manufacturing. The woman who took the call at Stargel told him that she couldn't help him, that while he might be an employee's physician, she could not over the phone disclose any information of a personal nature.

"I can't seem to get hold of his wife, you understand . . ." Barrett tried explaining.

"I understand, but I'm afraid there's nothing I can do." Then she paused. "Wait. Mr. Sandor does have a friend who works in his division. Let me put you through to him."

The friend's name was Bob O'Connor and his secretary informed Barrett that he was unavailable. "He's out sick today," she said.

And, of course, she couldn't give out his home phone number. It was information of a personal nature, after all.

That route apparently closed, he decided he would forget about Beth Sandor for the time being and attempt to obtain an autopsy without her permission.

So he put through a call to the coroner. The coroner, a man he barely knew, agreed that he presented an impressive case. But then he said, "Still, when you get right down to it, I think it'll turn out to be nothing more than some weird pneumonia. I can sympathize with your dilemma, but in the absence of the widow's permission—"

"But I keep trying to tell you, I can't find her. She hung up on me and never got back to me."

"That's why I'm in the business I am—the wackos I have to deal with are mostly dead. Keep in touch."

The only option left for Barrett was the chief medical examiner's office, but he enjoyed so little clout there that he very much doubted it was worth his while to explore the possibility of their taking on the case.

Late in the day, however, Mrs. Preston buzzed him with a message that Dr. Heisler was on the phone.

"Are you sure you've got the name right?"

"Positive, doctor."

Of course she had the name right. Mrs. Preston always had everything right.

As a resident, Barrett had once studied under Heisler

and found him to be an exacting taskmaster, by turns exciting and indifferent; a month of high-voltage lectures would be followed by a month in which he would send his grad students, like subalterns dispatched to the colonies, to speak in his place. At one moment he would display great warmth and encourage his students; at the next, he would regard them with glacial indifference.

Since that time the two had come into contact, but their association, while correct, was never going to blossom into a friendship.

And not once in the eight years Barrett had had his practice at Westside had Heisler ever called him.

"I understand through one of my med students that you had a patient with a peculiar pneumonia," he began.

News travels with exceptional speed through the corridors of Westside, Barrett thought. He confirmed the report.

"The reason I'm calling you is that I'm told that the pneumonia was characterized by acute liver failure."

"That's true. A very baffling case."

"Since my lab has been doing a considerable amount of research into alcohol-related liver diseases, I thought I'd talk to you and see whether this case had any relevance."

"I don't know whether he was an alcoholic. There's no indication that he was. His wife, on the other hand, was treated here for alcoholism over a year ago, according to her chart."

"I see. Well, I would like to get a look at the liver tissue, even so." .

"I'd like to oblige you, Leo, but I can't find the widow, and the coroner just turned me down."

There was a brief pause on the other end. Then Heisler said, "You know, Matthew, I don't think that should be a problem. I have a friend at the medical examiner's office who might be able to help us out. Let me give him a call, and I'll get back to you as soon as I know anything."

Barrett was ready to hang up when Heisler said, "Oh, there's one other thing. I almost forgot to tell you. A very unpleasant piece of news, I'm afraid to say."

Barrett couldn't imagine what news Heisler could tell

him that he'd find that disturbing, but still his breathing became shallow and something seemed to drop into the pit of his stomach. "Yes?"

"You were a friend of Dr. Voyles's, I believe."

More than a friend. Less than a friend.

When he allowed that she was, even if their friendship had diminished to an exchange of formalities whenever they passed each other in the corridors of Westside, Heisler said, "It appears that she drowned herself." He waited for Barrett to say something. But Barrett didn't know what to say, and so he resumed, "Her rented car was found not far from Lakeshore Drive close to Lake Michigan. Empty vials of prescription pills, apparently stolen from my lab, and an empty bottle of cognac were found in the car. I'm told by the Evanston police that there were traces of vomit in the front seat and all the way down to the lake. They also discovered a skirt that belongs to her and one of her shoes on the beach. The lake's partially frozen over, so it may be some time before they can dredge it for the body."

"When did you find this out?"

"Just this morning. A detective called my office right after he'd traced the car and discovered that Helen had rented it in San Francisco."

"Have you any idea why she might have done this?"

"None whatsoever. But then, she was always a little unstable. It doesn't come as a complete surprise."

Only after he'd hung up was Barrett struck by how emotionless Heisler had sounded. Almost as if Helen Voyles's death had been a matter of indifference to him.

But the more he thought about it, the more he realized that emotion hadn't been absent. It wasn't indifference Barrett had heard from him. It was satisfaction.

5

Kris Erlanger had been to Helen's apartment only once before, two weeks previously. Located among a complex of buildings reserved for students and the staff at Westside, it had only a number to distinguish it from those above and below and on either side of it. The buildings were designed the same, the apartments—all one- and two-bedroom—were laid out the same, and while the color scheme sometimes differed from floor to floor, the only colors to be found were pastels: blue, rose, green, and a pale yellow that stared at too long tended to produce headaches in the observer.

Somehow the residents of these buildings seemed to look much the same too, as if their environment had little by little sapped them of their individuality. They shared a vaguely somber, self-absorbed air and their skin had the sallow cast that comes from too much time spent indoors.

Kris stood out; she gave off a restless energy that was almost palpable; she scarcely seemed able to stand still. She was in her thirtieth year, good-looking enough to give men pause and prompt a second glance on Fifth Avenue, but not so glamorous as to discourage their approaches.

Until she had stormed out of Matthew Barrett's apartment, she wore her hair halfway down her back; the next day she'd had it cut so that it hung, dark blond and shot through with streaks of silver, shoulder-length. More mature, she thought. More *something*, anyway. She had good breasts and better legs, and hips that she considered a little too wide.

People passing by her on the concrete paths that led from one high-rise to the other gave her thoughtful glances. She didn't look like she belonged. Of course, she imagined that neither had Helen.

It had taken a day and a half for the message Helen had left for her at *America Now* to reach her. Bureaucratic inefficiency. She guessed that Helen had tried calling her at home too, but had evidently gotten disgusted and hung up when she heard the answering machine.

Kris and Helen had met through Matthew in the days when Kris was living with him and Helen was still on speaking terms with him.

There was every possibility that they would not get along; Helen was obviously jealous of Matthew, but surprisingly, she'd taken to Kris, recognized in her a kindred spirit perhaps, a renegade like herself who just didn't fit in.

She was trying est at the time, urged Kris to do the same. Kris said that she didn't want to sit in a room for hours, which was mandatory at introductory seminars, and wait for someone's permission to use the bathroom. She'd gone through that in grade school.

But then Helen's involvement in est lasted no longer than her involvement in transcendental meditation or in Freudian analysis. She was always desperate for a religion to follow, a cause to believe in, a leader to look up to. Maybe that was why she had never left Leo Heisler's employment. She hated him, but she believed in him.

Helen was brilliant, but she had no grounding. Common sense was something alien to her. Her personal life was in so much disarray that Kris was sure it couldn't have gotten that way without a great deal of work on her part. Helen wouldn't know what to do if everything around her should suddenly become tranquil—not that that was ever a danger.

She was generous with her emotions, fell in love constantly, slept with a bewildering number of men, then one day discovered that she had no more to give, was completely drained.

Incapable of sustaining a love affair, she was little better at sustaining a friendship. A year had gone by since she and Kris had last been in touch, which was why her phone call two weeks previously had come as such a surprise.

Helen said she had a story for Kris. A story of fraud and illegal experiments on patients. "I'll fill you in on all the details when I get back from San Francisco," she'd said.

But it seemed that she hadn't gotten back. The message she'd left at *America Now* had been as ominous as it was cryptic. What did she mean, she was never coming home? Where, then, was she going? The calls Kris had made to the Melkis Pavilion, where Helen worked, had been unavailing; no one there had any idea what had become of her or when, if ever, she'd be back.

When Kris tried phoning Helen's apartment, all she got first was no answer, but this evening she'd obtained a busy signal. The problem was that the busy signal persisted for hours. Either Helen was home and engaged in a very long conversation or else had taken the phone off the hook. In any event, Kris decided she had little to lose by traveling uptown to see if she might be home.

She had half a story, a quarter of a story, maybe less. Only Helen could provide her with the facts. Kris imagined that she might one day have enough to present to her editor at *America Now*—something that would be front-page material. Her ambition was to leave behind the Contemporary Living section to which she'd so far been confined: articles presenting home-decorating hints, gardening tips, and new-wave fashions for suburbanites.

The entrance to Helen's building was badly lit and it was with some difficulty and much squinting that she found the bell she was hunting for. She rang it twice without hope.

A moment later she was buzzed in.

Maybe, she thought, I pressed the wrong bell. But she proceeded up to the twelfth floor and walked all the way to a door at the end of the corridor and knocked.

A few seconds passed before the door opened. A man peered out. Kris had no idea who he might be.

"Yes, can I help you?"

Kris quickly explained who she was. "I thought that Helen might've come back."

The man drew the door open wider. He had a curiously expressive face that was capable of appearing both handsome and ugly, depending on the way he turned; it was a face that seemed somehow not to belong to this century, but was more likely to turn up in a medieval painting or on an icon. His eyes were sunk into hollows, with circles around them, giving him a haunted appearance. He had a lean frame and his hands were thin and white with long, beautiful fingers.

"I regret to have to tell you this . . . but Helen is dead."

"What?" She stepped back as though she'd been hit.

He told her that she'd drowned herself, that her car had been located by police on the shores of Lake Michigan. "No one knows why she did it," he said.

There was a long silence.

Finally Kris asked who he was.

"I'm terribly sorry. My name is Isaac Ninn. I was a friend of Helen's . . . I was cleaning out her apartment when you rang. Please come in."

Only now did she detect a slight British accent in his voice. There was something oddly formal about his manner, too, which she associated with Englishmen.

She walked into an apartment that looked almost exactly the same as it had two weeks ago when she'd visited Helen. There was little hint of the disorder that obtained in her life here.

"There's really not much here," Ninn said. "But you can look around if you'd like. Tell me, how well did you know Helen?"

Kris told him, revealing more than she ordinarily would have to a man she'd only just met. But the circumstances seemed to invite an immediate exchange of confidences.

"Have I seen anything you've written?" he asked when she was through.

"I doubt it. But soon you will.

"You have good connections, then?"

She couldn't figure out whether he was actually interested in her journalistic career or just being polite. At any rate she felt somewhat odd being in a dead woman's apartment with a strange man. But on the other hand, he didn't look like the type who would attack her, and what was the point of throwing away an opportunity like this? She had nothing to lose by spending a few minutes looking around.

While Ninn continued packing in the bedroom, Kris rummaged through the drawers of an antique chest, where she discovered half a dozen photo albums. Skimming through them, she came upon a picture of Helen as a little girl standing hand-in-hand with her mother, very solemn, her hair fashioned into a ponytail, already looking as if she were ready to do battle with the rest of the world. A few pages later, Helen had turned into a frowning adolescent waiting impatiently to become transformed into a great beauty. On the last page Kris found a graduation picture: for once Helen was smiling, mortarboard clasped in her hands, her body shapeless in the folds of her gown. Standing next to her was a short, balding man with a timorous expression on his face. A relative, Kris guessed.

The next album she opened was not devoted to Helen at all, but rather to Leo Heisler: publicity photos, P.R. releases announcing the discovery of a new protein or the completion of a successful genetic experiment, news clippings, tear sheets of articles he'd had published in a multitude of professional journals. It was the sort of scrapbook a teenage girl might keep on her favorite male movie idol.

She looked up to find Isaac Ninn glancing over her shoulder.

"I can't understand why she'd have something like this," Kris said. "She told me she loathed Heisler, she said he'd plagiarized some of her research and claimed it as his own."

None of this seemed to surprise Ninn. "She had a very complicated relationship with Dr. Heisler. We talked about it on a number of occasions. It was true she loathed him, but she couldn't bring herself to leave him. She might have loved him too. The evidence is right there in front of you. We sometimes admire people who can get away with what we cannot."

"It sounds as if you knew Helen a lot better than I did."

"We were—how would you put it?—involved for a short time."

That was what Kris had suspected from the start.

Her eyes fell on a sheet of printout paper with clusters of lines which resembled a graph of some kind and extended the entire length of it, nearly six feet when unrolled completely. At the bottom of the page was the notation "T-protein: Mice/Sample 7."

Kris picked it up, but on examining it, she couldn't make out any more than she could from a distance. "Do you know what this is, by any chance?"

It appeared as if Ninn were only waiting for the opportunity to display his knowledge. "It's a computer printout of amino acids. There are four types of amino acids in each strand of DNA. With electricity you can break up the genetic material. The DNA is tagged with radioactivity so that once it is broken up, you can photograph it. Then you put the results into a computer for analysis. Apparently this one describes the composition of a certain protein in mice."

"Do you know what it means, though?"

He shrugged. "I have no idea. Helen generally didn't discuss her work with me."

"But you seem to know a good deal about this sort of thing."

"I have my own laboratory in London. We do similar genetic work there."

"Do you know Dr. Heisler, then?"

He acknowledged that he did. "From time to time, when his laboratory becomes very busy, he'll ask me to do the occasional test assay or analysis for him. That was how I happened to meet Helen."

"Do you share her feelings about him? Or is that prying?"

"It may be prying, but since that is the obligation of any respectable journalist, I certainly don't mind. The answer to your question is that to a large extent I do. Dr. Heisler is unquestionably brilliant, but along the way he has destroyed many careers. I hold him partially responsible for Helen's suicide. He subjected her to a great deal of emotional stress and worked her mercilessly."

Kris deliberated for a moment before she asked the next question. "Did Helen tell you anything about illegal experiments he was conducting on patients?"

"The double-blinded study on alcohol disease? Yes, as a matter of fact she mentioned it. But she was so vague I can't say that I made much sense out of what she told me. She had the unnerving habit of starting to tell you something, then suddenly stopping and refusing to say more."

"I know," Kris said. "She'd do the same thing to me. Did she tell you about the four men who died in the study?"

He shook his head, looking very puzzled.

The disappointment must have shown on her face, for he quickly added, "But perhaps at some later date we could sit down and talk about it. By then things might be clearer." Glancing about the apartment, he shook his head gravely. "Having just learned myself that Helen is dead, I find it difficult to discuss her association with Dr. Heisler."

Kris said she understood. She was being overanxious again, jumping in to get her story when some gentle coaxing might produce much better results.

"If you'd like, we can exchange cards, and the next time I'm in New York, I'll ring you up."

Kris had no card and was obliged to write her address and number down on a piece of notepaper.

Isaac Ninn's card bore the name of his firm: Torquay Research, Ltd., 65 Bolingbroke Road, London, England.

"Would you mind if I looked around a little more?"

He had no objection, but told her that he'd have to be getting on his way shortly, so she shouldn't take long.

Not that there was any reason to. What she found in the bedroom held no interest for her, although it was possible that in the cardboard boxes Isaac had packed there was something of consequence; nonetheless, she resisted the temptation to go through them.

The medicine cabinet in the bathroom was cluttered with prescription drugs of all kinds; it was like a miniature pharmacy. As she reached in to extract one mysterious-looking bottle, she felt something sharp graze her thumb.

She didn't feel the pain at first. Then she drew her hand out, observing that she'd cut herself on a razor.

"Shit!" she yelled.

For such a small cut it was bleeding profusely. Ninn rushed in to see what had happened.

He held her hand under the tap, releasing a stream of scalding water that caused her to cry out.

Peering into the medicine cabinet, he said, "Damn, you'd think with all the rest of this rubbish Helen would have some Band-Aids."

In their absence he gave her some tissue paper. "I don't believe you'll bleed to death," he said.

She waited until the flow had diminished sufficiently for her to remove the paper. "I always feel like an ass when I do these things to myself," she said.

"It happens—you have no cause to feel embarrassed."

She thanked him and told him she'd be on her way. "I hope we can see each other soon."

"Of course we will. I'm in and out of New York all the time."

Once he'd closed the door behind her, an idea occurred to Ninn. He proceeded to the bathroom and gathered up the blood-soaked clumps of tissue paper Kris had just discarded, and placed them in his pocket. He would have her blood analyzed later that night.

It was just possible that the result would be positive for the T-protein. Not that he had any idea what he would do if it turned out to be so, but it was always helpful to know such things. Under the appropriate circumstances, she, too, could be put to good use.

6

ISAAC NINN WAS DEAD DRUNK when he entered Heisler's laboratory on the fifth floor of Westside's Melkis Pavilion. Being drunk was such a common condition with him that he'd long ago accommodated himself to it; he held himself erect and walked with a precise and careful step; when he spoke, he sounded so lucid that it would have come as a great surprise to his listener that he really had little idea what he was saying.

It was late and the floor was almost completely deserted save for the Ukrainian and Polish cleaning women stooped over their mops.

Surrounded by cages filled with gray and mottled mice and white rabbits, Leo Heisler sat perched on a stool peering into an electron microscope in the solitude of his laboratory.

When Ninn walked in, he raised his eyes from the microscope and swiveled about on the stool to regard his visitor.

At the age of sixty-three, Heisler had the look of a colonel who's ruled over some backwater South American republic for so long that he cannot imagine anyone replacing him. His eyes were a smoky blue, the eyes of an inquisitor, revealing nothing; his brow was high, emphasized by a receding hairline, and glowed when the lights shone on it; his posture was correct, and even his most casual movement seemed calculated; this was a man who would not cross a leg or light a pipe without thinking of what impact the gesture would have on his audience.

"I didn't expect you back from London so soon," Heisler remarked.

Ninn gave a shrug. "It happens that my business there was finished for the time being." He was looking beyond Heisler at the caged mice.

"Let me show you something." Heisler guided him over to the cage he'd been staring at. Of the half-dozen mice inside, one was obviously dead, belly-up; the others looked as if they might be joining it soon. If they moved at all, it was feebly, and their eyes were yellow from liver failure.

"You've infected them with the virus," Ninn said.

"Only hours ago. But not directly. I used the mice over in that cage."

He gestured toward another cage with three mice inside it. By contrast, they were still active, scampering from one end of their prison to the other. "I'm testing different dosages to see their effect. So far the result is always the same in every case: death. For some it takes longer, that's all." Turning back to Ninn, he said, "Have you any news from London for me?"

"Everything is in place. The arrangements with the Inverness Courier Service are finalized, the escorts are on their way to the States. I have a plan to deploy them in selected regions—urban areas, primarily—throughout the country. I can give you all the details—"

Heisler stopped him. "I don't want to know."

They were, in effect, about to test-market the virus, initiate what might become an epidemic if it was not carefully controlled. But Ninn was the operations specialist, the pilot who dropped the bombs; Heisler was the man who sat behind the desk thousands of miles away and gave the orders.

But Ninn was drunk and not so easily discouraged. There was much that he wanted to say; he was actually quite pleased with the strategy he'd contrived, and he needed to tell somebody. Given the secrecy that was incumbent upon him, Heisler was the only person he could confide in.

"I decided we needed to begin with a bang, kill off someone with a large public following . . ."

Heisler's only reaction was to raise his eyebrows. Otherwise his face remained expressionless.

"An actor, a movie star," Ninn continued.

"You don't need to tell me his name. I'm certain I'll know who it is as soon as it happens."

"You don't sound pleased, Leo. Do you think I'll screw up on you, is that it?"

"It's not that," Heisler muttered, his eyes focused on a second mouse as it pawed at the walls of its cage, emitting faint whistling noises the likes of which Ninn had never heard from a mouse. All at once it toppled over. For several seconds afterward its limbs continued to twitch; then it convulsed in a final spasm and lay still.

"What is it, then?" Ninn was becoming irritated.

"I am beginning to think that Helen is alive."

"Helen is what? You told me yourself that she's dead, drowned in Lake Michigan."

"Did you find anything of consequence in her apartment?"

"Nothing—some computer printouts of no importance, that was it."

"As I suspected. I believe she staged her suicide. This afternoon I discovered that she took a good deal of data from this lab when she left for San Francisco two weeks ago. Some of it we have copies of, but there's a body of original research in her possession for which we have no copies. While I'm certain I can synthesize more of the virus, without her data I might not be able to find a cure for it for many months, even years to come."

To Ninn this was of scant importance when weighed against the possibility that the virus might run out before they could fully profit from it. "The more that die," he said, "the more money we make."

Of course, Heisler wanted more than money; he wanted the fame that would certainly be his should he produce a cure for his own disease. But that was not Ninn's concern. To his mind Heisler had far more fame already than he deserved.

"That's not the point. I don't like to see this get out of control. Helen's a loose end. If she really did commit suicide, where are the data? Why can't we find them? They weren't in her car, they weren't in her apartment, they're not in her office. She must still have them, don't you understand?"

Ninn understood—but only to the limit that the whiskey in his system would allow. "I tell you what I'll do for you, Leo, if you're so concerned. I'll try to find her for you."

Heisler gave him an incredulous look.

"I just made the acquaintance of a young woman—a free-lance writer—who says that Helen contacted her before she left for San Francisco. Evidently she was prepared to tell her about the double-blinded studies."

Heisler's face turned noticeably pale. "How much did she tell her?"

"From the sound of it, very little. Tantalizing shreds of information, that's all. Nothing for you to lose any sleep over. It occurs to me that if Helen was already in touch with her, and if what you say is true, that she's still alive, perhaps she'll attempt to contact her again."

Heisler began to relax. "I see. You'll have her watched?"

"I have just the person in mind for it, too. A good man, follows orders, no questions asked. And there's one other thing . . ."

"What's that?"

"I found the opportunity to run a test on the blood of the young woman in question. She's positive for the T-protein."

"And just how, may I ask, did this opportunity arise? You didn't slash her open with a knife, did you?"

Ninn smiled, although Heisler did not quite mean this as a joke. "No, Leo. Just as you have other people to do your dirty work for you, so do I."

7

EARL WHEELOCK WAS A SLIGHT, battered man accustomed to spending his days in badly lit doorways, freezing his ass off in February cold or wilting in August heat, all without complaint. All he required was Isaac Ninn's praise and enough money to feed his habit.

There was about his scarred face a certain roguishness that endowed him with an odd sort of appeal that he used effectively in dank establishments that went by the names of the Anvil, the Sewer, and the Hellfire Club. He had practically no interest in women, though if Isaac wanted him to, he would happily seduce one and bed her down.

Most of all, Earl was an inconspicuous man; one minute he looked to be in his thirties, the next he could easily be mistaken as a teenager. Maybe it was the smack he'd collected in his blood that made him so youthful, for he was actually past forty. He did not think he had long to live, but the prospect of an untimely end did not bother him in the least.

Having waited for five hours in the bitter chill, he was finally rewarded for his patience when the woman he'd been watching finally emerged from her apartment building.

It was close to five-thirty and she appeared to be in a hurry.

Ah, he thought, this may be it.

It was probably hoping for too much to think that Helen had phoned her and that she was now rushing off to meet her.

Nonetheless, he began to follow Kris to the end of the street. She was so intent on finding a cab that she had no idea someone was tracking her movements.

His car, an olive-green Pontiac, rusted and almost as dented-in as its owner, was parked at the corner of the block.

He got in and waited.

Venturing halfway out into the street, Kris gestured frantically for a cab, but it was rush hour and it took her ten minutes before she acquired one.

And because it was rush hour, with traffic uptown so clogged, Earl had little difficulty keeping her taxi in sight.

She got off much farther uptown than he'd expected, just a block away from the Westside Medical Center.

Parking illegally, because in New York City there seemed to be no other alternative, Earl started to follow her. When he saw that she was heading into the parking lot reserved for medical personnel, he grew puzzled. She appeared to be searching out a particular car.

Apparently she found the one she was looking for, because she abruptly stopped in front of a blue Cutlass, and after examining the license plate, rooted herself to the spot.

Well, he concluded, something is about to happen here.

But for a good long while, as he lingered, keeping far away from the glare from the mercury vapor lights, nothing happened at all.

Kris shifted her feet and hugged herself to keep warm, but it was clear that she was just becoming colder. Unlike Earl, she wasn't used to prolonged vigils in the winter twilight.

It wasn't until six-fifteen that the person she was waiting for showed up.

Earl, concealed behind a spanking white BMW (which

he'd resisted hot wiring only with the greatest reluctance), was close enough to see that it was not Helen, but a man.

"Excuse me, miss," he called out. "Would you mind moving? You're standing in front of my car."

Kris didn't reply. The man approached within a couple of yards of her. "Oh," he said, "it's you!"

It was impossible for Earl to tell whether he was pleased to see her or not, but he was certainly damned surprised.

One way or another, Earl wasn't interested. His purpose was to locate Helen for Isaac. He decided he would drive back downtown, and now that the opportunity had presented itself, he would slip into Kris's apartment and see whether anything of importance awaited him there.

Barrett didn't know what to think of Kris's sudden reappearance in his life. He was nervous, expectant, and curious to see what would happen next.

"It's good to see you," he managed to get out. "How long have you been waiting here?"

"Not long. I thought I'd surprise you."

"You did that, all right." She was always good at surprises. "Would you like to go somewhere? It's pretty cold out here." He began to unlock the car door.

"Sure."

He knew there must be something she wanted to talk to him about, but he wasn't sure he was prepared for it.

Although her face was partially submerged in shadow, Barrett was struck at how attractive she still was, though two years had passed since they'd last seen each other; if anything, she was better-looking. Her hair was shorter, he realized, and restyled. In spite of the parka she wore, he had the sense that she'd lost weight in the interim. And there was in her eyes a measure of experience and perhaps even wisdom that hadn't been there before.

Or was he only imagining all this because that was what he hoped for?

It was odd: having so much to say to her, he found he could say practically nothing at all.

"Where are we going?" he asked.

He'd just begun to drive in the direction of downtown without any particular destination in mind.

"Wherever you'd like. How about an uncrowded bar where we can talk?"

Neutral territory, he thought.

But certainly the anger she had held toward him, anger which he'd fully reciprocated, could not have sustained itself for all this time. If there hadn't been so much feeling between them, there wouldn't have been so much emotional tumult.

He found a bar that he'd always meant to inspect, should the occasion ever arise. It was located a block from the Museum of Natural History, which in the gloom rose like an abandoned Gothic edifice of another century.

"I'm sorry to hear about you and Miriam," Kris said when they'd taken their seats at a table far enough in the rear to ensure they would not be disturbed.

He'd long since come to the conclusion that the only reason he'd married Miriam was to forget about Kris. It was a pointless gesture, unfair to Miriam, unfair to himself. "At least it ended amicably," he said. "As amicably as these things ever end. And how've you been doing?"

"Still writing."

That wasn't what he meant, but he figured that eventually he would find out what he most desired to know.

"I thought you would've gone back to acting."

Because it was acting (primarily in commercials: TV spots at two in the morning for collections of forty-eight great country-and-western hits and for assorted household products) and modeling that had first drawn Kris to New York. The writing had come later.

"My hands." She held them out.

"What about them?"

"They're not soft enough to convince viewers that I benefited from the dishwashing liquids they hired me to plug. So I decided why not use them for writing? Actually, that's what I wanted to talk to you about."

All at once he felt immensely disappointed. "I don't know whether I have any advice to give you about writing."

"No, but you might about medicine. Specifically, the way things work at Westside Hospital."

In the time they'd spent together, Kris had expressed only vague curiosity about his work, and it was the last thing he'd expected she'd want to discuss with him. Another surprise.

She got out a notebook and opened it to a blank page. He wasn't certain he liked the idea of being quoted. "Who is this for, exactly?"

She told him she hadn't tried to place her story yet—for that matter, she wasn't even sure she had a story—but that she hoped it would eventually appear in the pages of *America Now*.

"That's the new national daily, isn't it?"

"That's right. But so far the only pieces I can sell them are on decorating ideas and fat farms—nothing that's about to win me a Pulitzer."

"What about Westside do you want to know?"

She fell silent for a moment, her face darkening. "You heard about Helen?"

He nodded.

"I wasn't sure whether you knew."

"It came as a shock, but somehow it seemed inevitable."

He really didn't care to talk about Helen. It was like conducting an archaelogical expedition into his past. There was a great deal he had no wish to dig up and expose to the light.

"She called me just a couple of weeks ago."

This astonished him. "I had no idea you were in contact."

Kris proceeded to explain the circumstances surrounding the call and her subsequent attempt to discover whether there was anything to Helen's story—that part of the story, anyway, that Helen had revealed to her.

"So you're asking me whether I could shed some light on what she told you?"

"Let's just say that you might be able to clarify some things for me. You told me you're a member of the Human Investigations Committee."

The Human Investigations Committee—HIC—oversaw

experiments conducted on hospitalized patients. Many of these experiments entailed the use of new drugs that carried a high-risk factor. Barrett was somewhat taken aback that she would remember something like this. She had a more retentive memory than he'd supposed.

"I'm still sitting on the committee," he told her. "But what has that got to do with Helen?"

"Dr. Heisler sits on it also, doesn't he?"

Now he could make the connection. "That's right."

"But Helen told me he never shows up at meetings and that he rarely turns in progress reports on the course of his experiments."

"He does show up at some meetings, but not many. About the progress reports, I wouldn't know."

"Can't someone be suspended if he constantly ignores HIC?"

"In theory, I assume so. It's never happened. And I doubt that it would ever happen with Dr. Heisler. He's too famous, he brings in too much grant money to the hospital."

"Could Dr. Heisler be operating in violation of federal guidelines governing genetic experiments?"

"The guidelines are not exactly engraved in stone, Kris. But to my knowledge, no one's ever accused him of doing something like that."

"Helen claimed that he was involved in testing drugs that had not been approved by the HIC in one of its double-blinded studies."

He realized he was becoming irritated. Helen Voyles was hardly a creditable source. There was no telling what grudges she bore Heisler. "Are you sure you know what a double-blinded study is?"

"It's a study in which neither the patient nor his doctor knows whether he's receiving the test drug or a placebo, so the patient's psychological attitude won't be a factor in the result. Am I right?"

"That's correct so far as it goes. But all double-blinded studies are subject to rigorous scrutiny by the HIC before they're approved. Then the experiments are coded. But there's always a moderator who has the key to the code, so that if anything ever goes wrong—the patient develops an adverse side effect, say—he can find out whether he's been receiving the drug or the placebo. The moderator is almost always a member of the HIC, and all the codes are kept in the HIC office. So I can't imagine that an unsanctioned double-blinded study could be going on like Helen says.''

Kris looked dubious. She thought she had the makings of a story and she didn't like the idea of anyone punching holes in it.

"Have you considered the possibility that Helen might have been trying to get back at Heisler for some reason or other and came to you for help in accomplishing her purpose?'' he asked.

"Are you implying that she assumed I was gullible enough to believe anything she told me?''

He adamantly denied this. The last thing he wanted was to start fighting with Kris. They would be right back where they left off two years ago, with scarcely an hour's ceasefire to interrupt the war.

"They have fact checkers at *America Now* who are just as scrupulous as your collegaues on HIC. Maybe more so,'' she went on.

"I wasn't implying that you were gullible. I was just suggesting that Helen's emotional state at the time might have colored her thinking.''

Even in the best of times, he recalled, Helen could become unreasonable, even hysterical, without warning, her moods as sudden and unpredictable as New England weather in midsummer.

"But isn't it also possible that whatever drove her to commit suicide had to do with what she'd told me?''

"Yes, of course it is. But if she knew something was wrong, she could have gone to the head of HIC—or informed the president of the university, for that matter. In fact, she had an obligation to do so.''

"I think she was afraid.''

"Afraid?''

"Of what Heisler might do to her.''

"Well, he couldn't have done anything worse to her than she did to herself, could he?"

Kris shook her head. "I'm not so sure about that, I'm not so sure at all."

Barrett really didn't believe that Kris had a story, but now that they'd met after all this time, he didn't want another two years to pass before they saw each other again. He was determined to maintain contact with her no matter what stratagem he had to resort to.

"There are two people you should speak to, Kris," he advised. "One is Helen's only living relative, an uncle who lives out on Long Island somewhere, named Henry Loomis. I know I have his number at home."

"I'd appreciate that. And who's the other?"

"Leo Heisler."

Her eyes brimmed with excitement. "You think he'll talk to me?"

"I don't see why not, so long as you pretend to be reasonably sympathetic toward his position."

"I'm good at that." She smiled.

"I'm sure you are."

"How soon do you think you could arrange it?"

"In a few days. I have to speak to him anyway."

He didn't know how long it would last, but he had assured himself that some connection, however tenuous, would remain between them at least for a while.

He drove her back to the Village, although he would have much preferred having dinner with her. But she told him she was trying to cut down on eating, though it was his impression that she didn't need to lose any additional weight. He half-suspected that she was anxious to get home in time for a date.

It was none of his business, but the prospect provoked in him a pang of jealousy. Two years and I'm still jealous of her, he thought with wonder.

She kissed him warmly on the lips and slipped out of the car, saying, "Give me a call as soon as you can. We'll do dinner next time."

Out of habit, he waited until he saw the light in her apartment window come on. He was about to drive away when she flung the window open, leaned out, and called down to him, her voice betraying her urgency. ''Matthew, could you come up here? Something's happened.''

8

THE APARTMENT WAS IN SHAMBLES. The desk and bureau draw-ers had been pulled out, their contents thrown to the floor. Papers lay ripped and strewn everywhere. Coils of cassette tape lay in tangled heaps and spilled out under the bed and chairs. The television was smashed so thoroughly that its tubes and wiring were almost entirely exposed. The stereo had been upended, the speakers gutted, many of the record albums removed from their covers and broken in such a way as to suggest that the intruder had jumped on them repeatedly. The telephone cord had been cut, the answer-ing machine demolished. From the walls an original Chagall print, an Air France poster of Montmartre, a photograph of Kris's mother, a charcoal portrait of Kris, and a Sierra Club calendar had been pulled down and slashed with a knife.

In the bathroom they found that the mirror on the medi-cine cabinet was now a spiderweb of cracks stained with fresh blood. There was more blood in the sink. Whoever had done this was willing to damage his own hands to inflict this kind of havoc.

Barrett doubted that this was any ordinary burglary. Somebody was either searching for something he could not turn up or else was intent on terrifying Kris, which led him to the conclusion that she might actually be onto something with her story.

"Do you have any idea who could've done this?"

She shook her head. She seemed incapable of reacting. She just stood where she was, dead center of the room numbly surveying the damage. It was too much for her to absorb at once.

At first she was just very pale, but then, gradually, almost imperceptibly, she began to shake.

Barrett took hold of her and pressed her close to him. He would've liked to say that it would be all right, but there was no evidence of that, so he wisely refrained.

He had no idea how long they remained together, her head buried against his shoulder, her body trembling uncontrollably, but at last he drew apart from her, saying, "We're getting out of here."

She didn't ask where they were going; it was enough that they were leaving.

Barrett decided that they would notify the police later; if the perpetrator had left any fingerprints behind, they would still be there tomorrow.

In the safety of Barrett's apartment, Kris's spirits improved. A couple of stiff drinks—poured from a bottle of Martell she'd forgotten when she left two years ago, which had remained untouched—undoubtedly contributed something to revitalizing her as well.

She reconnoitered the apartment while Barrett prepared dinner. "Everything looks exactly the same as I remember it," she said, examining the African sculpture she'd given him, knowing his penchant for the exotic and the ancient.

He saw that she was pleased he hadn't removed the statuary she'd given him. But he didn't believe in that kind of purging.

Running her hand along the head of the unhappy-looking Ashanti doll, she frowned slightly and said, "Even the dust is exactly the same."

"No," he countered, "I've replaced it with brand-new dust."

She turned and fixed her eyes on Helen's fog-shrouded island. "You once loved her, didn't you? Funny, even when we were together, you didn't talk about her much."

How was he to explain to her—or to anybody—what Helen had represented? She would eventually have driven him mad, she would've deceived him and run off with other men, being no more capable of settling down with one man than she was of leaving Heisler's employ. But for a brief period of ten months, just when he was on the verge of completing medical school, she'd made the world seem full of high adventure; every day with her was a revelation. She proposed that they travel together—South America, Mexico, Central Asia, the steppes of Russia— anywhere where he could indulge his passion to dig up history. She told him she'd forgo her own career to support him. He would've asked her to marry him, if only because he believed that the excitement she would bring to his life would more than compensate for the unhappiness and craziness, but she asked him first.

It took him by surprise, and in the end, when he thought it through, he recognized that life with her would be impossible. She never forgave him for rejecting her. The last thing he'd expected to have happen was for the woman abandoned at Cornell to turn up at Westside Medical Center as a graduate student five years later.

Kris sensed that he was still disinclined to speak about her, and in any case, she was so distracted, even giddy with fear that simmered right below the surface, that she couldn't concentrate for too long on any one subject herself.

She barely touched her food, although she wanted Barrett to know that it wasn't his cooking that was at fault. He would've put it in the refrigerator to save till the next day, but he'd done that with this chicken once already.

The drinks, together with the trauma of discovering her apartment torn apart, succeeded in knocking her out. Barrett found a gown belonging to his ex-wife for her to wear. It was interesting, he considered, the things women left behind in his place; maybe they all expected to come back someday.

He told her that she could take the bedroom, while he would sleep on the couch, surrounded by ghost masks from Nigeria and carved leopards from the Central African Republic. Kris was too dazed to question the arrangement.

Though he generally did not have any difficulty falling asleep, tonight he lay awake, thinking, all too aware of Kris in bed just beyond the door. He felt as if he had, without knowing, stepped out of one phase of his life and right into another, just in the course of a few hours.

He must have dozed off, because sometime in the middle of the night he heard his name being called.

It took him several seconds before he realized that this was actually happening and not just a dream, that Kris was in the other room and that it was she who was calling to him.

Sometimes gazing into her eyes was like looking across an immense chasm into another world, unknowable, forever beyond his reach. He'd forgotten how uncanny the experience could be, how exhilarating and terrifying too it was to try to leap across that chasm to get to her.

The only light in the bedroom was seeping through the part in the drapery, light from Manhattan reflected off the icy Hudson, and in this faint light he could see that she'd been sleeping badly, that she'd ended up in an awkward position, with Miriam's nightgown twisted and bunched about her waist. The blankets and sheets were in disarray at the end of the bed, and when Barrett placed his hands on them, he found that they were moist with her sweat.

With his palm he felt her forehead. It was warm, a little feverish. Her eyes were big, larger now in the darkness, and they followed his movements. "I don't want to be alone," she said almost in a whisper.

All of a sudden she raised her arms above her head and slid off the nightgown, dropping it to the floor. She held out her arms to him, her nipples pink and large against the ghostly white skin of her breasts.

He watched her, surprised by her action, a bit uncertain, thinking that this would not have happened like this, not so quickly anyhow, were it not for the psychopath who'd violated her home. He had him to thank.

Her body, so familiar to him once, was a stranger's now. He'd forgotten so much. And when he traced a line of kisses from the hollow of her neck to the crest of hair between her legs, he felt as though he were reclaiming territory lost to him. But he never knew, the whole time he was with her, whether he'd managed to cross that chasm that separated them or whether he'd simply dropped down into it, unaware where he would finally land.

9

FROM HIS LIVING ROOM Lew Congdon could gaze out onto the Pacific Ocean, which, when it wasn't behaving, threatened to wash away all of Malibu beach and his house with it. But today was sunny and the waters benign. It was his plan to go for a walk, but he lacked the energy. He thought instead that he would stay put.

Upstairs the woman who'd been spending the last four days with him was getting dressed. He could hear her footsteps as she traipsed from one end of the bedroom to the other. When she finally appeared, she was wearing a sarong and a bright pink shirt knotted above her stomach. She was a dazzling sight.

Not that Congdon wasn't used to beautiful women. Even if he were only an ordinary middle-class businessman, he would have attracted a great many women; he had chiseled features and an athletic body that he maintained with the fervor of a religious zealot. In his blue eyes his admirers saw soulfulness and vulnerability, perceptions that Congdon did his best to encourage.

But the fact was that he was not someone ordinary. At a million-five a film, with points, Congdon was one of the five or six male stars in Hollywood with guaranteed box-office potential. His name on the marquee alone was judged to be worth forty million in rentals before the picture opened.

Although he'd enjoyed the luster of fame for several years, he'd never quite gotten accustomed to it. He was sure that one day someone would tell him it was all a sham and return him to the obscurity from which he'd emerged.

"Are you feeling all right?" the woman asked, leaning over his chair to plant a kiss on his brow.

"Why do you ask? I'm feeling fine," he said.

She was blond, but in a particularly dramatic way; she belonged in movies. In real life she didn't seem quite as real as she would on the big screen. She was too nubile, too alluring. He couldn't take his eyes off her.

"Oh, I don't know." She gave him a long scrutiny. "You look pale." She had a small mirror in her hand and held it up so he could see.

Pale? His tan was legendary. But when he caught his reflection in the hand mirror, he saw that the tan was visibly fading. His eyes were sunken. He thought he looked like a fifty-year-old man, though eight more years would have to pass before he reached that age.

"Put it away," he commanded. "I tell you I'm fine."

He knew he sounded petulant. He also knew that he sounded hoarse, his voice dipping an octave or two from its normal range.

"Maybe you should call a doctor," she said. "Just a suggestion, darling. It's your health."

She went out onto the terrace and stared idly at the ocean. Her name was Sheila Hammond. Whether that was the name she'd adopted for modeling purposes or whether her parents had given it to her at birth, he had no idea. He'd come to suspect everyone of falsifying his or her identity in this town. He wouldn't have been surprised to learn that even her lilting English accent was phony. Not that it made any difference to him.

He'd been introduced to her by his agent, Lee Myers, at

Ma Maison. Lee's explanation of how he'd recently met her was somewhat mystifying.

"Why don't you come back in here?" he called.

When she turned, the morning sun diffused itself through her pink shirt, so that he could clearly see the way her breasts lifted with the motion of her arms. "But why? It's so nice out here. You should come outside."

But he declined. He couldn't move out of his chair. Maybe he really was ill. He tried to recall the last time he'd seen a doctor, but couldn't.

The phone began ringing. His number was a very private one; only four people had access to it. Not even his ex-wives, of whom there were three, knew it.

He reasoned that it must be Lee.

But it was not. It was a man's voice he could not identify.

"You must have the wrong number," he said.

"I do not. Would you put on Sheila on, please?"

Congdon was thrown into confusion. Except for Lee, no one was supposed to know that Sheila was here.

"Sheila!" he said angrily. "Did you give anyone this number?"

She gave him a very odd look. Then she said, "Not that I know of."

"Well, there's someone who's asking for you."

He was so upset that he hung up.

When the phone rang again, he refused to answer it.

"I don't have any idea how anyone would know I'm here," she asserted. "It must be a mistake. Maybe he wanted a different Sheila."

He wasn't convinced. "Where are you going now?"

"To the loo, is that all right?"

She chose to use the facilities upstairs, although there was a master bathroom just to the right of the living room. Although he might have been imagining it, he thought he heard her voice.

Quietly he picked up the receiver. His suspicion was correct; she was on the phone to someone.

He heard the same man's voice. "I want you to go back

to Inverness. You've overstayed your welcome," he was saying.

"Right now?"

"Right this minute."

"I can't just walk out on him."

"Yes you can. Of course you can."

Then the man hung up.

There was no way that Congdon intended to let her leave without an explanation.

He heard her coming down the stairs. He saw that she had her overnight case in hand. It seemed that she wasn't even going to say good-bye. Her idea was to simply slip out.

"Wait a minute! You bitch, where do you think you're going?"

His voice had no strength left to it; it was a wonder that he could make himself heard.

But while she glanced back at him, she didn't stop. He tried drawing himself up from the chair. It was such a taxing effort that it nearly knocked the breath out of him.

He started after her, but she was faster. She was half-way down the path before he could get to the door.

She was lost to him. He realized he couldn't go any farther.

Dazedly returning to the living room, he threw himself down on the couch. Who or what was Inverness? he wondered. Maybe everything would come clear if he knew what the hell Inverness was. But that would have to wait. Right now what he wanted most was a long, long sleep.

10

IN THE SAME ISSUE of the morning paper that announced the death of actor Lew Congdon in Hollywood, Barrett discovered two other items of interest. The first concerned the late Dr. Rollins Hazard, chief of immunology at San Francisco's Coleman Memorial Hospital, who'd died the previous week of what the *Times* referred to as "a severe viral infection which claimed two other Bay Area victims, including an Oakland physician, Douglas Rosen, 38."

According to reports from the Centers for Disease Control, based in Atlanta, a private research laboratory used by Dr. Hazard was ordered closed by the authorities. Spokesman Dr. Alan Schwartz was quoted as saying, "There is a remote possibility that the viral infection involved in the deaths of the three victims might have originated in Dr. Hazard's lab. Investigators from the CDC are pursuing this matter and should make their determinations by the end of the week." He added that he did not believe there was any cause for alarm and that the lab's closing was undertaken "purely as a precautionary measure."

The second item that caught Barrett's interest appeared

under the headline "New York Researcher To Be Named to
Presidential Post."

> Dr. Leo Heisler, an internationally known gene-
> ticist, is to be named to a special Presidential
> Blue Ribbon Panel this week, according to
> sources at the Department of Health and Human
> Services. The panel is to recommend to the
> President more efficient and economical ways of
> delivering health care to the American public.

Only minutes after he put the paper down, a call came
through to his office. Mrs. Preston told him that Dr.
Heisler's office was on the line.

It wasn't Heisler speaking, though; it was one of his
secretaries. "Dr. Heisler wanted you to know that he has
obtained some preliminary data back from the medical
examiner's office regarding your patient Mr. Sandor. The
evidence so far points to a viral process involved in hepatic
failure. It appears as if whatever precipitated the pneumonia can be traced to the liver failure."

This was nothing that Barrett hadn't already deduced for
himself.

But there was more. "Dr. Heisler has called a press
conference for this afternoon to discuss your patient and
other related cases. It will be held at three in the Jacobi
Building, Conference Room Four."

Related cases? Barrett thought. What related cases? He
returned to the paper and reread the article about Hazard.
Then he went back, and giving it more attention, reread
Congdon's obituary. Now he was almost sure that whatever had killed off Sandor had killed these men as well.

This should be one press conference worth attending, he
thought, and then proceeded to call home. Kris had been
asleep when he left, so he had no idea whether she'd still
be there. She was.

She sounded as if it would take another three cups of
coffee before she'd grow fully conscious, but she could
communicate all right. In any case, she said she felt well
enough to contend with cleaning up her apartment.

"Before you do, I thought you might be interested in attending a press conference Heisler plans to hold this afternoon. Who knows, we might be able to wrangle an interview for you when it's over."

She promised him she'd be at Jacobi at a quarter of three. She sometimes could be infuriatingly late, but he did not think that that would be the case today.

Next he telephoned Mrs. Preston from the hospital and instructed her to cancel all his appointments after two-thirty.

She didn't sound especially pleased about it, but she said she would do what she could.

Jerry Perretta was back from vacation, the tan he had acquired endowing him with an exaggerated air of prosperity. He had seductive good looks to begin with; all his midwinter tan did was to give him the appearance of a model who'd stepped out of the pages of *Gentlemen's Quarterly*. The problem was that, in some way, Perretta had never gotten over how glamorous he was, how much he attracted women. Calls in the night for Barrett were from people seriously ill or dying. Calls in the night for Perretta were from women he'd ditched who were desperate to get him back.

If he hadn't been a highly competent doctor, it would have been possible to dismiss him. But he was competent and quick. Maybe a little too quick. He'd boast of finishing an acute gall bladder in under an hour and whipping off an appendectomy in less than half the time it took others.

Barrett thought that he could like Jerry Perretta, but hadn't quite found the knack of doing so. It occurred to him that it might never happen. But they were together because the two had once considered themselves friends and had opened a practice on the basis of that assumption.

When Barrett walked in to see him, an hour before Heisler's press conference, he was busy sifting through his mail. A dozen of his patients—easy to pick out, being young, pretty, and female for the most part—were sitting in the waiting room, and he was opening his letters.

He greeted Barrett effusively. "I feel rested, I feel relaxed, I feel like I shouldn't be back. You look like winter. You bring into this office the stench of decay and maladjustment."

He nearly always spoke like this, like he had the world on a string, or maybe, more likely, by the balls. It seemed to Barrett that he didn't mean his last remark to be entirely taken as a joke.

But Barrett laughed anyway. "Decay and maladjustment are what you get paid for, Jerry."

"Look what I come back to." He spread his hands over the mound of papers heaped on top of his desk, like a magician about to perform an interesting trick. "Just look at all those bills, will you? I thought that they would have disappeared in two weeks. I sat on a beach picking up some rays under the impression that I wouldn't be coming back to this shit."

"Things have been a little hectic around here," Barrett explained. Perretta was trying to make him feel guilty. It wouldn't do him any good. Barrett had problems feeling guilty except when it came to women. Then he got all the guilt he needed, enough to make up for the other times.

"Things are always a little hectic."

Scooping up a sampling of the bills, he appeared ready to toss them on the floor. But he did nothing of the kind. He simply put them back down on the desk. And when he spoke to Barrett now, it was not about the bills, neither the ones that hadn't been sent out nor the ones that hadn't been paid. "Do I know somebody named Beth Sandor?"

"You do. She's a patient of yours." Barrett added that her husband had also been, but he was no longer to be counted on for future business. He added that Sandor had chosen a very unusual way to die, one that seemed to have resisted diagnosis.

Perretta seemed uninterested. Unusual ways to die were all well and good, but he was just back from his vacation and he'd really prefer not to have to talk about them just yet. Barrett could see his point.

"But why'd you bring up her name then?" he asked.

"Because she called me last night and left word with my service that she'd call again. I couldn't for the life of me remember who she was. She also mentioned somebody named Bob O'Connor. Am I supposed to know who he is? I don't have any patient by that name."

"He's some guy who worked with Sandor. But why she'd mention him beats the hell out of me."

"My service says she sounded drunk."

"Look, Jerry, if she calls again and you speak to her, I'd like to know what she has to say."

"Hell, if she calls again, you can talk to her yourself. I don't much care to talk to drunks unless I'm drunk too. Makes communication a lot simpler that way."

At a quarter to three Barrett found Kris pacing in front of Jacobi, waiting for him.

She appeared distracted, not quite with it. Taking his arm, she said, "Millions of people keep going in there. If we don't hurry, we won't get a seat."

She was right. The conference room was nearly filled to capacity, and while Barrett had no difficulty recognizing the people who usually turned out for these affairs, today there were a great many he'd never seen before.

He and Kris were obliged to stand in back. Barrett found that they were right next to Fromm, the resident who'd gotten him up in the middle of the night to inform him that Sandor was dying.

"Looks like a movie set," Fromm observed.

It did. A bank of lights was directed on the podium with its three vacant chairs. The front rows had been taken over by a small army of camera crews and reporters. This was obviously going to be no ordinary press conference.

At five past three the door to the left of the podium came open and two men walked in and quickly assumed seats behind the lectern. They looked very nervous with all the lights on them.

"Who are those guys?" Kris asked.

Barrett had no idea. They certainly were not associates of Heisler's.

Another minute passed before Heisler himself appeared. "The grand entrance," said Fromm.

Heisler strode confidently to the podium. He was wearing a somber brown suit, offset by a splash of color from his red tie. In the glare of lights his glasses sparkled brilliantly, at the same time virtually hiding his eyes from view. While he was obviously conscious of the attention he was drawing, he acted indifferent to it all. This could have been another graduate-student seminar as far as he was concerned.

Half a dozen microphones bristled from the top of the lectern, partially obscuring Heisler's face. He began tapping each one in turn to check if they were all functioning.

"May I have your attention, please," he began, gripping the lectern with both hands. "First of all, I wish to thank you for coming here on such short notice. I promise not to monopolize too much of your time in return. But before I proceed with my announcement I would like to introduce the two gentlemen sharing the podium with me this afternoon. On my left is Dr. Lawrence Wingate, the deputy director of the Department of Health of the city New York." He nodded for Dr. Wingate, a pale, neurasthenic-looking man of about forty, to rise.

"And sitting right next to him is Dr. Dennis Ross, who is attached to the Epidemic Intelligence Service of the Centers for Disease Control based in Atlanta."

Dr. Ross followed Dr. Wingate's example and stood briefly in acknowledgment. He was a man also in his forties, but he gave the impression of having the capacity to move straight to the heart of a problem. The problem he seemed to be trying to solve right at that moment was exactly what he was doing on the podium with Wingate and Heisler.

Barrett was frankly astounded; it had taken him probably no more than forty-eight hours to gain the support of both the federal and local authorities. He had never realized that Heisler possessed this much clout.

"Ladies and gentlemen," Heisler went on, "I would like to use this opportunity to dispel any fears that might have been sparked by an article appearing in today's New York *Times*. The impression a reader might obtain from the article was that this pneumonia of unknown origin might crop up all over the country. One case received special attention.

"That case involves the death of the chief of immunology at San Francisco's Coleman Memorial Hospital, Dr. Rollins Hazard. Dr. Hazard was engaged in research that involved recombinant DNA and there is some speculation that he and one of his colleagues were infected by a neuro organism accidentally created in his lab. As a precautionary measure, the Centers for Disease Control in Atlanta have sealed the lab while the source of the viral infection is investigated. However, it seems unlikely that Dr. Hazard's lab can be implicated, for the simple reason that a third man who died from the same pneumonia was in no way connected with the lab or with either Dr. Hazard or his colleague. The third victim, Michael Andrews, in fact, did not live in the city but was only passing through when he came down with the pneumonia.

"In addition to the three victims in San Francisco, there have been outbreaks in the Los Angeles area; in the Evanston-Chicago area; in Santa Fe; Denver; and, closer to home, at least one, possibly two instances in New York City. The total of victims now stands at twenty-eight. The reason that the disease has not been identified as the causative agent in all these cases until now is that it has been variously misdiagnosed, mostly as a pneumonia-type infection."

There was an audible stirring in the audience, but Heisler continued as though he wasn't aware that there'd been any reaction. "My interest in these cases may already be known to some of you. For several years I've been involved in genetic research related to liver disease. The twenty-eight cases so far recorded have all been characterized by severe liver dysfunction. The disease may be in fact refining new viral particles on the site of the liver.

"We've been able to obtain serum from seven of the victims, as well as various tissues. We are hoping to receive tissues from many of the others, but in the meantime we've been analyzing what we do have. The hypothesis I'd like to venture at this point is that we are probably dealing with a new illness, probably a new type of virus."

Calling to the projectionist, he ordered the lights killed.

The slides he proceeded to show for the most part depicted diseased liver tissue with suspicious white spots that Heisler believed to be the new viral particle. These white spots looked curiously innocuous, like drops of milk spattered over the tissue's surface.

Heisler did not linger over the slides; many of those seated in the auditorium wouldn't have known what to make of them in any case, and Heisler was not about to become technical.

Once the lights were raised, he announced that, in consultation with the CDC and New York City public-health authorities, his lab would become the coordinating center for all research relating to the new disease. For the convenience of the media a press packet would be distributed at the end of the conference.

"Now I will take any questions you might have," he said.

The first man who sprang to his feet represented the *Times*. "There's nothing that you said that would contradict the possibility that an epidemic might break out. Is that a correct assumption, doctor?"

"I would not wish to characterize it as an epidemic at this point. Since we know so little about this disease, however, I could not completely rule out the possibility that it might become one."

A WPIX reporter asked if the disease were invariably fatal.

"In all the cases that have come to our attention, yes, but the sampling is too small to draw an absolute conclusion."

"All the victims have been male," another newsman pointed out. "Does this mean that only men are affected?"

"Again, twenty-eight is too small a number to make any determination like this. Don't forget that legionnaire's disease was initially thought to be exclusively male. Now we know that it has no special propensity toward gender."

A UPI representative now rose to ask Dr. Ross how he could be convinced that the virus did not originate in Dr. Hazard's lab.

"We've gone over the research Dr. Hazard was engaged in and examined the specimens available in his lab and there is nothing we've found to relate his work to the disease. The closing was merely a precautionary measure."

The last phrase was as much a favorite of Heisler's as it was of the CDC people, Barrett thought.

"Does that mean his lab will be reopened?"

"I would expect so, although that is a matter for the CDC investigators to decide."

A correspondent for the *News*, noting again that twenty-eight cases was a very small sampling to draw any conclusions from, said that he had two questions for Heisler.

"One, doctor, have you any reason to think that any of these twenty-eight cases was related to any other?"

"Not at this point. They may, in fact, be altogether unrelated," Heisler conceded.

"If that is the case, then the disease might very well not turn out to be contagious at all."

"That is a possibility," Heisler said, "but on the basis of my previous experience working in the area of infectious diseases, I tend to think that we are dealing with a contagious disease in this instance."

"Your name has been mentioned in connection with an advisory panel on health and medicine the president is preparing to form," a WINS reporter observed. "Do you think, Dr. Heisler, that this honor and recognition by the president has helped you in obtaining the cooperation of the Centers for Disease Control?"

Barrett was surprised; the questions were somewhat harder on Heisler than he would have expected. On the other hand, anytime someone announced the discovery of a new and fatal illness, he had to anticipate a rather heated reaction.

"First of all, let me say that my appointment to this

panel has not been confirmed. Until the members of the panel are announced by the White House, I will have no comment on the matter. As to your suggestion that political influence is responsible for the cooperation federal authorities are providing me, I will let Dr. Ross answer that."

Dr. Ross looked astonished to be put on the spot like this. But he quickly recovered and answered with aplomb, "While we are a federal agency, we are also an autonomous body whose primary aim is to identify and to arrest infectious diseases. To that end we rely on all resources at our disposal. As Dr. Heisler has already told you, his laboratory is one of the best in the country to research a disease of this type. It would take a good deal of time for the Centers of Disease Control to gear up to the stage which Dr. Heisler's lab has already reached. That is why we are more than happy to be working with Dr. Heisler. No politcal influence whatsoever is involved here. I cannot emphasize that fact too strongly."

The WINS reporter did not appear quite satisfied with this explanation, but resumed his seat in any case.

Heisler signaled the end of the press conference by thanking everyone for coming. Photographers in the front row responded with a final assault of detonating flashbulbs, as if they feared they would never have another opportunity to put him on film.

Barrett and Kris struggled against the flow of the crowd to get to him before he vanished through the door to the left of the podium.

But Heisler spotted his former student and stopped long enough to greet him. His eyes, however, were on Kris.

Barrett introduced them, adding that Kris was a reporter.

"A much better-looking one than these others," he said, indicating the few members of the press still lingering around in the front rows.

"I'd like to interview you at your convenience, Dr. Heisler," she said.

"I see no reason why that can't be arranged."

It was obvious that Kris's presence had a more pronounced impact on his decision than if Barrett had interceded for her on his own.

"Should I call your secretary?"

"No, I tell you what. Why don't you come by my office at the Melkis Pavilion around seven this evening? We might have to do your interview on the run. I hope you won't mind."

"Not at all. I do a great many things on the run."

He looked from Barrett to her and said, "Yes, I imagine you do at that."

When they were alone, Kris turned to Barrett and said, "He tries awfully hard to be charming, doesn't he?"

"To you maybe, to other pretty women. But his reputation does not rest on his charm, not at Westside."

"I wouldn't trust him as far as I could throw him."

But he suspected that she wasn't above carrying on a mild flirtation with him if she thought he'd be more forthcoming. He wouldn't dare tell her this. She was so elated by the prospect of the interview that she seemed almost to forget that he was there by her side. And it was he who'd arranged the interview, after all.

"I should go home and look over my notes before I see him," she said. "I only have a few hours."

Barrett reminded her that, given the condition of her home, it was hardly likely to be a conducive place to do anything, let alone review her notes.

She laughed. "You know, I almost forgot about that. I suppose I can use the university library for a few hours."

Barrett left her at the steps of Jacobi, wondering what else she'd forgotten from the previous night. Had she wanted him with her simply to comfort her? Or had she intended something more? If she didn't let him know, he would have to ask her directly. But he'd wait. He might wait for a good long time, because he didn't think he was ready for the answer.

Shortly after returning to his office, where he'd begun to work on bills he'd been procrastinating about, Mrs. Preston buzzed him.

"There's someone on the line for you, Dr. Barrett. It sounds to me like an elderly man. He won't give his name, but he says it's urgent. He says it's in regard to Dr. Heisler."

"I'll take it."

The voice could have been an old man's, but it could also have belonged to someone younger, even to a woman. It was harsh and grating.

"Who is this?"

"Never mind that now, Matthew. You'll find out soon enough. I just want to tell you that you should watch out for Leo. He can kill you so you won't even know when you're dead, Matthew."

"What are you saying? Why don't you tell me who you are?"

But the caller ignored him. "And if he doesn't kill you, maybe I will."

The line suddenly went dead.

A crank, Barrett decided. But the thought gave him no comfort.

11

As SOON AS KRIS stepped off the elevator on the fourth floor of the Melkis Pavilion, a research assistant, probably a graduate student, appeared to greet her.

He escorted her down a corridor flanked on either side by doors she was sure must lead into laboratories, and motioned her finally into an office that looked too sparsely furnished to be Heisler's.

Digital computer rested on a table opposite her, its dead black screen framed in a pristine white casing. Next to the chair there was a table piled high with documents and books. The most prominent object was a cellular model: a strand of wire that climbed like a vine, to which Styrofoam balls of red, blue, and green had been affixed.

Her eyes caught sight of a computer printout that reminded her of those she'd seen in Helen's apartment. She unraveled it.

Clusters of lines radiated up and down its length, and while it made little sense to her, she remarked on the label: "T-protein, VDV-21: Primates (Sample 2)."

Hearing footsteps in the corridor outside the office, she refolded the printout and put it back where she'd found it.

Heisler entered and gave her a warm smile. For someone who'd been besieged by the press all day, he looked surprisingly relaxed, as if he had just returned from a long holiday in the country.

"How are you this evening, Miss Erlanger?" he asked.

"Very well."

"I decided that the best thing to do would be to take you on a tour of the lab, and you can ask me whatever you'd like while we walk."

It was an agreeable enough proposal; she only hoped that she wouldn't make an ass of herself or allow him to evade her questions. She realized she felt intimidated. Having not for an instant thought she would ever get to Heisler, she had the sense that no matter how much she'd read, he'd have no trouble showing her up, proving her ignorant and naive.

But then she thought that maybe it was better if he thought her so; she might learn more.

She followed him first into one lab, where Heisler pointed out incubators filled with cultures: mouse cultures, rabbit cultures, human cultures, some of them maintained at special temperatures, others kept in perpetual motion. He told her that there was a squat brick building across the street where the mice and rabbits were bred for the express purpose of providing these cultures. Where the human cultures were obtained, he neglected to say.

He then showed her rooms where chemical reactions could be retarded or accelerated, and rooms where the temperature could be adjusted from arctic to tropical depending on the requirements of the particular experiment going on. He brought her into rooms where centrifuges with heavy rotors separated out various substances at speeds dizzying even to the men who raced the Indianapolis 500.

"One centrifuge room he pointed out to her was especially designated with a biohazard warning.

"Only one person is authorized to use the centrifuge here," Heisler said, "under a protocol approved by the National Institute of Health."

"Why is that?"

"The specimens that we're working with can be highly dangerous contaminants. Since we know so little about this new virus, we don't want to take any chances. Much of the lab is operating in hyper-P-2 conditions, which means that we're taking maximum precautions to insure against the risk of exposure."

"How much federal funding are you getting for all this, Dr. Heisler?"

"I can't quote you the exact amount, but you may be sure that it's substantial."

"Six figures?"

"The high six figures. But it doesn't come in one lump sum. Also, the final amount will be to be determined by need. I don't want you to come away with the impression that this is the first time the government has funded us. In the past, we've received grants to study a variety of disease processes."

Although she was not especially interested, he proceeded to tell her about what some of those studies entailed. One involved bethalassemia, a genetic blood disease, another herpes simplex, another bovine leukemia, another melanoma. "Did you know that there are some individuals who suffer from a melanoma so severe that even exposure to fluorescent lighting can trigger it off?"

"You mean their skin is that sensitive?"

"That sensitive. It's caused by a recessive gene that usually manifests itself only when its victims are in their twenties. Otherwise it would have evolved itself completely out of existence. If people were born with it, they'd soon die, and that would be the end of it. But diseases can be as tenacious as human beings in holding on to life. It's possible that evolution wouldn't have taken place without disease, that disease is such an integral part of the process of life that we couldn't have one without the other."

She tried to draw him back to the subject at hand. "Dr. Heisler, you said at your press conference that your lab was selected because of previous research you've conducted on liver disease."

"Correct."

"Were there any other labs ever in consideration besides yours?"

"Not that I know of. I think I mentioned that even the CDC hasn't developed their research capabilities to the extent that we have here at Westside."

"Dr. Heisler, has your lab ever been linked to any irregular practices?"

He stopped in his tracks and regarded her with an expression of bafflement. "I'm sorry, Miss Erlanger, I don't understand your question."

"I mean that sometimes laboratories become embroiled in controversies, particularly when genetic experiments are going on. I don't want to imply that there's anything wrong with your lab facilities. I just wondered whether you've been involved in any such controversy."

She was trying to be as tactful as possible and still get her idea across. But she had a feeling that she hadn't quite succeeded. Certainly she didn't care to antagonize him this early on the interview.

"I'm not aware of any kind of controversy. The United States government isn't in the habit of giving out funds to laboratories that engender controversy."

His peremptory tone seemed to put an end to that line of questioning.

"In fact," he said, "let me show you just how safe this laboratory is."

He led her past a succession of doors with labels embossed on them warning either of radiation or of chemical hazards or of both, into a stairwell.

The stairs were hard concrete, the walls steel and concrete, emphasizing the fortified nature of the building. Kris had the feeling that after a nuclear war, when all the rest of the city lay smoldering in radioactive ruins, when the vast honeycomb of structures making up Westside Medical Center had been reduced to rubble, the Melkis Pavilion would remain standing, and the people who worked inside it, oblivious of catastrophe, would go right on with their experiments.

As they were ascending the stairs, Kris asked whether

he thought the disease would claim hundreds, even thousands of victims before it could be brought under control.

"We're working on this twenty-four hours a day," he replied. "I hope that we don't see a level of casualties that high. But there are no guarantees."

Opening the fire door, he announced, "We are now entering the containment area."

Access to the area was achieved only by inserting a personal computer card into a slot by the door and punching out a code on the digital panel underneath it.

Beyond the computer-activated door there was another warren of laboratories. Once again she was greeted by the sight of incubators, biohazard shields, scintillators, balancing scales, petri dishes, and trays filled with gels, in which gene splicing was conducted.

Then he led her to a window and had her look out. What she saw was a second window half a foot distant from the first; between one and the other there was a sheer drop-off, nothing but space. Beyond, there was a patch of sky, river, and New Jersey.

"What we're in is actually a building within a building. A shell of reinforced concrete has been wrapped around this one. That's to make certain that there's no danger of contamination to the public."

"That was why Dr. Hazard's lab was closed down in San Francisco, wasn't it? Because contamination was feared?"

"That's right. It proved unnecessary, but that was why it was done."

He guided her out the same door they'd come in and took her to the other end of the corridor to a small room which contained a console and two chairs and not much else. "I want you to tell your readers that we've taken other precautions as well."

There was no one inside the room at present, although a jacket was thrown over the back of one chair, evidence that someone would be back before long. The console held an impressive array of small bulbs emitting green, red, and amber light. Under each bulb there were switches and tags indicating their function: Biohazard Room 2; Chemhazard Room 5; Main Incubators; Cold Room 1; Centrifuge 1, 2, 3. Three toggle switches were labeled under the heading "Emergency Operations." Whatever happened when you pulled these switches was not immediately apparent.

She asked Heisler.

"First off, it's necessary to insert a key, of which there are only two existing copies, before these switches will have any effect. That's to make certain that they can't be pulled down by accident."

"You have one of the copies?"

"The chief of security has the other."

"So what does happen?"

"In case some contaminant does indeed leak out, by activating emergency operations we can destroy it."

"How?"

"Formaldehyde bombs. They're set into the walls and ceiling just like a sprinkler system. If they go off, they kill any living thing present."

"What if there are people working in the containment area?"

"I have no doubt everyone will be evacuated in the unlikely event that should become necessary. But of course, people *do* fall into the category of living things."

They returned to the fourth floor. All the while, Kris was trying to make up her mind whether to ask him about Helen. In the end she decided not to. There was no reason to believe that he would be truthful if she did, and it might only cause him to suspect her motives. She decided she would stick only to issues dealing with him and his research.

"In your official biography, published in *Who's Who in American Medicine,* it says that you were a consultant to the U.S. Army epidemiology staff from 1968 to 1971. What exactly was the nature of your job?"

"The U.S. military deploys its forces throughout the world, as I'm sure you're aware. There are regions in which malaria, typhus, even such exotic diseases as Green-

Monkey fever are endemic. I was in charge of testing possible antidotes.''

"You were working with Dr. Rollins Hazard, then, weren't you?"

Heisler said that this was true. "An outstanding researcher," he commented.

"Did you ever do work on biochemical-warfare projects—binary nerve gas or anthrax, for example?"

"I had nothing to do with anything like that," he said. There was an edge to his voice, and she had the feeling he was lying. But she realized she'd gain nothing by pressing him. "Is there anything else?"

"Just one more question."

She might be treading on treacherous ground here, but she figured she had nothing much to lose.

"What is it? I have to get back to my office."

"What is a T-protein?"

The question obviously took him aback, because something changed in his expression, his eyes narrowed, and he regarded her with renewed curiosity. "How did you happen to come across a reference to the T-protein?"

His smile was strained. She'd gotten to him in some way, but she had no idea how.

Unable to fabricate an explanation on the spot, she said she'd noted it on a computer printout in his office. "I was just curious," she said, attempting to be as offhand as possible.

She couldn't tell whether he believed her or not. "There are thousands and thousand of proteins in the human body. The T-protein is just one of many."

That told her precisely nothing. "Is the T-protein related to the virus you talked about today at the press conference?"

He gave her a defiant look that made her fear she had overstepped her bounds.

"There's absolutely no connection," he said. She'd made him angry, no question. "And the next time you're invited somewhere, I would suggest you refrain from nosing about among your host's personal effects. If you're found out, you may not be invited back."

12

Isaac Ninn. who used to be Colin Thomas, found himself once again walking along the banks of the Charles. The last time he'd been here was six years before, prior to his exile to England. As Colin Thomas he'd been a pathologist; before that, a surgeon. But everything had changed since then: his name, his face, the manner in which he carried himself, even his accent. Everything except for his desire to destroy those who'd attempted to destroy him.

It was likely that his antagonists did not even believe that he was alive. The truth was that he'd contemplated ending his life when he'd been forced to retire as a surgeon. But he'd not succumbed to the temptation. Even when he was finally disbarred from the practice of medicine in the United States altogether, the notion of suicide was something he found preposterous. Or rather the notion of a swift, melodramatic suicide. For certainly he was sufficiently self-aware to understand that his drinking was a form of suicide, that in his effort to obliterate so much memory and pain he was also obliterating himself.

Nonetheless, Ninn was convinced that once he'd achieved his objective and seen to it that his former self, the self who used to be Colin Thomas, was avenged, then he might free himself from the need for alcohol. But until then he needed it to ease himself through the days and make bearable the interminable hours of the night.

Unmindful of the wind that was blowing steadily from Cambridge across the Charles, Ninn began walking toward the Beth Israel–Brigham Young medical and research buildings which dominated several blocks of Boston real estate.

It was in this center of advanced medical science that Colin Thomas had spent several years of his life enjoying the status of a brilliant, if erratic, surgeon. There was a time when his opinions were eagerly sought out by his colleagues; there was a time when he was invited on public-affair shows, aired on WGBH, to present his views on a wide variety of subjects: the causes of American legionnaire's disease, the impact of toxic-shock syndrome, the role of hospices, the problems of rising medical costs. It mattered less what he said about any of these things than that he had such an air of authority. People tended to believe what he said.

But all the while he felt as if he were living in the shadow of Leo Heisler, who for a brief period in the mid-1970's held a position in the renowned Lewis Sandburn Institute for Cancer Research. It was at Sandburn that Heisler pioneered some of the techniques in gene splicing that would eventually be adopted for use by labs throughout the world.

What no one knew was that the cultures were derived from fetuses stockpiled in the rear of an abortion clinic shut down by authorities when it was learned that abortions were being carried out as late as the third trimester. It was alleged that several fetuses were born live and then killed. Thomas both performed the abortions and supplied the fetal tissue to Heisler, without government authorization.

By the time Thomas became associated with the clinic, he had already resigned from the staff at Brigham Young under circumstances the newspapers referred to as "cloudy." Thomas had become an embarrassment to the very same colleagues who'd once come to him for a second opinion.

People attributed the botched operations, the neglect of his patients, and the frequent unexplained absences from meetings and work to his drinking. Two malpractice suits were instituted against him before he was compelled to step down.

By becoming a pathologist he opened himself up to a number of tasteless jokes on the part of the people who ousted him. He'd been killing off his patients so that he could be sure of having enough work later on, they said.

Yet, in a way, he preferred the dead to the living. The dead provided him with opportunities to make money that the living hadn't. The dead included the aborted fetuses. Without them, Heisler would never have developed his celebrated techniques, would never have discovered how cats fall victim to leukemia and transfect it, would never have identified at what point a virus produces tumors and lymphocytes in humans, and would never, as a consequence, have been able to go into the marketplace and raise the venture capital to finance his own private research company.

But Heisler possessed a certain magic—or perhaps it was just luck, a matter of stars, the fall of a deck of tarot cards—which Colin Thomas lacked. Why else would Heisler be appointed to a White House panel, while Thomas, reborn as Ninn, was reduced to a life of anonymity and disgrace? The corruption that tainted Heisler had attached itself to Colin Thomas, but Heisler had known how to keep his reputation. Perhaps he had a portrait hidden away in his closet that revealed the true state of his soul.

When the volcano of Soufrière had erupted on Guadeloupe many years before, sending lava spilling down into the villages below, leaving no one alive in them, only one man was spared—a condemned murderer committed to solitary confinement. Heisler and that condemned murderer had much in common.

Heisler would just as soon have been long rid of Colin Thomas, but Thomas refused to give him that satisfaction. He went to London, and taking advantage of the more relaxed rules governing the practice of medicine in the

British Isles, established his own research facility, recreating himself in the process.

Tenaciously he kept on Heisler, threatening him with exposure, forcing him to rely on him for assays and chemical analyses—for vast sums of money. He'd courted Helen so he would have a way of knowing what Heisler was doing. It was from Helen that he'd learned about the virus, though it was only later that he and Heisler understood what it could do and how they both could profit from it.

And whether or not Helen was dead, Ninn wasn't concerned. He had found another spy to work for him in Heisler's lab.

One day he would see to it that Heisler was ruined every bit as thoroughly as Colin Thomas had been. But until that day, he would willingly collaborate with him and reap the benefits from the virus that he and Helen had created.

There was a restaurant close by the Sandburn Institute to which the medical staff would repair in the evenings on a regular basis. It was favored for its reasonable prices, for its casually romantic ambience, and for its pasta, which, whatever it lacked in subtlety of taste, more than made up for it in sheer quantity.

It was a strange, even eerie, experience for him to walk into the restaurant, called simply Tony's after its late founder, and find himself among the same people with whom he used to be friends. In the days when he was a surgeon and still respectable, he would sit up in the front where he could be seen. In the days when he was a pathologist, he would sit in the rear, closeted in a booth, where he was all but invisible. For some reason, perhaps just obstinacy, he refused to stop coming here.

Today, however, he could sit wherever he wished; no one would know him. For the first time he could recall, he was enjoying the anonymity the plastic surgeon in Mayfair had given him.

He sat down and ordered what he customarily had ordered five years previously—veal scaloppine. Once he'd settled in, he scanned the faces around him. It was surprising how many of them he knew. Bill Hodgkiss, deputy administrator at Sandburn. Carl Elkin, specialist in immunological diseases. Avery March, oncologist. Jack Whittenhouse, genetic researcher and member of Sandburn's governing board. Hal Lawrence, professor of psychiatry and retired physician. Morris Tannenbaum, pediatrician and specialist in congenital defects in children.

These were men who'd either been responsible for his ouster or else had deliberately snubbed him once his station in life had been reduced. He could stare at them now, and he did, smug in the knowledge that they had no idea who he was. He caught Elkin's eye and smiled.

Elkin did not smile back. Ninn could see that he was trying in his mind to place him, but it wouldn't come to him.

These were men who believed that Colin Thomas was out of their lives forever. These were men who would say that they had always thought him a reprehensible individual, who would adamantly deny that they'd once been friends and associates of his.

These were the men whom the former Colin Thomas intended to kill. Realizing that in his excitement he'd lost his appetite, he left the table and strode to the rear of the restaurant, where the public phones were situated. It was time to call some of his friends from Inverness. He'd prefer Sheila, in spite of her congenital inability to follow directions, but if not, Georgia would do. She was proficient enough and certainly dazzling enough to ensnare the likes of Elkin, March, Lawrence, Tannenbaum, and Whittenhouse.

13

THE HUMAN INVESTIGATIONS COMMITTEE convened once a
month—in this case, on a Wednesday morning at ten on the
fourth floor of the Clayton wing. The view from the windows
of the conference room yielded a panorama of the Hudson
River, brilliant under a strong winter sun, and a glimpse
of the Palisades on the Jersey shore.

Twelve members of the Westside staff sat on HIC,
including representatives of the administration, the hospital
lawyer, a contingent from the medical school, a scattering
of researchers and physicians, and, to serve as ethical
watchdog, an Episcopalian cleric as well.

Deputy administrator Herman Rauh brought the meeting
to order promptly at ten, disregarding the fact that one of
the HIC members had failed to show up. Rauh assumed
that he would never show up at all, and so there was no
reason to delay the proceedings for him.

The absent member was Leo Heisler.

Barrett, sitting at the far end of the conference table so
he could, when boredom set in, stare out the window,
realized that this must be at least the fifth meeting in a row
that Heisler had failed to attend. Not until Kris had brought

his attention to the matter had he given any thought to his attendance record.

As usual, the meeting plodded along without managing to stir anyone from his torpor. No one bothered to read any of the reports in full. Instead, a committee member would summarize the results of each study and make a recommendation that would in turn be voted on. Occasionally someone would ask a question, but that was the extent of it.

Forty-five minutes into the meeting, Craig Ahearn, the hospital lawyer, took the floor as chairman of a three-man subcommittee assigned to investigate the progress of a double-blinded drug study conducted by Dr. Heisler's lab.

Just the mention of Heisler's name was enough to invigorate the proceedings; the expressions changed, so did the postures.

Ahearn had a mellifluous baritone voice that could easily lull the listener into forgetting what it was exactly he was saying. His presentation was made with dispatch; briefly outlining the nature of the double-blinded study, approved six months previously, he noted that four men who had volunteered for it had died during that time. There was no hint in his voice or in the manner of his delivery that these deaths were cause for concern.

"The subcommittee reviewed the circumstances surrounding these deaths and fully examined the relevant charts and autopsy findings," he stated. "We concluded that the deaths were all within normal parameters of a study of this kind and that there was nothing about them to implicate either the drugs being tested or the protocol governing their disposal. Accordingly the subcommittee recommends that the study should be continued as is."

As chairman of the full committee, Rauh moved for a vote.

Barrett interrupted him. "I'd like to ask a few questions before we vote on this."

Rauh and Ahearn shot him looks of annoyance.

"All right," Rauh conceded. "But let's not take too long, we have a lot of other business to get to this morning."

"Isn't it true that all the drugs involved in this study are kept on the premises of Dr. Heisler's lab?"

"That's correct," Ahearn said. "But I hasten to remind you, doctor, that with budget cutbacks the hospital pharmacy has had a difficult enough time maintaining and distributing the necessary supply of drugs for the medical center's routine needs. By assuming the responsibility for the drugs employed in this double-blinded study, Dr. Heisler is actually doing us a favor. May I remind you that this arrangement was worked out at the inception of the study and voted on by this committee? If my memory serves me, you were one of those voting to approve it."

Barrett had forgotten this, but was quick to rejoin, "My vote six months ago is not relevant now."

"Well, what's your point?" Rauh asked impatiently.

"My point is that we've had four deaths in six months using a drug that the medical center doesn't have direct access to."

"Dr. Kramer is moderator of the project," Ahearn said, nodding to the bespectacled man who sat impassively on his left, "and he's in possession of the code for the double-blinded study. Do you have any cause to believe that the test drug was responsible for the deaths?"

Kramer appeared surprised, as if he'd just been stirred from a sound sleep. "No, not at all. I've consulted frequently with Dr. Heisler on this and I can assure this committee that he has taken all the necessary precautions. I don't recall hearing any complaints in the past about the conduct of his work. I doubt very much whether the CDC would choose his lab to pioneer research into this new viral disease if that were the case."

"So at no time did you break the code?" Barrett pressed him.

Kramer shifted uneasily. "I think that Craig's report covers everything. There was nothing found in the four auotpsy reports to indicate that anything was amiss or that the deaths might be attributed to the test drug. I don't know why you feel compelled to raise this issue, Dr. Barrett."

Barrett registered the insult. Since Kramer and Barrett

had known each other for years, they customarily addressed each other by their first names. Referring to him as "doctor" underscored his irritation.

Barrett glanced at a copy of the subcommittee report. Ignoring Kramer's last remark, he said, "Now, it states here that this experimental drug was intended to alleviate the symptoms of alcohol-related liver disease, if not cure it."

"That's correct," Kramer agreed.

"It also notes that there was no proof that it did so."

"That's not unusual. Most such experimental drugs turn out to be disappointing. It's a pity, but it happens to be true. Surely you know that."

Barrett refused to let go. "What I would like to know is why Dr. Heisler isn't here to defend his own work. He hasn't attended a single HIC meeting since early last fall."

"Dr. Heisler is a very busy man," Ahearn broke in.

"We're all very busy men," Barrett replied evenly. "But no matter how occupied Dr. Heisler is, I don't believe that four deaths should be so casually dismissed. I move that we postpone a vote on the subcommittee report until such time as Dr. Heisler can do us the honor of appearing before us. If he can't find the time, I see no reason why he should remain a member of this committee."

Were it not for Helen's insinuations that there was some kind of fraud involved in this particular double-blinded study, Barrett would never have pressed this. Even though he had serious doubts as to whether there was any basis of fact in what she'd said, his conscience still wouldn't allow him to remain silent.

There was always the possibility, however remote, that Helen had been telling Kris the truth.

"Let me look at this for a moment," Barrett said, taking hold of the report. He was rather amused by the heightening impatience among the other members.

After skimming through the document, he had additional questions for Kramer, who now had the look of a suspect undergoing a merciless police interrogation.

"Four men received the experimental drug and two the placebo, is that correct?"

"It's right there in front of you," Ahearn said, answering for Kramer.

"And three women received the drug and three the placebo?" It was a rhetorical question. He was building up to something. "It says here that the only patients who died were the four men who were given the drug."

It was Kramer who responded this time. "May I point out that the four were suffering from advanced stages of alcohol poisoning. Three of the four had acute and incurable cases of cirrhosis. In no case were they expected to survive. As I said before, using experimental drugs entails a high risk, and generally they don't work any miracles." Kramer sat back, looking remarkably satisfied.

"You'll also note that three women were given the drug and that nothing untoward happened to them," said Ahearn. "Their records clearly state that their disease was not nearly as advanced as the men's. So it should follow the drug had very little, perhaps nothing at all, to do with whether these patients lived or died."

Rauh had had enough of this. "Gentlemen, may I assume that everyone who wants to have his say has had it?"

"I believe I have a motion on the floor," Barrett said.

"It hasn't been seconded."

The Episcopal priest raised his hand. He might have thought it an obligation to do so.

Raugh sighed. "All right, we'll take a vote on it. All those who favor delaying consideration of the subcommittee report until Dr. Heisler can appear at this forum raise your hands."

Two hands—Barrett's and the priest's—shot up.

"The motion is defeated. Now, do you wish to present your second motion, that Dr. Heisler be removed from this committee for chronic absenteeism?"

Recognizing that it would be a pointless gesture, Barrett withdrew it. The others looked vastly relieved.

Now Rauh returned to the subcommittee report. Not the

slightest doubt existed that it would carry—as it did, by a vote of nine to two.

Barrett refused to give up. The least he felt he could do was consult the records of patients involved in the double-blinded study.

From the Clayton wing he went straight to the record room on the top floor of Jacobi and asked the secretary to find the records not only on the four deceased men but also on all of the other eight patients who'd been a part of the study.

He waited for several minutes for the secretary to retrieve them, but when she came back she was empty-handed. "I'm sorry, doctor," she said, "but I can't find any of them. They've all been checked out."

It did not come as much of a surprise to learn that it was Dr. Heisler who'd taken them.

14

By late afternoon Wednesday Kris had succeeded in making her apartment livable again, as livable at any rate as a cramped studio apartment in Manhattan ever got. The locksmith had come and gone, leaving behind enough locks and bolts attached to her door to keep the Mongol hordes at bay should they choose to turn up anywhere in the West Village. A doe-eyed woman with an impressive array of gadgets strung along her belt showed up from the telephone company and within five minutes had returned her phone to service. The books and papers had been placed back where they belonged, there were new pictures to go up on the walls, the bathroom was newly scrubbed, and the shattered mirror had been taken down and a whole one installed in its frame.

But still it seemed to Kris that for all her efforts, the picture her apartment now presented was an illusion, that the devastation the intruder had perpetrated was hidden just below the surface, ready at any moment to reassert itself. The one thing she was not—the one thing that you should absolutely feel in your own home—was comfortable.

Yet she wasn't prepared to move in with Matthew.

What they knew of each other was based on knowledge gathered from two years back; about who they were now, they were still in the dark. From experience Kris recognized that it was much too easy to slip into the very same habits that had proved so ruinous to their relationship.

He hadn't opposed her returning to the ransacked apartment, but he insisted on lending her money so she could get her apartment back in order without going into hock. "Pay me back when you can," he'd said. "And let me know if you need more."

She appreciated the offer, really had no choice but to accept it, given the grim state of her bank account, but resented the dependency at the same time. Mainly it was her frustration about not being able to make money that was at the root of it.

He also told her that he'd check up on her, that if a day passed and he didn't hear from her, he'd start to worry.

"You don't have to worry," she told him. "I don't want you worrying."

"Nobody can tell me not to worry about my friends," was how he answered. Which was, she supposed, in its own way true.

Before she'd left, Matthew gave her the telephone number of Helen's uncle, Henry Loomis, who lived in Copaigue, Long Island. The first call she made, once the woman from the phone company had hooked up the service, was to Loomis.

He sounded old, as though his lungs had dust in them. After she explained how she'd obtained his number and her purpose in wanting to speak to him, he told her that he very seldom left the house. Coming into the city was not something he'd done in years, and he wasn't about to break with precedent now.

"That's all right, Mr. Loomis," she said. "I don't mind coming out to see you in Copaigue. Just give me the directions from the train station."

The directions seemed simple enough, although the cabdriver Kris found at the base of the platform had to radio back to his dispatcher to locate the address.

Loomis lived in a dull brick condominium complex that bordered a channel in which two power boats were berthed. Come summer, there would doubtless be a great many more.

Evidently Helen's uncle preferred to live without the intervention of sun in his life; shades were pulled down on the upper floor, while curtains shrouded the windows on the ground floor.

She rang the bell, but hearing no sound, tried knocking.

After a while a frail little man appeared and peered out. Kris recognized him at once from the photograph of Helen's graduation; he'd evidently done all his aging already, because he looked no older than he had in the picture.

"You must be Kris," he said, beckoning her in.

As she'd surmised, the house was mostly submerged in darkness, save for a single ornate lamp by which he'd been reading; a book lay open on a table nearby.

There was a musty smell in the house; it could use an airing. Much of the furniture was covered over with plastic. To Kris the place had the atmosphere of a small museum that had seen its last visitor five or six years ago.

"Can I get you something? Coffee? Some cake? It's very good cake. My neighbor made it for me."

Kris declined politely.

Loomis slumped down into a cushioned chair enormous enough for him to get lost in. Although he told her he didn't get out much, he was still very well dressed, in a gray vest and tie and a pair of slacks that looked like they once must have cost a great deal.

Kris began by expressing her sympathy over Helen's death, but Loomis stopped her with a brusque wave of his hand.

"It was painful," he said, "but what can you do? It was the kind of life she was living." He looked at her, frowning. "Did you want to talk to me because you were a friend of hers or because you are a reporter?"

Kris said that she was both a friend and a reporter, that she wouldn't be here at all if she didn't care about Helen.

"We can talk, but I don't like the idea of seeing my name in print."

"It won't be necessary. I'm just hoping to find out about Helen's past as background."

This appeared to satisfy him. "She told you that her boss stole her work, didn't she? Plagiarized it and denied her credit."

Kris said she'd heard about this. "Why do you think Helen stayed with him, then?" she asked. It was the one question she put to everyone who'd known her.

"He threatened her, said he'd make trouble for her if she complained or went somewhere else. I told her this was nonsense, that he wasn't god. She was a smart girl, she could've gotten a job with any lab, but no, she stayed with Heisler."

"Is it possible they were lovers?"

He shook his head vehemently. "I know she had many men in her life, but not him. He had a hold over her, but he was no lover. Maybe he convinced her that without him she would never get anywhere. She wanted desperately to believe in somebody. She had no confidence, she was insecure. That was why she went from man to man, always looking for something from them. Some were very present-able young men. I was disappointed that my niece and Matthew didn't marry. I was so sure they would."

Kris refrained from saying that marrying Helen would probably have been the worst thing Matthew could have done. No matter how "presentable" a potential marriage partner might be, he could never have made Helen happy. From all Kris knew about Helen, no one could have made her happy.

"Have you ever heard of a man named Isaac Ninn?"

"He was a friend of Helen's? Never. But except for those few she knew I would approve of, I never met her male friends. And of course she had so few girlfriends. I'm surprised you two got along."

"Maybe that was because there were long periods of time when we didn't see each other."

"Absence makes the heart grow fonder." He uttered

this cliché and smiled as if he had just invented it on the spot.

Thinking of Matthew, Kris allowed that this was often the case. "Have you ever seen the thesis Helen claimed Heisler plagiarized?"

"Yes, I have a copy of it. She left it with me. I think she meant to pick it up but never got around to it. Wait here, please."

He rummaged about in the other room for a few minutes, returning with a thick sheaf of yellowing pages held together with string.

Attached to it was a Xerox copy of an article authored by Leo Heisler, which had been published in *The Annals of Viral Medicine,* Vol. XLVII, Number 6.

"This is the plagiarized article?"

Loomis nodded. "You can turn on that lamp over there and read it if you want."

She began to do so while Loomis observed her. The intensity of his gaze unsettled her.

"Could I make copies of these, Mr. Loomis?"

"I don't want them leaving the house. I have so little left of Helen's, you see. You can take notes, though."

In theory, that was fine. But the truth was that the article from the journal was so abstruse that she could barely comprehend it. The thesis was no clearer to her. Only someone qualified could tell her what this was about. The most that she could deduce was that both Helen's thesis and Heisler's article concerned the composition and behavior of certain types of virus and how these viruses attached themselves to animal cells.

None of it seemed revelatory enough to bestir readers of *America Now.* Even if an expert could prove that the article was plagiarized from the thesis, it was not going to sell very many papers.

But one reference did capture her attention. It came at the very end of the thesis on a page that was otherwise blank except for the words "Appendix 1: The T-Protein Factor in Viral Transmission."

This was the third time she'd come across mention of

the T-protein, and for a moment she thought she might be onto something.

Turning the page, she discovered that the contents of Appendix 1 were missing. There was an Appendix 2 and an Appendix 3. But no Appendix 1.

She carefully went through the entire thesis, thinking that possibly the pages were out of order, but they weren't there.

She pointed this out to Loomis.

He had no explanation for her. "I just put it away for her," he said. "I don't know anything about it. What you see there is all I have. Has it been of any help to you?"

Not to hurt his feelings, Kris said that it had. "I don't want to take up any more of your time, Mr. Loomis, but if you think of something else that you would like me to know, please give me a call. Even if you would just like to talk to somebody."

She had a feeling that he spent most of his time in solitude and that he was more disposed toward company than he would care to admit.

He tried to persuade her to stay longer. "Are you sure you wouldn't like some coffee? A soda maybe? I have some Pepsi in the refrigerator."

"No, thank you, Mr. Loomis, I have to get back to the city."

He stood watching her from the door until she'd disappeared from sight. When he closed it shut and turned around, he was startled to see that there was someone standing behind him.

"Who are you?" he stammered. "How did you get in?"

Earl Wheelock gave him a broad smile that could have done with a couple of additional teeth. "It's not important how I got here. What's important is where your niece is."

He shook his head. "You're mad. You don't know what you're talking about. My niece is dead."

The smile wouldn't give up; Earl didn't seem to know how to get it off his face.

He had Loomis backed against the door. He had very little time to discover what he needed to know; it was imperative that he be on the same New York–bound train that Kris was taking. Isaac wouldn't like it if he lost her.

"I'm a very impatient person," he said. "If I don't find what I'm looking for, there's no telling what'll happen."

The truth was that he often didn't know himself. He'd had no idea until he'd accomplished it that he would tear apart Kris's apartment the way he had. It was a compulsion, a *need*, and he couldn't see the slightest reason why he shouldn't give in to it.

"You have to leave," Loomis said, his whole body quivering with terror. "You can have all the money I have, but please, you have to go."

Earl was tiring of this. He snapped open a blade and touched the point of it to Loomis' neck, a quarter of an inch below his Adam's apple. "No excuses. Tell me where Helen is."

Loomis hardly dared breathe, let alone speak, with the knife pressing against him.

When he said nothing, Earl applied just the slightest bit of pressure. A single drop of blood formed at the tip of the knife. Loomis gasped.

"Now, shall we try again?" Earl asked quietly.

15

KRISS HAD NO IDEA how depressed her visit to Henry Loomis had made her until she was already on the train heading back toward Manhattan. His despondency was like a disease, communicating itself to her.

Lights were coming on all over Queens as the train proceeded in the direction of Manhattan, but they did little to dispel the gathering midwinter gloom. Icy rain drummed against the train, spattering the windows so that when you looked out all you saw was a blurred bit of darkness and ghostly haze formed by the lights; it was like a television station badly tuned in.

As soon as the train pulled into Penn Station Kris found herself being pushed out, forced by the crowd toward the escalators. She was convinced that she was being followed. But there was no one behind her.

Even so, she believed a stalker was there. She needed to have people around. Among a lot of people, she felt, she would not be in much danger. The only place she could think of was a bar. Any bar would do, really, just so long as a single woman was welcome.

The bar she chose was in the Broadway area, a dozen

blocks north of Penn Station. At this early-evening hour it was spilling over with people who'd just left work. There was hardly any room at the bar, and Kris found herself squeezed into the corner almost directly beneath the color television set. It was turned on to the local news but ignored by the customers, who were occupied in conversation.

While the bartender was pouring out a shot of Rémy, the anchorwoman's face was replaced on the screen by a familiar-looking building. It took Kris a second before she recognized it as the very same building she'd visited two days before—the Melkis Pavilion.

Now the reporter was standing inside in one of the laboratories that Kris remembered from her visit. With him was Heisler.

"Could you turn up the volume, please?" Kris asked the bartender when he brought her her cognac. Happy to oblige any single lady at his bar, he did so.

"Dr. Heisler," she heard the reporter say, "two days ago at your press conference you declined to commit yourself about the prospect of an epidemic here in New York City. Do these latest incidents change your view?"

Heisler, his eyes directed at the camera lens, responded quickly, obviously prepared for the question. "Although these new cases are troubling, I wouldn't want to say that we have an epidemic."

"But three of those cases involved delegates attending the National Republican Leaders Caucus now being held in Manhattan. Doesn't that mean that this disease is in fact contagious and that an epidemic is not just a remote prospect?"

"I regret to say that the possibility of an epidemic is greater now than it was on Monday when I gave my press conference. But as to whether this disease is contagious or how it's transmitted, I can't tell you. It's too early to speculate."

"Is there any precaution people can take to avoid contracting this disease?"

"I wish I could tell you, Gary, but right now I have no advice to give."

"Is this disease always fatal, Dr. Heisler?"

"Again I would like to caution your viewers that we know too little about this disease to say for certain that it is invariably fatal. All those who have fallen ill with this particular virus have died from it. That much is true. But it's possible that others who haven't been diagnosed have experienced similar symptoms and lived. And in some instances people may have the disease and not know it."

"Are you saying that there may be people out there who are silent carriers of the disease?"

"It's something we're considering, certainly."

The reporter turned away from Heisler. "This is Gary Fisher for *Action News* at New York's Westside Medical Center."

That was the extent of the story. Kris finished her Rémy and left the bar.

Until she was on the street she didn't know where she would next go. She had a great need to talk to Matthew. It was likely he was still having office hours, but she felt certain he wouldn't mind her paying a surprise visit.

When she arrived at his office there were only a few patients yet to be seen. In the office adjoining the waiting room Mrs. Preston was on the phone. Another secretary, one Kris did not recognize—a mousy-looking woman with reddish-brown hair—was rushing back and forth with manila envelopes and files tucked under her arm.

There was one woman in the waiting room who immediately drew Kris's attention. It wasn't simply that she was stunning; it was the way she was dressed. Not provocatively, by any means, but with such expensive good taste that it was hard for Kris to take her eyes off her. She wore a tweed suit with a waist-length jacket; her shirt was crisp and white and ruffled down the front, with enough buttons left undone to reveal a smooth graceful expanse of neck. Her shoulder-length hair, the color of maple syrup, was swept back with tortoiseshell combs. Her face called out for a photographer to capture it, particularly the eyes which were large and brown and liquid, although at the moment they were half-hidden behind fashionably tinted glasses. The woman was jotting down notes on a yellow legal pad perched on her lap.

Kris assumed she was one of Perretta's patients.

"Is Dr. Barrett about done for the day?" Kris asked, poking her head into the office that Mrs. Preston considered her private dominion.

"He has one more appointment, Miss Erlanger."

"Could you tell him I'm here when he has a moment?"

Mrs. Preston nodded.

An elderly patient emerged from Barrett's office. Mrs. Preston wished him a good evening and addressed the alluring woman filling her pad full of notes. "Miss Payne?"

"Yes?" She seemed ready to leap from her chair.

"Dr. Barrett will see you now."

Depositing her pad in the leather bag she carried slung over her shoulder, she strode across the waiting room after Mrs. Preston, her slim slit skirt showing off her legs to excellent advantage.

The dramatic way she moved across the waiting room caused Kris to remark that Barrett was getting a new type of patient. She realized that some resentment carried in her voice.

"She's not a patient, dear," said Mrs. Preston.

"Not a patient?"

Mrs. Preston held out a printed card for her to read:

Sheila Payne
Representative
Carey Pharmaceuticals and Lab Equipment, Inc.
New York City–Elizabeth, New Jersey
212 555-4001/201 555-0098

"She makes a good many sales, I imagine," Kris commented.

"Perhaps," Mrs. Preston said noncommittally.

"You told Dr. Barrett I was here?"

"I did." She didn't say what his response had been.

Waiting for Barrett, waiting for anybody at this point,

was something that Kris could not do for very long. Ten minutes she could have abided, not twenty. How long, she wondered, did a pitch for pharmaceuticals take? Had it been a man, he probably would have come and gone by now.

She stood up, and ignoring the looks of the two patients still in the waiting room, asked Mrs. Preston if she could use the phone.

Kris began by phoning home to see if any messages had been left for her on her machine. There were two: one from her editor at *America Now*, Marcie Lewis, the second from Isaac Ninn.

Marcie's message was expected. She was undoubtedly calling to discover why Kris's article—about female bodybuilding—was three days late. Every time she tried to tell Marcie that she was working on something much bigger and would soon have a proposal on her desk, Marcie would react with only mild interest and her favorite words, "We'll see."

The hell with her, I'll call her tomorrow, Kris decided.

She was surprised that Ninn had phoned at all, and more surprised still that he'd left a message inviting her to dinner that evening. He was staying at the Sherry Netherland Hotel on Fifth Avenue and asked her to call if she could meet him there.

He wasn't in, but she left a message to say that she'd be at his room by seven.

Hanging up, she turned to Mrs. Preston. "Would you do me a favor and tell Dr. Barrett I had to go, but that I'll call him later?"

She took one last glance at the door to Matthew's office. Sheila Payne had yet to come out, although she'd been in there for nearly half an hour. I wonder what she's selling him? she thought. But it would be more interesting to know whether he was buying.

16

FROM HIS ROOM Isaac Ninn could gaze out onto Fifth Avenue and observe the procession of New Yorkers back and forth. As it was now half-past six, the flow had ebbed; most of those on their way home had long since crowded onto buses or else vanished into holes in the ground.

The woman he was waiting for was twenty minutes late, but this delay he felt was probably due to the traffic. All the way up and down Fifth Avenue, nothing was moving; with a terrific protest of blaring horns, cars and buses sat immobilized in a sea of exhaust fumes.

At last the logjam broke and the traffic gradually began to move. Two blocks away Ninn spied the limousine he'd seen an hour and a half earlier: a two-toned stretch Lincoln, maroon on top, gray on the bottom.

It seemed to take forever to reach its destination. When it came abreast of the hotel the chauffeur quickly got out to open the rear door. Georgia, her breath suddenly visible in the frigid air, emerged, and without a word to the man, hurried into the hotel.

Georgia was not actually the woman's name; it was just the name Ninn had given her. She was blessed—or perhaps cursed—with a lovely, indolent face that promised long hours of expensive sex. Her body was a thing to marvel at, and when she entered his room five minutes later, she immediately dropped her lynx coat so that Ninn could do all the marveling he cared to.

She wore a red silk dress so sheer and flimsy that it was a wonder she hadn't caught a death of a chill, even with the fur. A gold crux ansata dangled beguilingly between her breasts. She smelled of sex, he thought; she smelled of insatiability.

"How did it go?" he asked, facing away from her toward the window.

"I've had better, I've had worse. But he does have energy for a man of sixty-seven, I'll say that for him. Maybe it's true what they say about men with power. How powerful is he, by the way?"

"Oh, very. He's chairman of an important committee in the House of Representatives."

"American politics always confuses me."

"It confuses everybody else—why should you be an exception? Did he divulge any state secrets to you?" This was meant as a joke, but she took it seriously.

"What do you mean by state secrets? All he said was that he was bored with the whatever it is they're having here in New York."

"A Republican National Leaders Caucus."

"That's right. He told me he was tired of speeches and that he was happy to take an hour off."

"Good girl," Ninn said, turning around. "Now, collect your wrap and go back to your room. You can't stay here."

She looked disappointed. He didn't know what she had in mind, and he didn't much care. "Go on, now."

"I'd like to see something of the city," she said. "I've never been here before. The Statue of Liberty, the top of the Empire State, Studio 54, the things all tourists see."

"Sorry, you'll have to see the city another time. To-night you stay in your room until I get back. I don't imagine I should be too late. You'll be in time for your flight."

"I'd rather stay another day, if you don't mind."

"I do mind." He smiled pleasantly enough, but his voice was firm. "You don't have any choice in the matter. That was the agreement. Now, be a good girl, watch television, order up whatever you'd like."

She stormed out the door without another word.

Satisfied that everything had worked out as well as could be expected, Ninn made himself a whiskey and soda.

The phone by the bed began ringing. He wasn't surprised, as he was expecting several calls this evening. It seemed to him that he lived a great deal of his life on the phone. Making arrangements for several women at a time was a complicated business; having to keep track of them all was harder still. If he could ever bring himself to trust someone else, he would happily have delegated much of the responsibility. But for him trust was always a luxury, and it was not one he considered wise to indulge in.

The woman on the other end identified herself as Meri. She was by no means as strikingly beautiful as Georgia or some of the others, but she was more companionable and more intelligent. "I'm here at the St. Moritz where you told me to be," she said, "but our client hasn't shown yet."

"He'll be there. It's the weather that's making everybody so late tonight. If for some reason he fails to appear by seven, call me back and we'll work out another plan of action."

No sooner had he put the phone down than it rang again. He cursed it.

"Yes?"

"This is Sheila."

She was the best-looking woman among the contingent currently operating in New York.

"Where are you?"

"I'm still at his office, but I'm pretty sure I can get him to invite me to dinner."

"Excellent. Take all the time you need, just so long as you're back here by tomorrow morning at eight."

"I don't think I'll need that much time."

"No, I don't imagine you will, at that. But call me if there's any problem. And don't linger there."

"I promise," she said. " 'Bye now."

A man used to things blowing up in his face in the past, Ninn was determined that in this operation, every risk would be hedged if at all possible. His first objective was to make an enormous amount of money from what he would siphon off from the grants flooding Heisler's lab. His second objective was to destroy his enemies, not only those corruptible colleagues of his at the Sandburn Institute but also Leo Heisler himself. No amount of money could compensate for the satisfaction of witnessing Heisler's downfall.

Yet he now found himself in the uncustomary role of having to protect Heisler from exposure. He would not permit anyone else to bring down Heisler; that was his privilege. Having heard of Matthew Barrett's performance at the HIC meeting, he realized that he posed a real threat. There was no telling what he might discover about the double-blinded study. If he forced the administration to undertake an investigation of activities proceeding in the Melkis Pavilion, then it would place the whole project in jeopardy. That could not be allowed.

His thoughts were interrupted by a knock on the door. He assumed that it might be Georgia back again to complain; then he glanced at his watch, saw what time it was, and remembered that he was expecting another visitor.

He threw open the door and gave his visitor a welcoming smile. "Come right in, Miss Erlanger. Let me take your umbrella."

PART TWO

17

BARRETT WAS HAVING THE DAMNEDEST TIME trying to shift his vision from Sheila Payne to the fancy, lavishly colored brochures she kept pushing across the desk at him.

Of the four drugs she'd told him about, he could remember barely a single one. He was tired and his concentration was less than it should have been, but that wasn't the problem. The problem was her. He had the sensation of being in a movie; women like Sheila Payne seemed to belong nowhere else but on celluloid. There was something unreal about her. Even her voice had a certain hypnotic quality, low, breathy, as though her words were coming out in bursts of cigarette smoke.

In fact, the quality of her voice was entirely appropriate to the drug she was now in the process of describing to him. "It's a tranquilizer," she said, "which we're about to put on the market this spring. We call it Anodex. It's a specially formulated tablet very similar to sedatives currently available. Its advantage is that it can be administered in a single dose at bedtime and remain effective for twenty-four hours. It can help your agitated patients get a good night's sleep. The clinical trials we've completed have revealed no adverse reaction or depression that might be associated with it.''

She bent down—way down—to extract yet another brochure from her attaché case. In doing so, her blouse fell open to provide him with a far more generous view of her breasts than he really thought he should have. As embarrassed as he was, he couldn't stop himself from staring.

Raising her eyes at him quite suddenly, she flashed a curiously conspiratorial smile at him, as though they were in on the same joke. "Here," she said, presenting him with a stapled Xerox copy of a magazine article of some kind. "This is a paper that ran in the *Journal of Therapeutics*, which shows that Anodex can be very effective in arresting anxiety in adults. It's much better than Valium, and tests have shown beyond a doubt that it doesn't lead to the same type of dependency that Valium does."

Barrett nodded and smiled agreeably. Whatever this woman wanted to say was fine with him. He thought he might actually buy one of these drugs she was peddling, just because she was so astonishingly pretty. If other pharmaceutical houses hired women like this to be their sales representatives, they would reap fortunes even greater than the ones they were already making.

"The usual dose is thirty milligrams," she was saying, "which can be adjusted gradually within a range of fifteen to sixty milligrams, depending on the reaction of the patient. Prolonged administration of high dosages was found to have no toxic effects, nor were there any noticeable adverse reactions following abrupt cessation of the drug."

She paused, but only for a moment, before producing yet another one of her brochures. "There are a few more products of our company I'd like to discuss with you . . ." Suddenly she broke off, an apologetic smile on her lips. "I'm sorry, doctor, I'm getting carried away. I didn't realize how late it is, and I'm sure you've had a long day."

"It has been long," he admitted.

"Well, then, maybe all this should wait for another time." She regarded the brochures held in her hands. "I could leave these with you and you could look them over." She didn't sound too happy about the prospect. "Though I would prefer to discuss these products in person. I know from experience that physicians tend to ignore a lot of material that winds up on their desks. There's just so much you can cope with, and no more."

"You're a most unusual salesman—excuse me, salesperson. It's rare to find somebody who's as enthusiastic about his work as you are."

"Maybe that's because I'm so new at it. I've only been with this job two months. I wonder . . ."

"You wonder what?"

"Oh, nothing. I just thought that maybe if you had an hour or so free we could go somewhere and I could tell you about the rest of our line. It would save me the trouble of coming back." Evidently she felt a need to further clarify her position. "See, I've just been appointed Carey's representative for the area that covers this part of the Upper West Side. I've been speaking to a number of physicians who work at the medical center, trying to persuade them to prescribe some of our drugs, particularly Anodex. Maybe if you could prescribe it to your patients you might help set off a demand for it. I don't know whether it's too much to hope for, but it would be nice if we could get it on the hospital formulary."

Drug companies were always monitoring the volume of their sales in certain test areas, and perhaps Carey thought that with Anodex it might have a best-selling sedative on its hands.

Barrett realized he felt sorry for her. She really did seem inexperienced, stumbling a bit over her words, striving to be convincing about drugs she probably knew very little about. The idea of spending an additional hour with her certainly was very appealing.

"I'd like to do that," he said, "but I'm afraid I have another commitment this evening. Will you excuse me a moment?"

"Of course." She retained the smile, but her voice hinted at disappointment.

He stepped into one of the adjoining examining rooms to buzz Mrs. Preston. "Could you tell Miss Erlanger that I'll be right out."

"Oh, I'm sorry, doctor, I forgot to tell you."

"Forgot to tell me what?"

"She said she had to run off and would contact you later."

"What?" He tried to think what could have arisen that would have caused her to leave so hastily. "Did she say where she was going?"

Mrs. Preston didn't answer right away. "Well, I heard her on the phone arranging to meet someone for dinner."

"You don't recall the name of this person, do you?"

"Let me think. I believe it was a Mr. Ninn, doctor."

"Ninn?" The name struck no bell. "Are you sure?"

"That's what I heard."

It didn't make any sense; he hadn't expected her to show up at the office in the first place, but then to call up a man he'd never heard of and agree to have dinner with him before disappearing again was too much for him to absorb. He still couldn't figure that girl out, and sometimes he wondered whether it was worth trying. "The hell with her," he muttered under his breath, and went back into his office.

Sheila Payne gazed up at him with a shy, hopeful look in her eyes.

"It seems that I am suddenly uncommitted for this evening," he announced. "Where would you like to go?"

Just as they were preparing to leave, Perretta came out of his office and locked the door behind him.

Only then did he look to see that Barrett wasn't alone. For a moment he stood frozen; Barrett had the feeling that he didn't believe his eyes. The sight of the Carey Pharmaceutical Company representative was dazzling enough to throw him off kilter.

"Are you going to be civil and introduce us, Matthew?"

With a trace of irritation Barrett proceeded to do so. Sheila bestowed a winning smile on his partner, holding her hand out for him to take.

When Perretta discovered what her job was, he expressed amazement. "I'll buy whatever you're selling," he declared.

"You're kidding." She threw her head back, laughing.

"I'm not kidding. I always do things impulsively. Ask Matthew."

"It's true," Barrett agreed, hoping that this conversation wouldn't continue too long in this vein. He did not like to be a party to these little seductive dramas that Perretta insisted on playing out every time he got within ten feet of an available lady. Even an unavailable lady, for that matter.

In which category Sheila Payne would prove to be was not immediately clear. But it was Barrett's impression that she was available—very available.

"She's trying to convince doctors working for Westside that we should prescribe a sedative called Anodex to our patients."

"Just so long as you're not around when they take it," Perretta said. "Otherwise it wouldn't do them any good."

Sheila laughed as though she found this vastly entertaining. She was one of those women who had the knack of always seeming genuinely interested in what men wished to tell her. She was also one of those women whose expression and posture suggested that she was ready at the slightest provocation to jump into the bed with them. Barrett wondered just how smart she really was.

"Well, Dr. Perretta, maybe you should take a look at some of our material too. I managed to pull Dr. Barrett away from his work for an hour so I could make my presentation to him."

"Oh?" Perretta gave Barrett a look that he didn't much like. "I'd be very interested in your presentation."

It was hard to miss the double entendre, but it appeared to have passed right over her head. "If you'd like, I could make an appointment with you too."

"Why don't you save yourself the trouble of making the same speech twice. I have nothing pressing to do at the moment. I could join you—that is, if I wouldn't be intruding. I don't want to butt in on something private."

"There's nothing private about this, Jerry. It's only a business meeting over a few drinks."

"Then it would be all right if I came along?"

Barrett glanced at her, but there was no way to determine what she was thinking from the expression on her face.

"I don't see why not," he said, but with such a hint of annoyance in his voice that he thought sure Perretta would realize he wasn't wanted and would find a way to gracefully disengage himself.

That was expecting too much, however. Once on the trail of a woman, there was practically nothing that could persuade Perretta to disengage. He might not even have picked up on just how annoyed Barrett was.

It was Perretta who now assumed command of the situation, proposing that they go in his car to one of his favorite restaurants, a small, dark haunt not far from Columbia University. With its intimate ambience, characterized by flickering candles on all the tabletops, it scarcely seemed appropriate to a serious discussion about a line of pharmaceutical products manufactured by a company that up until an hour ago Barrett had never heard of. Actually the lighting was so dim that it was just about impossible to read more than the big print in the brochures that Sheila kept extracting from her bag.

After their first drink Perretta succeeded in drawing the conversation away from the subject at hand to how Sheila came to be doing something as improbable as representing a drug company.

Barrett was surprised how easily she abandoned her pitch and began to talk about her life. She said that her father had been a doctor and that she'd once considered going into nursing, but that she'd gotten married instead, a remark that wasn't lost on Perretta.

"Are you still married now?"

"Oh, no," she said. "That ended years ago." She seemed puzzled at the question, as though she assumed that all marriages ended years ago and that this was common knowledge.

Perretta sat back, visibly relaxed.

"But once Charles and I broke up, I had to do something to make a living."

"So you applied for a job in the pharmaceutical industry?" Perretta said, monopolizing more and more of the conversation.

No, she explained, there were other odd jobs until "this thing at Carey," as she termed it, came along. It was one of those jobs she fell into by chance.

"You know," Barrett said, "you have something of an English accent. Did you live in England for a while?"

She laughed. "I thought no one could tell, but occasionally it slips in—the accent, I mean. Charles and I lived in Cambridge for a year. He was studying late-Victorian literature there. It's a very easy accent to pick up, isn't it?"

"Very," Perretta said, anxious to get the discussion back on track.

Whenever she wished to make a point, she would emphasize it by leaning forward so that her breasts pressed against the edge of the table, then dancing her fingertips lightly on either Barrett's hand or Perretta's, depending on whose attention she wanted at the moment. From time to time Barrett felt her legs move against his, and almost automatically he would readjust his position to break the contact. That didn't stop her from repeating the gesture, and Barrett could only assume that it was intentional. He wondered whether she was favoring Perretta the same way.

Complaining that she found it too warm, she removed her jacket and draped it over her chair. Barrett didn't think it was very warm, but there was no doubting the effect she created by dispensing with the outer garment; her nipples, dark circles against the white fabric of her shirt, were plainly visible.

All she needed to do now was undo her hair, Barrett thought. If there'd been any question that she was prepared to seduce anyone before, it was gone now. The only question remaining was who her victim would be. By the way she cast her eyes from Barrett to Perretta and back again, he reasoned that she was having a difficult time resolving this herself. It was his sense that she was partial to Perretta—and why not? He was the ladies' man, the charmer; it was he who dominated the conversation and was undoubtedly prepared to prescribe Anodex to all his patients. Even so, she still gave Barrett considerable attention as well, either because she didn't want him to feel left out or because she still hadn't finished making up her mind which man was the more suitable to take to bed.

Was all this necessary just to sell some tranquilizers and antibiotics? Did she flirt this outrageously with every physician she paid a call on? Or maybe it was all a tease that she would suddenly cut short?

Whatever her motivation or objective, Barrett wanted no part of it. But as much as he wanted to, he could not quite bring himself to leave. Every time he started mumbling some excuse, she stopped him before he managed to get three words out; it didn't take much. All she had to do was clutch his hand and address him directly. He wasn't even conscious of what she was saying; he just enjoyed the melodiousness of her voice.

Perretta, meanwhile, thinking that she might have lost interest in him, would reassert himself anew. "I think we're ready for dinner," he declared.

"That sounds like a wonderful idea," she said.

"I'm not sure that I can—" Barrett got no further.

"Of course you can," Sheila said. "You must!"

"See that," Perretta said, as though she'd made his point for him.

So they ordered dinner and Barrett continued to sit there, drifting in and out of a conversation that had less and less to do with him. Even the Muzak, which had been playing ever since they entered this place, seemed to him strangely obtrusive now, and he began to have difficulty hearing what the two were saying.

Excusing himself, he went to a phone and dialed first

Kris's number, then his own. But all he succeeded in contacting was a tape-recorded message and the sound of his phone ringing in his empty apartment.

No sooner had he rejoined the other two than his beeper went off in his pants pocket.

Perretta smiled. "Glad it's you and not me."

Returning to the phone, he put through a call to his service. He learned that one of his patients, a Mrs. Eldridge, had just been brought into the emergency room suffering from chest pains and a shortness of breath.

Knowing Mrs. Eldridge, a woman in her mid-sixties, from previous experience, Barrett doubted she was having a heart attack. More likely an attack of angina exacerbated by chronic hypochondria, which kept her coming back to see him and Perretta half a dozen times a year. But for once he was grateful to her; she'd unwittingly given him all the excuse he needed to remove himself from a potentially sticky situation.

Perretta said he was sorry Matthew had to leave, especially since they'd just begun dinner. But it was obvious he was happy to have this delicious-looking woman all to himself. "Forget about the tab, it's my treat."

"Oh, no, it's my company's treat," put in Sheila. "I'm taking both of you out to dinner."

There was a sudden silence. Then Barrett said that he had to be getting on his way.

She sprang out of her chair and kissed him on the cheek. "You take care of yourself. I'll call you soon and then we can finally get around to discussing the rest of our products. And I do hope you will prescribe Anodex."

He promised he would. With a nod to Perretta, he rushed off to attend Mrs. Eldridge. If he'd had the time, he might have entertained some suspicions about this woman, but lacking the time, all he could do was wonder what might have happened had he stayed.

In the first few minutes after Barrett's departure, the conversation between Perretta and the woman turned somewhat awkward; they had to readjust themselves to take Barrett's absence into account.

A second bottle of Cabernet Sauvignon succeeded in putting an end to any lingering anxiety.

"I really should make a phone call," Sheila said.

Perretta took her hand, knitting his fingers into hers. "Is it absolutely necessary that you do?"

"Well . . . no, I guess not."

"Good, then let me settle up here, and we can go somewhere else. That is, unless you've got other plans."

"No, I don't have any other plans at all," she said.

It was exactly what Jerry Perretta wanted to hear.

18

NINN WAS DRINKING SANTORI ROYAL, and given the origin of the Scotch, its choice was entirely appropriate to the setting, a new Japanese restaurant located just off Park.

This restaurant was designed like a Tokyo house constructed during the age of the shoguns, with tatami rooms enclosed within still larger tatami rooms, one shut off from the other by curtains of bamboo and embroidered silk. You could make out the voices of other customers, hushed, almost reverential, but only rarely catch a glimpse of them on your way in or out.

The waitresses, with smooth glistening skin, hair coiffed in the classic manner of geishas, came and went in a silence so profound that it was possible to hear the tips of their robes whisper against the lacquered surface of the floor.

Ninn was a friend of the owner of the restaurant, and it was not unusual for the proprietor to close it at eleven at night so that his clients could make what use of it they wished. Anytime Ninn required an environment that offered private facilities and efficient—and discreet—service, he would call upon the owner. For the money he was paying him, there was never any question of obtaining a room—or several rooms if necessary.

Tonight, as he sat cross-legged on a mat across from Kris, he could, if he listened closely, hear Meri on the other side of the bamboo. Her client had made his belated appearance and was now—from the sound of his laughter, high-pitched and frequent—enjoying the attentions Meri was lavishing on him.

Kris seemed not to notice. She was flushed from drinking too much saki. He could sense her nervousness, realized that it was accountable to his presence. He understood that she was attracted to him and didn't really care to be. Also, she was telling him much more about herself than she had had any intention of doing. It happened all the time with him. He could be an excellent listener, but only because he believed that sooner or later he would be able to discover an individual's vulnerabilities by attending to his every word.

Yet, as much as he thought himself superior to people, detached, his emotions kept at bay so that he could judge every situation that arose with dispassion, he realized that he was attracted in turn to her. In comparison with the Meris, Georgias, and Sheilas of the world, she had a certain freshness about her. It was not that she was innocent, it was just that she suffered from the illusion that it was possible for her to change the way things were, and in doing so, change herself.

He would dearly like to transform her, to recruit her and compel her to love him.

Carefully, methodically, he led her on, feeding her facts and falsehoods in equal measure as he described the life of Leo Heisler and related his sordid history. He did not forget Colin Thomas' part in Heisler's career. About Boston, the fetal tissue, the disgrace and exile of Thomas, he left out nothing.

His object was to set her up so that when the time came she could act on his behalf and expose Heisler to the public.

"Where is Colin Thomas now?" she asked.

"No one knows. They say he fled to Brazil or to Switzerland, but there are others who say he's dead. It's my belief that he's dead."

She was so intent on his words that she'd ceased eating, the chopsticks held pinched between her fingers.

"Did you find out anything about the double-blinded study Helen was involved with?" she asked.

Here he was on dangerous ground. If he was too ambiguous or evasive, she might look elsewhere for her information. But he could not tell her too much. The sound of Meri's voice reached him through the bamboo. Even she, who was intimately linked to the double-blinded study, had no idea what it was about, didn't even know that there was such a thing as a double-blinded study.

"I've done some digging," he said, "and it seems in fact that Heisler might be conducting experiments without the approval of the HIC."

"That's what I kept trying to tell Matthew."

"Matthew?"

"Matthew Barrett," she said, slightly embarrassed. "He's a friend of mine—an old friend." Seeing the change on Ninn's face, she asked, "What's wrong? Aren't you feeling well?" Her eyes focused on the bottle of Santori.

"I'm fine," he said. He smiled, but all the while he was attempting to absorb this new revelation. At this very moment Barrett was being lured to his death.

"Just how much of a friend is he?" he asked, hastening to add, "I don't mean to pry, I'm just curious."

"Well, it's hard to say. We lived together for almost a year. But that was two years ago. It's only recently that we saw each other again. In a strange way, it was Helen who brought us together. I mean, if she hadn't died, I might not have had the courage to see him again."

"I'm not sure I understand."

"He was almost going to marry her when he was in med school, and it was through him that she and I became friends. So when I heard she had died, I thought immediately of Matthew. I needed to see him. It was more than just the story. The story was important—it still is—but even after two years, I wanted to see him again. Just to talk."

"I see," Ninn said tonelessly. "But it got to be more than just words."

She nodded. "I have no idea what'll happen next."

What'll happen next, Ninn thought, is that he'll be dead. What'll happen next will be up to me.

A long silence passed. "Isaac?"

"Yes?"

"I don't mean this to sound insulting . . ."

"But?"

"But why are you helping me, giving me all this information about Heisler?"

"Because of Helen," he replied quickly. "I think I told you when we met at her apartment that I believed Heisler might have been responsible for what happened to her. I can't prove it, but you know as well as I that he placed tremendous pressure on her. Finally it got to be too much. So if I'm helping you, it's really for her."

She accepted his explanation, not just because it sounded plausible but because she was sentimental enough to believe it.

The truth was that while Ninn had met Helen, he'd never been one of her lovers. But with the number of men in her life, many of them with nothing else in common save their anonymity, how was Kris to find this out?

When they left the restaurant, he could no longer hear either Meri or the client. The conversation must have concluded, he thought, the business of pleasure begun.

It was no longer raining; what had been rain had now turned into a foggy mist, making for the closest thing to a romantic evening that February can offer.

Kris took Ninn's arm and allowed him to decide on the direction they'd take.

They began walking uptown toward his hotel. At the southeast corner of Madison and Fifty-third he caught sight of a familiar figure. Earl Wheelock. No one was more certain to dispel any notion of a romantic evening than Earl Wheelock.

Had the opportunity presented itself, Ninn would have gone over to him. Earl evidently hadn't gotten it clear in his head that this evening there was no need to trail Kris. Ninn had explained that he would be with her, that Earl could better spend his time browsing uptown saloons in search of Beth Sandor.

Like Helen, she was another wild card in the pack, uncontrolled and an ever-present danger to the operation.

He suspected that the real reason Earl was tagging along after them was that he was jealous; he didn't care for the idea that Ninn might prefer Kris's company to his.

Although Earl was signaling to him, tipping his cap in a manner that even the most oblivious observer could pick up, he chose to ignore him.

Ninn glanced at Kris out of the corner of his eye and noted with satisfaction that she'd failed to notice Earl.

As they passed him on the other side of the street, he gave a slight nod.

"It looks like I'm walking you back to your hotel," Kris said a couple of blocks farther on.

"We'll find a taxi for you there. It's never any problem."

He had the feeling that she'd expected him to invite her up to his room. But while the prospect held some interest for him, if only out of curiosity to see what would develop, it was really impossible. After all, he couldn't have her in the room as he repeatedly answered phone calls from half a dozen women. It wouldn't quite square with the impression he wished to leave her with.

Once they'd reached the Sherry Netherland, he had the doorman, a broad-shouldered man with the face and brusque manner of a drill sergeant, flag down a taxi.

Giving her a kiss as chaste as a mourner would bestow on a relation lying in an open coffin, he told her he'd call her just as soon as he was back in town. "It shouldn't be very long, I'm always in and out," he said.

She thanked him for the evening, but he was suddenly distracted by the sight of Georgia walking out of the lobby. "Good night," he called to Kris as the taxi door slammed, then ran after Georgia.

Either Georgia was too high to understand that while it may have been an uncharacteristically benign night for February, it wasn't exactly warm out, or else she was just unaffected by the chill in the air. Because all she had on was her silk dress.

As he came abreast of her at the corner, he said, "What are you doing out here?"

She spun around, angry that her escape had been aborted. "I told you, I wanted to go dancing. It's boring staying in my room."

He gripped her arm hard enough to make her wince and cry out. "Stop it, you're hurting me!"

It was then that he saw that Kris's taxi was sitting at the light, waiting for it to change, and that she was looking at them with an expression of incomprehension on her face.

"Come on, Georgia, I don't want you out. You have to go back," he said, abruptly relaxing his hold.

The light changed, the taxi shot out into the traffic. With no one else in the vicinity to concern himself with, Ninn balled his hand into a fist and drove it hard into her stomach.

She gagged, doubling over, while he stood there and quietly spoke to her. "You know the rules, Georgia. You mustn't break them."

Steadying her with his arm about her waist, he led her back to the hotel without further resistance on her part. "It'll be all right, you'll see," he said in a soothing voice. "We'll have a drink and then you'll go to bed."

"Can I stay with you, then?" she asked.

"No, you stay only with whom I tell you to," he said. "That's what you're getting paid for, after all."

19

WHEN PERRETTA WOKE UP, he discovered two things. The first was that Sheila was gone, the second was that he was late. He did not remember whether he'd set the alarm or whether he'd shut it off when it had rung and gone back to sleep. Not that it mattered. He was reconciled to the idea of being late; it was worth it.

The scent of her perfume was everywhere in his bedroom. There was another odor, one much less agreeable, the odor of stale alcohol. He spied two glasses on the table across the room and a bottle of Chivas Regal. There did not appear to be anything left of the Chivas. Which might explain why there was such a terrific hammering in his head.

He searched for a note and presently found one held by a magnet to the refrigerator door: "Late for work, call you soon. Love, Sheila." He would like to see her again, to be sure; her ability in bed was a source of wonder; he'd had very few women who were anywhere near as beautiful or as proficient. But there wasn't any emotional connection. While she pretended to be fascinated by whatever he said— and with his imbibing, he had said a great many things—he

127

was shrewd enough to see through it. She was acting out a role. In fact, he had the sneaking suspicion that she might have been a professional. But that didn't make any sense. If she were, she would have made it clear from the outset; certainly she would have demanded payment.

In a surge of panic he checked his wallet, but there was nothing missing from it.

He didn't know why his thoughts were taking him in this direction. There was no plausible reason why she wasn't what she said she was, a representative of a pharmaceutical company based in New York and New Jersey,

His suspicions didn't dissolve with his shower, but on the other hand, he didn't act on them. Sheila Payne, he concluded, was a nice piece of ass, a one-night adventure, that was all. Though who could tell? More than one woman he assumed to be nothing more than a one-night stand had surprised the hell out of him by calling him a few weeks later. It was endlessly flattering to know that even on the verge of middle age he could still excite the attentions of attractive women.

The shower helped to get some of the juices flowing again, but the exhaustion he felt, coupled with the hangover, would not be swept away so easily. Coffee and juice and the addition of a few uppers to his system alleviated the pain to some degree, but he realized that nothing less than a good night's sleep would repair the damage.

Turning on the television, Perretta was rewarded with the image of David Hartman on *Good Morning America*. He was conducting an interview with a senator about the latest budget battle in Congress. The only interest Perretta had in this was how it would affect the stocks he owned. The market had been behaving erratically lately and the only thing he could rely on his broker for was bad advice.

As late as he was, he could barely get his body to move. It just wasn't in any kind of functional mood today. Every movement he made entailed a terrific amount of strain. He kept downing cups of coffee, but all he succeeded in doing was churning up his stomach.

David Hartman had vanished from the screen, to be

replaced by two very distinguished-looking gentlemen sitting on either side of a freshly scrubbed newswoman. She was introducing the two interviewees as doctors, one from Sloan-Kettering, the other from Columbia Presbyterian. "With the alarming increase in the number of deaths from Heisler's Disease in the New York metropolitan area, do you think we are in the midst of a full-scale epidemic?" she asked the two.

The doctor from Sloan-Kettering hedged, saying that it was premature to make such a flat statement, echoing Heisler, while his counterpart from Columbia Presbyterian was inclined to say that it now was definitely reaching epidemic proportions. "The first week here in New York, all we saw was one, maybe two deaths from this thing. Now, I understand, in the last few days the number of cases has grown markedly. And as more physicians have come to understand the nature of this disease and to identify it correctly, many additional cases are coming to light. Four deaths were recorded yesterday. Overnight that count has risen to five. That now makes seventeen here, one hundred and thirty-six nationwide. I regret to say that we will probably see a dramatic increase by the end of the week. And then there will be no question about an epidemic."

Perretta, listening to these remarks, had the sinking feeling that he would be confronted by patients sure they had this disease. Evidently no one had been able to save any of its victims, and it always angered him when he was helpless to effect a cure or at least prolong a life.

"Are we getting any closer to a knowledge of what this disease is?" the moderator was asking.

"I am confident that we are doing all we can to find out," the Sloan-Kettering man responded. "The federal government is putting all the resources at its disposal to work. Dr. Heisler's laboratory at Westside Medical Center is coordinating all of the research in a twenty-four-hour-a-day battle to find a cure. I'm informed that the government is speeding a sizable grant through the pipeline to Dr. Heisler so that he can pursue his investigation. I think you can safely say that no effort or expense will be spared."

"And remember that while there have been several deaths from this disease, in comparison to the population at large, their numbers have been quite small," pointed out the man from Columbia Presbyterian.

It looked as though they might go on for another few minutes; Perretta had no time to watch. Switching off the set, he put on his coat and hurried out of his apartment.

It seemed unusually cold out this morning. Generally the cold didn't bother him; even when the temperature was in the thirties, barring the presence of a stiff wind, he could dispense with an overcoat without any discomfort. Not today. Today he doubted he could ever get warm.

He managed to get through rounds at the hospital, though half the time he was in a haze. One or two of the nurses asked him if he felt all right. "You look pale, doctor," they'd say. "Are you sure you're okay?"

"A hard night last night," he'd reply.

And right away they knew what he meant; they were well aware of his reputation—especially the nurses—and his explanation never failed to draw a smile accompanied by low laughter.

Seeing Barrett in the afternoon at the office was enough of a psychological boost to lift his spirits. Although it had been an emergency call that had removed Barrett from the competition, Perretta had never had any doubt that of the two men, Sheila would choose him. The problem with Barrett was his lack of adventure; once he found a woman he could get along with, he clung to her as long as he could. He was afraid to experiment, afraid to compete.

"How did that coronary of yours turn out?" Perretta asked him.

Barrett shrugged. "It was just as I suspected. There was nothing wrong with her. She was probably hyperventilating and made herself panic. I admitted her overnight and released her this morning. And how did your night go?"

His smile gave him away. All Barrett had to do was take one glance at Perretta's face to get a very good idea how his night had gone.

"I hate to say it, Matthew, but you don't know what

you missed by not sticking around. That Sheila Payne was something else.''

"I'm not surprised.''

"Once that lady gets going, she doesn't stop. Between you and me, I don't think I could handle someone like her every night of the week. Talk about energy. Jesus!''

"I'm glad you enjoyed yourself, Jerry. I'll see you later.''

By four in the afternoon Perretta told Mrs. Preston to cancel the rest of his office hours. He just couldn't cope any longer. Placing his hand to his brow, he was astonished to discover how feverish he was. I must be coming down with something, he concluded.

With so much to drink last night and so little sleep, he decided that he must have lowered his resistance and had very likely set the stage for this Russian flu that was going around. He was furious that he would now have to curtail his schedule for the next few days. His only consolation was that he probably could induce one of his more solicitous female friends to come over and take care of him.

Never one averse to treating himself, he rummaged through the medical-supply cabinet and helped himself to a handful of antibiotic samples, some antihistamines, and uncoated aspirin. He realized that the antibiotics wouldn't do him any good if it turned out it was a viral syndrome he was suffering from. But hell, if he prescribed them to his patients, there was no reason he couldn't sample them himself.

As he was on his way out of the office, Mrs. Preston gave him a measured glance, narrowing her eyes to emphasize her disapproval. "I think, doctor, that it wouldn't hurt if you let Dr. Barrett have a look at you. It would make me feel better.''

"It's nothing, really, Mrs. Preston, just a bad cold. I'm sure that with a good night's sleep I'll be in fine shape tomorrow.''

The phone was ringing when Perretta walked into his apartment. He ran to answer it.

"Jerry?"

"Yes?"

"This is Sheila."

"I didn't recognize your voice for a moment."

"I was wondering if I could stop by this evening?"

As terrible as he felt, he could not bring himself to say no.

To keep himself alert, he dropped an injudicious quantity of uppers into his stomach, chased down by an equally injudicious quantity of Scotch. But the combination was enough to put him at one remove from whatever was afflicting him.

She was late by an hour, and even with all the chemical tinkering he'd done with himself, he could barely stay awake. She was a blur unless he concentrated hard to see.

Yet, to his amazement, she was skillful enough to arouse him even in his depleted condition. The problem was that he was practically numb. He had to assume that from the way she held him, and from the look in her half-slitted eyes, and from the sounds she was making, that he was still capable of performing, but he really didn't know. It was like having some peculiar, hallucinogin-induced out-of-the-body experience.

Then, suddenly, it all got away from him. He fell away from her with a groan.

"Jerry, what's wrong? What happened? Is it me?"

He tried to get an answer out, but the words died on his lips. He realized quite suddenly that he couldn't see her; he couldn't see anything at all.

20

Jolted rudely awake, Beth Sandor gazed blurrily into the eyes of a man who loomed above her. A bartender.

"Miss, you can't sleep here. You have to do your sleeping at home."

"I wasn't sleeping. I was just sitting here thinking."

"If that's thinking, then you'll have to do *that* at home."

"Don't worry about me," she snapped.

Not about to provoke an argument if he could help it, he tried to be conciliatory. "All right, but if it happens one more time, I'll have to throw you out of here. Understand?"

She returned to her drink. She'd days before lost count of how many she'd had, how much vodka had gone down, how much gin, how much wine. She'd even lost track of which bars she'd been in, couldn't even say for certain which one she was in now.

It had started when some doctor had phoned her in the middle of the night to tell her that Jim had died. It somehow hadn't surprised her. She didn't know why he'd died. Something about pneumonia. That was enough for her.

At first she couldn't figure out why she hadn't at least called the doctor back or gone to the hospital to see to the disposal of the body. What would they've done with Jim anyway? Buried him up in potter's field where they buried all the paupers? She didn't know.

But it was guilt that was at the heart of it. Guilt. When the doctor had woken her she'd been with another man. A friend of Jim's. His best friend, as a matter of fact. Bob O'Connor.

She felt that she was being punished because she was so happy to have Jim gone and Bob with her in bed. Evidently the punishment wasn't enough, because now God had taken Bob away from her too. Killed him like he'd killed Jim. Pneumonia.

And now where would she ever get another man? She'd once been attractive, and there were traces of beauty left, but the booze and an unhappy marriage had sabotaged her, so that now her face bore the look of a woman in her forties, though Beth was only thirty-one. Her blazing red hair should have been cut weeks ago, because now it was a tangled mess, giving her the appearance of a madwoman. What man would so much as look at her now?

Even if she managed to find a man, he wouldn't want to have anything to do to her once he found out about Jim and Bob.

She was afraid of what a doctor might say. She detested doctors, detested hospitals. For years she'd succeeded in staying far away from them, until she'd gotten sick with all the drinking.

She'd been at Westside three times, but they never could cure her of her addiction to the bottle. The doctors described her as a hopeless case; they said if she kept on, she would kill herself.

They asked her to take part in a study—a double-blinded study, they called it. They said they were going to give her medicine which would remedy not her drinking, but the damage she was inflicting on her liver because of it. It was experimental, but it didn't matter to her. She didn't want to die. She just didn't want to be with Jim. Only she couldn't say this to anybody. Jim would have killed her if he ever found out.

When Jim had taken sick, she thought nothing of it. She even persuaded him to go to the hospital when he insisted that he stay at home and sweat it out. But when Bob, too, had taken sick like Jim, she began to think that maybe it had something to do with her, that she'd caught some kind of germ in the hospital and passed it on to them. She'd heard that there were millions of germs floating about in hospitals, that you could get sicker in there than you could out on the street.

She was sure she was carrying something terrible inside her. It was funny that she hadn't come down with some weird pneumonia too, but it hadn't happened. She might die of all the booze she'd been putting in herself, but not of pneumonia.

Finally she found enough courage to put in a call to her doctor. She lurched over to the phone booth, composed herself, and dialed information.

With immense difficulty she wrote down the number the operator gave her. To her disappointment, she was informed that her doctor, Jerry Perretta, could not be located.

"He doesn't answer his beeper, I'm afraid," she was told by his service. "I'll try to reach his partner for you, Dr. Barrett. Could you give me your number, and I'll have him get right back to you."

Beth was unhappy about this solution but read off the number to her anyway.

A few minutes later the phone rang. She didn't immediately answer it, because in truth she'd momentarily forgotten she was waiting for a call.

"Is this Mrs. Sandor? I'm Dr. Barrett, Dr. Perretta's partner. How can I help you?"

"I need to come in and talk. Listen, I killed Jim and Bob. I gave them this pneumonia thing."

"You mean your husband, Mr. Sandor, and Mr. O'Connor?"

"I can't talk now. I don't like talking about these things over the phone. Can I come in and meet you someplace?"

"Just calm down now, Mrs. Sandor. It'll be all right.

Can you meet me at the emergency room of Westside Medical Center in about half an hour? Can you get here in that time?''

''All right, I can be there.'' She didn't like the idea of an emergency room, nor did she have any idea how long it would take her to get there, since she had no inkling of where she was now. ''You wait and I'll be there.'' With that she slammed the receiver down.

She decided to wash up, and headed toward the ladies' room. She couldn't very well present herself to a doctor looking the way she did.

Earl Wheelock observed her weaving in the direction of the men's room, entering, then a few moments later realizing her mistake and switching rooms to the one with the silhouette of a female on the door.

Having seen to it that Kris had gone immediately home after her walk with Ninn, he'd come all the way uptown to find Beth. He'd done this for the last few nights, tracking her from bar to bar, but tonight was the first time he'd actually gotten to a place and found her still there. Usually he'd be told that she'd been there but was now gone.

Tonight if she was going anywhere, it was with him.

Beth spent fifteen minutes scrubbing her face, combing her hair, applying lipstick and rouge. But when she stepped back to observe the results in the mirror hanging above the ladies' room sink, she was hardly satisfied. She didn't know whether anything would help.

When she reemerged, she was greeted by a young man, younger than she at any rate. He wasn't bad-looking; his hair was black and thick and straggled down his neck; his smile was so winning that she had the sense that maybe she'd run into him before. There were a great many men she met during binges like this, whom she couldn't recall.

He was wearing a brown leather jacket and a set of keys jangled at his hip. He looked like he might be a member of a bike gang; he was a type she wasn't very well acquainted with.

''How are you?'' he said. ''You looking for someone?''

She shook her head vigorously.

"You look like you were looking for someone. But if you're not, I'd like to buy you a drink."

Maybe her impression of herself in the mirror had been wrong; maybe she'd fixed herself up enough to attract the attentions of a man. "I don't know," she said.

"You don't like me?"

"No, that's not it. I like you. It's just that the bartender here refuses to serve me another."

The man nodded understandingly. "There are other bars. We don't have to stay here. I have a car. We can just go."

She considered this for a moment. It came back to her that she had made an appointment with this doctor at the hospital. "There's somewhere I've got to be in a little while."

The man shrugged. "So, no problem. I told you I have a car, I'll drive you wherever you're going."

It all sounded much easier to her. To search for a cab or a bus at this hour was too tortuous an exercise to contemplate.

"All right, all right." She held out her hand and introduced herself.

The man said that his name was Earl. No last name. But then again, in encounters like this, who expected last names?

Earl said he had an idea. He would buy a bottle from the bartender and they could drink it on their way to wherever Beth wished to go.

There was something odd about this, Beth thought, something off balance. But it was enough that this Earl fellow seemed to like her. She needed to have someone take her mind off things.

Just as Earl said, he had no difficulty purchasing a bottle of vodka from the bartender. It wasn't a pint, as she expected, but a quart. "I don't know whether I can drink all that," she said.

"If you don't, it'll keep," he replied, taking her arm in his, at the same time steering her out of the bar.

Once they were in the car, they began passing the bottle

back and forth. Beth realized she was doing all the talking, but every so often she'd sense that Earl was paying absolutely no attention to her. She'd grow upset and sometimes jab him in the shoulder. "Are you listening to me?" she'd demand.

He'd laugh and say, "I'm listening, sure, I'm listening, what do you think I am?"

It was only when he pulled the car to a shuddering halt that she became conscious of her surroundings. They were parked at the very edge of a pier overlooking the Hudson. It was dark all around. She had to look back, out the rear window, before she saw any lights. "Where is this?"

"Somewhere," he said. "Just somewhere."

The bottle was half-empty. She was surprised how fast they'd drained it. Actually she'd been the one to do most of the drinking, too.

She fell into a sullen silence. She decided that she didn't want to be with Earl any longer. She wasn't afraid, she was just bored with him. "I ought to go talk to that doctor," she said.

"What doctor?"

"See, what did I tell you!" she shrieked. "You haven't heard a word I've been saying."

"What's your hurry? We'll finish the bottle, then I'll take you to where you're going."

"I got to go pee."

"Go pee. There's no one around. I won't look."

She thought about this for a moment, then got out of the car and went around to the rear of it, where she pulled down her pants and squatted. Raising her eyes, she saw that he was peering at her from the car.

"No fair!" she shouted. "You're cheating."

"I was curious," he said when she returned. She grabbed the bottle from his hands. "Where are we?" she asked again.

He didn't reply. Instead he brought something cold and sharp up against her throat.

It was a blade. "I'm going to fuck you," he declared. "I'm going to fuck the shit out of you."

"No, no, no," she was saying, "you don't want to do that. I'm telling you, you're fucking crazy if you do that."

But he was already ripping at the buttons of her blouse, scooping out one exposed breast, which he kissed greedily. But his concentration was not so distracted that he allowed the knife to loosen from his grasp.

She struggled against him, but the alcohol made her woozy, her strength was gone. It was easier to let him do what he wanted. Most of the time she had no idea what he was doing; he fumbled with his clothes and hers, and all she did was lie there, propping her one leg against the dashboard while the other was cramped under his body. She caught a glimpse of his cock, but she could barely feel him when he entered her.

She was astounded at how much effort he was going through, how labored his breathing was as he strained to come. He seemed to be taking such a long time that she finally decided she should help him. She closed her eyes, pretended that the man was Bob, and reared up and moved hard against him. A moment later she was rewarded with a deep sigh. Looking down, she could see nothing but the wayward curls of his hair. For some reason, she almost felt sorry for him.

The knife didn't frighten her. He still held on to it, but it was at his side. Maybe he no longer remembered he had it.

But when he lifted his head from her breasts, what she saw was a pair of cold, empty eyes. "Did you like it?" he asked.

"Yes, yes, it was all right." That wouldn't be enough, she supposed. "Really, it was terrific, it hasn't been that way for a long time."

"I'm glad." He planted a kiss on her lips, and it was almost sweet, almost imbued with tenderness.

Then he pulled away. " 'Bye, sweetheart," he murmured.

She assumed that he was very likely going to kick her out of the car and leave her stranded. But that was not what he meant at all.

At first all she felt was a sharp pain, then a dull throbbing, to which she reacted by jerking up. Her eyes caught sight of the blade. He'd buried it in her almost to the hilt.

"No, no, you fucking bastard," she said, but low, almost in a whisper, because she did not—could not allow herself to—believe that this was happening to her.

His expression did not change. With his right hand he was beginning to move the knife up toward her breasts, as though she were something to be flayed.

She thrashed and hammered him with her fists and clawed him with her nails, producing deep, bloody welts along his cheeks, but he maintained his knife on its steady, inexorable course. The pain altered direction, but it was always unbearable.

Blood showered him; his face had become all but invisible with so much blood spattering it. He was the one who looked hurt. But already she was losing focus. The pain was too searing, burned too deep, for her to remain conscious. She screamed once and threw back her head against the hardness of the seat, and then lost consciousness.

The man removed his knife, and opening the door on the passenger side, pushed her out. She fell with a thump to the pier. As he watched, enough blood drained from her wounds to form a small pool about her. But it was not such an interesting sight that he cared to remain and watch it for long.

In seconds he had the motor running; then, with a squeal of tires, he drove off, heading toward a place where there were a great many lights.

Barrett was growing impatient. He hadn't been overly optimistic that both would arrive in the emergency room in the half-hour they'd agreed upon, but still he was convinced that she would appear eventually. From the way she'd sounded over the phone, there was little question in his mind that she was in desperate straits, that she was serious about needing to talk to somebody. Actually he suspected that she was in a borderline hysterical state, which was why he'd proposed that they meet in the emergency room. She very well might need to be admitted for observation.

Yet he knew from experience that if he should decide to leave the E.R., he'd no sooner get back home than there'd be a call for him, saying that Beth Sandor had arrived, and he'd have to turn right around. Given how drunk she sounded, it was reasonable to expect that time meant nothing to her. He promised himself he'd wait just twenty minutes longer and then cash it in for the night.

Ten minutes later an ambulance sped up the drive to the E.R., followed by a police cruiser.

Emergencies being so common, Barrett was scarcely impelled to look up from the magazine he was reading in the nurses' station to see what this one was all about.

But something prompted him to abandon his post, and as the stretcher was being wheeled through the corridor toward the operating rooms, he asked one of the police officers what had happened.

He shook his head. "Raped and stabbed. Some fucker did a real number on her. It's a wonder we picked her up alive."

He asked the cop for her name, hoping his hunch was wrong. It was not. His first glimpse of Beth Sandor was likely to be his last.

A small army of residents and nurses had been rounded up to attend to her. Tatters of her clothes still clung to her when she was hoisted onto the operating table. With no time even to scrub and don masks, the residents began to go to work on her, their primary concern to staunch the bleeding.

But they'd scarcely hooked her up to the EKG machine when one of the attending staff looked up, shrugging, and said, "We can't go on here, this woman is dead."

Barrett regarded her helplessly. He felt that he ought to have done something more, that somehow he had made a grievous mistake and that he might not catch on to what that mistake was until it was too late.

21

IT USED TO BE that you could walk up Columbus Avenue in the Seventies and Eighties and find a neighborhood that hadn't quite made up its mind what it wanted to become. You'd see a succession of cleaners and barbers and bakery shops that identified themselves by the sweet smell of their bread long before you reached them; you'd pass by laundromats filled with old women carefully counting out their quarters for the machines; you'd pass by Chinese restaurants that in their architecture tended to resemble grand old movie houses, baroquely colored in reds and golds; you'd pass by grocery stores and delis so cramped you could hardly squeeze through the aisles to your destination. In the secondhand bookstores, people with bad eyes would skim through the pages of worn books all day long and end by buying nothing. Immigrants from half of Europe ran such places; they spoke English so badly sometimes that it was easily mistaken for another language, and they seemed to know every one of their customers by name.

At the same time, this neighborhood was marked by blight, by blocks filled with decay and the threat of violence. There were apartment buildings whose rooms held tales of mayhem and unspeakable misery, and transient hotels whose windows represented points of departure for men and women whose luck had long since run out.

But the rents had soared; the tailors, the barbers, the bakers and foundry workers had been forced out, moving elsewhere or retiring; the old shops were obliterated, replaced by boutiques, gourmet food emporiums, pet stores, and antique dealers.

But most of all the gentrification, as this phenomenon was called, manifested itself in the appearance of a multitude of restaurants. These restaurants offered mediocre nouvelle cuisine along with glitzy decor—their walls were lined with abstract art, mirrors, and chrome. The waitresses in these places were winsome, the waiters winsome too, and gay. On fine summer nights people would spill out onto the sidewalks, but in winter they displayed themselves in the windows, like merchandise exhibited for sale, luring inside the singles seeking sex for the night or maybe even a love affair to last a lifetime.

One of these establishments, which had sprung up as recently as the previous spring, was known as PieceMeal. PieceMeal looked like half a dozen other such places along Columbus, with a glass-enclosed café, a bar, and a restaurant large enough to accommodate maybe fifty people. Because it was so new, it hadn't worn out its welcome among the pool of potential customers, almost none of whom was over forty years of age. On the contrary, they gravitated to it in great number, so that on weekend nights you could barely get into the bar, let alone find a table.

It was no secret to Barry Canowitz that he attracted the attentions of good-looking women. He was good-looking himself, husky, muscled, with a thick head of hair and a mustache he felt gave him a certain rakish air, like an updated Errol Flynn. He knew how to dress so meticulously that the end effect would seem casual. He sported a thin gold chain around his neck, but he didn't find it necessary to open his shirt down to his navel. Because PieceMeal was turning into something of an actors' bar— Richard Gere, Christopher Reeve, and Richard Dreyfuss had all been spotted here, at least in its earlier days last spring—he hoped to be mistaken as an actor. Most often, however, women guessed that he was connected in some manner to the garment industry. In fact, he was pulling down seven hundred a week as a copywriter at an advertising agency located, predictably, just off Madison Avenue.

He came into PieceMeal practically every night; he would often come away from it with a woman in tow, but he'd never been known to arrive accompanied.

Friday night, by convention, was the night when everyone came out. This had been the case twenty years ago; it was the case now. Worlds might rise and fall, heads of state might be assassinated, cybernetic and biological discoveries might revolutionize the world, but nothing was going to tarnish the popularity of Friday night in bars like this.

Women came generally in twos or threes, uniting for protection. Which was why Barry took particular note of one woman sitting by herself almost at the very end of the bar, not far from the serving area.

She was stunning enough in her own right to distract a man, but the attire she'd chosen made certain that she would not be overlooked even amid a score of other alluring women. It was, Barry thought, something like an insurance policy.

For one thing, she was all in white. White might not have been appropriate to the season, but it was nonetheless appropriate to her. The jacket she wore was buttoned halfway down her chest, but whenever she leaned forward to allow the bartender to light her cigarette, he was gratified to observe that she had nothing on underneath.

In spite of the confusion that surrounded her, she remained aloof, paying no attention whatsoever to the man earnestly attempting to make conversation next to her. She spoke only to the bartender, who was more than happy to reciprocate her interest.

There was a second bartender on duty, one not quite so preoccupied, and it was to him that Barry addressed his question. "Who is that woman over there?" He had decided she might be an actress. She had the looks and bearing of an actress, certainly. "I've never seen her in here before."

"Her name's Jackie. Jackie what, I don't know. She comes in here from time to time. She's quite a piece of work, don't you think?"

Barry agreed. "She's not from around the neighborhood, is she?"

"I'm not sure, but if she is, she's new. She has a bit of an English accent."

"All the girls you meet who have an English accent—ever notice how intelligent they sound, even the stupid ones?"

The bartender said that this was something he'd observed in his time too.

Undeterred by the prospect of rejection, Barry sidled toward her. "You're from London," he said to her.

She half-swiveled about on her stool to regard him. She was not, Barry saw, altogether uninterested. "What else do you know about me?"

"That your name is Jackie."

The man next to her glared at Barry; he could not comprehend what he was doing wrong, and resented this intrusion.

"You've been doing your homework."

She was faintly amused.

"That's me. I'm a very good student."

"What else?"

"What else? You have an attitude."

A smile was his reward. "An attitude?" She seemed to consider this. The way she positioned herself caused her jacket to separate. When she caught the direction of his gaze, she drew it closer together. The smile hadn't gone anywhere. "What are you looking at?"

"You."

When she momentarily turned her attention back to the bar, Barry plucked the top button of her jacket from its hole. A breast, submerged in shadows, came into view.

Jackie turned back to him, her eyes narrowing. With no

special haste she redid the button. "That was uncalled for."

"Just wanted to get a better view, that's all."

"You're very sure of yourself, aren't you?"

"The name's Barry Canowitz. Can I buy you a drink?"

"I can pay for my own, thank you."

"Can I take you to St. Thomas?"

He was intrigued to see the sort of reaction he'd get.

She was silent for a moment. "Is that the line you use on all the girls? That you'll fly them to St. Thomas?"

"Who said anything about flying? I had something more on the order of a dugout canoe in mind."

"Cute." She was making up her mind about him, he could tell.

"If you don't like the idea of St. Thomas, we can go to West Seventy-eighth Street."

"Oh, and what's there?"

"My place."

Another silence. Longer than before. "Why would I want to go there?"

He was beginning to appreciate her. "Because you'll have a lot more fun than you will if you stay here."

"I bet." Her eyes flashed. She abruptly returned to talking with the bartender. Barry stood by, wondering whether he'd lost her. He might have misjudged her and come on too strong, although that was what her manner seemed to invite.

After several minutes had gone by, she once again regarded him. "You still here?" But before he'd had a chance to reply, she said, "All right, my dear, let's go and see what West Seventy-eighth Street is like."

22

In a paper to be published today in the Annals of Infectious Diseases, Dr. Leo Heisler, spearheading the drive to find a cure for a mysterious new viral infection, contends that he has isolated the infectious agent responsible in citrus fruit. The virus, characterized by severe pneumonialike symptoms and liver failure, has struck down several victims in various parts of the country, including New York City, in recent weeks. All known cases—totaling 151—have been fatal and all the victims have been male. The disease was first described at a press conference by Dr. Heisler of the Westside Medical Center and now bears his name. The paper, entitled "Suspected Citrus Link in Heisler's Disease," maintains that the recent ingestion of citrus fruits, specifically lemons, is the common agent found in patients with this disease. "It therefore appears that this type of citrus may be the vector carrying the virus," he writes.

This relatively understated report in the New York *Times* contrasted markedly with the banner headline over the story in the *Post*: "PANICKED SHOPPERS AVOID KILLER FRUIT."

The story had a sidebar advising drinkers to avoid using slices of lemon or lime in their cocktails. "Alcohol can kill bacteria, not viruses," it said. The author of the story, Kris noted, was otherwise employed as a restaurant reviewer.

Kris didn't believe a word of it. True, it was possible that a virus could be spread by fruit, vegetables, or anything else people might happen to consume, but it just didn't make sense to her. Even so, she decided for the while to forgo fruit and fruit juices. Why tempt fate?

Throughout the day the all-news radio stations, WINS and WCBS-AM, broadcast continual bulletins on the reaction to Heisler's paper. Though only lemons were named as the common agent, people were beginning to boycott all fruit. On the floor of the Commodities Exchange in the World Trade Center, orange-juice futures plunged below their daily limit, registering declines worse than those that had resulted from the disastrous frosts in Florida's citrus groves a year previously.

As word of the report spread, the supermarkets and neighborhood groceries and fruit stands began to feel the impact as well. Bins full of grapefruit, limes, oranges, and lemons went to waste as consumers passed them by. Grocers were openly despondent and predicted in interviews with the press that they might be driven under if the boycott of citrus fruit continued for any length of time. "Things are tough enough," one man, the proprietor of a Gristede's on the Upper East Side, remarked to a WINS reporter, "but this is crazy. People stop eating fruit, what happens next? They stop eating vegetables? They stop eating meat because someone says it's poison? Then what do they do, starve to death?"

A woman was stopped at random in the aisles of a supermarket and asked why she was refusing to buy fruit. "I know women aren't supposed to get this sickness," she said, "but something could happen to my husband. I'm just not taking any chances."

Told that the link between citrus fruit in general and lemons in particular and the virus was still tenuous at best, she repeated, "I'm not taking any chances. You do what you want, but I can live without fruit for a while."

There were inevitably references to the Tylenol affair, when someone had deliberately contaminated several bottles containing the extra-strength pain reliever. But this contamination was a disease, not a poison; it was not just a matter of finding the perpetrator and bringing him to justice.

By the final bell, a number of fruit concerns on the New York and American stock exchanges had sustained ten-point losses. In three cases, the Securities and Exchange Commission had suspended trading until the situation was clarified.

Kris was at her apartment in the Village while all this tumult was raging. She was trying to sort out her notes, see whether she was any closer to sitting down and writing her story than she was when she'd begun. After hours of studying what she had so far pieced together, she decided that she had a long way to go.

Her only hope was Isaac Ninn. No one, apart from Heisler himself, knew as much about the operations of Heisler's lab as Ninn did. But she couldn't figure him out. On the one hand, he'd seemed genuinely interested in helping her; at the same time, whenever she pressed him, he turned vague. She had his London telephone number and there were moments when she was ready to place a call to him. But what would she say? She needed additional facts, but how she was to go about obtaining them?

She'd been thinking about the phone so much that when it rang she was almost jolted from her chair.

It was Matthew on the other end. He sounded out of breath. "Kris," he said, "could you do me a big favor and come with me to Jerry's?"

She was bewildered, but said of course she'd come with him. "What's the matter?"

"I've been trying to reach him at home all day and there's been no answer. He wasn't feeling well when he left here yesterday, and I'm worried about him. I checked with the service, and they can't get a response either. I'd

like to go over and see whether he's all right. I'd appreciate it if you'd come with me.''

''Sure.''

''Good. I'll pick you up in half an hour.''

She could sense the anxiety in his voice; he was far
more concerned than he'd let on.

It was on the way uptown to Perretta's that Barrett first
mentioned Beth Sandor.

''The wife of the man who died of Heisler's Disease?
The drunk?''

''That's right. She's dead.''

''Dead? What happened to her?''

He began to explain.

They sat in silence for a while. The traffic was heavy—no
surprise, given the fact that rush hour was upon them. It
looked as though they'd be waiting on Eighth Avenue
between Thirty-seventh and Thirty-eighth streets until the
middle of May. Horns blasted away, taxi drivers screamed,
none of it did any good. Pedestrians weaving their way
through the paralyzed vehicles gave small smiles of triumph.

''What exactly did Beth say to you?'' Kris asked.

''She said she was the one who killed both her husband
and Bob O'Connor. She was so drunk she was nearly
incoherent.''

''You mean she didn't know what she was saying?''

''That was my impression.''

The traffic had begun to inch forward. The frustration at
the delay was clearly visible on Barrett's face. Kris had a
feeling that he blamed himself in some way for what had
happened to Beth Sandor. She feared that if enough anger
built up in him he might take it out on her. Her proximity
alone made her a likely target.

''But why would she say something like that—that she
killed both men?''

He shrugged. ''Guilt, I suppose. Some women believe
that they've driven their men to their graves.''

''Some men, I imagine, have the exact same feeling
about women who die on them,'' she rejoined.

* * *

Perretta should never have bought the condominium he lived in; it cost too much for one thing, and the maintenance was staggering. His income never could match his extravagant ways. Still, his home was an impressive-looking affair, fifteen floors up, overlooking enough of Central Park that he could, if he felt like it, ring someone up and report the traffic conditions from the park's entrance on Fifty-ninth Street and Columbus Circle all the way to its northern border on 110th Street.

The doorman viewed the two visitors with skepticism. "Can I help you, sir?" he asked, deliberately ignoring Kris.

"Could you call Dr. Perretta and let him know that his partner would like to see him?"

Tapping out a digital code on a console, the man held the receiver to his ear.

Kris could hear the steady ring on the other end.

"I am sorry, sir, Dr. Perretta isn't answering."

"You haven't seen him come down today, have you?"

The doorman shook his head.

Barrett than appealed to him to be allowed up. He displayed his identification, which the doorman stared at long and hard. Then he scrutinized them, not Barrett and Kris so much as the clothes they had on, as though the nature of their wardrobe was the only criterion he needed to make his judgment. At last he relented. "I'll send Marco up with you and he'll let you in."

Marco was a short, stubby fellow with a slightly moronic grin. As he rang the bell at 15R, Kris thought she detected the drone of a television set going inside. "Maybe he's asleep," she suggested.

Barrett didn't say anything.

Marco managed to unlock the door, only to discover that Perretta had secured a chain across it. "Dr. Perretta?" Marco called out.

There definitely was a TV on.

"Dr. Perretta?"

No response.

"Wait here," said Marco. "I go get something."

Barrett called his partner's name but failed to receive a reply.

When Marco returned, it was with a sharp sawlike blade, which he used to break through the chain. As soon as it snapped, the three of them entered.

The local news was on; even from the foyer they could make out the television. The picture was clear enough, but the colors were distorted, endowing the anchorman's face with a jaundiced look. "The American Fruit Growers Association representative said that Dr. Heisler's contention was unsubstantiated," he was saying. " 'There is no reason to avoid the consumption of any kind of fruit,' the industry spokesman stated. Dr. Heisler was unavailable for comment."

They went farther into the apartment, hesitant, still calling out Perretta's name.

Liquor bottles, some nearly empty of their contents, were set out on the living-room table. Unwashed dishes lay stacked in the sink. A single medicine container, unlabeled, was on the kitchen table, a scattering of tiny white capsules surrounding it.

From what Kris knew of Perretta, it was unlike him to leave a mess like this.

They found him in the bedroom. At first he seemed to be asleep, but that was before they came closer. Then they observed that his face was colorless. His eyes, still open, were yellow; foam and traces of blood, where he'd bitten into his lips, were visible about the lips and on the chin. His whole body was contorted, the legs splayed out, while his head was thrown back against the bedboard. He smelled of sweat and a hard death. His expression at the end disclosed both anguish and rage that such a thing could happen to him.

Marco hung back; he might not have been very bright, but he had eyes.

Barrett, out of form, if nothing else, took hold of his partner's wrist, but of course there was no pulse. He allowed no emotion to register on his face; he was strictly in his professional role now. Then gently he closed Perretta's eyes.

Looking again at Perretta's ghostly face, Kris felt an overwhelming sadness and regret. It was surprising, because she had never liked him very much.

She went to the window and drew open the drapes. She didn't know why; there was no light left in the sky any longer; it just seemed that it was something that should be done.

"You want an ambulance?" Marco asked.

"No," Barrett snapped. Then: "Yes, sure, all right, call an ambulance." His voice disclosed anger and incredulity at the same time.

Like Kris, he was having immense difficulty accepting the fact that his partner had died.

Dazedly Kris left the bedroom and wandered into the other room, thinking that she might pour herself a shot of something from one of the liquor bottles on the living-room table. When she went to the refrigerator for some ice, her eyes fell on a note pinned by a magnet to its door: "Late for work, call you soon. Love, Sheila."

Barrett had come up behind her. "Sheila," he muttered.

"You know her? Was she one of Jerry's regulars?"

"I met her. She works for some drug company in New Jersey. Strange bird."

Now Kris recalled the dazzlingly beautiful woman she'd seen a few days previously in the waiting room. Sheila Payne, Carey Pharmaceuticals. She was developing a good memory for details.

"And Jerry picked her up and brought her home?"

"It was more the other way around. I think she was ready to seduce any available man. It just happened to be Jerry."

"How about you?" Kris was amazed that they could be talking this calmly, with Perretta lying dead in the other room.

He shrugged somewhat abashedly. "Let's just say I escaped."

23

JERRY PERRETTA'S FUNERAL was well attended. More people showed up than could be accommodated in the church, which was situated between Madison and Fifth, an expensive location from which to depart the world. Barrett hadn't known that his late partner had had so many friends and relations. Girlfriends, yes, but not friends.

Barrett had once met Perretta's parents, two graying souls weighed down by memory and fat, but he was unprepared for the brothers and sisters, for the nephews and uncles and aunts and cousins. In each one of them he could see something of Jerry Perretta: a nose in this one, the eyes in that one, the mischievous twist of the lips in another. Perretta's youngest brother, Joseph, looked so astonishingly like him that for a second Barrett thought he might be hallucinating, that his partner had come back from the dead to inform everyone that it was all one big joke, that death was not such a dark, inexorable thing that it couldn't be outwitted. Besides, there was such a dearth of good-looking women on the other side, what was the point?

There were those among the crowd that Barrett recalled

seeing before but whom he could not identify; some were Perretta's cronies who played poker and golf and traded execrable Polish jokes with him. They all bore the same slightly embarrassed look in shared recognition of what Jerry Perretta's untimely death might mean to them. The virus that had felled him had no respect; it could bring them down in the prime of life just as it had him.

Barrett noticed Perretta's stockbroker. He looked like the most miserable person in attendance.

The object of the ceremony lay exposed in a polished casket made of redwood, surrounded by flowers that emitted a cloying sweetness. In his casket, Perretta appeared in far better shape than on the evening Barrett had discovered him dead. The mortician had worked a miracle, giving him back the illusion of health and something of his youth too in the process.

Kris was wearing a dark gray suit that Barrett had never seen before; with her hair pulled back, she looked somber and certainly older. Not less attractive, but older, like she had become a woman he'd yet to meet.

''You know, if we could find this woman who slept with Perretta—Sheila—I'm sure we'd learn what really happened to Jerry,'' Kris said.

Barrett was so preoccupied that he scarcely heard her. ''Maybe,'' he said, ''but I wouldn't count on it. There were a lot of women in Jerry's life.''

''But I'd bet anything that this one mattered more than the others.''

''She was pretty, all right,'' he started, but just then the ceremony began and he had no opportunity to finish his sentence.

The funeral was quickly over—it seemed that the priest did not know Perretta and consequently kept his eulogy as brief as it was vague. On the way out, a number of the mourners, some Barrett knew only distantly, came over to him to offer their condolences. His association with Perretta seemed to have made him a part of the family, at least on this occasion. Others had nothing to say to him, but rather regarded him with great sadness and shook their heads; maybe they felt that if Perretta could be so easily taken by this virus, then it was likely he was next.

It was only when Barrett and Kris had gotten out of the church into the leaden gray afternoon that Barrett saw her.

Or thought he saw her.

She was wearing a red coat and a kerchief about her hair, but that was the only thing he could say for certain. And placed on the stand in a court of law, he would not be able to say that it was her at all.

But for one long moment, in which time seemed to fall away, he'd discerned in the crowd of mourners descending the church steps, the face of Helen Voyles.

24

"THAT'S A RATHER INTERESTING thing you've got there. What is it?"

Carl Elkin lifted the necklace away from the woman's chest to see it better.

"A crux ansata," she said. "They tell me it's an ancient Egyptian symbol of fertility, but I don't know. Somebody gave it to me as a gift."

Allowing the necklace to drop back into place, Elkin gave her an appraising look. "I imagine you've been the recipient of a great many gifts in your life."

She was certainly not the sort of woman that Elkin was accustomed to seeing in the academic circles of Cambridge and Boston. It was not only her English accent, but a kind of self-confidence. It was also something in the very nature of her beauty, in the lushness of her body, the high breasts and generous hips, the dark eyes and promising lips and the sweep of auburn hair.

"I've never seen you before," Elkin said. "How did you come to be at the Ellises' party?"

The party was large and, with the exception of this one woman, predictably dreary. The same people who had showed up for the last half-dozen parties Elkin and his wife had attended had showed up for this one. They had nothing new to offer, nothing new to say.

A woman in a black dress and white apron kept coming around offering them canapés and refilling their glasses with white wine.

"I'm a friend of Dave Finegold's," she said.

"Oh, yes, I know Dave. Funny he never mentioned you, Georgia. I didn't realize he knew such an enchanting woman."

She laughed brightly at the compliment, which, Elkin suspected, she was undoubtedly used to. "I suppose the reason he never mentioned me was that I'm from out of town."

Elkin didn't know whether this followed, but he let it go. "Where out of town? England?"

"Originally. Now I live in Los Angeles."

An actress, he thought. Or a would-be actress. How had Dave, a colleague at Sandburn, found her? "Where is Dave, by the way?"

"Oh, he's not coming until a little later. He told me to come ahead on my own."

"I'm glad you did."

Now Elkin became conscious of his wife giving him frequent surreptitious glances from the other side of the room.

He asked Georgia if she were a model or an actress.

"A little of both. Perhaps you've seen me. I've done some TV commercials."

"For what?"

"Selling discount tickets to Acapulco."

"Have you ever been there?"

"No," she said, laughing, "but that doesn't stop me from selling tickets."

"I'll buy one."

"And what do you do, Dr. Elkin?"

"I don't know whether you would really be interested."

"But I am. Please tell me."

She was staring so directly at him that it made him a

little unsettled. "Well, my specialty is diseases of the immunological system." He wondered whether she even knew what the immunological system was. She didn't seem stupid, but she didn't seem especially bright, either. Nonetheless, he did his best to explain.

After several minutes he realized he had gone on far too long and stopped himself. "Forgive me, I must be boring you. You probably would like to circulate."

She had a way of turning down her lips to express dissatisfaction that he would've found an endearing trait had he been her lover. "Why should I want to do that? Do you want to get rid of me?"

"No, no, not at all," he protested. "I just thought you'd be bored . . ."

He wished his wife wouldn't look at him like that. He adjusted his position so that he was no longer facing her. Not that it mattered; he could still feel her eyes on him.

"When I'm bored, people know it." She touched his hand lightly.

Her touch was electric.

"Actually, to really get an idea about what I do, you'd have to see the laboratory where I work."

He was just throwing this out. He didn't believe she would take him seriously.

"I'd like that very much."

He was all but struck dumb, then decided that she was just being polite. "Well, then," he said, "you'll have to come by. I'll give you my card."

"What time's best for you?"

"Generally, late afternoon, early evening. I take a break around then."

"I'll stop by tomorrow, then," she said, examining the card carefully before slipping it into her bag.

She held out her hand, which he promptly took. Only by exercising restraint did he manage not to bring it to his lips. "It's been nice meeting you, Georgia."

"Nice meeting you too, Dr. Elkin."

"Carl."

"Carl." She smiled and disappeared into the crowd.

Elkin was charmed. He was more than charmed; he was exhilarated as only a man can be who has never considered himself particularly attractive to women, being short and balding, with eyes searching out the world behind thick lenses.

It was only when he was driving home that evening, with his very irritable wife beside him, that he remembered that he hadn't seen Dave Finegold the whole time he was at the party. But then, there were more than a hundred guests, and it was a big house. He'd probably just missed him.

25

Matthew Barrett never bothered to read the *Post*. For that matter, he never read the *News*. One reason was that he lacked the time; he barely had a chance to skim through the *Times*. Another reason was that he believed the other two papers were beneath him, particularly the *Post*. He was convinced that the *Times* gave him all the important news.

But Kris found the two tabloids more to her liking. The *Post* especially was an indulgence. Like eating too much chocolate, it got to you after a while, but she had to admit she enjoyed it. Where else could she learn about scandalous divorce cases complete with incest, adultery, homosexuality, and drug abuse?

The *Post*, the day after Jerry Perretta's funeral, did not devote its front-page story to Heisler's Disease. Heisler's Disease, however, occupied two of the inside pages, with more stories about the reaction of the grocers and supermarket chains as well as shoppers. It ranged from deep-rooted skepticism to terror. Hundreds of people across the nation were turning up in hospital emergency rooms—women too—saying that they'd recently eaten a grapefruit or had a glass of orange juice or lemonade, complaining of fever and aching joints. So far no one had been found to have contracted the disease, though that alone was not enough to allay their fears. The disease was still claiming victims, after all—in New York, in California, in parts of Louisiana and Mississippi, in Massachusetts and in Appalachia. There seemed to be no pattern to it, and sometimes only one or two deaths would be reported from each area. But one thing remained the same in all cases: the victims were always men.

Of course, it could be that Heisler was correct, that citrus fruit was in fact the source of the virus.

Kris's doorbell rang, disrupting the flow of her thoughts. As it was close to eleven in the morning, it could only mean that the mailman had arrived. The mailboxes were inside the front-hall door and, having no key, he had to rely on one of the tenants letting him in.

The mail brought Kris three bills, one of them with a stinging reminder from Con Ed that she'd forgotten to pay the two previous months' bills. She also found in the hallway a large, bulky manila envelope with her name on it; there was no return address. What was curious was that there was also no postmark, nor was her address written on it. It must have been delivered by hand.

Tearing open the envelope, she discovered a tattered manuscript whose title page had been torn off. But as soon as she'd thumbed through the pages she knew very well what it was: Helen's thesis.

But having already seen it at Henry Loomis' home, she was more curious as to what had prompted him to send it than in the contents, which she could scarcely begin to understand.

Yet when she turned to the back she found something that she hadn't seen before: the entire Appendix 1—"The T-Protein Factor in Viral Transmission"—was included.

Henry must have located it, she thought.

Her elation didn't persist for long, for she was no better able to figure out the appendix than she was the main body of the thesis. Apart from the fact that T stood for "transfer" and that it was something that could be isolated after undergoing certain chromatographic procedures, whatever they might be, nothing made much sense to her.

Finally she gave up, realizing she would need Matthew to help her out.

Still, she decided she ought to phone Henry and thank him for going to so much trouble for her.

The phone in Loomis' Copaigue home was picked up on the second ring. But Henry wasn't on the other end. It was a woman—an older woman, from the sound of her.

"Hello, is Mr. Loomis there?"

"No."

She thought she might have gotten the wrong number and started to read off the number she'd dialed, but the woman cut her short. "He's dead. He was killed Wednesday night."

Wednesday night was when she'd gone out to see him. "Who are you?"

"I'm a neighbor, Tilda Amando. I'm cleaning things out here. There aren't any relatives, so I get everything. God knows what I'll do with this stuff."

"Who killed him?"

"No one knows. Police figure it was a robber. Knifed him. Lots of blood, big mess. Lots of cleaning up to do."

"Thank you," said Kris, hanging up.

She sat down on her bed. She sat there for fifteen or twenty minutes, staring into space. The thesis was open on her desk. It had come while she slept last night or early this morning. Henry Loomis could not possibly have delivered it to her. It had to be somebody else, and she wasn't absolutely certain she wanted to find out who.

As a form of therapy, because she needed to think, because she'd really prefer not to have to do any thinking at all, she took a long walk.

She walked uptown, knowing that eventually she would wander over to the West Side and catch a bus to the Westside Medical Center. She didn't care to disrupt Matthew's office hours, and in any case, she had to compose herself before she sat down and talked to him. Her handbag bulged with the thesis she'd crammed inside it. It made her nervous having it with her; it was like carrying thousands of dollars in cash.

She only wished she understood what it was about.

At a quarter to four, as she was crossing Fifty-eighth Street, she happened to notice a row of limousines idling in front of the main entrance to the Plaza. Several policemen were in evidence; there were other men, in plain clothes, who stood by, scrutinizing the milling crowd, with automatic weapons—machine guns of some kind, Kris realized—prominently displayed.

She stepped up to one of the cops and asked what all this commotion was for.

"Vice-President's in town," he replied. "He's meeting with some dignitaries."

There was no way of determining whether the Vice-President had already gone into the Plaza or was at any moment expected to emerge from it.

In either case, the spectacle held little attraction for Kris, who continued around to the other side of the Plaza, walking toward Columbus Circle.

Then she stopped dead in her tracks. She wheeled about, looking behind her. Her first thought was: I know that woman.

It had been such a fleeting glance that she retraced her steps and followed the woman into the Central Park South entrance of the Plaza to be sure. The lobby was thronged with more security men, but there were a number of wealthy-looking tourists and businessmen too. There was an atmosphere of confusion and expectation, as if some event were about to occur or else had already happened and nobody had quite gotten over it yet.

In the midst of this gathering she spotted the woman she'd seen only a few moments before on the street. Kris stood back, near the magazine stand, so that the woman wouldn't notice her.

The woman was sitting patiently in a chair, obviously

waiting for somebody to meet her. She seemed oblivious of what was happening around her.

Although she was no longer wearing the business suit Kris had last seen her in, and her hair had been pinned up, there was no doubt in Kris's mind that this was the same woman who'd been in the waiting room of Barrett and Perretta's office. The woman who purported to be a representative of the Carey Pharmaceutical Company. The woman who had slept with Jerry just before his death. Sheila Payne.

Kris was about to go up to her when a man approached Sheila and spoke to her. He had the air of a plainclothesman or private bodyguard. Kris guessed that this wasn't the man she was waiting for, but probably his messenger. In any case, she got up from her chair and followed him to the elevator.

Whatever else she is, Kris thought, she isn't a rep for any pharmaceutical company.

By the time she reached Matthew's office it was a little after six. There were still seven patients to be seen. With Jerry gone, Matthew had had to take over his partner's patients until he could make other arrangements. The additional money he'd be making in the interim was little compensation for the amount of excess work he'd been saddled with. A bad time for him all around. Kris knew she would have to tread softly, even on the neutral ground of an overpriced restaurant.

Mrs. Preston was very subdued. Though her sense of duty did not allow her to mourn Jerry Perretta's untimely demise, her attitude, even her posture, testified to her grief. "How are you, Miss Erlanger?" she said in greeting. "I'll let Dr. Barrett know that you're here."

"Don't bother him. I'll wait until he's through."

Kris very much wanted to express her condolences, but the facade of cool, brusque diligence that Mrs. Preston had erected over the years made such a gesture impossible for her. She sensed that Mrs. Preston had favored Jerry over Matthew—she had been Jerry's discovery—and that she resented, maybe consciously, maybe not, the fact that it was Matthew who was still alive.

"Oh, Mrs. Preston, could I ask you a favor? Do you still have the business card that woman from the pharmaceutical company gave you?"

"What woman might you be referring to?"

Kris had a feeling she knew, but nonetheless she proceeded to describe Sheila Payne, without, however, mentioning that she remembered her name. Mrs. Preston's curiosity was aroused enough already.

"Oh, yes, I think I do have that card. Let me look."

With her compulsive penchant for classifying every piece of paper that found its way into the office, Mrs. Preston naturally had little difficulty locating it.

Kris memorized the numbers on the card and went to look for a telephone she could use in privacy.

Perretta's office was unlocked. No one had gotten around to cleaning it out, however, and a sharp pungent odor filled the air.

It originated from the wastebasket behind Perretta's desk. Inside she saw buried within the plastic bag that served as the liner chunks of squeezed lemon. It seemed Perretta had been drinking a good deal of tea, for there were several used tea bags in the wastebasket as well.

She didn't like it. It was logical that Perretta would have consumed copious amounts of tea to ease his sore throat. It was possible that he'd contracted his fatal illness from the lemons. But it was too neat somehow.

Forgetting for the moment about the phone calls, she went back to Mrs. Preston. "Did you know that Dr. Perretta's office was open?" she asked.

It came as no surprise to her. "I know, I unlocked it myself. Some investigators from the CDC wished to inspect the premises. They're still here, I believe."

She was right. When Kris returned to Perretta's office, she discovered two men emptying the contents of the wastebasket into a polyurethene bag. Several similar bags, stuffed with other items from the office, were visible through the opening door of the adjoining examining room, which was where she guessed the two men had come from.

"Can we help you?" one of them said.

His companion continued working.

"Are you from the CDC?"

"That's right."

She thanked them and retreated down the hall until she located another free phone.

It might be too late to find anyone in, but she was interested to see whether either telephone number on the card was in service.

To her astonishment, the first number she tried—the New York one—was functioning. After the third ring, someone picked up, a woman. "Carey Pharmaceuticals, may I help you?"

Kris asked for Sheila Payne.

There was just the slightest hesitation; then the woman said, "I'm sorry, but Miss Payne is out in the field at this time. Can somebody else help you?"

"I'd prefer to talk to Miss Payne directly. Do you have any idea when she'll be back?"

"I really couldn't say, but if you leave your name and number, I'm sure she can return your call."

Kris said she'd call back, but before hanging up, she asked the woman to tell her where Carey Pharmaceutical Company was located.

The woman rattled off an address in New Jersey that meant absolutely nothing to Kris. "It's just off Route Seventeen, above Rutherford, right before you get to the airport."

Before Kris could ask her which airport, she terminated the conversation.

Out of curiosity, she dialed the second number, only to reach the same woman. She replaced the receiver without saying a word.

While it would take a trip out to Rutherford to prove it, Kris was convinced that Carey Pharmaceutical Company did not exist, that it was simply a front with an answering service and a mailing address.

On her way to the waiting room she passed the two investigators hauling their find from Perretta's office. The smell of rotting lemon hovered over them like a cloud.

Barrett had been informed in advance about the investigators' visit. But when Kris spoke to him, he seemed unconcerned about their findings.

"Aren't you worried that your office might be contaminated?" Kris asked him. "They found fruit in Jerry's office—lemons."

"Lemons?" He sounded mystified. "What were lemons doing in his office?"

"Why ask me? He was your partner, not mine. Maybe he liked lemon in his tea."

"Tea? Jerry drink tea?" He laughed.

"What are you saying, Matthew? If he didn't ordinarily keep lemons in his office, what were they doing there? Do you think the same investigators who found them might have put them there in the first place? Planted them?"

It occurred to her now that they weren't from the CDC at all, but from Heisler's lab.

"Well?" She gave him a searching look.

"I don't know, Kris."

"Matthew, I have to talk to you."

She didn't know where to begin—with the thesis? with Loomis' death? with her sighting of Sheila Payne?

"I'd love to, Kris, but I can't right now. There are half a dozen people out there I've got to see. I can meet you later—around nine?"

"I've got an idea. There's a Mexican restaurant called El Pueblo I once reviewed for *America Now*. The manager liked what I wrote, told me I could come back anytime I wanted for a dinner on the house."

"Sounds terrific. Where is it?"

"On Columbus at Seventy-third, the west side of the street."

As she was leaving, she asked him if everything was all right.

"I'm just busy, but otherwise I'm fine."

He was always busy; it was a state so constant with him

that she ruled it out as a factor in his behavior. She knew he hadn't adjusted to the loss of his partner. It wasn't the loss of a friend that got to him—for Jerry and he hadn't been friends for a long time—but the fact that they were the same age.

Yet Kris intuited that there was something else nagging at him. The problem was finding out what.

26

"I SEE that you've lost her too," Heisler said.

"I'll find her. Jacqueline's not so clever as all that," Ninn answered, using Sheila's real name as if that might help him pin her down better. "Like an animal, she leaves a spore behind her. She's nothing like Helen. I found Beth Sandor for you, didn't I?"

They were meeting in Heisler's office in the Melkis Pavilion; Heisler was spending so much time here that it had become his second home.

"I was under the impression that you were firmly in control of your girls."

He stepped across the room to refill Ninn's glass. Ninn knew what he was doing: keeping him in an alcoholic haze so that he would be more susceptible to his influence. But even so, he couldn't bring himself to refuse.

"How did she escape, if I may ask?" Heisler went on.

"I couldn't really tell you. She turned up at the Plaza—"

"The Plaza?"

"She had an appointment to see Martin Frazer, you recall. Frazer had an appointment to see the Vice-President."

"And?"

"And Frazer is a dead man." Ninn glanced at his watch. "Give him a couple of days, he's a dead man."

"She couldn't have gotten to the Vice-President, could she?"

"Jacqueline's very capable, but he was with his wife and several Secret Servicemen, so it wasn't in the cards. A United States senator, though—that isn't bad. I'm sure his death will have the desired effect."

The death of a politician from the virus would alarm other politicians and cause them to authorize funding in a hurry.

"Then where did she go from there?"

"I don't know. She may have a rebellious streak, but I didn't think she'd go off on her own like that. I suppose she feared retribution."

"Retribution?"

"She was instructed to go home with Matthew Barrett."

Heisler frowned. "You never told me anything about this."

"He was becoming a problem—he still is. He made trouble for you at the HIC meeting, he's tried to locate the records on patients who participated in the double-blinded study. It was only because Jacqueline's so impulsive, so easily swayed, that he's still alive. I regard it as a temporary setback. I'll find another way—and another woman—for him."

Heisler didn't like it. "There's no rhyme or reason to what you're doing. You're spreading the virus wherever you feel like it. That can't be allowed to happen."

Ninn was unconcerned. "What possible difference does it make at this point? There are now over two hundred fatalities, with another hundred or so infected. I think I've done an excellent job."

Heisler wasn't convinced. "There are limits. When are you proposing to stop?"

"When the virus runs out. I don't see why you're complaining, Leo. The more people dead, the more you stand to gain."

"I thought that when we originally planned this the idea was to take it just so far."

"That was a tentative arrangement. Now that things are working so well, I can't see any reason to stop."

Heisler rose from his desk, glowering at Ninn, but Ninn did not react. He might have been too intoxicated; he might not have cared.

"So what are you proposing—that we kill off six hundred men? A thousand? Half a million?"

Ninn glanced up at him with amusement in his eyes. "What's got into you, Leo? A sudden burst of conscience? By this point I can't imagine it possibly matters. Have you made enough money from all your investments? Is that it?"

"What investments are you referring to?"

"Oh, come on, Leo. You know very well what I'm referring to. It was only a couple of months ago that you found someone to buy short in orange-juice futures, knowing full well that the market in them would plunge precipitously. Ascribing the cause of the disease to fruit was brilliant, Leo—you might as well take credit for it. If you can't cure it, the least you can do is purport to know its cause. A stroke of genius!"

"How did you find out about that?"

"I keep telling you, I have my sources. I know everything that's going on in your lab."

Heisler realized that he wasn't about to make any headway with him. He would have to determine who Ninn's spy was on his own. "If you're so knowledgeable about my operations, then you must also know that we'll soon exhaust our current supply of the virus."

"What about the tissue from the Sandor woman? You told me that it was possible to reconstitute the virus from the livers of the ones we've already infected."

"First of all, it appears that we can reconstitute it only within a short period after the woman is initially infected, so that whatever we could have derived from Sandor wouldn't have done us any good. Second, the body was immediately sent off to the chief medical examiner's office and I couldn't get to my man there in time, so the tissue was lost in any case.''

"You're saying that you don't know how long the viral particles remain viable once the virus is introduced?"

"I assume it's approximately forty-eight hours, but that's merely a hypothesis at this point. Helen probably knew, but if she ever wrote it down on paper, she must have taken it with her.''

"Then I'll just have to find her."

"You keep saying that.''

"I have an idea where she's been. She's beginning to leave a trail behind her." He refused to elaborate. Instead he asked Heisler exactly how much of the virus he still had left on hand.

"Not nearly so much as you seem to want.''

"You have to produce more. By stopping now, we'll have lost an unprecedented opportunity. The outbreaks will die down, interest in the disease will diminish, soon you'll be forgotten . . . forgotten even before you can effect a cure. Think of it, Leo. If we can get the number of fatalities to reach a thousand or more, and then you succeed in finding a cure, you'll have guaranteed yourself a place in medical history. It's what you've wanted, isn't it? To be regarded as an equal of Salk, of Fleming, of Best.''

Ninn realized that this line of argument could move Heisler even more than the prospect of increasing wealth, that no matter how much the secret intelligence networks of the United States government might honor him for his work in biochemical warfare, nothing could rival the fame achieved by the discoverers of the cures for polio, bacterial infection, and diabetes.

"But a thousand deaths . . ." he muttered.

"Some of the mutant viruses you developed for the army might one day kill off hundreds of thousands, millions of people." Then he got straight to the point. "For the time being, I will require at least another hundred capsules."

Heisler remained silent, but it was evident to Ninn that he had them in his possession. At last he said, "Tomorrow

I'll have them ready for you. But that will have to be it until I determine how to produce more."

"I don't want you to think you are doing me any favors. We are in this together, after all. When I benefit, so do you."

As Ninn was leaving, Heisler called to him, "Isaac, what do you intend to do about Barrett?"

"Since Jacqueline proved unequal to the task, I will just have to find someone who is, won't I?"

"Watch it, Isaac. I don't like things getting out of our control."

Ninn looked back at him. His eyes weren't focusing properly, and he saw two Heislers, one with more substance than the other. "Things may be getting out of your control, Leo, never out of mine."

Then, before Heisler had any chance to reply, he left the office.

On the fourth floor he found Owen Barnes peering through a microscope and jotting down a succession of figures on a sheet of graph paper on the counter in front of him.

"Owen?"

Barnes turned around quickly. "God, you gave me a start," he said.

Barnes was a researcher whom Heisler had hired ten months previously; he was in his mid-forties and had a face too large for the features contained in it; there was simply too much milk-white skin. That, and the oval shape of his face, gave him the aspect of a four-year-old in adult form. There was something so bland about his appearance that when he was angry he looked little different than when he was pleased.

It was only after thoroughly analyzing the profiles of the researchers, technicians, and lab students employed in the Melkis Pavilion that Ninn had selected Barnes as his eyes and ears.

Barnes was soft, he was greedy, he was endowed with a fervent lust that went unanswered in the woman he had for a wife.

He was certainly ripe for an affair; he was diligent and tireless in his work, but away from his work, he was nothing. He was devoid of personality, he had no hobbies, no interests; in the outside world, the mind that was so inquisitive in the laboratory went unused. A vacation to the Adirondaks for two weeks every summer was his idea of an adventure.

Ninn used a woman to snare him. He hooked him on the woman, and in so doing, gave him the illusion that he could step out of himself, becoming the Owen Barnes of his imagination. The heroic Barnes, the potent Barnes, the ladykiller Barnes. The Owen Barnes who had escaped his destiny.

Barnes, however much he owned Ninn, still resented him. He believed—or half-believed, anyhow—that the woman, whose name he thought was Lucy, truly loved him and would go anywhere in the world with him. But Lucy, like Jacqueline, like Georgia and all the others, was a performer who had nothing but contempt for her audience of one. But she was too skillful an actress to allow it to show.

"I didn't know you were in town," Barnes said.

"I clearly am. Have you anything new to tell me?"

Barnes was looking over his shoulder, fearful that he might be observed talking with Ninn. "Nothing since the last time."

"I want you to find out two things for me."

"What is it? We're kept awfully busy nowadays. I can't go poking around for you with all this work we've got to do."

Ninn ignored him. He wasn't interested in Owen Barnes's workload. "I would like you to see if you can locate a certain viral strain that I imagine should be kept on the premises. It is designated by the code VDV 21. And then I'd like you to find out what quantity of it is available."

"I don't ordinarily have access to the rooms where the viruses are stored."

"Owen, I have faith in you."

"When do you want this information?"

"Whenever I'm next in town."

"And if I don't have it by then, what happens?"

He was being as truculent as he could manage, but his position didn't permit him the luxury of outright rage.

"You lose Lucy," Ninn said. "On the other hand, you still have your wife, don't you?" Then he proceeded out the door, leaving Owen Barnes to consider his choices.

Half an hour later Lucy phoned. It might simply have been a coincidence. But Barnes knew better. Even so, he couldn't refuse her. She told him she would meet him at the lab around ten.

She was a dark, sultry girl with wondrous legs, and she made every appearance a small drama. No sooner had she entered the room where he was working and thrown off her coat, revealing a V-necked dress that held him in awe, than he knew without a doubt that he would be willing to do anything to find the virus if the alternative was losing her.

Noticing how somber he looked, she said, "What's wrong, Owen? Aren't you happy to see me?"

He *was* happy to see her. And that was exactly what was wrong.

27

DINNER PROCEEDED SMOOTHLY until Kris told Barrett about Henry Loomis.

"You're saying that you think he was killed because of this thesis?" Barrett asked. He held the copy she'd given him in his lap, but now he regarded it with new respect.

"It's possible."

"Kris, I know how important this story is to you—"

"But you think I should stay away from it."

Barrett chose to order another beer before he resumed. "I didn't say that. But it seems to me that a pattern's developing. The break-in, Henry Loomis' death . . ."

"And Sheila Payne."

"What does she have to do with it?"

"She killed Jerry Perretta." She was polishing off her third margarita and so she was putting things a bit more bluntly than she customarily would. Barrett understood the effect too much alcohol had on her.

"I don't get you."

"I've thought a lot about what's being called Heisler's Disease, and I'm sure it's sexually transmitted. Like AIDS."

Acquired immune deficiency syndrome, a breakdown of

the body's defense system, had only recently achieved the kind of media attention ordinarily given to cancer and heart disease. Prevalent among homosexuals, but infecting other populations as well, including Haitian refugees and hemophiliacs, AIDS was transmitted, in some cases, by transfusion of contaminated blood, but primarily through sexual contact.

"It's an interesting theory, Kris, but I'm not sure it holds up. On the other hand, I don't buy the possibility that citrus fruit is the cause, either."

"But suppose it *is* sexually transmitted . . ."

"Let me think about it. I'm not saying I'd rule it out, mind you." Still, it was hard for him to imagine that something so lethal, and so rapid, could be attributed to sexual intercourse. Even AIDS took up to two years to incubate. From all of his readings in medical history, he'd come across nothing that resembled Heisler's Disease. It appeared to have sprung from out of nowhere. "The problem," he said, "is determining where it originated, what's behind it."

"Like locating the bacteria in the water towers above the Bellevue Stratford Hotel when all those men came down with legionnaire's disease?"

"That's right."

"If I were Leo Heisler, I'd be trying to track down the source at the same time I was trying to find something to either cure the disease or at least arrest it. That is, unless I had another motive."

"What kind of motive?"

"I don't know whether Helen was right, but I have a feeling that with any number of experiments Heisler's tried to short-circuit HIC and government guidelines. He's an impatient man, more interested in fame and money than pursuing a tortuous routine of lab tests. For all I know, he might be playing some kind of game, putting on a show to collect government money. Maybe in the end he doesn't give a damn about the virus. But what hope is there to cure it, then?" she asked, draining her second margarita.

"Well, remember, Kris, Heisler isn't in this on his own. The CDC and other labs around the country are also trying to figure this out. It's not like he has a total monopoly on this thing." Holding up the thesis, he promised her he'd read it as soon as he could. "Maybe it'll lead to something."

"Take a good look at Appendix 1," Kris said. "I keep seeing references to something called a transfer protein, but I can't figure out why it's supposed to be so important."

Barrett agreed. But his mind was already on other matters. "We have to talk, Kris. Not about Heisler's Disease. About us."

She said nothing, but her posture changed, becoming more rigid. She held herself very still, her lips pursed. He knew she wasn't looking forward to what was coming.

"You know," he began quietly, "I'd like to believe that what happened between us the night you stayed over wasn't just a unique event, never to be repeated. And I don't just mean sleeping together, I mean all of it, the way we were together. I keep thinking about you, Kris, all the time. And it didn't just start when I found you by my car in the parking lot. It's been going on for a long time now, maybe ever since you left—"

"You wanted me to leave," she said in a soft voice.

That wasn't quite the way he saw it, but on the other hand, he didn't want to engage in an argument over the past, over who was right and who was wrong. That would just be counterproductive.

"Maybe . . . maybe I did," he said, conceding the point. "But that was two years ago and I was wrong, dead wrong. I thought that I would find somebody else who was just like you, but without your faults."

She laughed uneasily. "What you got was somebody with different faults, right? I know how that works."

He looked at her carefully. He believed her. "What I found was that there was no one like you. I'd rather have you with all your faults than someone like Miriam."

"I never doubted that."

"If we hadn't gone our separate ways, there would never have been any Miriam in the first place. But I can't figure you out. One day you're responsive, the next you're on another planet. I want you back, Kris, but if that's not possible, then I can't be sure I can continue going on like this, never from one moment to the next knowing where I stand with you. It's like living in a constant state of limbo.''

He fell silent. It was her turn.

"You don't make it easy," she said. "But then, you never did. I wish I could say yes or no. I wish I could make up my own mind. But I think in order to do that, I'd have to stand back, get a little distance—''

"What do you mean by distance? Going to India and meditating in an ashram for six months?''

"That's not the worst idea I've heard, though that sounds more like Helen's style than mine. It could be physically removing myself from everything, it could be just giving myself some time off to do nothing, not even think. I think too much. Or I brood too much and call it thinking. I love you, Matthew, and yet I'm not certain that I'm ready to be involved with you. Or with anyone else, for that matter. Not right now.''

"When, then?" he demanded.

He didn't want to lose his patience, but there he was, losing his patience nonetheless, watching it vanish right out of sight.

She shrugged, looking very pained. She didn't want to hurt him, he sensed that, but she was establishing conditions that would hurt him even so, imposing on him the very unhappy choice of remaining in limbo until she decided, or giving up on her.

"Maybe when I'm done with the story.''

It seemed arbitrary to him, and not especially relevant to her emotional state. "That could take months, maybe a year. And I doubt whether at the end of that time you'll know anything more than you do right now. Besides which, I think you should watch it, Kris. It might be a bad idea for you to cross Heisler. He has a lot of connections and he can bring a great deal of weight to bear on people he considers his antagonists.''

"Are you saying I should forget about the story?"

He could see she was becoming angry. Even the mildest suggestion from him she was tempted to see as a threat to her independence. That was why he was trying to be so circumspect, not to come right out and tell her that, as a precaution, she'd better lay off, whether or not Loomis' death and the break-in at her apartment were related to the story she was pursuing.

"No, I'm not saying that, Kris. What I'm saying—"

Here he was broken off by someone calling out his name.

He looked up to see a waiter passing by. "Is there a Dr. Matthew Barrett here?"

Barrett hadn't informed anyone that he was coming to El Pueblo; anyone who wished to reach him could do so through his service, which would in turn beep him. But his beeper lay silent in his pocket.

"I'm Dr. Barrett," he said.

The waiter told him he was wanted on the phone. "It's right in back by the rest rooms."

Barrett disliked being interrupted in the middle of such an intense and important conversation, but he was on tonight and he couldn't ignore the call. Still, he couldn't help wondering how the call could have reached him here.

He took the phone, putting a hand to his other ear to blot out some of the noise and jukebox music coming from the dining area.

"Hello, this is Dr. Barrett. To whom am I speaking?"

"Hello, Matthew, how are you this evening?"

The voice was sultry, the kind of voice an actress would use to try to sell a product no one was interested in buying. He knew the voice but couldn't quite identify it.

"Who is this?"

"Don't you know, Matthew? You saw me the other day at Jerry's funeral. You looked straight at me."

Helen? He was afraid to say her name.

"What do you want?" He attempted to keep all trace of nervousness from his voice, but he wasn't sure he was doing a very good job of it.

"I want you to stay away from Kris. You belong to me. You all belong to me now, you and Leo and Isaac. All of you. Stay away from her and she'll be all right, Matthew. Otherwise . . ."

"Otherwise what, goddammit?"

But he wasn't speaking to anybody. The woman on the other end had hung up. It sounded like Helen; he reasoned that it actually *was* Helen. Returned from the dead, never dead at all. But ghost or fully human, she was stalking him, haunting him. And he didn't know what on earth to do about it.

When he got back to his table, he was pale and shaking and there wasn't very much he could do about that, either.

"What's wrong, Matthew? What was that phone call all about?" Kris asked.

They were sitting by a window. He realized now that they must have been followed. He didn't immediately reply. Instead he looked across the street and then up and down the block as far as he could. But if she were anywhere close by, she was concealing herself from view.

"We've got to leave here," he said.

Since they hadn't finished their coffee, Kris was mystified. "But why? . . . All right, we can go, but I have to first thank Nina for the meal."

"Nina?"

"I told you, she's the manager who offered me the freebie."

"Right. Could you make it quick?"

Utterly perplexed, she said she would, and went back into the kitchen to find the manager.

Nina would've preferred to be an actress, but that was a story so often duplicated among women coming to New York that she rarely mentioned it. It seemed to Kris that she no longer entertained fantasies about a career in movies or on the Broadway stage and that she'd done reasonably well for herself as manager of El Pueblo. She was smart and pretty and there were a number of customers who came to the restaurant just because she was to be found there.

Tonight Kris found her in a despondent mood.

"I came in to say thank you. It was excellent, particularly the tostada supreme."

Nina, perched on a stool by a broiler, gave her a wan smile. "I'd tell you to come back anytime, but I'm not sure there will be another time."

"I don't understand."

"Some people from the Board of Health came in today . . ."

Kris thought that maybe they'd discovered some violation of the city standards—rat droppings or a faulty sprinkler system, blocked exits maybe. But it turned out to be none of these things.

"There was also a man with them who identified himself as an investigator for the disease-control authority."

"The Centers for Disease Control?"

"That sounds right. They've been going up and down Columbus and Broadway, looking into every hot-dog stand and three-star restaurant anywhere around here. They're talking about closing a lot of places down, maybe even us."

"Heisler's Disease?"

She nodded. "The other night some guy in the place across the street dropped out of his seat and died on the spot. But he's not the first one who's died of this thing in the neighborhood. He's the first one who checked out so dramatically, though. It was awful. This whole business is awful. They confiscated all of our citrus fruits for analysis. Did you try ordering something with fruit in it?"

Kris said she'd noticed that the margaritas had been served without lime, but had merely attributed that to the bartender's indifference. "They told you they were closing you down?" she asked.

"Not in those words. But that was the implication. They say they're trying to keep a tight lid on it so as not to cause a panic. But you know as well as I do that you get a few more people dying of this thing on the West Side and the deaths are in any way connected to the restaurants and bars in the area, then we might as well forget it.''

"I'm sorry it took so long," Kris said when she rejoined Barrett.

He didn't say anything. She'd never seen him look quite so distracted, at loose ends. "Do you mind if I said good night to you? Something has come up, and I have to deal with it right away.''

Kris didn't know whether she was surprised or not. "We've left a lot of things hanging, haven't we?''

"A lot of things. We need to talk, but not right at this minute.''

"Why don't you call me later tonight?" she said. "Or sometime tomorrow.''

He said he'd like to drive her home, but because he was going in the opposite direction, he'd prefer to put her in a cab. It was some minutes before he found one, and during that whole time he hardly spoke a word.

She noticed that his eyes kept darting about, as though he were searching for something—or someone. She was certain his edginess was due to the phone call. She doubted he'd act any different if someone had just announced his death sentence.

"Matthew," she said, taking hold of his hand and gripping it tightly, "I meant what I said before, that I do love you.''

"I know," he said, but sadly, as though the knowledge of the fact only burdened him more. "I know you do. And I feel the same about you. And where does that leave us?''

A cab came abreast of them and halted.

She kissed him. It was her way of answering.

"Where to?" the driver asked.

"Jane Street and Greenwich," she instructed him.

Half a dozen blocks farther downtown she said, "Wait a minute, I've changed my mind. I'd like to go back to where you picked me up.''

The driver could only shrug. It was all the same to him, and it was likely that Kris would not be the oddest fare he picked up that night.

She got out on the other side of the street from El Pueblo. The restaurant where the man had dropped dead was crowded. Every table was full and the bar was so jammed that if someone should choose to topple over from his stool and die, he'd never be noticed.

It was not difficult for Kris to strike up a conversation. Actually, all she had to do was stand in one place and have the conversation happen to her.

"Somebody told me a man died in here last night," she said to the first man who approached her. He had the dazed, drugged look of a man who's gone into hock over cocaine.

"That's right," he said. "That's exactly right."

"You know him?"

"I knew him. He used to come in here all the time. It was weird. He wasn't what you'd call old. But when you go, you go, I suppose."

She asked him if he knew of any similar incidents elsewhere in the neighborhood. He didn't. But a man standing not more than two feet from her had.

He was big and bearded and obviously looking for any opportunity to break in on the conversation in order to have a chance with Kris.

"You have?" she asked.

"Some clown six blocks up the street at Winston's died a week ago. He wasn't at the bar at the time, but he came in there almost every night. I have a friend who was a friend of his. One night he comes in, says I'm not feeling well, goes home, takes to his bed, and when he doesn't feel any better, he calls the doctor."

"Didn't do him any good?" the first man, with the burned-out eyes, asked.

"I guess not. He died, didn't he?"

"Of pneumonia?" Kris asked.

"Something like that."

It wasn't much to go on, but it was all Kris had.

Winston's was less densely packed, but that didn't make it any easier to attract the bartender's attention. She tried another tack; rather than ask about the victim, she'd try asking about the only person she knew who might be the perpetrator.

"What can I do for you?" the bartender asked.

"I was just wondering if you've ever seen a woman come in here with blonde hair, very pretty?"

"We see pretty women in here all the time."

"This one would have an English accent."

He shook his head. "I wouldn't know. I work here days most of the time, I'm only filling in for tonight."

She tried another bar called Electricity. The sign for the bar glowed lavender in the window; a neon lightning bolt hung on the wall opposite the bar and was reflected in the mirror that extended along the bar's length.

The bartenders at Electricity told her that her description reminded them of a woman they'd seen, but they were so imprecise in their recollection of her that it did Kris no good.

In a place called Greensleeve's, the bartender was a woman, big-breasted and wide-hipped, with an open Irish face. From experience Kris was inclined to trust a woman's observational powers over a man's.

After Kris had described Sheila Payne to her, the woman nodded and pursed her lips. "I think I've seen somebody like that, but I don't think her name was Sheila. I once heard someone call her Jackie, though I could be mistaken."

"She could be using another name."

"An actress? We get lots of actresses in this neighborhood."

"I suppose she could be one."

"Well, whatever she is, I haven't seen her around in a while."

"But she did have an English accent?" Kris wanted to be as certain as possible they were talking about the same person.

"Honey, she could've had a Chinese accent for all I know."

Kris then asked if this woman had come in alone.

"Oh, sure, she came in alone, but that was never the way she left."

By this point Kris was growing tired, tired because she hadn't had enough sleep and tired because it took more and more energy to keep men at a distance. She was also somewhat drunk; she didn't feel right about soliciting information from bartenders without ordering at least one drink from them, and the result of this policy was beginning to tell on her.

It was just after midnight when she walked into PieceMeal. This, she resolved, would be the last bar—for tonight anyhow. Why she thought it possible to survey all the singles bars in the area in the course of only one evening was beyond her. She just hadn't imagined there would be quite so many of them.

Once again she described Sheila to the bartender on duty, but this time mentioned that she was also called Jackie.

"Real looker?"

"That's right, a real looker."

"Hey, Don, you remember that English gal who came in here the other night?" he called to the other bartender.

Don evidently remembered. "Yeah, she was one hell of a piece of work."

"She was in here recently?"

"As recently as last night. You a friend of hers?"

"I used to work with her downtown."

It was the kind of nebulous statement that no one would question.

"Right. Well, I can't guarantee you she'll be in. She was here three or four nights running, but tonight I don't know what happened to her. If you want to wait around, maybe she'll turn up."

Kris waited. Her waiting was accompanied by many more drinks than she really cared to have. The bartender continued to replenish her glass without asking her whether she wanted another drink. Except for the first one she'd ordered, they were all on the house.

It was only inertia keeping her seated here, or else the influence of all the white-wine spritzers she'd been consuming. She didn't even want to ask what the time was, but she suspected it must be getting close to two.

Suddenly she raised her eyes to discover that one of the bartenders was gesturing to her. She thought that maybe she'd gotten lucky after all and that Sheila—or Jackie, if that's how she wanted to be known in these parts—had come in. But when she looked down to the other end of the bar, she saw that it was a man the bartender was talking to, not a woman.

The bartender then approached her. "A friend of mine was with that woman you asked about last night. I figured maybe you might want to meet him."

She sensed that the bartender was trying to help her because it was getting late and he might want to have someone to take home with him once the bar shut down. But she didn't let it bother her. "Absolutely," Kris said. "What's his name?"

"Barry Canowitz. Nice guy, works in advertising. I'll send him over here."

Barry looked a bit unsteady on his feet; his face was pale, his eyes bloodshot; when he stepped up toward Kris, he smiled wanly.

Kris's first thought was that he must have been drinking too much before he got to PieceMeal, but then it occurred to her that Barry had very likely spent the night with Sheila, and in doing so, had contracted Heisler's Disease.

He will be dead in two days, she thought numbly.

"Hey, girl, how are you doing?"

He was obviously so accustomed to charming unattached women and seducing them within a few hours of meeting them that he wasn't going to let a little thing like a fatal illness intrude on his style.

The realization that she was facing a dead man all but paralyzed her; she couldn't speak for several moments.

"Something the matter?"

He took the stool beside her.

"No, nothing." her voice was small, almost inaudible. "How are you? I'm Kris Erlanger."

"Barry Canowitz. Why have I never seen you in here before?"

"I don't live around here."

All the while, she was thinking how she could tell him that he might be critically ill and that he should see a doctor immediately. At the same time, she knew that it would probably do him no good, that whether or not he received medical care, he would die anyway. Then there was always the possibility that he was simply suffering from the flu, that she was just imagining things.

It took her some time to draw him around to the subject of the woman he'd been with the previous night. Clearly he would have much preferred to continue trying to seduce her.

"You know Jackie?" he said, but without much interest. "What a strange chick."

"How so?"

"I don't know, maybe it's different knowing her just as a friend. How can I put this? She does some very kinky numbers in bed. I'm not saying I mind, it just takes some getting used to is all."

Yes, Kris thought resignedly, he *is* a dead man.

"You met her right here?"

She didn't know why this detail mattered.

"That's right. You're her friend?"

"We hung out together," she said, adding, "downtown," as though this made it all the more plausible.

Turning to the bartender, Barry called for another shot of one from the brown bottle. The brown bottle turned out to contain some very smooth tequila. "I think I'm getting a cold," he said. Taking the glass of tequila in hand, he announced, "This helps."

Nothing helps, Kris was about to say, but she held back. "So you went back to your place with her?" This might have been the wrong thing to say, she realized. Maybe he'd think her a bit too interested in his one-night stand.

But he was apparently too sick and dazed to consider the

implications of what she was saying. "I said I had a good view." Looking straight at Kris, he said emphatically, "And I do. You can see the river." His face went blank for a moment; his mind might have gone somewhere very far away. "You want to know something? I think your friend is hustling."

"Oh?"

"She never came right out and said it, but I had the feeling she was in bad shape. Financially, I mean. I don't mind helping somebody out, you know, but I don't like some bitch coming around and hustling me, no offense."

"None taken."

"I got money, I like spending it on women. Speaking of which, are you going to let me buy you a drink?"

Since she was seeking information from him, she decided to accept the offer, although she had no idea how she was going to drink it and still walk out of the place without making a fool of herself.

"You didn't give her any money, did you?"

He shook his head. "No, but I suggested that I wouldn't mind helping her out if she told me where I could get in touch with her. I said I'd like to see her again. Some broads you find here, you don't want to see again. I can be honest with you, can't I? But then you get somebody like Jackie . . . well, she interests me. To tell you the truth, she turns me on. There was something she did with an ice cube."

"An ice cube?"

"Yeah, but you're going to have to forgive me if I don't go into details."

"So did she give you a phone number?"

"Told me she was staying in a hotel uptown. The Windemere? You heard of it? Up on Ninety-third Street. Ninety-third, Ninety-fourth, something like that. I had a girlfriend who used to live there once."

"She tell you what her room number was? I'd like to see her again."

"She owes you money too, right?"

He smiled, but the smile he produced only contorted his

face, which was white as a sheet, but a sheet that no amount of washing was ever going to completely get the stains out of.

"Something like that," Kris said.

"Just so long as you don't say I told you."

"Not a word, I promise."

It won't matter anyway in a day or two, she thought.

"It's 22H. That's the extension she gave me, I assume it's the room number too."

"You make a date?"

"For tomorrow night. We're meeting for drinks."

"I really appreciate this, Barry."

"Hey, no problem. How about another drink?"

"I haven't finished this one yet. And I do have to get going. I have to be up early."

"So have I. Then again, I might just take the day off and rest so I can get rid of this damn thing. Everybody in my office has this Russian flu." As if to corroborate his point, he suddenly threw his head back and sneezed three times. "Damn," he muttered as he blew into a silk handkerchief. "And I never get sick."

Kris felt terribly guilty. It was not her obligation to let this man know that he was very likely fatally ill. Even his personal physician would be reluctant to pronounce that diagnosis. Yet she knew she had to say something. "Look, Barry, maybe you ought to see a doctor first thing tomorrow morning."

He gave her a cross look, swept back a lock of hair that had fallen over his brow, and said, "A couple of days go by, and I'm still not feeling any better, then I'll call in a quack. But I've had this bug before. Twenty-four hours, and it's gone, kaput!"

Kris sensed that he would have liked to continue their conversation; he struck her as a man who would regard a night as a disaster if he couldn't score a piece of ass. But the disease he unknowingly harbored had so exhausted him that all he could do was issue a perfunctory invitation: "You know, I think I like you a lot better than your friend Jackie. Maybe you might like to come back for a little while and talk. I've got some fine smoke and half a gram of coke I've been saving for a special occasion. This could be a special occasion."

Kris explained again that she had to be back home, but she was apologetic. And the apology was genuine enough. After tonight there would be no more women for him.

"I'll see you another time," he called after her.

"I'm sure you will," she said, turning and waving. What else could she say to someone who within forty-eight hours would be resting in a funeral home?

Although it was three in the morning, many of the bars Kris passed were still occupied by customers either plagued by insomnia or such late sleepers that a glimpse of daylight would be as rare an experience as a trip to Tierra del Fuego.

It was possible, Kris thought, that Sheila, aka Jackie, had provided Barry with the wrong address, one that would prove no more reliable than Carey Pharmaceuticals had. On the other hand, maybe she'd been honest with him when she'd said she'd run low on money and would like to see him again.

It was cold, but the weather appeared not to have intimidated either the bums who made their beds in the doorways of ShopRite and the West Side Shoe Repair or the hookers who idled at strategic corners, their coats open and their long naked legs exposed to the air and the occasional scrutiny of a frozen passerby.

A sign at the West End entrance to the Windemere advised all guests to announce themselves at the desk. But the one man behind the desk exhibited no interest in Kris when she entered, so she hardly felt constrained to obey the injunction.

She waited for several moments outside the door where Barry said Jacqueline lived. It was not just the thought that she might not find anyone in that caused her to hesitate, but the very real problem of how to tell her that her body harbored a fatal virus and that if ever a man made love with her again he would lose his life.

How can you tell someone that she is a killer? An unwitting killer perhaps, but a killer nonetheless.

Kris had no idea, was too tired to puzzle it out. She listened, heard nothing, knocked, then, gathering her resolve, knocked again, louder.

28

"EARL? Earl? Are you in there?"

Ninn didn't anticipate any response and would have been as surprised as hell if one had been forthcoming.

The hallway was dark—where the light should have been, there was only an empty socket—and smelled of urine and of something less identifiable, spilled alcohol or ammonia maybe, that hadn't quite dissipated into the air. A dog was barking furiously from somewhere and the sound of it was carried up through the airshaft opposite Earl Wheelock's apartment.

Ninn unlocked the door. As soon as he opened it, the smell hit him with the force of a sledgehammer. By contrast, the hall smelled like a fresh spring morning.

Earl had never smelled too terrific in life—a shower was evidently an alien thing to him—but in death he exuded a stench that Ninn would expect to find in the most squalid precincts of Calcutta.

Earl hadn't been dead for long, and on the outside he appeared intact; it was cold in his apartment and it was the cold that was probably preserving him. But on the inside he was decomposing.

He had a one-room place with a bathtub in the middle of it, and it was in the bathtub that he'd ended up; the bathtub, which he'd painted all black, wasn't quite large enough to accommodate him, and so he'd had to draw his legs up against his chin. He was stark naked, his body bluish-white like a statue too long exposed to the elements, and the way he was curled up in the tub, he resembled a little boy waiting for his mother to come and scrub him.

There was still some water left in the tub; with the cold in the apartment, a thin coating of ice had formed on its surface.

Earl, even in the best of times, was almost all skin and bone. But now he was so emaciated, so diminutive in appearance, that Ninn felt as if he would have no trouble picking him up in his arms and carrying him out. But he had no intention of removing him from his final resting place.

He gaced into Earl's face. His eyes were still open, but filmed over; his lips were cracked; mucus was caked below his nostrils. One hand gripped the side of the tub, suggesting that in his last moments of life he'd tried hoisting himself up out of it.

He would have had no idea that by killing Beth Sandor the way he had, he had guaranteed his own end.

It occurred to Ninn that he would miss Earl. He had never known anyone quite so eager to perform mayhem for so little money. He would do anything demanded of him. He had a knack for insinuating himself into other people's lives, for rooting them out of their hiding places, for filling them with terror. Ninn would miss Earl terribly, no doubt about it.

Earl was—had been—a junkie, always looking for a score. True, there were thousands of others like him between Avenues B and D; it was no problem finding someone who would cut up a man or torch a building—or rape a woman. But even so, there were very few who were as obedient, as eager to please, as much in love with him, as Earl.

Yet he'd had to be sacrificed. Neither discreet nor possessed of the merest shred of honor, he'd learned too much in the time he'd spent in Ninn's service. He was, like Matthew Barrett, someone in the way, someone who could cause a needless mess when you weren't watching.

He'd lived simply, sparsely; there was practically nothing of any value in his apartment to be found except for those goods—a Sony Trinitron color TV, a huge tape deck, a Pioneer stereo system—that he'd stolen, probably from apartments very nearby. There were also, Ninn noted, a great many skin books, copies of *Honcho* and *Blue Boy,* strewn about the floor.

All this while, Ninn did his utmost to breathe only through his mouth; this was not a smell one could ever adapt to, this dead Earl smell.

He now opened the refrigerator, and taking two lemons from a paper bag, he placed them inside. A third lemon he cut in half, squeezing the juice into a glass he found in the sink. Among his other purchases were a pint bottle of Gordon's gin and a bottle of Schwepp's tonic water. With these he prepared a gin and tonic, which he set by the side of the tub, close to where Earl could reach it should he miraculously be resurrected. When someone found Earl—and sooner or later, once the stench began leaking out into the hall, someone would—it would appear as though he'd been drinking it before he died.

It would not be long before the CDC or another researcher with more integrity than Leo Heisler would discover that there was absolutely no connection between citrus fruit and the virus. But until then, Ninn would go right on planting false evidence wherever necessary.

He bid a silent farewell to Earl and went on his way. Somewhere in the world he would find another Earl, a man who would be every bit as subservient and ruthless. But until such an individual turned up, he would have to go it alone. Without Earl, he knew, he would have to kill Jacqueline Hanratty himself. First, though, he had to find her.

29

"I DON'T UNDERSTAND what you're telling me."

Kris was about to explain all over again, but realized that what Sheila—or Jackie, as she was now calling herself—was really saying was that she didn't believe Kris, didn't want to believe her.

They were sitting some distance away from each other; Kris was perched on the edge of a shabby overstuffed chair, while her reluctant hostess lay recumbent on the bed, her head propped against a pillow. She was obviously worn out and frightened. Lacking makeup, her face was pale and her eyes ringed by shadows.

"Look, I don't want you to worry, but I think it's important that you see a doctor. I'm not saying for certain that you have anything wrong, but it couldn't do any harm to check."

"I've been checked a million times by doctors," she snapped. "No one's found anything wrong with me yet except for a yeast infection once. I'm taking an antibiotic regularly, so I don't see how I could have picked up this thing you're talking about, much less given it to someone else."

"Antibiotics don't necessarily protect against viruses," Kris pointed out.

Jackie shook her head; she wasn't interested in such details.

"I feel fine, a little tired maybe, but if you ran around like I do, you'd feel tired too. If I thought I was sick, I'd see somebody. But I don't, and that's the end of it."

"Look, Jackie, people give other people measles and mumps too and they feel just fine. They're carriers. All I'm saying is that it's possible you may be a carrier."

"Hey, I watch the news on the telly," she countered. "I saw where that doctor said citrus fruit caused it. I don't know where you get off coming here at God knows what hour of the morning telling me that just because I fucked some guy—what did you say his name was?—he's going to end up dead."

"Barry, and I didn't say that he was going to end up dead."

That was what she had meant to imply, but she couldn't bring herself to put it quite so frankly.

"What are you, some kind of Moral Majority nut? We've heard of you people over in England, so piss on that."

"I assure you I have nothing to do with the Moral Majority. I'm not even a churchgoer."

"You know something—I'm not sure I know which one was Barry."

"Broad-shouldered, mustached, not bad-looking, he said that he had a date to see you tomorrow night."

"Oh, right, I remember."

It was possible that it was not just sleeplessness that accounted for her abstracted behavior. "Can I ask you something, Jackie?"

"Sure, anything." She suddenly seemed no longer resentful of Kris; maybe she even welcomed the company so long as there was no further talk about mysterious and fatal illnesses.

"You said you were working for an escort service."

"That's right. They call it a courier service, but it's just a fancy name."

"But you're not working for them anymore?"

"No, it was bloody murder, it's like you're a doctor, on call twenty-four hours a day. Fly here, fly there, go pick up a john at some hotel, turn a trick, and split. The pay's pretty good, but you never see bloody half of it. Why are you asking me all these questions?"

"Curious, that's all. I never met anyone who worked for a service like that."

"It's a business, you know, like any other. It's not so special."

"Are you planning on staying here long?"

"I don't know. Some bloke I met said I could stay here for a few weeks while he was in South America, but I have no idea really how long I'll be here. I could split tomorrow."

"I assume you could go wherever you like with the money you've saved up."

"Money?" She laughed. "What bloody money? I've got no money saved up. It goes through my fingers like water."

"Where does it go?"

"Cocaine, grass, ludes, nothing unusual—just very expensive. Sometimes it's all right, though, sometimes people—men—just give me stuff. But then I always want more. You do something?"

"Some grass now and then, that's all."

She was nodding with satisfaction. "Everybody does something," she declared. "The bloke who runs us—"

"Runs you?"

"Operates the escort service, I mean."

"What about him?"

"Drinks," she said. "Drinks like a pig. You don't want to cross him."

"What happens if you do?"

"You wouldn't want to know. *I* don't even know, to tell you the truth. Maybe nothing, maybe he just makes a lot of noise."

"What's his name?"

"It wouldn't mean anything to you. Look, if you don't mind, let's talk about something else."

Kris, however, didn't want to talk about something else. But she decided that she would have to alter her tactics, try a more roundabout approach. "Bet you do a lot of traveling in your business."

Jackie nodded. "A lot. I told you it's murder. Minute to minute, you never know where you're going to be. That's why I got out of it."

"Where were you before New York?"

"All over. England, mainly I'm always going back there."

"What did you say the name of the service was?"

"Jesus, you're one curious bird, aren't you, now? It's called the Inverness Courier Service Limited."

She was silent for several moments. Kris realized that she might have lost the train of her thoughts. "You were telling me about your travels."

"Well, then, before London, where was I? It's hard to remember, really. You wake up in some room with some bloke next to you, you look out the window, and you know, you can't for the life of you figure how you got where you are. It can be disorienting as hell. I've had to turn the telly on or go out and look for a newspaper to find out sometimes."

"So, let's see, before London I was in Denver. Before Denver, in L.A. I like L.A. I didn't think I would, with all those freeways and those people trying to become movie stars, but it was fun actually."

There was no way that Kris could put the next question very delicately. So she came right out with it. "You slept with guys out there, in Denver and in L.A.?"

"What of it?"

"You recall their names?"

"Maybe."

Jackie was beginning to sense that she was being led somewhere, and from the expression on her face, she didn't particularly like it.

"If you could, it might help enormously."

"Oh? What have you got in mind?"

"Just a little experiment."

"An experiment?"

"That's all it is, an experiment. Tomorrow I'd like to try it with you."

The new midtown branch of the New York Public Library impressed Jackie mostly by how well-lighted it was. "The last library I was in, you couldn't see a bloody thing, it was so goddamn dark."

"You should have no trouble seeing here."

Jackie suddenly looked perplexed.

"What is it?"

"I was just thinking that I've seen you somewhere before."

Kris was surprised she hadn't recognized her before from the waiting room of Barrett and Perretta's office. "I don't think so."

"Maybe not, then."

Jackie couldn't help jumping from subject to subject, never sticking to one for longer than a few minutes before growing bored with it. Kris didn't know whether she'd ever met anyone so distracted before.

"You were in Denver and Los Angeles in the last few weeks, weren't you?" she asked.

"Oh, that again. I guess so."

Maybe, Kris thought, her dissociated manner was a pose too, calculated to deceive.

The library had copies of the Los Angeles *Times* and Denver *Post* as far back as the first of the year; prior to that, issues were on microfiche.

"Now, tell me the exact dates you were out there, Jackie."

They were standing by a table with the *Post* spread out in front of them.

"How am I supposed to know the exact dates? I told you I can't keep track of time."

"Let's try to calculate it, then."

"I don't think I like your experiment."

"We haven't even started, Jackie."

"I know I'm not going to like it." She made as if to walk away, but Kris gripped her arm gently but determinedly.

"Come on, this is no big thing."

But it was; it was a very big thing.

"You were in London when?"

She thought for a moment. "Last Wednesday—that was when I left for New York again."

"And how long were you in London?"

In this tortuous manner Kris was able to pin Jackie down at least to the approximate days when she had been in the two cities in question.

That was the easy part. The hard part was convincing her to divulge the names of the men she'd slept with.

"I'd rather not say."

It was odd how at certain moments, last night and again today, Kris was under the impression that she'd established a certain friendship with the woman, only to find that it was nothing of the sort. The woman was a stranger to her, and while she spoke the same language, albeit with an English accent, she was as removed from Kris's experience as a Tibetan would be.

Kris couldn't be sure which argument would work with her. If she said that by cooperating she might help save lives, would that make any difference to her? She tried another strategy. "Don't, then. Forget it."

"Zachary Hackett."

Kris turned questioningly to her. "Who was he?"

"The first bloke I picked up in Denver. He wanted to take me up into the mountains, but we never got farther than the tenth floor of his hotel."

Kris looked up from the obit page of the *Post*. "He was from out of town?"

"He was a dentist, I think, from St. Paul, St. Louis, someplace like that. They all lie anyway, don't want their wives to find out."

That wasn't going to do any good at all. She needed the names of men who lived in the Denver area. "Anyone else?"

"Let me think. There was an oil executive. Daniel something. Wait, it was Daniel Thompson or Thomas."

Kris scanned the obituary pages in the February 13, 14, 15, and 16 editions of the *Post*. She assumed that if this Daniel Thompson or Thomas held a corporate position of any significance at all she should have no difficulty in spotting the notice of his death. Jackie had said she left Denver on the 12th. From what Kris knew of the course of Heisler's Disease, it usually manifested itself by the second day after contact and killed off its victim no later than the fourth.

At last she was rewarded for her patience. The Denver *Post* of February 18 carried a short article on the death of Daniel Towner, 47, former chief operations officer of the Lewis-Cole Petroleum Company. The cause of death was listed simply as pneumonia.

"Would it be Daniel Towers?"

"That sounds right."

"He's dead."

Jacqueline stared at the notice and shrugged. "I don't know what that proves. People die all the time."

"Anyone else in Denver?"

"Davis."

"Davis what?"

"Just Davis—could have been his first name or his last name, I'm not sure." She sounded petulant, but at least she hadn't clammed up altogether.

"Did Davis live in Denver?"

"Part of the time. He was a ski instructor, I think. Quite a hunk."

That wasn't much to go on. Kris decided to try the L.A. *Times* instead.

Jackie was stumped. She read the obituaries with the same interest she would have bestowed on a textbook in accounting.

"Don't you remember any name at all? Doesn't one of these obits ring a bell?" Kris was becoming so frustrated that it was all she could do to keep from wringing this childlike woman's neck.

She was shaking her head. "No, no," she said.

"All right, then, I guess that's it." Kris got up from the table.

"What are you going to do?" Jackie asked.

"Go home."

"Wait a minute."

Kris stopped. "I'm waiting."

"I might have something that could help you." When Kris didn't say anything, she began searching through her bag. A few moments later she produced a small pink datebook. "The names are all in here," she said. "My memory's bad; I figured I'd better put everything down so I'd know when I got to a new town who to call."

"Why didn't you tell me about this before?"

Now Kris was positive she was going to wring her neck.

"I don't know." She shrugged.

"Well, let's have a look."

Her handwriting, just like her psyche, could have belonged to a child; the letters were large and full of loops and curlicues.

But the relevant information had been noted down with care: city, date, client, client's age, address, telephone number. In addition she'd made sure to include a detail or two about the men's individual preferences. "Likes gloves," one stated cryptically. "Dresses in drag, loves musical comedy," was another. About Frank Holly, "actor, unemployed," she'd written: "Straight, but Greek OK."

There was one name that leaped out at her. Lew Congdon. ("Straight, but not averse to leather.")

Kris looked quizzically at Jackie. "Did you sleep with Lew Congdon?"

"Stayed with him three days," she replied with evident pride. "He was all right. I've seen a couple of his films. Everybody in the world has."

Kris flipped back to the front page of the edition she was reading. At the bottom of the page she found this headline: "CONGDON'S DEATH FROM NATURAL CAUSES, SAYS CORONER."

She showed it to Jackie, who read it with an indifferent expression. "Doesn't surprise me. He didn't look well at all when I left him."

Kris had an idea. As Jackie divided her address book by city, she had no difficulty finding New York. Among the names was Jerry Perretta's. "How do you know this man?"

At first Jackie seemed not to recognize the name. Then she said, "Oh, right, he was kind of sweet. I just sort of bumped into him."

"He's dead too, Jackie."

Her face darkened. For the first time Kris thought that maybe she was getting through to her.

"You think I've got this disease they're all talking about?"

"I think it's possible you're a carrier of it."

"Then maybe I should see someone." Her voice was flat. "I want to see the best."

"The best?"

"The man they're always interviewing on the telly."

"Heisler?"

"That's the one."

He was the last person Kris would want to recommend anyone to, but Jackie grew insistent. "He's the expert, isn't he? Any other doctor I go to is only going to send me to him."

She had a point. Kris agreed to phone the Melkis Pavilion and see what could be done.

As soon as she mentioned that she knew of a woman who might have a connection to the virus, she was put through to Heisler.

"Miss Erlanger, what a surprise!" he said. "When's your story going to appear?"

"Soon, I hope. But in the meantime I have a favor to ask of you."

She half-hoped that Heisler would decline to see her.

But on the contrary, he told her to bring Jackie in. "This sounds most intriguing," he said. "What did you say her name was again?"

"Jacqueline Hanratty. She wants to see you because she says you're the best."

"Oh, but I am, Miss Erlanger. I am the best."

30

MATTHEW BARRETT was used to going without sleep. He'd grown accustomed to functioning up to forty-eight hours without it, though it could not be said that by the thirtieth hour he was functioning very well.

But it was not an ailing patient who'd kept him up through Monday night and all through Tuesday afternoon. He decided he wouldn't go to sleep until he talked to Kris. If he could've gotten his hands on her goddamn answering machine, he would've had no compunctions about demolishing it. Though she'd told him she'd be home, every call he made went unanswered.

But Kris was not so much in his thoughts as Helen was. He was convinced that it was Helen who'd called him at El Pueblo. It would not surprise him to discover that it was she who'd devastated Kris's apartment, not, as he'd originally believed, to retaliate against her for some offense—real or imagined—but rather to show him exactly what she was capable of.

In the best of times Helen was a wild woman, headstrong and compulsive, and in some way, demonic. But these were patently not the best of times, not for her, not for anybody.

He was afraid for Kris, afraid for himself. His first impulse was to say the hell with Helen and stay with Kris as much as possible, although this raised other problems having nothing whatsoever to do with Helen. His second impulse, however, was to maintain a discreet distance from her until such time as Helen could be brought out into the open and somehow stopped. Imagining her locked away in a psychiatric institution for the rest of her life provided him with only momentary surcease from his worries.

It was obvious that Helen was, as many psychopathic individuals are, capable of pursuing her objective with so much boldness, so much cunning, that it put most relatively well-adjusted people to shame. To keep Kris's company might truly place her in danger. And if anything happened to her he would never forgive himself.

Tuesday morning he went into the hospital and performed his rounds in a daze. Nurses and residents observed him gravely, as if they suspected that he might have succumbed to Heisler's Disease as his partner had.

By Tuesday noon Kris still wasn't at home. Failing to find her in, he got into his car and drove down to the Village and rang her bell. But the mail hadn't been collected, a good sign she had never been home.

Everywhere he went he kept looking for Helen. And there were times during the day that he was sure he saw her, just a glimpse of her, darting through a crowd or else observing him from behind a parked car. But then it struck him that he was hallucinating, that with his lack of sleep he was projecting her image onto the faces of a score of women who only in build and hair color happened to vaguely resemble her. Should he keep on without sleep, he'd end by seeing every woman as Helen—except for the real one.

What the hell had he done to her that she would come after him like this? he kept asking himself. He had backed out of marrying her, but that was years ago, and anyway, was that such a heinous sin that now, more than a decade later, he—and Kris—had to suffer for it? But of course the motives guiding her were probably so devoid of logic that they were as inscrutable as they were dangerous.

When his thoughts turned to Kris, his paranoia (if paranoia it was) turned in a different direction. All along he'd been thinking that she might be in trouble, that that was why she hadn't come home. But something else preyed on his bewildered mind—that there was another man, a man she might have known and fallen in love with during the two years they weren't seeing each other, or maybe someone whom she'd met only in the last few days. Was it possible that she was with him now, finding him to be a far more sympathetic, understanding ear than Barrett had been?

To distract himself he decided to turn on the television. It proved to be very little distraction. All he could find were nightly news programs, each one with its own special reports on the progress of Heisler's Disease. The daily death tolls, ranging from fifteen to twenty-five a day, reminded him of the tallies the National Traffic Safety Council issued after holiday weekends; they sounded almost as routine. People might get used to them, he thought, and accept Heisler's Disease as simply another risk in their lives, like poisonous dioxins in the ground where they lived or PCB's in the water they drank.

Another lab had been shut down, he learned, this time in Boston. The Lewis Sandburn Institute for Cancer Research had temporarily closed its doors pending a CDC Epidemic and Intelligence Unit investigation into the causes of the death of three of its researchers, Carl Elkin, Hal Lawrence, and Avery March, all victims of Heisler's Disease.

He shut off the television and turned instead to the thesis that Kris had given him to read.

Little of it was capable of holding his attention. It might be a brilliant piece of work, but it was dry and occasionally impenetrable. Since he was no biochemist, large chunks of it were beyond his comprehension altogether. So he skipped ahead to Appendix 1, which Kris had expressed the most interest in.

The T—or Transfer—protein, he read, was found in approximately fifty percent of all females. Its importance lay in the fact that it gave this fifty percent greater-than-normal resistance to certain viral diseases.

The T-protein evidently bound to viral particles, several of which comprised a whole virus. In essence, it locked up the viral particles and threw away the key.

This meant that women who had the T-protein were capable of carrying the virus, but not displaying any symptoms of if.

Helen cautioned that considerably more research had to be undertaken before the whole mechanism of the disease process was understood. "At this point it is impossible to say with certainty how the virus is transmitted," she concluded.

It was just possible that this appendix held the clue to the nature of Heisler's Disease. Kris could be right; it could be transmitted sexually. But perhaps there were other ways too. The mystery was still there.

He hoped that Kris would phone soon. He knew she'd be anxious to hear that he'd divined the meaning of Appendix 1. It was only then that the thought occurred to him that, with half the women in America in possession of the T-protein, Kris might have it as well.

But that wasn't worth worrying about, he decided. Only a tiny minority were probably infected. The question, of course, was who?

31

NINN THOUGHT he might be going mad. He couldn't locate Jacqueline for the life of him. Having traced her to the Upper West Side, he'd found himself at a dead end. She seemed to have disappeared. Losing her would confirm Heisler's impression of him as incompetent, a man who in the final accounting proved to be as much a loser as Colin Thomas was.

He continued drinking from his flask as he drove toward Westside Medical Center. The liquor wasn't going down well, it was burning his gut. Probably he should see a doctor about it, but there were no doctors he trusted.

When he reached the Melkis Pavilion, he proceeded by elevator to the fourth floor; once there, he made his way down the corridors to the stockroom where much of his derelict equipment lay, still in the crates shipped from England. A short passageway from the stockroom led to a seldom-used rear door of Heisler's office.

Heisler was alone at his desk when Ninn entered. He failed to register his presence until Ninn spoke his name.

"I thought I told you not to use that entrance," Heisler said. He sounded not irritated, but very tired.

"It was easier."

Ninn came around to the other side of the desk. Heisler followed his movement with his eyes, but said nothing.

"I wanted to know if you'd managed to reconstitute any additional amounts of the virus."

"Nothing so far."

Ninn was incredulous, but before he could speak, the phone buzzed.

Heisler picked it up. "Yes, what is it?"

He listened for a few moments, then said, "I'll meet them in the conference room."

When he replaced the receiver, he gave Ninn a smug, self-satisfied look. A smile was slowly forming on his lips. "Your friend Jacqueline Hanratty has come home."

"I don't understand."

"Jacqueline is here, in the company of Kris Erlanger. Erlanger did your work for you, Isaac. You lost Jacqueline, she found her. A clever girl."

"That's impossible," he muttered.

"Perhaps, but it is a fact. I'm to meet them in the conference room. If you'd like, you can watch from the projection booth. There's no way they'll see you there."

Ninn hastily composed himself. "It seems to me that Jacqueline might be the source we need for that tissue, Leo."

Heisler would not reply, probably because he was not yet willing to consider the implications of Ninn's words.

The two woman were escorted into the conference room where Heisler waited. He welcomed them with elaborate formality and asked if they would care for some coffee.

Kris was evidently in no mood to suffer through an exchange of small talk. She did not want coffee, nor did Jacqueline.

Heisler turned his eyes to Jacqueline. She still had her coat on, as though she hadn't quite made the adjustment from the cold, outside. It seemed that only now did he recognize how remarkably attractive the woman was.

"I'm told that you have some information regarding the possible origin of the virus."

Ninn, sitting in the projection booth overlooking the conference room, strained to hear every syllable; he was afraid of what the answer might be.

Kris answered. "That's right. I'm inclined to believe that Jackie is a carrier of the disease."

The rigidity with which Heisler held his body suggested that he was every bit as apprehensive as Ninn. "How did you come to that conclusion?" he asked after a long silence.

Kris supplemented her explanation with photocopies of the obituary notices she'd compiled from the Denver *Post* and the L.A. *Times*. Heisler examined them carefully, but there was nothing to indicate what his reaction was.

"You're quite certain you don't want any coffee?" he asked.

"Positive." Kris sounded exasperated.

Jacqueline continued to sit there with a blank look on her face; it was as though none of this had anything to do with her.

"What do you say to this?" Heisler directed his gaze toward Jacqueline, who started.

"What?"

"Are you convinced you're a carrier?"

She shook her head. Her eyes were very bright, almost luminous. It would be drugs giving so much light to them, Ninn thought.

"You slept with these men?" He held up the photocopies.

"Yes, I slept with them. I don't remember them, but I slept with them."

Heisler studied the copies for another moment. "Some of the obituaries say that these men died of pneumonia. There's no proof that the pneumonia was caused by the virus we're studying here. I don't wish to question your motives, Miss Erlanger, but I do wonder whether you're not jumping to conclusions. For all I know, Miss Hanratty here may not even be telling the truth——"

"I am telling the bloody truth," she burst out in the first display of emotion she'd shown since sitting down.

Heisler held up a conciliatory hand. "Please, I'd very much like to believe you. I want to see this disease cured more than anyone else. My reputation is on the line, and I would certainly not overlook any possible clue to the origins of the infection. But these obituaries do not constitute proof that you are a carrier. Even you don't believe you are a carrier, as you just admitted."

"That's because it's damned hard for someone to accept, doctor," Kris said.

"Wait, let me make a suggestion."

Kris gave him a dubious look, but held her silence.

"Just to make sure that nothing is the matter, I'll admit Miss Hanratty and run a few tests—"

"I don't want to stay in a hospital," she protested.

"We're not talking about a prolonged stay—just until later tonight. The tests are quick and painless, I assure you."

"Well, in that case . . ." Jackie said. "So long as I'll be out in a few hours."

Glancing at his watch, Heisler maintained it wouldn't be later than ten or eleven o'clock at night.

"I'll come and pick you up then," Kris said, rising from her chair.

Jackie gave her a sidelong glance, a very abstracted expression on her face. "Sure, I'll wait for you," she said.

Ninn watched all this with a growing sense of satisfaction. It was as if fate were collaborating with him, a phenomenon that occurred so rarely that it was a signal event of the first order. Having pursued Jacqueline all over town, he'd been rewarded by having her brought directly to him. And now he had not only the opportunity to punish her for her defiance but also the prospect of putting Heisler to a small but intriguing test of his own devising. He'd long been interested in seeing how well Heisler would perform when forced to make an impossible choice. He would finally find out.

32

ATTACHED TO THE LABORATORY FACILITIES of the Melkis Pavilion was a four-bed research unit where individuals undergoing observation or participating in tests were put up overnight. Unlike the hospital, this facility maintained no admitting records.

Jacqueline Hanratty was the only occupant of the research unit that afternoon. Heisler had personally escorted her to her bed. He'd given her a green hospital gown to wear, and watched while she'd taken a Valium, telling her that it was important she be relaxed. He appeared uneasy, but maintained a strained smile the whole time he was with her. "There's nothing you need to worry about," he repeated enough times that she felt certain there must be a great deal to worry about.

She'd taken Valium before, but it had never had quite this effect on her. It didn't put her to sleep, but it succeeded in making her more tired than she could ever remember being. It felt as if she were tortuously making her way underwater, struggling to get to a place where she could breathe freely again.

How many minutes or hours passed until Heisler

reappeared, she had no way of telling. Time was an abstraction, and in the absence of windows and a watch, there was no way it could be otherwise.

He was pushing a stretcher when he entered the research unit. She wondered at this even in her groggy state. Wouldn't this be done by an orderly?

The smile was gone from his face now. He acted as though she were no longer conscious.

He extended his arms, and taking hold of her by the waist, attempted to lift her from her bed to the stretcher. She didn't resist him, but she had no energy to help him. She realized, in fact, that she had little control over her body at all.

Obviously he wasn't accustomed to doing this sort of thing; his grip was unsteady. She slipped. She didn't fall, though; he was quick enough to stop that from happening, but the gown came undone, revealing considerably more of her body to his view.

She was used to men staring at her, but not like this, not when she was deprived of any power over the situation. For a moment he seemed aroused; his hand was poised, ready to cup the breast that had fallen out of the garment. But then he reconsidered and simply drew the gown up so that it covered her.

His second attempt to get her onto the stretcher went more smoothly.

She asked him where he was taking her, but either her words were inaudible to him or else he refused to acknowledge them.

He wheeled her down a corridor that turned once before culminating in a door with a sign reading "Pathology Lab."

Inside there was a room smelling faintly of antiseptic, with an examining table and a trough at its base. Cabinets, their shelves full of specimen bottles, lined the wall at the opposite end of the room.

He managed to transfer her from the stretcher to the table without incident. He then proceeded to hook up an IV line. The substance he introduced into the IV was milky white in color; there was no way she could know that it was morphine, but the impact of it made itself felt quickly enough.

She was just about to go under when a second man entered the lab. As debilitated as she was, she had no difficulty in recognizing him.

She struggled to hold on to consciousness, as though knowing what was happening to her would in any way alter her fate. But she could not do it. Not that consciousness faded completely, but what remained of it wasn't of any use to her.

Heisler regarded Ninn, waiting for him to initiate the procedure.

Ninn was preparing a solution to inject her with. Heisler demanded to know what it was.

"Pancuronium bromide."

"Curare?"

"I need to have her muscles paralyzed. I don't want her squirming while I do this."

"But, my God, man, that's inhuman. You mean to say that you intend to cut out her liver while she's still alive?"

Ninn appeared rather surprised by the question. "Have you suddenly become squeamish? Yes, that's precisely what I mean to do."

"I can't allow that."

"Well, then, you kill her. It's the same to me. It's not so hard, Leo," Ninn added. "You ought to know what it's like. You've been killing people all along—but always from a distance. It's time you dirtied your hands a bit."

Heisler remained silent.

"You have a choice," Ninn went on. "You could use air or potassium chloride."

"No."

"No? All right, then. I'll go ahead."

But as he was about to direct the needle containing the curare into her vein, Heisler stopped him. "Why don't you use the potassium chloride yourself?"

"I don't choose to." Recognizing that this was not likely to satisfy Heisler, he explained, "I see no reason why I should relieve her of any excess pain. She defied me. She deserves the pain. But if that repels you, you are free to use it. I don't mind. That way I can observe your pain instead.''

Heisler didn't answer.

Once the curare had entered her bloodstream, Ninn didn't wait until she became fully paralyzed, but straight-away made the incision.

The thin ribbon of blood welling up from the wound was enough to mobilize Heisler to action. ''Dammit, I can't let you do this.'' Brushing Ninn aside, he proceeded to introduce air into the IV line, little by little. The bubbles began to descend through the tube, one, then another, then another; nothing could have looked so innocuous. Heisler continued to increase the quantity.

At first there was no visible reaction from Jacqueline. She lay rigid, her eyes slitted but still open. It was impossi-ble to tell by looking at her whether she was at all aware of what was happening. But then, as the level of air built up to nearly one hundred cc's, she started to seize. Heisler wasn't looking at her; his eyes were concentrated on the IV line: 125 cc's.

She bucked from the table in a grotesque parody of the sexual act, saliva frothed from her mouth. At 150 cc's the seizing stopped.

Heisler turned angrily to Ninn. ''All right, now, get on with it.''

PART THREE

33

BY THE TIME Kris reached the Conrad Building at Forty-sixth and Park, lights were coming on all over the city. To the west, tatters of blue were still visible in the sky; a sliver of moon hung delicately in the darkness to the east.

The thirty-second, thirty-third, and thirty-fourth floors of the Conrad Building were newly occupied by the offices of *America Now*. Designed with every available piece of new technology, they scarcely resembled the newsrooms Kris had visited years before, with typewriters clattering away, teletype machines ringing every few minutes, and copyboys rushing through the aisles, dropping off tear sheets and picking up corrected galleys, all accompanied by a constant din of phones no one ever seemed to want to answer.

The offices of *America Now*, by contrast, were eerily hushed, often producing no sound more noticeable than the electronic hum of word processors. A national newspaper, *America Now* was actually compiled and printed in several locales around the country, with satellite hook-ups feeding the finished page proofs into printing facilities based in Louisville, Atlanta, and Los Angeles.

Headquarters for *America Now* was in Washington, D.C. The second-largest office, in New York, was responsible for covering most of the cultural, financial, and sports news in addition to news related to the New York metropolitan area.

In charge of this office was the patriarchal figure of Mackenzie Walker, whose luxuriant white mustache contrasted dramatically with the high red complexion of his face. He was a slave to fashion and took great pains to dress with elegance. He preferred to wear three-piece suits, even at the height of an August heat wave, and he carried a cane that masked a thin rapier. But as far as his actual body went, he didn't seem to care what kind of impression he made. The beneficiary of a large expense account, he ate out constantly, and to show for it he had a paunch beginning to bulge over his belt.

A veteran of the *Brooklyn Eagle,* the *World Telegram & Sun,* and the *Journal-American,* he'd grown weary of editing newspapers that folded. He would sooner reject an idea than accept it, because accepting it meant more trouble for him.

Kris seldom had to deal with Mac, as he was familiarly known. The articles she was regularly assigned were commissioned by Marcie Lewis, a woman in her late forties whose abrasive manner concealed a soft heart for her writers.

Marcie joined Kris for her meeting with Mac in expectation that she might need someone to mediate for her. Mac had a reputation for exploding suddenly in the middle of editorial conferences, and there was no telling, from one hour to the next, how he was going to respond to something.

He was sitting behind his desk, a cigarette in his mouth, his bushy white eyebrows exaggerating the look of astonishment in his eyes as he scrutinized Kris, apparently taking her measure. "Sit down, please," he said.

Marcie pulled over a chair for herself. Kris anxiously glanced toward her, not knowing who would give her the signal to begin.

"You're the gal who wants to write about this Heisler

business?'' Mac said. He fumbled among the papers on his desk until he discovered the proposal Kris had sent along to Marcie.

While Kris looked on uneasily, he reread the proposal, not a flicker of emotion showing on his face.

"Interesting," he said. But whether that meant he was interested or not, Kris couldn't say.

"You can substantiate all of this? You can prove that Heisler is conducting unauthorized experiments, these double-blinded studies?"

"I think I can. But there's more than what I wrote there—information I only just found out."

"I'm listening."

She then proceeded to tell him about Jackie and the London connection. She had a feeling she was going on for too long, but each time she looked up, Mac seemed to be absorbed in what she had to say.

"I'm not sure I understand what the connection is between these gals who keep running back and forth from London and what Heisler is up to."

"It's my contention that the couriers are transmitting the disease. I don't know exactly how they were infected, but I'm sure they're carriers. Heisler is claiming that the disease is caused by fruit."

"So what you're saying is that you have two parts to your story. The first part focuses on these unauthorized studies that are allegedly taking place in Heisler's lab. The second part relates to what you believe is the real cause of Heisler's Disease, namely these couriers. Have I got that right?"

Kris allowed that he had.

"Well, it's all a bit complicated, especially for our format. You've been working with us long enough to know that we don't like to go over fifteen hundred words or so. Our readers don't have much time and they have a damn short attention span."

"Mac, suppose she forgets about the lab and just goes for the sex link? That seems to be the crux of the story, that's what'll sell papers. Nobody gets much excited about a corrupt researcher, someone doing some obscure experiments no one authorized. But if you can prove the thing about how sex leads to death—now, that's what I call news.''

To people like Mac and Marcie, disaster could always be translated into circulation figures. Kris didn't especially like that, but she recognized the reality of it.

''Besides, Mac, you know we need to gain a foothold in the New York market. This could do it.''

Mac wasn't saying a word. He was busy chewing on his cigarette, not smoking it, maybe because he was simultaneously trying to satisfy his oral craving and cut back on tobacco. At last he said, ''It seems to me that Marcie has a point. Forget about the lab for now. Concentrate on the sex.''

Kris realized that her proposal was about to be accepted—at least in part. She hardly dared believe it.

''It also occurs to me,'' he continued, ''that you'll need to go to London, see what this courier service is about.''

Kris agreed that going to London was an excellent idea but added that she lacked the resources to do it.

''We'll foot the bill, there's no need for you to pay,'' Mac said, obviously puzzled that she would even think of having to use her own money.

Marcie, too, was excited. Having urged Kris to come and pitch her story to Mac, she had staked something of her own credibility on its value to the paper. ''Should I have a contract drawn up for her?''

Mac nodded. ''Standard rates. I'd say that we could run it in two parts, two thousand words each. Have Accounting issue Kris a check for five hundred in expense money tomorrow. And wire London and have another five hundred in contingency expenses waiting at our office there. That should be enough to cover you for half a week or so. We'll put you in touch with our man in London, Peter Morris. I'm sure he'll do what he can to help you out.''

He rose from his chair, indicating that the meeting was concluded. ''I'm taking a gamble on you, Kris, because I think you're onto a juicy story. But I warn you that we're going to have whatever you turn in gone over thoroughly by our fact-checking people. If we find more than a couple of spelling errors, we won't run it. So bear that in mind."

Kris, having just made the leap from the ghetto of the Contemporary Living page, was confident that her story would stand up under the scrutiny of the Library of Congress.

Emerging from the Conrad Building, she felt that after nearly ten years of struggle she had finally made it. Although not exactly certain what "it" was, she liked the feeling very much. She rushed home and began to call everyone she knew, beginning with Matthew.

"How long will you be gone?"

He didn't sound pleased, although he said he was happy for her.

"Less than a week. I don't know, four or five days. Depends on what I find."

"Will we see each other before you go?"

"I plan to leave Friday." That was still two days away. "Why don't I come see you tomorrow night? I'll call you and let you know exactly when I'll be there."

He agreed, but she had the impression he didn't like being slotted into her time schedule like someone she was interviewing for her story.

She next called Isaac Ninn in London, only to be informed that he was in New York and that she could try him at the Sherry Netherland.

She was surprised to find him in.

Once she told him about the assignment, he expressed delight—far more than Matthew had. "When are you leaving?"

"Friday."

"If you'd like, we could fly together. I was originally going to return on Saturday, but it really makes no difference. It would be a pleasure to have the company. Then, once you've established yourself in your hotel, I can show you a bit of London. Maybe even help you research your story."

All this sounded appealing to her.

"I'll make the arrangements and get back to you tomorrow as to when and where we'll meet."

It seemed to her that nothing could go wrong, that this was one of those days that made up for the days when catastrophe and disappointment threatened at every turn.

Feeling rich in spirit, though not necessarily in dollars, she indulged herself in a cab ride up to the Melkis Pavilion.

Even though it was half-past ten when she arrived, the night security guard at the desk in the lobby didn't question her presence. She was asked to sign in and allowed to go on her way. Maybe he was getting used to seeing her face.

The receptionist on the fourth floor must have gone home. Kris took the liberty of wandering into the lab facilities to see if she could find someone to help her.

"I'm looking for Dr. Heisler," she told the first person she saw, an intense young woman with eyeglasses on a chain around her neck.

The woman regarded her with some confusion. "I think Dr. Heisler's gone home for the night. But if you wait here, maybe I can find someone who can help you. Who should I say is looking for him?"

Several minutes passed before someone emerged to talk to her. He was a plump man with anonymous features. He introduced himself as Owen Barnes.

"I'm here to see a friend of mine, actually," Kris explained. "Her name is Jacqueline Hanratty. Dr. Heisler admitted her for tests this afternoon."

Barnes nodded absently. She suspected there would be yet another delay while he went and checked to see who this Hanratty woman was, but it seemed that he was acquainted with the case. "I'm afraid you're too late."

"Too late? What do you mean?"

"Once the tests were done, she checked herself out." He glanced at his watch. "She must've left an hour or so ago. I saw her myself. A very attractive woman."

"She was supposed to wait for me."

He shrugged. There was nothing he could do about this.

"At least she could have phoned."

She was talking more to herself than to Barnes. But then, what did she expect from someone like Jackie? She was so impulsive, it was possible she'd even forgotten that Kris was coming for her.

"I'm sorry," Barnes said. "You might try her at home."

Home? she thought. In Jacqueline Hanratty's life there was no such thing. "Tell me, do you have any idea what the test results were?"

"Yes, I do, as a matter of fact. They came back negative. Miss Hanratty is free of the disease. She's definitely not a carrier."

"Are you sure?"

"Dr. Heisler ran the tests. That's what he told me."

It was her conviction that either the tests had not been done properly or Heisler was lying. And if that were true, then it might mean that he was lying about Jackie's departure too.

She decided there was no reason to linger here any longer. Thanking Barnes, she made as quick a departure as the speed of the elevator would allow.

Barnes dismissed the encounter from his mind. The woman didn't mean anything to him. Of course, he'd never so much as laid eyes on Jacqueline, had only repeated what he'd been told to say by Heisler.

At the far end of the lab he worked in, there was a large rectangular container filled with water that was at present shot through with high-voltage electricity. Radioactivity tagged genetic material was slowly being broken down into amino acids; by tomorrow it would be ready to be exposed to photographic film for analysis by computer.

The DNA material had been given to him earlier in the evening; it was designated by code and was referred to only as human liver tissue in the accompanying data. He had been advised to take extreme precautions handling it, as it was infected with viral particles. He suspected where this liver tissue had originated, but he'd never inquire, not because he thought he wouldn't learn the truth, but rather because he thought he would.

He did Heisler's bidding and he did Ninn's, and he had Lucy. It was enough for him. There was no reason to ask questions.

34

WHEN GENERAL PARKER GREY telephoned to request a meeting with him the next afternoon, Heisler had no choice but to agree. Immediately canceling all his appointments, he went home to his duplex on Thirty-second between Park and Lex to wait for him. He preferred, as he assumed the general did, that they conduct their meeting in a spot less public than an office in the Melkis Pavilion.

Heisler hadn't heard from General Grey for six years, although he was kept informed as to his whereabouts. Grey was, more or less, retired from active service, but there was every reason to believe that he still maintained good connections with the Pentagon and intelligence circles.

Grey had been in command at Fort Detrick during the years that Heisler had been under contract to the army. Prior to that Grey had served in Korea and in the Far East during the Second World War. Later he'd undertaken a commission in Vietnam in '68; it was rumored that he'd had a role in the Phoenix Program, whose purpose was to round up and terminate suspected Vietcong sympathizers. It was natural to tie Grey into clandestine affairs, even though he might have had nothing whatsoever to do with them. He was a man who would be lost without intrigue.

Over the phone Grey pretended that his visit was entirely impromptu, a mere matter of his being in New York and wishing to pay a call on an old friend.

Heisler knew very well that Grey was frequently in and out of the city; had friendship been his motive, he surely would have come to see him earlier and not have let six years go by. And in any case, unless he'd changed drastically from the last time they'd met, Parker Grey was not a man to indulge in casual courtesy calls.

It so happened that when he arrived home at three—half an hour before Grey was due—he found Tina waiting for him. He was not expecting her until evening, but then, she was a woman whose habits were as unpredictable as they were infuriating.

"I wasn't expecting you so soon," Heisler said. "An old friend is stopping by."

"What would you like me to do?" She was not interested in who the guest might be, no doubt assuming that it was some scientist or another official from the CDC, for they were always coming around.

"Disappear. You can stay here if you'd like, but I think it would be better if you remain out of sight. I'm sure it won't take long."

She shrugged. It was all the same to her. Stretching, she got up from the couch.

A woman like Tina Hanover would never come into his life were his life not filled with money and fame and power. It was no secret; Tina had admitted as much. But Heisler was a realist. He demanded beauty and glamour in a woman, Tina Hanover was perfectly suitable for his needs; her hair was red as blood and it gave to her sculptured face a theatrical quality, impressing the observer with a sense of high spirits and reckless opportunism. Most important, in bed she gave herself over to him as though her life depended on satisfying him.

They'd been together for five months, and sooner or later the affair would end; he dreaded the recriminations and indignities that would accompany the breakup. Were it not for his terrible need of women, he thought, he would give them up entirely.

At half-past three the bell chimed. Parker Grey was precisely on time.

He wasn't in uniform, and Heisler didn't know why he'd expected that he would be, but he held himself in that stiff, immobilized manner that betrayed a long-term regimental career. In appearance he wasn't greatly altered from six years ago; his hair had grown whiter but was cut every bit as short, and the individual strands protruded like small spikes from the pinkness of his scalp; his face was deeply furrowed, dead in places with precancerous leisons, and was, like leather, stretched too tautly over his skull. Bushy eyebrows, whiter than his hair, almost joined together over the ridge of his nose, which was long and angular and gave every sign of having been badly broken at one time. He was taller than Heisler and seemed to tower over him.

They shook hands, exchanged a perfunctory greeting.

Grey scanned the foyer, took in the Pissarro in its gold-leaf frame hung over the umbrella stand, then allowed himself to be led into the study.

Over drinks, Grey said that he'd heard much of Heisler's success and wished to congratulate him. "You know, I like to think of myself as your guardian angel."

"Guardian angel?"

"While we haven't often been in contact, Leo, that doesn't mean I haven't kept track of you."

"I'm not surprised. I expect that you've done the same with all the graduating class of Fort Detrick."

"Graduating class" was just an expression of his. One didn't exactly graduate from Fort Detrick.

"It's a pity about Rollins, isn't it?"

Heisler didn't like the way he said this. "I was saddened to learn of his death. At one time we were very close."

"I remember. Although it seems to me that you always had more ambition than Rollins. There was never any question in my mind that of all those we contracted for the Dropwind project, you were the best.''

"I have always appreciated your confidence.'' All the while, Heisler was wondering when Grey would get to the point. His stomach was in knots and he registered an unpleasant fluttering in his chest. He had only the vaguest idea of what was coming, but he knew that whatever it was, he wasn't going to like it.

"What struck me as curious was why, with such an exceptional mind, you needed to resort to fraud to gain your ends.''

Heisler was about to protest, to give a great show of indignation, but as soon as his eyes met Grey's, he recognized that this would be pointless. "If you believed that to be true,'' he answered instead, "why did you continue to support me? Why remain my guardian angel?''

Grey smiled coldly. "Because you were good and because the nature of my occupation calls for fraud on a regular basis. You might say that I can identify with your vice. However. . . .''

Heisler shifted uneasily in his seat.

"It now appears that you have gone a little too far. I suppose that, having gotten away with so much in the past, you were convinced you could go right on doing it without any repercussions. I'm afraid, Leo, that this time you've overextended yourself. I might have no choice but to abdicate my role as guardian angel.''

"Do you care to elaborate?''

"I think you know exactly to what I'm referring. But to make it clear, I'll say first off that researchers down in Atlanta have discovered that Heisler's Disease is not caused by eating citrus fruit, that it is, in fact, sexually transmitted. I see by the look on your face that this does not come as a revelation to you.''

"It's not unknown for a researcher to make a mistake.''

"Whom are you talking about? The researchers in Atlanta or you?''

"Either one.''

Heisler felt now as he had in Ninn's presence. It was all he could do to maintain his grip.

"I think that in this case the burden of proof lies with you. I wouldn't be surprised if the government severs all connections with your lab, and very quickly. You've created quite an embarrassment. I hope you can see that. We know about the orange-juice-futures contracts you bought short prior to announcing that the disease was tied in with fruit. We know you made a fucking fortune once the market in those contracts went to hell."

"There's no evidence of that."

"I know that. You were cunning enough to have a third party buy those options in your behalf. I'd have expected nothing less of you. But the point is, you see, that we know."

"What do you intend to do?"

"None of this is my decision, understand. I came here as an admirer of yours, an admirer and an old friend. I didn't have to. What I believe will happen is that the funding will stop and you will be quietly dropped from the White House panel."

"I assumed that that would happen."

"Other than that, the government will do nothing."

"Nothing?"

"Let's say nothing *overt*."

"But it might act in another way?"

Grey sat back. He allowed a long minute to go by before speaking again, knowing very well that he'd put Heisler on edge. "We understand that your research has led you in some very intriguing directions."

"My research? On alcohol-related liver disease?"

"Yes, exactly. There might be some very substantial interest on our part in the results of this research."

Right then Heisler knew that Grey was onto what he was doing, that he'd somehow gotten wind of where the virus was originating. Heisler also had a sense of what he was being asked to do in this very circuitous fashion. "I'm sure something can be worked out," he said.

"If you are willing to help us, supply us not only with the relevant documentation but also with the substance in question, then I'd expect we could arrive at an arrangement pleasing to all parties.''

"I can assure you of my cooperation right now.''

"That's very good to hear. Naturally, we are constrained in some ways. It's possible that Westside Medical Center might decide to initiate an in-house inquiry of its own. But I wouldn't let that worry you. What I'd suggest is that you announce your retirement and leave New York. We have someplace in mind where you could enjoy your retirement and at the same time continue your research undisturbed.''

Heisler realized that even if in time he should learn how to cure the disease that Helen had created, he would never be recognized for it. He would be denied public honor. But perhaps he could come to enjoy anonymity after so many years in the spotlight; it could be that a life in the shadows, such as Isaac Ninn had, was his true destiny.

His message delivered, Parker Grey rose from his chair, his drink still unfinished.

"Tell me, when do you suppose the CDC will release its findings?'' Heisler asked.

"In the next few days, I imagine.''

"That's not much advance warning.''

"Ah, but, Leo, how much advance warning did you give your victims?''

‖‖ **35**

IT WASN'T IMPOSSIBLE that she was dead. Certainly some important part of her had died in the snows of Illinois. If she hadn't thrown up she would be six feet under. Yet her body had, by expelling the toxins, insisted that she live. She took it as a sign that God intended her to go on.

When she lay caught between dying and living, in a limbo state that was neither pain nor revelation, that contained the presence of neither man nor angel, it seemed to her that she could perceive, as if in the distance, a light. The light was not like any light she'd ever seen before; it was luminously blue, bluer than blue, and it beckoned her to come forward. The light somehow wanted her.

Thrown violently back into a life and a consciousness she thought she'd forever put past her, she vowed that of the old Helen Voyles there would be nothing left.

And that was why she'd abandoned her job and her apartment, everything she owned, keeping only the money she'd saved up, because money was anonymous, untainted by identity, hers or anyone else's, and because she needed money if she were to accomplish the purpose that now fell to her.

She hadn't known that she had it in her, to come and go in the shadows, to live like an outlaw, a pariah. She'd once read in a book by an Indian religious leader that it was possible to make oneself invisible, even in a room among friends.

After leaving Illinois, she had in fact gotten the knack of becoming invisible, enjoying a freedom she never thought possible. And she did not believe that it was just the disguises she fashioned for herself. Because people considered her dead, they were not looking for her, not suspecting she would be there. And in a way, they were right: she was dead. It didn't matter what she'd do henceforth.

There was nothing she would face that held more fateful consquences than what she'd already done on the day she'd first infected herself.

It was such a little thing, an incident so trivial that it became clear to her only in San Francisco what had happened.

She decided that she must have cut herself and that somehow, while she was preparing a solution of the virus for testing in the secret double-blinded study, it had infiltrated her bloodstream. She could think of no other explanation.

But by then two men in San Francisco were dead and one was dying.

Previously she and Heisler had deduced that the four men who'd died in the double-blinded study had succumbed to the drug they were experimenting with. It was only later that they understood that the genetic material that composed the drug contained a new virus, hitherto unknown in world history.

What neither of them had suspected was that it could be transmitted indirectly, too—by women. Moreover, only one exposure to the virus was necessary to remain contagious. This was something that even Heisler hadn't realized.

For all the pleasure sex had given Helen, it had caused her infinitely more pain. She stood ready to sacrifice everything for a lover, and she had, but in the end, he always left her. It seemed to her that she must trigger something off in men; it was as if she held the key to a mechanism which, once activated, would inject them full of hatred and scorn for her—or worse, with utter indifference.

She hated. Until the night she had attempted suicide, she never realized how passionately, how deeply and irrevocably she could hate.

She had a mission now. It was to kill, to use her body as she'd always used it, but now her body had become a weapon immeasurably more lethal than it had been before.

As Helen Voyles or as a woman with a past she simply invented on the spot, she returned to her ex-lovers, running them down one by one, wherever they lived in the country—no matter that they'd aged, married, turned into fat, complacent husbands and fathers. To a man, like Roger Moss, who recognized her, she said that she'd been thinking of him during all the years that had ensued since she'd left Minneapolis and was anxious to renew their friendship. To those like Peter Sawyer who failed to recognize her, she assumed the role of a woman traveling on a business trip who was simply looking for company for the night.

It was surprising how eager men were to believe the flattery she lavished on them, how willing they were to discard their scruples and rent a motel room with her.

With the same diligence and attention to detail that she'd exhibited while working for Heisler, she pursued these men, never allowing herself a day off to rest. She had the feeling of time closing in on her; if she didn't use every minute, she would never have this chance again.

But now, back in New York, she'd had to change her tactics. It was no longer enough to practice the same simple deceptions she'd employed elsewhere.

She could no longer depend on the virus contained in her body to do her work for her. Heisler and Ninn were aware of the danger she posed to them, and it was possible that Barrett did as well. If she meant to kill them, then she would have to use other methods.

Her first victim was to be Leo Heisler. Ironically he was the only man who'd never slept with her, never shown any interest in sleeping with her. He wasn't averse to women;

that wasn't it. He just didn't want her. At least not her body.

But he seemed to want everything else from her. He pillaged her mind, he manipulated her emotions, he stole her work, and then he wouldn't let her go.

And she suspected now that he had long understood his power over her. He, more than the others, discerned that she could, by the act of sex, empty herself of any fantasies she might have been cultivating about a man. Sex was her way of obliterating the possibility of love. Only a very few men could break through and overcome the obstacle course she'd set for them.

But Heisler wouldn't even try; he used the sexual power he had by not using it. She longed for the day when he would fuck her and thereby give her her freedom. But of course, he never did.

But if she had little difficulty in locating him, she soon understood that she would have to forgo killing him. He was never alone. That came as no surprise to her, for he was a man who was terrified of solitude, needing always to be surrounded by people, especially those he could rely upon to shore up his confidence.

From her observation she saw that in addition to his customary retinue, he was also being watched by men who had the air of security agents. They were never very conspicuous, but she noticed them all the same; they were uniformly tall, impassive men, invariably in ties and jackets. Bulges in their jackets warned of the guns they were carrying. From time to time, whenever Heisler had to leave the fortress of the Melkis Pavilion or his home in Murray Hill, they would appear with two-way radios to monitor his progress.

It was even possible that they were agents working for the federal government. Whoever they were, there was no chance that she could somehow slip through them, to get to him.

Nonetheless, she was convinced that one day she'd succeed in destroying him. She regretted only that she could not make the destruction as drawn out a process as he had with her.

Yet she was not to be denied satisfaction. Though she might have to postpone the destruction of Leo Heisler, she still had the opportunity to achieve the destruction of his work.

In the six years that she'd worked in the Melkis Pavilion, Helen had come to know every inch of it; utilitarian as it was, its architects had built into it enough passageways, storerooms, and rooms within rooms to recall the layout of an English castle.

Having no intention of proceeding through the lobby, where one of the security agents, perhaps with a more discerning eye than some of her past lovers, might recognize her, she opted for a freight elevator. She reached it through a subterranean corridor, a part of the bewildering network of such corridors that extended beneath the Westside complex.

The freight elevator took her directly to the fifth floor. It was the middle of the evening, so there were not a large number of people about, and her passage went unnoticed.

Having already ascertained that Heisler was at home, she knew there would be no one in his office. That it was locked was of no concern for her; she'd made a copy of all of his keys. Her only problem was evading the security guards who monitored the control console directly opposite the office.

But this problem was hardly an insurmountable one; all she had to do was wait until one strode off to the men's room. The other, his attention riveted on the lights and switches in front of him, failed to notice her by the door of Heisler's office.

She quickly inserted the key, turned it to the left, and was in.

Owen Barnes had spent a good part of the last hour searching through the containment area for the virus coded VDV 21. Like all other viruses, it was stored in a container of liquid nitrogen, weighing close to fifteen pounds, and kept in a separate room to which only a very few researchers had access. Barnes had had a hell of a time finding someone who would help him get in—no questions asked.

It had never occurred to him that he would one day play the part of spy and unfaithful husband, that he would end up living out the movie version of his life instead of the real thing. Surely he would never have done either were it not for Isaac Ninn. Isaac Ninn was one of those people who step out of the blue, appearing unbidden and unannounced, to inform you that they intend to turn your life upside down.

Ninn had sent Lucy on ahead of him, his seductive emissary. Then he waited half a month before he appeared himself, by which time he knew he had Barnes addicted. He offered Barnes freedom from the drabness of his life and enslavement simultaneously.

And now Barnes was looking for a secret virus to please Isaac so that he could keep Lucy. He felt like a hero in an ancient Greek myth, but the problem was that this myth wasn't turning out right at all. For no matter how assiduously he looked, how scrupulously he examined the coded containers of liquid nitrogen, he could not find any marked VDV 21. It simply was not there.

When she'd last been in the Melkis Pavilion, Helen had had neither time nor opportunity to remove all the files pertaining to the double-blinded study she and Heisler had conducted on alcohol-related liver disease. Although she'd removed much of her material, in her haste she'd been unable to get at it all. There were still a great many relevant documents she needed if she were to make the record complete.

In some ways, Helen thought, Heisler was too much like the Nazi leaders who carefully recorded every war crime they committed, not necessarily because they believed they were right and that history would vindicate their actions, but rather because they were compulsive chroniclers; they couldn't stand the idea that events, however heinous, however barbaric and self-incriminating, might take place without their being duly noted.

Similarly Heisler had left behind him, in files and on microfiche in Fort Detrick, at the Sandburn Institute in Boston, and here at Westside, a trail of evidence that could one day, if it were all gathered together by someone who knew what he was doing, be more than sufficient to convict him in any court of law.

Helen had in six years discovered where Heisler maintained his confidential records, in particular all the records about the double-blinded study, records which she had borrowed frequently, given her involvement in the project. It was possible that, once she'd left, Heisler would have transferred the records to another location or else had the lock on the file cabinet changed. If that were the case, then there'd be nothing she could do.

But she found the records in the same place, although now there were many more than previously. Making certain that she had them all, she lifted them out of the drawer and placed them in a plastic bag.

Quickly drawing open the door, she peered out. To her surprise, there was no one manning the control desk; both security guards had apparently abandoned their post.

An idea occurred to her. It was such a wild and fantastic idea that she felt she had no choice but to act on it at once.

Shutting the door behind her, she walked straight into the control room, sat down at the panel, and began, one by one, to flick all the switches in front of her. Amber bulbs flashed to red, green bulbs flashed to red. In moments every single one of the bulbs was red. The sight was so dazzling that she failed to note that the lights above her had dimmed and gone out, as did the lights in the corridor adjoining the control room. She heard someone crying out; seconds later, alarms from every quarter began to shriek, setting off a tremendous din.

The security guards could be expected back momentarily. She would have to be gone soon if she wasn't to be caught. From the keys she'd duplicated from Heisler's set she selected one marked with a strip of red tape.

Sliding it into a slot below the words "Emergency Operations," she gave it a turn once to the right, once to the left, then depressed the three toggle switches beneath it.

That, she thought with satisfaction, should do it.

Hearing footsteps, she assumed that the guards must be on their way back. She moved so quickly to leave that she overturned the chair, but no matter, she succeeded in evading them in any case, taking advantage of the chaos and the darkness into which she'd plunged five floors of the Melkis Pavilion.

Just as she reached the fire exit, she heard a scream so terrifying that it froze her in place for several seconds; it was a scream that seemed to go on and on.

Gordon Levi, who'd been working at the Melkis Pavilion since its opening day, was the first guard to hear it. He wheeled about and shone his flashlight in the direction of the containment area. In the window of the computer-activated door he perceived the face of a man. At first he couldn't understand what the hell had happened.

"Dick!" he called to his partner. "Come over here!"

Dick Halloran, a former Pinkerton, suffered from a bum leg and couldn't run half as fast as Levi wanted him to.

When Halloran reached the door, Levi was already staring in at Owen Barnes. His eyes were bulging, his jaw had gone slack, the blood had drained from his face. He was evidently struggling to open the door, but somehow he couldn't work the lock.

"What's wrong with him?" Halloran asked, at the same time thrusting his computer card into the slot.

Nothing happened. The elimination of power had shut down the computer.

Barnes lurched up against the square pane of glass and then disappeared altogether.

Neither of the guards could figure out what was the matter. They heard his fingernails scratching the other side of the door in a desperate effort to communicate his distress.

Levi fumbled with his keys. There was a way of opening the door manually if the electricity failed, but it required the use of a special override system.

Between the two men they managed to get the door open. As soon as they did, they were immediately sent reeling by the acrid stench of formaldehyde.

In an instant both knew what had happened. Sputtering and choking, they seized Barnes by the arms and dragged him into the corridor. Halloran used his body to slam the door shut again.

It was all they could do to get Barnes into the stairwell beyond the fire door, where they could breathe freely again.

Levi, as soon as he got his own breath back, knelt down by Barnes to give him artificial respiration.

Halloran felt for his pulse. There was none. Levi labored hard, but he couldn't revive Barnes. He lay still, his eyes fixed in an incredulous stare that he would have taken with him to the grave if Halloran hadn't shut them. "He's seen plenty tonight, the poor bastard."

"Wonder what he was doing in there?" Levi remarked. "Hope it was worth it, whatever it was."

36

WHEN THE PHONE RANG, Kris was certain it had to be Matthew, but it wasn't, it was Mac Walker.

She was so astounded to hear his voice that she could only stammer out a greeting. Her first thought was that he'd decided to kill the story and apologize for having to disappoint her.

But that wasn't it at all.

"I just heard from one of our reporters that something happened up at the Melkis Pavilion about twenty minutes ago."

"What was it?"

"Looks like a massive power outage, but no one's sure what caused it. It's just the pavilion. The rest of Westside's unaffected. I thought you might want to go up and see what it's about, considering your interest in the subject."

"I'll start up there right now. Thanks for letting me know."

She threw on her coat and rushed out of the apartment, too much in a hurry to bother turning on her answering machine.

It wasn't more than a twenty-minute cab ride uptown,

but to Kris it might have been hours. She was afraid that by the time she got there, there would be no story left for her to cover.

A score of flashing red lights in front of the Melkis Pavilion, signaling the presence of patrol cars, ambulances, and fire-department vehicles, told her at once that the excitement wasn't over yet.

A crowd of onlookers and reporters stood with their eyes fixed on the darkened building, impatiently waiting for something—anything—to happen. Garbled voices from squad-car radios mingled with those of the people milling behind a police barricade.

No one Kris spoke to seemed to know exactly what had happened.

"Power shutdown" was about the only thing that everyone could agree on.

"I heard it was sabotage," commented one. "With all the publicity about this place, it's no wonder that you'd get some weirdo doing a thing like that."

"There was a fire, that's what caused it," another offered.

"Five or six people killed in it, too, is what they tell me," a third one put in.

But there had been no fire and there was no evidence that up to half a dozen people had been killed, either. Most of the lab's employees were visible on the other side of the barrier; having evacuated the building immediately after the power had gone off, they'd left their coats behind and were now stamping their feet and hugging themselves in an effort to keep warm.

Kris walked up to a police officer, hoping to hear the details.

"No one knows exactly. We've got men in there now looking to see if someone might have sabotaged the power source."

"Is there a chance this person might have escaped?"

"There's a damn good chance, lady, but we're looking anyway."

At that moment a black limousine pulled up and Leo

Heisler emerged. As soon as Heisler made his appearance, he was surrounded by eager reporters thrusting microphones up to his lips. For a moment he looked as if he might speak; but then all he said was, "No comment, I have no comment," and with the police pressing the way ahead for him, he proceeded into the pavilion.

Not many minutes later, paramedics and a pair of ambulance attendants came out of the building wheeling a stretcher with a man on it.

Kris was close enough to catch a glimpse of him. The face was still not covered. She recognized the man as the person she'd spoken to last night. How he'd died, she couldn't tell, but there was no question that his end had been an anguished one.

Little by little now the power was being restored to the building; lights came on first in the lobby and then began to appear in the windows of the second and third floors.

It seemed that there had been only one fatality, but that was enough to elevate the story to the front page of the three dailies.

"Kris!"

She looked about and spotted Isaac making his way toward her.

"What a nice surprise," he said. "I certainly didn't expect to see you here."

She told him why she had come, then asked him if he knew what had happened.

"Actually, I'm afraid not. I just got here. All I know is what I heard over the radio. It seems that it was a matter of sabotage, or at least that's what the police are saying."

"Do they have any idea who did it?"

"If they do, they're not making it public." Glancing up at the building, he said, "I was going to do some paperwork tonight, but it doesn't look like the appropriate time for it. Have you eaten?"

"I had some yogurt around noontime. I'm fairly hungry."

"I could do with a little something myself. There's a cozy place I know not far from here where the food is acceptable."

The restaurant he had in mind was located in the Nineties, off Amsterdam; it was small and dark and cavernous. In one corner a jazz quartet was playing an up-tempo version of "Smoke Gets in Your Eyes," while pretty, faintly anoerexic waitresses circulated among the tables.

Kris excused herself to call Matthew and let him know which bus she'd be taking. "I've just got a little more to do in the city," she said, without, however, mentioning what it was.

"Where are you? I can hear music."

"I'm using a phone in a bar not far from the Melkis Pavilion. Did you hear what happened there tonight?"

"I heard on the radio. A couple of people were killed, I hear."

"Just one."

"We'll talk about it when you get here. I'll be waiting for you at the bus station."

Returning to the table, she told Isaac that she wouldn't be able to stay long. "Anyway, we'll be seeing each other for the next few days," she reminded him.

He nodded, but it seemed that his attention was elsewhere.

She drew it back by lightly touching his hand, saying, "Isaac, I just want to get something clear between us—before London."

He gave her a disquieting look, then allowed his features to relax. "What is it?"

"I know there's an attraction between us, but I'd prefer we remain friends. I wanted you to know that so you wouldn't get the wrong impression. One thing I don't want to do is mislead or hurt you."

"I understand," he replied.

But she wondered. He was probably a man accustomed to getting the women he wanted, and she sensed that he might turn cold to any who rebuffed him. Since he was her principal source of information, she didn't want that to happen.

After a long silence he said, "I assume then that you're getting along with your friend Matthew."

"Well, yes and no. I'm not exactly sure what'll happen between us."

"I'm confident you'll work things out between you." He smiled. "And there's no reason to worry about our friendship. I should think we'll have a splendid time in London." As strained as he sounded, Kris was still gratified to hear him say this. She only hoped he meant it.

"I'm sure you know a London that most tourists rarely have a chance to see."

"I know a London that most Londoners don't ever get to see."

Excusing himself, Ninn walked to the rear of the restaurant, passing by the jazz quartet just as they were reaching the last few bars of Billy Strayhorn's "Lush Life," and entered the men's room.

Locking the door behind him, he proceeded to remove a vial from inside his jacket pocket, and from it selected one capsule. With a razor blade he sliced it in half, and using tap water so that the granules would better adhere, he contaminated the razor edge.

At last his decision to test Kris's blood was paying off. Since she possessed the T-protein, he was assured that she would become a carrier.

He realized that he was doing this out of jealousy. While Barrett had once loomed as a threat to the project, he'd so far done nothing to disturb its successful operation. Nonetheless, Ninn did not like to lose a woman unless it was his choice. Besides, he reasoned, to defeat one's rival in love was a tradition that extended far back in history. The only difference was that this time he was using the object of that rivalry to achieve victory. A Pyrrhic victory, of course—since he would be denied the object too unless he felt suicidal—but a victory nonetheless.

In any case, he had the feeling that Kris might not like him at all. She was more clever than she let on, and certainly she was determined to obtain her story. Just as he was leading her on, drawing her in, how could he be sure she wasn't doing the same to him? The more he considered this possibility, the more impassioned he became in his anger. Even the death of Owen Barnes hadn't made him this enraged. By the time he emerged from the men's room, he realized that he truly loathed her.

"I'm sorry, Isaac," she said, "but I really have to get going."

She was reaching in her wallet to get out some cash to pay.

"I insist." He declined the money she offered him. Then he told her that he wouldn't hear of her taking a cab to Port Authority, where she was to catch her bus. "It's no problem for me to let you off there. I'm headed in that direction anyway."

"But you haven't finished your dinner."

"I'm suddenly not very hungry," he said.

When he stopped in front of the terminal entrance on Eighth Avenue, he leaned across the front seat to give her a kiss that was perhaps more lingering than she'd been expecting from someone who has just agreed that they would be no more than friends.

With her eyes locked to his own, he allowed his left arm to drop, a gesture that she failed to notice. Then he quickly drew the razor blade across no more than half an inch of flesh below her knee. The pressure he applied was just sufficient for it to penetrate her nylons and break the skin.

She felt practically nothing, he could tell by looking at her. The kiss had her too much distracted and the pain was negligible, the pain that a pinprick might produce.

For a second she winced, retracting her right leg. But that was her only reaction.

"We'll see each other tomorrow, then, at the airport?"

"Absolutely. Thank you for dinner, Isaac."

"My pleasure."

Then she was out of the car and running toward the door, anxious not to be late.

Ninn glanced down at the blade he held in his gloved hand. He noted with satisfaction that there was a slender ribbon of blood along the edge. She won't notice it until later, he thought, and by then it shouldn't make any difference. He sincerely hoped she and Barrett would enjoy their lovemaking tonight; he hoped it would meet their every expectation. Ninn could think of neither a more pleasurable way to be killed nor a more pleasurable way of killing someone—more pleasurable still because neither the murderess nor her victim had any idea of the roles they were playing together.

37

BARRETT KNEW she was out there somewhere. He'd given the super and the three doormen who worked in his building each ten dollars, asking them to let him know should anyone, man or woman, come inquiring about him. He also asked that they occasionally check to see whether his apartment was secure when he was at work.

Only one of the doormen had registered any surprise when he made his requests; the others acted as if they were long accustomed to dealing with problems of this kind.

But taking such precautions was hardly enough to reassure him, particularly since he wasn't worried just about himself, but about Kris as well.

Each time he heard the phone ring, he was certain it would be Helen on the other end. Each time he took a step out on the street, he felt that she was tracking him. Even if he got home before the light had gone from the sky, he'd draw the curtains, though he didn't realistically believe that she was peering in through his window with a telescope from across the Hudson River.

It was not only deeply disturbing, living like this, it was

also infuriating. For so long as he didn't know when she would next strike, or in what manner, he could do nothing. She seemed to hold all the cards.

Half the time he was agitated, half the time depressed.

Tonight he didn't know in which state he was; it might be a combination of both.

On the one hand, he was heartened by the prospect of seeing Kris, although he had no idea how, at half-past eleven at night, with both of them exhausted, they would be able to resolve their differences.

On the other hand, he was apprehensive that by coming to see him, she was putting both their lives in peril. If Helen wasn't following him, maybe she was following Kris. He thought constantly of notifying the police, but his was not the sort of case that would warrant a round-the-clock surveillance. Besides, he didn't see what he could possibly tell them that would make it sound like he faced a real threat.

Lacking the patience to wait for Kris's phone call, he left his apartment and drove to the bus station. With only the last bus from New York scheduled, the station, never a bustling terminal even in the middle of the day, was practically deserted.

As he waited, he was constantly assailed by new doubts. He was torn between telling Kris about Helen and saying nothing. By the time she arrived, he'd decided that he was better off keeping quiet. Since she'd be out of town, there were no immediate grounds for concern, and in spite of his apprehension over her leaving for London, he couldn't discount the possibility that she'd actually be safer there.

And maybe when she did return Helen would no longer present any danger to either of them.

Kris was in a voluble mood when she arrived, excited about her impending trip.

She was interested in his summary of Helen's thesis, particularly Appendix 1, but he could tell that she was becoming impatient with the details.

She was looking for a smoking gun, and somehow the

T-protein didn't seem to be it. Its connection to Heisler's Disease was too remote.

All the way back to his apartment she talked about how she would go about finding the Inverness Courier Service and determining whether it was used as a base for spreading the disease.

Barrett had the feeling she was getting way out on a limb, but he was content just to listen. What did disturb him was her repeated mention of Isaac Ninn in connection with her story. It provoked him enough to break his silence. "Just how close are you to this man, Kris?"

She shot him a look that contained a certain measure of amusement. "You're not jealous, are you?"

"Of course not."

She wasn't convinced. "I told him tonight that we could only be friends, so you shouldn't worry."

He wasn't reassured. And who was she to tell him when to worry and when not to, anywhow?

As soon as Helen saw Barrett leave his building, she stepped up to the lobby entrance.

The doorman was slender and in his fifties and his face held an expression of permanent unhappiness that might have come from too many Christmases of dismal tips.

"May I help you?"

She offered him a warm smile. There was nothing in her manner to indicate that she'd been responsible this evening for the death of a researcher and the partial ruin of a laboratory facility across the river. On the contrary, she gave every appearance of being a successful career woman a little late coming home from work.

Still, the doorman did not recognize her and was not about to let her in without learning whom she planned to visit.

"I'm here to see Dr. Barrett in 7K."

She noticed something change in his face. His eyes had narrowed and he was subjecting her to a more scrupulous appraisal. She guessed at once that Matthew had warned him to be on the lookout for a strange woman.

"I don't think that he's in."

"I'd like to surprise him. If you could just let me into his apartment?"

"You'll have to wait outside. I'm sorry, but you can't wait in here."

"I see." She still hadn't moved. "If you could do me a favor, I might be able to do you one."

He shook his head, but that didn't necessarily mean he wasn't interested. "I could lose my job," he said.

"Look, I'm not going to take anything."

"I'm sorry, miss. I'm going to have to ask you to leave."

In spite of her calm facade, she was desperate. Sleep was impossible for her; she kept having to do things. She had to do this. And now.

She remained where she was. He would have to throw her out physically, but he'd made no move to do so.

When he raised his eyes, he seemed surprised to find her still there. "What sort of favor?" he asked. He couldn't let it pass.

"Almost anything you want."

"Anything?"

"That's right. And all you have to do is just let me into his place so I can surprise him. Do I look like I'm going to do any harm?"

He regarded her for a moment. "No, no, you don't."

"If he asks, say you never laid eyes on me. How will he prove otherwise?"

He seemed to perceive the logic in this. "I have a little office in back," he said. "There's a cot that sometimes I use during my breaks."

"I'm sure it'll do just fine. You're sure the tenants won't be surprised to come in and not find you here?"

"It happens now and then. We're here as kind of like insurance."

She didn't know that when Matthew returned he would be with anyone. As soon as she heard a woman laughing, she realized it was Kris. That changed everything.

Leaving the closet door only slightly ajar, she waited, standing very still. A moment before, she'd planned to knife him as soon as he fell asleep. She had no wish to confront him, to accuse him of anything, only to kill him and be done with it.

Now she wasn't certain. She needed Kris alive. Kris would have to tell her story to the world.

In the meantime, she watched.

They were still laughing. She envied them their laughter. She couldn't quite make them out; she could see their shadows, catch a glimpse of someone's arm or leg, but as they were in the adjoining room, it was difficult to get them in view.

"Can I get you anything to drink?" she heard Matthew say.

"Not now. Why don't you come over here, Matthew? You're too far away."

There was a long silence; Helen imagined them exchanging a kiss; she imagined a great many things. She scarcely dared breathe, and when she did, her breathing was shallow.

He was now leading her into the bedroom, his hand gripping hers. She'd tossed off her shoes, her skirt was all rumpled, her blouse half-unbuttoned.

Helen watched them helplessly, without wanting to. It was all she could do not to scream.

Matthew switched off the light overhead, but it wasn't so dark that she couldn't see them perfectly well.

He was saying nothing, but his hands were busy undoing the last few buttons on her blouse. Kris had her back to the door, so Helen couldn't see what her face was like, but she could picture it. Kris's head lolled back; Matthew was kissing her on the neck and on the ear, and she gasped and clutched him more fervently.

The blouse fell at her feet. Helen could feel their embrace, and for an instant she had the urge to expose herself and join them. The heat rose in her, her legs shifted, and instinctively she closed her eyes.

When she opened them again, Kris was wearing only her panty hose.

Their posture suggested that at any moment they would fall onto the bed, but instead Kris detached herself from him long enough to get onto the bed on her own accord.

Discarding his clothes as quickly as he could get them off, Matthew joined her on the bed. Kris's legs shot up into the air, then scissored his.

Matthew cupped one breast and lavished all of his attention on it, eliciting from her such sounds of pleasure that tears sprang to Helen's eyes. She remembered how Matthew had been with her, but all that memory did was to sharpen the pain. It was all the worse because of Kris. Another woman, a stranger, she could have accepted. But Kris? Helen considered her a friend, she'd placed her trust in her, and now Kris was betraying her.

But at the same time, in another part of her mind, she recognized how foolish she was. How could Kris betray her? She, Helen, was supposedly dead, buried in the past, decomposing at the bottom of Lake Michigan. The only thing left of her was her landscape in oils that hung in the next room.

Helen looked down at the knife she gripped in her hands. There was so much sweat collected about the handle that she thought it would soon slip from her grasp and alert them to her presence. She knew she would have to act quickly, before she lost her nerve altogether. She only wished she knew what it was she should do.

At first Barrett was aware of only the warmth. Their bodies weren't touching, but the connection was there, energy flowing between them even while they slept. Her face was turned away from him, her hair was all he could see, the dark tangle and luster of it. With the blanket drawn partway down, he had a generous view of her back, from the graceful arc of her shoulder to the hollow at her waist. Her breathing was quiet, scarcely audible.

He didn't immediately go back to sleep, but rather allowed his mind to dip beneath the surface of his consciousness, where dreams were indistinguishable from reality.

Sometime later, he was drawn back to consciousness. His eyes half-opened. He saw, or thought he saw, a figure standing poised at the end of the bed. He blinked, strained in the dimness to see. A woman's face gradually came into focus, taut, ashen, contorted with rage.

Helen.

But he couldn't quite absorb what his vision had just disclosed to him. It was as if he were still in a dream, and in the dream Helen held a knife with both hands, ready to drive it into his body.

This must be a dream, he thought, and all I have to do is open my eyes and she'll be gone. But he'd gotten it wrong. All he had to do was *shut* his eyes—and she was gone.

It was only several minutes after the alarm rang that Barrett recalled what he had seen the previous night. It was another instance of his paranoia taking hold of him and causing hallucinatory visions that had no basis in reality. He noticed no evidence that Helen had ever been in his apartment, no sign of a forced entry.

I must be badly in need of a rest, he concluded. He said nothing about the dream, if dream it was, to Kris. He didn't wish to dispel her impression of him as a stable, rational human being, the port you could always head toward in the event of a storm.

In any case, she was as much in a rush as he was to get dressed. At one point he noticed her inspecting her leg. "What's wrong?"

"It looks like I cut myself."

He saw that it was a small cut just below the knee, slightly matted with dried blood. "It seems to be pretty superficial," he said.

"Is that your official diagnosis?" She laughed and then got on with the business of dressing. "I must've bumped into something," she said. "I'm always doing things like that."

Just then her eyes were drawn to something metallic that

had caught the sun. She leaned down and found a sharp knife. "Did you drop this, Matthew?"

He looked, then went suddenly pale. So it hadn't been a dream, he thought. The knife was real.

38

Barrett wouldn't hear of Kris taking the bus out to Kennedy, despite her objections. He told her that he wanted to see her off and insisted on picking her up Friday evening. Even when she relented, he suspected that there had been more to her objections than what she'd told him.

But at least, he thought, they were getting along much better than in the past. He believed her now when she told him that Isaac Ninn was only a source of information for her, and nothing more.

Still, he couldn't help warning her that from what she'd told him, Ninn didn't sound like someone who could be trusted.

That was when she nearly blew up. "Let me be the judge of the character of the people I know, okay?"

He backed off immediately.

They might have established peace with each other, but they still had the capacity to get on each other's nerves. If they hadn't been lovers, they would surely not be friends. They would probably, he imagined, still get on each other's nerves if they ended up spending their dotage together.

The more he considered that possibility, the more he concluded that he wouldn't mind doing just that.

But how she felt about him was a mystery. One night together every couple of weeks, when she could take time out from her story, wasn't going to tell him. Nor was he willing to simply let things work themselves out. Although he wasn't ready to present her with ultimatums, he wasn't about to give her all the time in the world to make up her mind, either. Presented with all the time in the world, he knew, she'd take it.

Toward the end of the afternoon, just as he was getting ready to leave his office, he realized that he had a sore throat. At first he thought it was just the dryness that signals an immense thirst, but drinking large quantities of water didn't help, and soon it began to hurt to swallow. Pressure meantime was building in his head, centering just above the ridge of his nose. All these developments he took as symptoms of an oncoming cold, which was just about the last thing he needed right now. That, he told himself, was what he got for running himself ragged.

He had to leave work early anyhow in order to pick up Kris and get her out to the airport before eight. That worked out fine with him, since he lacked both the energy and will to keep seeing patients.

On the way downtown he heard the latest theory regarding the events at the Melkis Pavilion the night before, according to WINS radio.

"Police investigators now say that there was a deliberate tampering with the power system controlling the containment area," the news commentator said. "Apparently the loss of power in that area caused a drop in power throughout the building. Detective Lieutenant Warren Davis, in charge of the investigation, told reporters today that police now believe it was an inside job. 'Somebody would have to have access to the system and know how it operates to shut it down,' he was quoted as saying. He added that police are questioning employees of the lab, but have no suspect so far.

"The sabotage caused the death of one of those

employees, thirty-eight-year-old staff researcher Owen Barnes, who was in the containment area at the time. WINS News has learned that he was killed by the release of formaldehyde bombs secreted in the ceiling. The purpose of these formaldehyde bombs is to prevent any dangerous genetic mutations from escaping and endangering the public, according to Dr. Harold Slattery, spokesperson at Westside Medical Center. He declined to speculate as to whether the researcher was the object of a murder attempt or the victim of a tragic accident. Funeral services for Barnes will be held tomorrow.''

A second commentator came on the air with a follow-up: ''Controversy has continued to shadow Westside Medical Center's Melkis Pavilion ever since its head researcher, Dr. Leo Heisler, announced the discovery of a new viral disease that has until now claimed the lives of 312 victims, all of them male. Asked if the sabotage would have a serious impact on his efforts to find a cure for the disease that now bears his name, Dr. Heisler said that it would have no impact at all. 'We are back in operation and proceeding with our work to eliminate this lethal infection,' he said.''

Barrett noticed that there'd been no further mention of citrus fruit as a causative agent of the disease, either on the part of Heisler or the reporters covering the story.

Kris wasn't ready when Barrett arrived. This didn't particularly surprise him; she was almost never on time. Whereas his problem was that he always got to places too early, her problem was that she put things off until the last minute, with the result that she occasionally missed her appointments altogether. She'd improved in the last couple of years, but her departures were still marked by the sort of confusion he ordinarily associated with the flight of refugees from a country about to be overrun by invaders.

She was on the phone when he walked in, talking to her editor at *America Now*. Strewn over the bed, a corner of which Barrett now precariously occupied, was an assortment of dresses, slacks, scarves, and blouses. Two suitcases yawned open on the floor, one half-full, the other completely empty. At his feet were deployed six pairs of shoes. A lot of decision-making, he saw, had yet to be done.

But it all got done in the end, and even with heavy traffic they managed to reach Kennedy Airport well in time for Kris to catch her nine-o'clock flight.

Just as Barrett was about to let her off, Kris groaned.

"Don't tell me you forgot something."

"Dammit, I forgot to put on my machine."

"I'll go back and turn it on for you."

"Would you?" She kissed him. "That'd be terrific." She kissed him again. Then, taking her two suitcases, she said, "Take care of that cold, Matthew, I want you well when I get back."

"I'll go park and wait with you," he offered.

"Oh, Matthew, I have to go through security clearance, and you can't come with me."

"Well, take care of yourself, Kris. You know I love you."

She smiled distractedly. "Yes, I know. 'Bye, Matthew."

He would have watched her from the car, but an airport bus, pulling up right behind him, was honking furiously, urging him to get out of its way.

He didn't like the way they were saying good-bye. More should have been spoken, some commitment established that could be counted on to hold across three thousand miles of water.

Without knowing what more he wanted to say, he decided that he couldn't leave like this. He found a parking space and returned on foot to the terminal.

Several people were still in line for Flight 704, piling their hand luggage on the conveyer belt for the security check. He spotted Kris, who'd just passed through and was now heading toward the departure gate.

She was not alone.

There was a man with her, a valise in his hand, and they were standing there having an animated conversation. At one point, he noticed, she took hold of his wrist to emphasize something she was saying. Clearly they had not just met.

Barrett was all but certain that this was Isaac Ninn. She'd said that he was always flying back and forth between London and New York.

Why hadn't she told him that she was planning to take the same plane with him? If they were just platonic friends, why should she fail to mention it? And why insist that he not accompany her to the terminal unless she feared him seeing them together? Was it because she didn't want to arouse his jealousy? Or was it because there was something else going on between them, and her story about their just being friends was merely a ruse?

He didn't know the answer, hoped it was the former, suspected it was the latter. He was, in either case, angry. Not just angry, furious. Enraged.

He stormed back to his car, drove it at a speed neither he nor the Cutlass was used to back to Manhattan. It was only when he came over the Brooklyn Bridge that he remembered promising Kris that he'd turn on her answering machine for her.

He could've murdered her at that moment, but it was an obligation nonetheless. In making the turn onto Park Row, he nearly sideswiped an idling Checker. He realized he ought to pay better attention to where he was going, but at this point he didn't much care. His head cold wasn't improving his disposition much, either.

If, in fact, his cold had been trying to make up its mind whether to strike him or leave him alone that afternoon, there was no question as to what its decision was now. His nose was clogged, the pain in his throat had spread and become so raw that somebody might have poured lye down it. Chills were beginning to beset him, and there was a disturbing numbness in the back of his neck.

When he reached Kris's street, he parked his car by a hydrant, although he was usually scrupulous about finding a legal spot. He just wanted to get this thing done and go home to bed.

*   *   *

Helen watched Barrett, unnoticed, from the other side of the street. She wasn't doing anything to conceal herself. She would have liked him to see her. It was an enormous temptation to step right up to him—or better, to have been in Kris's apartment to greet him. She'd broken in before; no reason she couldn't do so again.

But how was she to know that he would be back here? She'd left her gift for Kris, and now Kris was gone. She'd missed her by only a few minutes, the super had said. Well, it would be there for her whenever she returned.

She was tired. She didn't want to think about the night, about what she had done, about the death of the man in the containment area. She was too drained from pursuing Heisler and Ninn and Barrett. She realized that she was in danger of faltering, of surrendering to emotions she'd thought she'd buried forever on the night she woke with vomit all over herself, still unhappily alive. But maybe not.

She could not lose her momentum. For if she did, if she gave in to those insidious emotions, then her whole mission would have been for naught.

On the door of Kris's apartment a note had been Scotch-taped: "Kris, see me. I have package for you." Super.

After turning her machine on, Barrett went downstairs and knocked on the super's door.

A burly man, Hispanic, with a beard and streaks of grease on his trousers greeted him. His initial puzzlement changed to recognition. "Ah, you are a friend of Kris," he said.

"Dr. Barrett, that's right. Kris will be out of town for a few days, and I'm taking care of her place for her."

The super nodded, retreated inside for an instant, then returned bearing a large envelope that looked as if it might contain a great many papers.

Barrett, in taking them, sneezed.

The super frowned and gravely shook his head. "You'd better take care of that, doctor," he warned. "There's something bad going around this winter. Everybody I know has got it.''

Barrett assured him he would, and said good night.

Until he looked closely, he had assumed that this package had been messengered from the offices of *America Now*. Probably there'd been some foul-up, and it had been intended to reach Kris before she left for the airport. But now he noted that there was no label on the envelope, only Kris's name scrawled across it.

He walked back to the super's door and knocked.

The super wasn't quite so affable now. "What is it?"

"Who brought this?"

"A woman."

"What did she look like?"

"Just a woman. Maybe thirty, maybe older."

"Did she say anything?"

"Just that I should make sure Kris got it, that's all."

Barrett decided to go back to her apartment and read it there in privacy. On the first landing he opened the envelope and saw that it contained files that must have originated in Heisler's office. Excitement surged through him, and he began to read even as he kept going up the stairs.

There was no note accompanying the documentation, nor did there seem to be any particular order to it. But Barrett had no doubt who it had come from. The only conclusion he could draw was that if Helen had pilfered all this from Heisler's lab, it was likely that she'd been the one to shut down the power and set off the formaldehyde bombs that had killed Barnes.

The first record he selected belonged to a woman named Ella Maguire, a second to Anne Littleton, a third to Maria Fleming. He realized then that they were the names of women who had participated in the double-blinded study Heisler was authorized to conduct with the approval of HIC.

There were additional records. One belonged to a woman named Jacqueline Hanratty. The woman Kris had mentioned. The woman he'd met who'd assumed the name of Sheila Payne. The woman who'd slept with Jerry Perretta.

He found inside the record a detailed pathology report which concluded with the words: "Liver tissue extracted for viral culture," written in hand; the rest of it had been typed. There was no date indicated for this extraction, but since she had been alive until a few days ago, it must have been very recent.

Rereading the report, it struck him that there was something of extraordinary importance missing from it. There was not the slightest mention of what had contributed to her death. He was going on the assumption that the liver was removed after death had occurred, because otherwise the only inference he could draw was that it was the removal of her liver which had caused her to die. And that would mean he was dealing with a case of premeditated murder.

Returning to the other records, he noted that even when the cause of death was explicitly stated, the livers had all been extracted, again for viral cultures.

There were other similarities as well. In each medical report there was the notation: "T-protein: positive."

Although much of Helen's thesis had him baffled, he recalled that transfer proteins had figured prominently in it. What he couldn't understand was what importance they played, though he gathered that there was some relationship between its presence in the body and a susceptibility to certain viral infections.

Maybe it was his cold, maybe it was that he was going through this documentation too rapidly, but he was picking up only bits and pieces of it, unable to make much sense out of the information he had before him.

But he went on with it. Now he discovered another record relating to somebody he knew of: Beth Sandor. Here he found a sheaf of pages which laid out the details of the double-blinded study approved by HIC. The study focused on the testing of an experimental drug to alleviate and possibly arrest the degradation of the liver due to alcohol-related diseases. All very straightforward.

But there was more. Not only had there been an officially sanctioned double-blinded study but also there had

been a second, unsanctioned one, using a far more dangerous and untested experimental drug, composed of synthe-
sized DNA material. It was this material that contained the
virus.

Ironically, the objective of the secret double-blinded
study was the same as the study which was intended as a
cover for it: to find a cure for alcohol-related liver disease.

Heisler, as Barrett had previously suspected, was just
too much in a hurry to wait for the drug to be subjected to
scrutiny by the Federal Food and Drug Administration.

Among the records he found the six for the men who'd
been a part of the original test group. The four who'd died
might have died from liver disease anyhow, but from what
he could see, the test drug had hastened their end. Jim
Sandor's record was here too, although he had not been a
part of the study, only an inadvertent victim of it.

He was still far from certain, but he was beginning to
get the impression that Heisler's Disease, far from being
cured in the Melkis Pavilion, had actually originated in it.

It was more than just a matter of an unethical study or a
possible murder now.

There were still several more records in the envelope,
all marked "Active." That, Barrett had to assume, meant
that they weren't dead.

Of them, not one subject was without the mysterious
T-protein. In the personal data accompanying the records
there were two mailing addresses. One was the Inverness
Courier Service, London, the other was in care of Isaac
Ninn, 88½ Old Brompton Road, London. No fewer than
six phone numbers were listed in addition.

Seeing Ninn's name filled him with dread, but not
nearly so much as seeing the name he discovered on the
next record he came to.

Erlanger, Kris.

His nerves were betraying him; he could scarcely hold
the pages straight. She, too, it seemed, according to an
analysis of her blood, possessed the T-protein; she, too,
was considered "active."

Did active mean alive? Or did it mean infectious?

Suppose she had become a carrier of Heisler's Disease? He suddenly remembered his cold and wondered whether it was really a cold at all.

39

THE ONLY TIME that Kris ever saw the English sun was when she was twenty thousand feet up in the air, and then the sun was a fabulous orange star that shot the surrounding clouds through with a pure golden light. They were over Ireland when she first glimpsed it, heralding the new day that the Boeing's accelerated speed had hastened into existence.

After several hours of deliberation Kris finally decided to tell Isaac about her meeting with Jacqueline and the subsequent interview with Heisler. While she refrained from saying anything about her suspicions regarding Jacqueline's fate, she did tell him about the Inverness Courier Service. "I'm sure it's being used to spread the disease," she said.

Ninn listened intently. "This sounds astonishing to me. For all the time I've lived in London, you know, I've never heard of this Inverness Courier Service. But I'd be happy to try to help you find it."

She assumed that she could find it with the help of *America Now*'s London bureau, but told him that if she needed his assistance, she wouldn't hesitate to let him know.

The jet was beginning to make its descent, and in doing so, left the sun far behind. A thick layer of dark clouds extended for miles over the English countryside around Heathrow Airport.

"We'll have to separate at passport control, since I carry a U.K. passport," Ninn told her. "But when we're both through with the formalities, I'll meet you in the main terminal. My man will be waiting for us."

"Your man?"

What an anachronistic expression, she thought, but appropriate for the British Isles, perhaps.

"His name is Drake. He'll drive us into London and drop you off at your hotel."

Dazed enough from the events of the last several days, and already manifesting the first symptoms of jet lag, Kris was more than happy to allow somebody else to make the decisions for her.

Drake proved to be a thin man in his late twenties or early thirties; he was almost fragile in appearance, so that you would've been tempted to moor him with ropes and pinions to the ground lest a strong gust come and blow him straight across the Chanel. Not Kris's idea of what a chauffeur should look like at all, he wore a tan leather jacket and a checkered cap which he kept adjusting, never quite satisfied with the way it rested on his head. His face was baby smooth, and his emotionless eyes were a startlingly light blue.

"This is Drake," Isaac said.

Drake nodded and immediately he placed her suitcases in the trunk of the red Audi he was driving.

During the drive into London Isaac continued to talk to Kris, but Kris could barely hear him. His voice seemed far away; the words penetrated, but not their meaning. She gathered that he was telling her how they would go about seeing the city together. "First, I recommend you get some rest."

That was one thing she understood and agreed with.

Her hotel—the Royal Westminster—situated not far from

Buckingham Palace, was much better than she would have been able to afford if she were not on an expense account.

"I'll ring you later this afternoon," Isaac said. "Perhaps we can have dinner together."

"That sounds like a wonderful idea," she said.

Upon getting into her room she threw herself on the bed. It was a day for sleep, with overcast skies and nothing but a dull gray light seeping in through the curtains and a constant drizzle tapping at the window. But sleep was no more possible now than it had been on the plane.

Without moving from the bed, she began leafing through a telephone directory she found in the bedside table. No listing for anything called the Inverness Courier Serivce. It would've been too easy if there had been, she thought.

Next she called the *America Now* branch office on Oxford Street and asked for Peter Morris.

He'd probably just gotten in to work; he sounded like she did when somebody phoned her before she'd had a chance to finish her first cup of coffee.

"Morris here."

"This is Kris Erlanger."

Before she could explain who she was, he said, "Oh, yes, you're the young woman they sent over from the States. I wasn't expecting you so early."

"I just got in. I was wondering if I could come and see you sometime today."

"I don't see why not. If you could come before noon, though, it'd be more convenient."

By this point she decided that she could do without sleep for several additional hours. "I'm staying at the Royal Westminster, so however long it takes me, that's when I'll be there. Oh, by the way, Mr. Morris—"

"Call me Peter, we're very informal around here."

"Peter. Have you ever heard of the Inverness Courier Service? It's an escort service of some kind, very exclusive."

"Not offhand, but let me see what I can find out about it. I don't think it should be a problem."

She left the hotel in such haste, a map of the London

Underground system in her hands, that she failed to notice the red Audi parked across the street. Nor did she see Drake get out of it and begin to follow her. He wasn't walking fast; there was no hint in his manner that he feared he might lose her. It was as if he knew exactly where she was going.

40

A TORRENT OF RAIN was descending when Isaac Ninn emerged from the Underground at Tottenham Court Road. With the strong wind that accompanied the rain, umbrellas were turned inside out, mocking the efforts of harried pedestrians to stay dry. The rain only compounded the usual chaos that could be expected of a midday London rush hour.

"Worse than the monsoon," remarked a man coming out of the Underground at the same time.

Ninn gave him a cursory nod. "I wouldn't know," he said, and hastened his step.

Water was seeping into his shoes by the time he reached the pub on Bloomsbury Street. The pub had opened only fifteen minutes before, and already it was packed with customers and people who were simply hoping for shelter from the rain.

If there was one thing that Ninn disliked about London, it was the abbreviated hours the pubs maintained. Noon until two-thirty; five-thirty until eleven. Each time there was a move in Parliament to extend the hours, established in World War I to ensure that the work force would appear punctually and sober, the publicans themselves would oppose it. They assumed that their customers got in as much drinking in eight hours as they would during a longer period that would cost greater overhead.

The man Ninn was to meet was either not present or else had yet to make himself known.

Ninn had no idea what this man looked like, but had been given to understand that this would make no difference; the people he'd spoken to assured him that he could identify him without any problem.

Ninn had never been in this particular pub before, although he had managed, in his years of exile here, to have seen the insides of a good many of the more than five thousand pubs in the city.

He wondered if this pub was specifically favored by operatives of foreign powers. For it was an operative that he was supposed to meet here. How do you recognize an operative? Ninn presumed that they looked like everyone else; otherwise they would have chosen different professions.

After several minutes had gone by, he found a table in the corner and sat there impatiently perusing a copy of the *Mirror*.

"Do you mind if I join you?"

He gazed up to see a middle-aged man wearing a fedora and an overcoat. For some reason, he looked hardly damp at all.

"I'm sorry, but I'm expecting company."

The man didn't react. Instead he said, "There's a chance that I might attend the Three Choirs Festival in Worcester this September."

So this was the man—anonymous, easily lost in a crowd. He could have been a middle-level businessman.

"My plan is to attend the Three Choirs Festival in Hereford," Ninn answered, according to the prearranged script. "Please have a seat."

The man had a pint of half-and-half in his hand. Ninn was drinking neat whiskey.

"It is a pleasure to make your acquaintance," the man said.

He had a faint accent that Ninn decided was Slavic, Czech possibly.

"You know my name," Ninn said. "It would help if you gave me yours. One of yours, at any rate."

"Johann."

"Well, Johann, to put it bluntly, I'm interested in knowing whether you're empowered to negotiate terms and money."

"To put it bluntly, no, Mr. Ninn. This is merely a preliminary meeting, and should we find your proposition interesting, we will, naturally, pursue it."

"I want to caution you, Johann. I haven't much time. You might say that I'm operating under a great deal of pressure. There's a possibility that my position here might become untenable before long. I would like your people to be aware of that. I'm talking about a matter of days, not weeks or months."

"Let me assure you that we are not in the habit of delaying if we see an opportunity. We have the resources to respond within hours if necessary."

"In addition to money, I'll also need a guarantee of safe haven."

"In our country?"

"Don't mistake me, I think very highly of your country, but I'd prefer a warmer climate."

"The Black Sea offers a warm climate," Johann said. But it was just his way of making a joke.

"I don't know how much you've learned about the virus."

"Enough so that we are satisfied about its usefulness."

Ninn wondered how they could've penetrated the operation that he and Heisler had set up. But then, they were professionals, it was their business.

"Then you must know that it's completely effective. There've been no cases where it failed to take."

Johann nodded, but obviously none of this was new to him. "How much of the virus can you provide?"

Of the hundred doses that Heisler had last given him, fewer than half that number were left. Since no one, with the exception of Helen, was certain whether the virus would lose its potency after a period of time, a week or ten days perhaps, he had to keep supplying it to his couriers on a regular basis. Once the remaining doses were gone, he had no means of replacing them. It was too risky to go back to Heisler and appeal to him for more, and he doubted that Heisler would give him more in any case. He'd made his millions, gotten what he wanted from the virus, and he saw no further point in carrying on with the plan. With Barnes dead, and with the Hanratty tissue destroyed in the power failure, there was no source of supply of the virus available to him in New York.

"I can't be certain at this point," he hedged, "but it will be enough to enable you to produce more on your own."

Johann wasn't satisfied. "We need to know how the virus is produced. You have to show us."

Ninn was trying desperately to figure out how he could achieve this. He'd observed Heisler reconstituting the viral particles only once, but whether he could duplicate the process was another matter entirely.

Nonetheless, he hastened to assure Johann that this would not be a problem.

"There is another condition."

Ninn had come to this meeting in the belief that he would be in the position of power, but it wasn't working out that way.

"What is it?"

"That you relinquish your contract with the Inverness girls and put them under contract to us—beginning tonight."

He was unprepared for this development and uncertain at first how to respond to it.

"We need photographs and all pertinent data relating to them," Johann went on.

Ninn realized that once he left London, it wouldn't matter what became of the carriers. "I expect to be amply compensated," he said.

"What would represent ample compensation?"

There was nothing to lose by taking a long shot. "A million pounds." He almost choked saying it.

But Johann's expression did not alter. "That would be acceptable."

"When can we draw up a formal agreement?"

"This evening someone will be in touch with you."

After Johann left him, he lingered in the pub, puzzling out how he might obtain more of the virus.

He would need a woman who was accessible to him and newly infected. It occurred to him that he already had his source. He didn't have to look any further than Kris Erlanger. She met all of his qualifications.

41

NORTH OF OXORD CIRCUS there is a district known as Maida Vale, which is particularly distinguished by a canal running through it that eventually joins the Thames. Brightly colored houseboats are berthed here, but early on a midwinter afternoon they lie deserted, gently listing in the quiet current. Flanking the canal are stately houses with the drapes drawn in the windows so that the impression the visitor takes away with him is that no one lives in them either.

"You wouldn't believe all the scandals that go on in those homes," the rather overenthusiastic photographer was telling Kris.

His name was Harry Quint and he was probably a year or two younger than she was, possessed of great restlessness and idealism, a dangerous combination that she could certainly identify with. Were it not for the Leica slung over his shoulder and the black leather bag crammed full of lenses and flash attachments, he could easily have been mistaken for a student at the London School of Economics.

He was, in fact, a stringer for *America Now*, though that was only one of a dozen publications that he did assignments for in the London area. "Mostly I cover nightclubs, the social scene, and all that rot," he told Kris.

"Is that how you learn about where all the scandal takes place?" she asked.

He gave her a smile as an answer.

"So," she said, "tell me exactly what does go on inside these places."

As imposing and handsome as these residences were, there was something uninviting about them. She had the feeling that if she were to step up to someone's door and ring the bell and tell whoever answered that she needed to use the phone urgently, the door would most likely be slammed in her face.

"You see that one over there, with the Corinthian columns?"

"Yes?"

"An M.P. shot himself in there only a fortnight ago."

"Oh? Why?"

"Infidelity," he replied confidently.

"His own or someone else's?"

"All of the above. The man who betrayed him with his wife lives across the way." He pointed to an Edwardian-looking house of three floors on the other side of the canal. "He's a diplomat, an undersecretary at the French embassy."

Their objective in being in this part of London, which before late that morning Kris had never known existed, was to pay a visit to the Inverness Courier Service. According to Morris, it was located no more than half a dozen blocks from the Underground station. But Quint was too much the tour guide to want to get there without showing her the sights along the way.

As they passed one house he said, "There's a chap who lives here who used to work for the Home Office. He was implicated in the Profumo affair and was sacked. Nice chap, too, it was just that he couldn't stay away from the working girls. Still can't, I imagine."

"I don't see many people around here. Doesn't anyone even go for a walk?"

"It's cold and it's damp, love, and with so much happening inside, why go out?"

She supposed he had a point.

"Tell me, Harry, what's your next assignment once you're done here?"

"I have to cover a party this evening at six in Mayfair. It's for that ministerial meeting they're having here."

"I hate to sound stupid, but what ministerial meeting?"

He crunched up his face in a gesture of mock dismay. "Where have you been all this time, love?"

"Out of it. It's all I can do to glance at the headlines."

He shook his head. "And I thought all you reporters were supposed to be so well informed on current events too. OPEC—the Organization of Petroleum Exporting Countries? Ever hear of them?"

"I'm not that out of it."

"Well, they're having an emergency meeting here about lowering their prices. Of course, all their meetings seem to be emergency meetings."

He now looked to his right, up a side street dominated by town houses of red brick, with elaborate wooden-framed windows.

"This is it," he declared. "Number eighteen."

For the first time since they'd set out from the office, Kriss felt a twinge of apprehension. Having tried to picture in her mind what the Inverness Courier Service looked like, she couldn't quite believe that she was actually going to see it.

And then what? she wondered. She really hadn't a notion as to how she expected to go about linking Inverness to the spread of Heisler's Disease.

Quint didn't know what her interest was in this place, and she doubted that Morris was aware of it either. Mac would understand the necessity for discretion.

Number 18 wouldn't have stood out from the rest of the buildings on either side of it had it not been for the three gray Rolls-Royces parked in front of it.

There was no sign of life inside. The windows were

darkened by blinds, and if any lights were on, they failed to penetrate through them.

"Well," Harry remarked, clearly disappointed, "it doesn't look like much."

"What are you doing?"

"I'm crossing the street to have a look."

She hesitated. "Oh, hell, how could it matter?" she said to herself, and crossed with him.

Embossed on a polished brass plate so small you had to get right up to it to see what it said was the single word "Inverness." A bell was beside it.

Quint put his finger to it, but Kris shook her head. "I don't think that's such a good idea, Harry. Why don't you be good and just take your pictures?"

"Anything you say, love."

He backed down the stairs and took a position midway across the street so that he had a full view of the town house's four floors. When he'd shot as much as he felt necessary, he turned to her. "What else?"

"Take the Rolls-Royces."

He did so. She was running out of ideas. But now she observed in a window on the ground floor a blind being partially raised by hand. Someone was peering out—a man or a woman, she couldn't tell. But there was no question that Quint's photography hadn't escaped notice.

"So you don't want to go in?" he asked.

"Not now. I don't think they'd let us in, in any event."

"Oh, that's not true. Believe me, you can get in anywhere. I've never been here before, mind you, but I've covered people who are clients here. If I ask them, they'll get me in. You, too, if you play it the right way."

"What sort of people?"

"Powerful people. Sheikhs, diplomats . . ."

"Like the French undersecretary?"

"Oh, some are far more prominent, though no more faithful to their wives. But take my word for it, they're well-connected and quite rich. Otherwise they wouldn't have the three thousand quid per year you need to be a member."

She hadn't realized it was that much. "I'm lucky that you came along, Harry. You're a terrific source of information."

He thanked her, but she wouldn't have been surprised to learn that he heard this all the time.

Just then a Rolls, gray like the others on the block, appeared at the end of the street and began to make its way toward them.

In front of the town house it drew to a stop. Two women got out from the back and the Rolls pulled away.

"Wait a minute."

"What is it?" Quint asked, looking at them.

At first Kris wasn't sure what it was. Then she saw, as the taller of the two turned toward her, dangling between her breasts, a crux ansata, the ancient Egyptian symbol.

"I know that woman from somewhere."

"Oh, yes? You travel in more interesting circles than I thought, love."

"But where?"

The woman briefly regarded her, her brow crimpling for an instant, as if she, too, was having a problem remembering where or how they'd met.

Then she and her companion, an attractive woman but not nearly so stunning, turned and ascended the six steps leading to the door. The door opened for them; they had no need of using the bell.

"Office hours have begun," said Quint.

Now Kris remembered. She was the woman Isaac had spoken to outside the Sherry Netherland right after he'd put her into a cab. In their conversation he'd denied that he had any knowledge of the Inverness Courier Service. And yet she was sure that this was the same woman. She could've been wrong about the face, but she distinctly recalled the crux ansata.

If Isaac was, on the one hand, connected to Heisler, and, on the other, to a woman who worked for the Inverness Courier Service, exactly what was his role in all of this?

"What did you say, love? I didn't hear you."

"Oh, nothing, Harry. Look, where can I reach you later on, after the embassy party?"

"I'll give you the number of my service. Tell them it's important, leave a number where I can ring you, and I'll get back to you in ten minutes. Why, are you thinking of trying to get in there?"

"That's the idea, Harry. That's exactly my idea."

When she got back to the office she decided to place a call to the States at *America Now*'s expense and let Matthew know that she'd safely arrived. With all her other concerns, she didn't want him sitting around in New York worrying about her. It was now close to four, London time, which would make it close to eleven A.M. in New York. Matthew should be at the hospital now.

It took less than a minute for the hotel operator to put through the call.

"I'd like to have Dr. Matthew Barrett paged," she told the Westside operator.

"I'm sorry, Dr. Barrett is not in today. Dr. Cassidy is covering for him. Should I have him paged?"

Kris told her not to bother. She instructed the hotel operator to call his home in New Jersey. He must be out sick with his cold, she thought.

But his service picked up and told her the same thing, that Dr. Cassidy was covering.

"For how long is he covering?"

"I'm sorry, I don't know," the woman said.

Next she tried Matthew's office, hoping that Mrs. Preston might have some idea or at least be more disposed to telling her where Matthew was.

Certainly Mrs. Preston seemed no more pleased to hear from her than usual. "Your guess is as good as mine, Miss Erlanger," she said. "Dr. Cassidy informed me this morning that he'd be covering for Dr. Barrett and that until further notice I should cancel all his appointments. Frankly, I'm very concerned."

"I don't blame you. So you have no idea what's happened to him?"

"None whatsoever. It isn't like him at all." She sounded

positively indignant. "If you hear anything, I'd very much appreciate it if you would tell Dr. Barrett to get in touch with me."

"I will, Mrs. Preston."

Kris was as much in the dark as his secretary, but of one thing she was convinced: whatever Matthew was doing, it had to be completely out of character. He'd never just disappear like this. That was something Helen would do. That was something even she might do. But Matthew? Never.

42

"WAIT A MINUTE, sir, let me check. I think there's a later flight leaving from Baltimore for London."

It was 10:10 P.M., and Barrett was standing in front of a Pan Am airlines desk, trying to obtain passage to London on any available flight. The problem seemed to be that at this hour there were no commercial flights to London.

The Pam Am representative, a blandly pleasant woman, was leafing through a thick book with fine print in an effort to discover whether there were any connecting flights that could be of use to him.

She must have sensed his desperation; surely she would've had no problem perceiving his unhappy state of health. Even a cursory glance in the mirror of the men's room had given him all the indication he needed that he was very ill. The color had drained from his face and he was sweating profusely. Even in the warmth of the terminal he was still shivering; it was all he could do to remain vertical. But the worst part of it was that he could barely breathe. Every couple of minutes he'd sneeze. At first the woman behind the desk commiserated with him, but when he continued doing this repeatedly, she gave him a look that suggested that her sympathy was turning to revulsion.

Now she began to see if there was any possibility of catching a shuttle to Boston and getting on a flight out of Logan. But Boston, in that respect, was no better than Washington.

"Maybe Miami," she muttered.

But he could tell by the expression on her face that Miami wasn't going to help him.

"Let's see. I think there may be a late-night flight out of San Juan . . ."

"San Juan?"

He had been of the impression that London was one of the easiest places to get to.

She continued. "There's a flight from San Juan to Amsterdam with connections in Amsterdam for London that could get you in around midday, London time."

But as soon as she checked the Eastern schedule to San Juan she realized that it would get him in two hours after the flight had departed for Amsterdam.

"If you'd only gotten here twenty minutes sooner, I could've booked you on the ten-ten KLM flight to Amsterdam and you would've been in London by noon."

He didn't care to hear about missed opportunities. There was no way that he could've gotten from the Village back to his apartment in New Jersey, picked up his passport, and driven all the way to Kennedy in less time than it had taken him.

"About the only thing I can suggest, sir, is the British Airways flight at nine-thirty tomorrow morning."

"And when does that arrive?"

"Six-ten in the evening, London time."

"That's about one our time?"

"Yes, sir. But I should tell you that that flight is a Concorde and it'll cost you about two thousand dollars one-way."

That was not only steep, it was ridiculous, but he had his credit cards with him and he wasn't convinced he'd be making any return flight in any case, so he couldn't figure out how it mattered.

But the flight representative hadn't exhausted all of his choices.

"Or, if you'd prefer to wait a half-hour, there's a Pan Am flight leaving at ten tomorrow morning."

"And what am I supposed to do until then? Wait here?"

Even the coffee shops and bars in the terminal would close by eleven.

"There's a hotel right when you leave the airport, sir. You could stay there for the night."

He couldn't tell this woman that he didn't dare spend the night in a hotel for fear that when he awoke in the morning he'd be too sick to leave. On the other hand, the prospect of sitting for hours among hundreds of empty chairs was too depressing to contemplate.

"Well, I suppose you'd better put me on the Concorde if there's no other choice. I'll occupy my time some way."

As he was handing her his gold card, she suddenly said, "Wait, you may be in luck."

"That would be a change."

Again she opened her book of schedules and flipped rapidly through its pages. "Here we are. There's a flight on Kuwait Airlines due to leave at nine-thirty tonight—"

He reminded her that nine-thirty had come and gone.

"Yes, I'm aware of that," she said impatiently, "but there was a delay, so the flight's now scheduled to leave here at ten-thirty."

That gave him all of fifteen minutes.

"I'll make a call for you and see whether you can still get on it."

He was not convinced that his luck had changed; on the contrary, he believed it had slipped off into the night, wanting nothing more to do with him.

She talked to whoever was in charge at the Kuwait desk for an infuriating amount of time. But when she read off Barrett's name he began to think that maybe, at least in this instance, his luck hadn't entirely deserted him.

"You have ten minutes, Mr. Barrett. They're still taking on passengers. If you had any suitcases to be loaded on, we wouldn't be able to do anything for you, but with just that"—she glanced skeptically at the overnight bag he held in his hand—"you can walk right on."

He was not exactly in prime condition, but with what remaining energy he had left to him, he managed to get to the Kuwait Airlines counter in time to check in and still make the plane.

He knew where Kris was staying in London, but he wasn't sure he could locate her. And if he did find her, how was he to break the news to her that she was probably a carrier of Heisler's Disease and he probably a victim of it? All that mattered to him now was that he find her and be with her, no matter how little time there was for either of them.

It was easy to see that Barrett was ill. Having observed him throughout the day, from the moment he'd left his office until now, Helen noticed a marked deterioration in his condition. He was pale and listless and unsteady on his feet. Had he somehow contracted the virus?

If he had, then it was pointless for her to pursue him any farther. Not that she could. She had no passport, no credit cards. She lived among the dead and could not suddenly expect to be accepted back into the world of the living.

Better to return her attention to her original goal: the death of Leo Heisler.

To that end she decided to place a long-distance phone call to London. It required only a few seconds before the connection was established.

"Inverness Courier Service. May I help you?"

"Yes, you can. I'd like to speak to one of your girls. Her name is Georgia. Mine is Helen Voyles. Tell her I'm a friend of Isaac Ninn's."

"Is this personal or business?"

"Let's say a little of both."

43

NEWS REPORTERS, attempting to reach Dr. Leo Heisler for an elaboration of his statement about the sabotage of his lab, found themselves frustrated. All phone calls to the Melkis Pavilion were fielded by his secretarial staff, who asserted that he was still unavailable for comment. At his Murray Hill home a woman who wouldn't identify herself said that he was away and she didn't know when he'd be back.

It grew increasingly evident, as the day wore on, that Dr. Heisler, whose movements in the last few weeks had become a matter of public record, had dropped out of sight.

One newsman, Lew Shipley of the Associated Press, was told by a reliable informant with ties to the Pentagon that Heisler had vanished and that a unit of army intelligence was somehow involved. The Pentagon understandably refused to confirm or deny the story.

For two days rumors floated among the reporters covering Heisler and the course of Heisler's Disease that a big story was about to break that would make everything clear.

It didn't necessarily make everything clear, but it did break, on NBC's *News Overnight* program, at four A.M., an hour for insomniacs and unhappy lovers. Joanne Shepherd, a correspondent for Atlanta's NBC affiliate, reported that she'd just learned that the cause for Heisler's Disease had been discovered—and discovered not by researchers at the Melkis Pavilion but at the Centers for Disease Control.

"A prominent physician associated with the CDC, who asked not to be identified, told NBC News earlier this evening that the fatal virus, which has already claimed 425 lives around the country, is sexually transmitted. Researchers have found, after exhaustive tests, that a minority of women carry the disease in their bodies and are infecting those men that they come into sexual contact with.

"NBC News has also learned that the CDC has definitely ruled out citrus fruit as a source of the disease. It was Dr. Leo Heisler of New York's Westside Medical Center who first discovered the existence of the new virus and who has maintained that eating citrus fruits, especially lemons, would result in spreading the disease.

"The source I spoke to at the CDC cautioned that it was too early to say how many women are carriers or how widespread the disease may turn out to be. Officials at the CDC are expected to release their findings next week. Because of the sensitive nature of the report, no representative of the CDC is willing to speak openly to the press until then. This is Joanne Shepherd for NBC *News Overnight* in Atlanta."

The story was so sensational that the wire services picked it up immediately, and all over the country weary copywriters were overhauling the front pages of four-star editions. By six A.M. CBS, ABC, and the Cable News Network were all broadcasting reports on the CDC findings. Noted physicians, awakened at ungodly hours, paraded in front of the cameras to offer their speculations as to the nature and virulence of the disease in the absence of any additional hard facts.

Repeated telephone calls to the Heisler residence went unanswered; it was assumed that somebody had unplugged the phone. This did not daunt a battalion of reporters from assembling in front of his home. Throughout the early-morning hours they rang the bell on the outside gate but failed to elicit any response. In the windows of the house visible from the street level, no lights were on; the curtains remained drawn as if in defiance.

A second, and larger, group of reporters gathered outside the Melkis Pavilion when their entrance into the lobby was firmly discouraged by the security staff there. The revolving door leading into the lobby was continuously bathed by video-camera lights that made it glow like some kind of religious shrine.

Employees coming to work at the lab shunned the cameras as best they could and raced up the stairs, shielding their eyes from the intensity of the lights with their morning newspapers. Almost invariably they ignored the questions thrown at them, and if they did reply, it was to say that they had no idea what was happening, that they only worked there, and that they did not know Dr. Heisler personally.

Yet a third group of reporters was stationed in the more public lobby of the Jacobi Building, waiting for the administrators of the medical center to turn up. If they had hoped to escape embarrassment because of this affair, it seemed that they hadn't acted soon enough.

At eight in the morning WCBS radio stated that in view of the leak, the CDC had decided to release its report at a press conference to be held at noon in Atlanta. "Otherwise this thing could get out of hand," said a spokesperson for the federal agency. "We'd have a spate of groundless rumors that could fuel a needless panic," he added.

Even so, it seemed possible that it was getting out of hand, no matter how delicately worded the CDC presentation turned out to be.

The CBS news broadcast also mentioned, in passing, that the CDC had formally terminated all links with Dr. Heisler. And while there could be no confirmation from sources in Washington, it also appeared that any federal grant money due Dr. Heisler had been suspended. Already three congressmen, one a chairman of the House Ways and Means Committee, were calling for a probe to discover whether use of taxpayers' money had been abused.

And all this had happened before seventy percent of America's population had yet gotten out of bed.

At a quarter to nine in the morning, following an emergency meeting of the administrative staff of Westside Medical Center, presided over by the chief of medicine, Guy Banks, it was decided that some response was required on the subject. A statement was hastily composed, and a brave, or perhaps just luckless, administrator, Daniel Corcoran, was chosen to go out to face the reporters and read it.

It was possible he'd been selected because of his size and bulk. A former quarterback at Colgate, at six-foot-four, weighing 240 pounds, he made for an impressive—if not intimidating—sight when he emerged into the lobby of Jacobi.

The representatives of the media failed to quiet at his appearance. Holding up his hands, he appealed for silence. "Ladies and gentlemen, please, I have a statement to read. I will not reply to any questions regarding it at this time."

He blinked rapidly against the surge of lights on him, then lowered his eyes to the handwritten statement drawn up only a few minutes before.

"The administration of the Westside Medical Center has learned in the past few hours that the Centers for Disease Control in Atlanta has discovered the source of the virus commonly known as Heisler's Disease. According to the CDC report, which, we understand, will be released to the public this afternoon, this virus is venereally transmitted. It is well-known that Dr. Leo Heisler, in coordination with the CDC and state and local health officials, has been involved in research into the cause of the disease. At this point Westside Medical Center has no reason to believe that Dr. Heisler was in any way derelict in his duty in applying the full extent of his energies and resources to putting an end to this epidemic situation. The administration of this medical center believes that it would be a mistake to judge the implications of the CDC report until we have had an opportunity to study it. At any event, Westside Medical Center retains its full confidence in Dr. Heisler. Thank you and good morning.''

The official statement, while widely quoted on radio and in the afternoon newspapers, did nothing to defuse the controversy surrounding Heisler. On the contrary, it only succeeded in fanning it.

The Centers for Disease Control's headquarters is located in a squat brick building, with a bust of Hygeia, Greek goddess of health, positioned in front of it. Some of its sections are still housed in wooden barracks left over from the days when the CDC was the Malaria Control in War Areas agency, created in 1942.

It was in the CDC's unprepossessing headquarters, in Auditorium B, that the noontime press conference took place. The press conference was far better attended than a similar one in January 1977 to announce the results of studies conducted on American Legionnaire's disease. In addition to the inevitable journalists, a significant proportion of CDC staff members had turned up to hear Richard Ling, director of the Viral Diseases Division of the Bureau of Epidemiology.

Notably, not one of the CDC staff who'd worked, however marginally, with Dr. Heisler's group in New York was anywhere present in Auditorium B.

All the networks broke at noon to cover the press conference; it was hoped that the federal authorities would be more candid than their counterparts at Westside Medical Center.

After reviewing the facts, Ling announced that the CDC findings left no doubt that the disease was venereally transmitted. While maintaining that there were relatively few carriers implicated in the contagion, he warned that until those were identified, the virus still posed a threat.

"Any woman who believes herself to be a carrier should consult her physician," he advised. "Testing facilities do exist here in Atlanta to determine whether or not an individual is infected.''

He did not offer any suggestion to those who might in fact be carriers as to how they could, aside from refraining from sexual activity, avoid passing along the disease. It was a subject he didn't care to broach because neither he nor his colleagues had an answer.

44

GIVEN A FREE OFFICE in which to work by Peter Morris, Kris decided to spend the remainder of the afternoon sorting through her notes. Every time she felt as if she'd collapse from exhaustion, she caught a second wind and kept going.

The problem was with her concentration; it would abruptly flag on her and she'd find herself staring dazed at the same page of notes, trying to decipher it as though it were written in a foreign language.

She couldn't tell whether she was getting anywhere with this story or not. What puzzled and disturbed her was the place Isaac occupied in the equation. She was convinced, however, that he was leading her on, offering her tantalizing bits of information that, when collected together, didn't add up to that much at all.

Never one to keep her opinions for too long to herself, she was determined to confront him that evening at dinner and ask him straight out what his involvement was with Heisler and the Inverness Courier Service. She didn't for one minute believe that he'd tell her the truth, but she was sure she'd find his answers rather interesting.

Realizing that she would have no time to get back to her

hotel and meet him, she phoned his home in South Kensington and left word that he should pick her up at the office. The woman who answered had the sound of old age and obedience in her voice: Kris presumed she must be his housekeeper. At any rate she told Kris that she expected Mr. Ninn back at any moment and would convey the message to him.

As soon as Ninn heard the news on the six-o'clock BBC broadcast, he knew at once that Leo Heisler had gone underground and, no doubt, taken the supply of virus with him. He would've called his friends from the Fort Detrick days and asked them to come to his aid.

Ninn wasn't sure whether the disclosures by the Centers for Disease Control at the press conference would make any difference to Johann's people. He thought not. After all, aside from Heisler, he was the only one to have possession of the viral strain, and insofar as they knew, the only one to have the capacity to reconstitute the virus from infected liver tissue. That still left him in an enviable position.

His assumption was correct. When he met with Johann's representative at six-forty-five in front of Quo Vadis, an Italian restaurant in the heart of Soho, no mention whatsoever was made of the reports coming from the States.

The representative was a large barrel-chested man with a beard bushy enough to protect his face from the cold of a Siberian winter, should that necessity ever arise.

"Are we going inside here?" Ninn asked.

Above the restaurant there was a flat where Karl Marx had once lived. Ninn couldn't help wondering whether Johann had a better sense of humor than he'd originally supposed.

The man, who introduced himself simply as Rudy, said no, that they were going to take a short walk.

They walked in silence until they came to the end of Dean Street.

Then Rudy said, his eyes fixed on something only he

seemed able to see up ahead, "I have a quarter of the money for you."

Ninn remarked upon the attaché case he carried in his hand and considered it now in an entirely new light. "A quarter? Two hundred and fifty thousand quid?" In matters involving such large amounts of money, he never believed that things could be so quickly expedited.

"Yes, in cash. Untraceable, of course."

Where he was going, he thought, it shouldn't make any difference whether it was traceable or not.

"What about the rest of it?"

"Another quarter is to be delivered when you are out of the country."

"Out of the country where?"

"Tomorrow afternoon such a question will not be necessary. Let us make the arrangements. That's not your concern."

Ninn didn't particularly care to be left in the dark, but at this point, with the temptation of a quarter of a million pounds so tantalizingly close, he wasn't inclined to argue.

"And the final half?"

"That will be given to you when you've successfully demonstrated that you can produce the virus."

"And if, supposing, I can't do it?"

He wanted to know the risks he might be running.

"What would happen is not up to me." Rudy shrugged. "But I think that in such a case it would require more from you than to merely give back the money."

Veiled as the threat might be, Ninn didn't mistake its meaning.

"You must understand that the women you have under contract are to be used as we want. They will go with the men we designate. You will let them know that they are no longer answerable to you, but rather to whomever we appoint."

Ninn said that this was a term he'd already agreed upon.

"Tonight either Johann or I will find you at the club and we will complete the arrangements for you to leave the country." Glancing down at the attaché case in his hand, he said, "Also, please remember that by taking this money you are placing yourself under obligation to us. Someone will always be watching you. Any attempt to leave on your own will be regarded as a breach of contract."

They were now in front of a door that led into a dark, malodorous hallway which looked—and certainly smelled—as if it had been used for quick trysts by the hookers who worked in the neighborhood.

It was here that Rudy thrust the attaché case into Ninn's hand. "Enjoy your evening, Mr. Ninn," he said. He kept right on going until he turned the corner and was lost to sight.

Ninn looked across the street, then in back of him. He did not for one moment doubt Rudy's words, but he could see no one who might be assigned to tail him. But that, he supposed, was the point: you weren't supposed to.

By the time Ninn arrived to pick up Kris, it was getting on toward eight. The traffic in the vicinity of the *America Now* office had delayed him. It was a matter of little consequence; Drake was keeping track of Kris. His red Audi was parked illegally on Regent Street, half a block from the office.

Just as he'd done with Earl in New York, he'd found Drake on the streets. Like Earl, Drake was a homosexual and a heroin addict, although he had the benefit of a government clinic to satisfy his habit, whereas Earl had been obliged to steal and occasionally slit somebody's throat to satisfy his. And like Earl, Drake was grateful to Ninn not just for the money, although that was a part of it, but also for the status he enjoyed as his spy. He never questioned the orders Ninn gave him, he merely complied with them. It was enough for him to know that he was doing something important, regardless of what it involved.

Ninn located him by a stationer's within sight of the press building. He had his nose in a copy of the *Sun*, trying his best to make himself inconspicuous. In Ninn's eyes he wasn't doing a very good job. A professional like Johann or Rudy wouldn't be so easy to spot.

But for the purpose to which Ninn had assigned him, he was more than adequate. Kris would not be likely to see him, and even if she did, it was hardly relevant, not at this juncture.

"She's still up there," he said, gesturing toward a window on the fifth floor of an undistinguished building of steel and glass with lights at its top that read out the time and the temperature.

"I know, I'm meeting her."

Drake thought about this for a moment. "It wouldn't do to have me look after the two of you, would it, now?"

"Not at all. I have something else I'd like you to do for me, though."

Drake regarded him expectantly.

"Go over to the Inverness and tell Georgia that I want all of the girls there tonight. I'll ring you there in a couple of hours and let you know where I want you next."

Ninn proceeded into the press building. Behind the closed doors of the offices he passed he could hear the clatter of teletypes punctuated by a repeated ringing of bells, signaling the arrival of news commanding special attention. Some of the news would undoubtedly concern the revelations coming out of Atlanta. Ninn had the satisfaction of knowing that he'd been responsible for creating that news. It was unfortunate he couldn't take any credit for it.

Although the attaché case, full of bills in small denominations, was more cumbersome than he expected, its weight was little burden. Quite the contrary, it was comforting, and its presence in his hand contributed a marked buoyancy to his step and, most assuredly, to his spirit.

Kris, however, exhibited no buoyancy whatsoever, although her subdued manner might be due to her lack of sleep. Nonetheless, he sensed that something in her attitude toward him had changed. She was more guarded now, her greeting to him merely perfunctory.

But he decided to keep up pretenses. "Have you heard the latest?"

Looking up from the papers stacked on the desk in front

of him, she shook her head. "I've been working here all afternoon. I haven't heard a thing from the outside world."

"Isolated in the very heart of an international news center?"

"So what have I missed?"

He told her about the press conference that had taken place in Atlanta.

"So," she said, "they finally get around to the same conclusion I reached weeks ago."

"Are you angry that you couldn't break the story?"

"No, of course not," she replied quickly, then hesitated before adding, "Well, maybe a little."

"Reporters get scooped all the time, it happens even to the best. Come on and have some dinner, you'll feel better. I have a very small and rather charming Indian restaurant in mind."

The small and rather charming Indian restaurant, which did actually live up to its billing, failed to improve Kris's disposition. While turbaned waiters threaded their way through the cluster of tables, bearing curries and parathas, she just sulked and looked as if she might at any moment drop off to sleep. Her protracted silences were contagious, tying Ninn's tongue at a time when he felt most expansive. It was all he could do not to tell her about the contents of the attaché case, now planted on the floor between his legs so that he was constantly reassured of its proximity.

It wasn't just Kris's disquieting mood that was working on him, it was also the knowledge that he was being watched. The restaurant was small, which had caused him to choose it more than the quality of its food, but of the fifteen diners, he could not say which one looked as though he—or she—might be an agent. And who was to say that the agent was here at all and not outside, enduring the steady drizzle?

Finally he could abide Kris's silence no longer. "There's something you want to say to me."

She shot him a look of surprise, perhaps taken aback

that she'd been so easy to read. "Well, yes, there is," she admitted. "I went to the Inverness Courier Service today."

"I expected you might. Did you get inside?"

"I didn't try."

"Well, I think you should. From what you've told me, this escort service lies at the heart of your story. If the infection is originating with the girls who work there, you'll come a great deal closer to discovering how this virus is spread than the CDC has."

She agreed that this was possible, but it wasn't exactly what she wanted to discuss with Ninn.

"I saw a woman go in there this afternoon. A woman I saw you with in New York. Just after you put me in a cab that night we had dinner in the Japanese restaurant."

He smiled. "You must be mistaken. Until you told me, I didn't know that such a thing as the Inverness Courier Service existed, let alone know anyone who worked for it."

All the time, he was thinking that there was no way for her to be absolutely certain it was Georgia. He wondered whether this was all that was bothering her.

"No, I'm sure it was the same woman. Both the one I saw in New York and the one I saw here were wearing a crux ansata."

This additional piece of evidence was nothing that would hold up in a court of law. "Isn't it possible that they were both wearing necklaces and that they just looked a great deal alike? Did you see either woman close up?"

"No, I didn't. But my eyes are good. I don't think I was mistaken."

He relaxed. He could already sense that doubt was building up in her. "I don't want to question your reliability, Kris. But I know that when I get very tired my perceptions are affected. I'm not suggesting that you were hallucinating, but something trivial like the design of a necklace doesn't seem enough to me to jump to the conclusion you did."

She wasn't fully convinced that he was right, but she lacked the initiative to debate the point with him, and there was no way, in any case, that she was going to win.

"Is there anything else that's on your mind?"

"It has nothing to do with you."

"That's a relief."

She deliberated for several moments before she admitted that she was worried about Barrett. "He's disappeared. No one I talked to in New York has any idea where he is."

"I'm sure he'll turn up. From what you've told me about him, he doesn't sound like the irresponsible type."

It was all he could do to keep from saying that he was very likely in a coma, close to death. He longed to tell her that had she abandoned Barrett for him, then he would have been spared. Being no longer a threat to the operation, Barrett could have lived out the remainder of his life—only with another woman, not with Kris.

And looking at her now, he understood that it was his pride that had been affronted, that even from the outset, his one desire had been to transform her, to prove to her that life was in fact corrupt and unbearably painful, that she was no better than Georgia or Jacqueline. Her story didn't matter a damn; her ambition to become famous by sitting at a typewriter, pounding out muckraking stories, was no more honorable than what the girls at Inverness did for their clients. In the end, he thought, what would it gain her?

She still considered herself superior to the Georgias, Jacquelines, and Isaac Ninns of the world. It was no wonder she'd attached herself to a doctor; they were both doing the same thing, analyzing, making diagnoses, dissecting. Always standing at one remove from the blood and passion of life. It would be appropriate if her death and Barrett's coincided, the one dying in New York, the other in a strange land, their only link the hour, the minute, they took their last breath.

When dinner was over he asked her if she planned on going back to the Inverness town house.

"Not tonight," she told him. "I'm dead tired. If you could give me a ride back to my hotel, though, I'd appreciate it."

She was tired, all right, but he could not believe that she

wouldn't change her mind—if she hadn't already—and return to the town house. Her obsession with her story would give her a second wind.

Actually he was counting on her going back. If she did decide to spend the night in her room, he would have to make other arrangements. One way or the other there was nothing she could do, nowhere she could go, without his knowing about it.

It wasn't until they were in the car and he turned on the ignition that he had any idea where his tail might be located. Then all at once it was clear: in the rearview mirror he saw a pair of headlights flash on, creating a ghostly haze in the drizzle half a block away. As soon as he pulled out of his space, he heard the sound of the other car's engine surge to life.

Tonight, he thought, we are all under surveillance. Tonight not a single gesture we make, not a single movement we execute, will go unobserved.

Kris got no farther than the lobby of the Royal Westminster before turning around and going right out again. At a public phone booth she called the number Harry Quint had given her.

When the man who took the call heard her name he said, "Oh, yes, Mr. Quint was expecting you to ring up. If you'd like to meet him this evening, he'll be at the bar in the Savoy until eleven."

That left her with little more than half an hour, but she was sufficiently close by that she could get there by cab with fifteen minutes to spare.

She found Quint at the bar conversing with a man whose bloodshot eyes and world-weary demeanor marked him as a fellow newsman.

Quint brightened at seeing her. The man beside him signaled his interest by raising his eyebrows.

"Well, love, I didn't think you'd make it."

"I wasn't sure myself. To tell you the truth, I must be crazy for coming out. It's been a good forty-eight hours since I last had any sleep."

"Sleep," Quint's companion muttered with some disgust. "Never had much truck with it myself."

"Kris, meet Robert Constable. He's with the *Telegraph*. The two of us have been waiting for the last hour for Alfredo Noyes Cardoza. We've got someone posted in the lobby ready to run in and tell us when he arrives."

"I'm sorry, but am I supposed to know who this man Noyes Cardoza is?"

"Venezuelan oil minister."

The OPEC conference. She'd forgotten. Compared to what else was happening in her life, a ministerial meeting to discuss the price of a barrel of oil didn't seem particularly relevant.

"He's the one who's holding out for a lower benchmark price than the Saudis are willing to consider," Constable explained. "But it seems he's making some headway in bringing the others around, which would have the effect of isolating the Saudis."

Kris was barely listening. She was anxious to talk to Quint alone, see if they could get into Inverness.

"So that's why he's important?" she said to be polite.

"Not exactly. If the price of oil falls far enough, then the Soviets suffer. They're the largest net exporters of oil in the world, after all, bigger than the Saudis. If OPEC prices decline, to stay competitive, they'll have to bring their prices down too. They're not going to like that."

"A story with international ramifications renews Robert's spirit," offered Quint.

"Are we going to buy this lady a drink?" Constable said.

"I think not. I'll drop if I so much as have a sip of wine."

She managed to draw Quint off to the side. "Is there any chance of us going to Inverness tonight?"

"A very good one indeed, love. We'll wait here until Noyes shows, then we'll be on our way."

"You're sure you can get us in?"

He smiled triumphantly. "With the right name, you can do anything."

*   *   *

Noyes didn't appear until twenty past eleven. Unsmiling, he regarded with indifference the half-dozen photographers gathered to capture him on film.

"Have you any comment to make, sir?" Constable shouted to him.

"Only that we've adjourned for the evening and will meet tomorrow at noon to continue our discussions."

"Was any progress made at this evening's session?" Constable pressed.

"Some issues were resolved, yes."

"To your satisfaction?"

Noyes stopped in his tracks. After a long pause he said, "We are not displeased with the results."

Then he continued on, his security men hustling him toward the elevators.

Constable turned to Quint. "Looks like the price is going to come down, wouldn't you say?"

"You're the reporter, not me. I just shoot the bloke's picture."

It was ten to midnight when they reached the Maida Vale location of the Inverness Courier Service. Kris had dozed off and Quint nudged her awake. "We're here, love."

They were parked a short distance from the town house, but already they could see several limousines lined up on either side of the street. Chauffeurs in tuxes lingered outside their cars, waiting for their wealthy clients to emerge.

Now all the lights were on in the town house, testifying to far more activity than had been evident that afternoon.

"I found out a few things about this place," Quint said. "Even people who have the money to spring for membership are screened before they're accepted. Once they are, they have the use of all sorts of amenities—saunas, bars, swimming pools, private movie theater, the works. Of course, the girls are the most important inducement for joining."

"Of course."

"There are anywhere from twenty to thirty-five of them working on the premises at all times. Others are contracted out, say, for a weekend excursion to Paris, or even longer. In theory they're only supposed to be escorts, hang on some bloke's arm and look pretty, but that's not what happens. I'm told by my sources that anything you want, sexual or otherwise, you can get here. Anything extra, though, they charge you for."

"Whips and chains?"

"Don't laugh, love. Whips and chains might be the least of it."

"What's your interest in this place? I see you left your camera in your car."

From his pocket he removed a miniature Canon. "You didn't think I'd forgo an opportunity like this, did you?"

This all seemed much riskier than she'd imagined it would be. She feared that Quint would be found out, no matter how unobtrusive his camera was, and that they'd be sent packing.

She couldn't help viewing the idea of actually setting foot inside the Inverness Courier Service with great trepidation. "Maybe we ought to come back tomorrow night when I've had a good night's sleep and am better prepared for something like this."

"Don't start getting cold feet. Tomorrow night my contact might not be here and we'll have blown our chance."

"Who, by the way, is your contact?" When she saw how sly his smile was, she said, "Let me guess. The French undersecretary who lives around the corner. The one the cuckolded husband shot himself over?"

"The very same. Why, you're better at this than I would've thought."

He then took her arm and led her across the street and up the steps to the door.

One more reservation occurred to her. "I'm not really dressed for a place like this, you know."

He threw his head back, laughing. "In this place, I'm sure, how you dress could scarcely matter. Not when you're going to take everything off anyway."

She allowed as how there might be something in what he said.

"Of course there is. I've been around a bit, you know."

Then he put his finger to the bell, glancing at Kris, perhaps thinking that she might raise another objection.

When she didn't, he said, "Here goes," and pushed it.

45

THERE WAS NO WAY of judging what the interior of the town house containing the Inverness Courier Service would look like from the austere style of its facade. A vast atrium presented itself to Kris and Quint as they walked in, one which encompassed all four floors of the structure, rising dramatically to a skylight composed of etched glass. Water gushed from a fountain of terra-cotta, and around it bougainvillea and night-blooming plants rose in splendid profusion.

Paintings—Kris recognized Modigliani, a Degas, and a Picasso—were hung from walls of brass and travertine. A spiral stairway was visible in the background, coiling up to a balcony where men, most of them in tuxedos, could be seen in conversation with women whose necks and wrists dripped with jewelry.

Music, a tintinnabulation, barely audible so far from its source, was coming out of one of the upper rooms.

A console desk, with a black lacquered surface in which Kris could see herself as if in a pool at night, was strategically situated so that no one could simply wander in off the street and mix with the clientele. Behind it sat a woman with russet-colored hair, dressed in black. Her leather pants rustled when she crossed her legs. Eyeing the two visitors, she tried to smile, but the smile failed and settled into a scowl. It was obvious that she did not think that either of them belonged here.

Quint approached her, smiling with a confidence Kris didn't believe was at all warranted by the circumstances. "Hello, there. My name is Harry Quint. I'm here as a guest of Adam de Forest."

He motioned Kris up alongside him so that there'd be no doubt that she, too, was a guest of Adam de Forest.

"Please wait a moment, sir."

The woman lifted a telephone receiver and proceeded to punch out a series of digits. When someone picked up on the other end, she said, "Would you tell Monsieur Adam that there is a Mr. . . ." Here she looked up at Quint. Quint gave her his name again. "A Mr. Harry Quint to see him."

It took some time before the confirmation was forthcoming, during which a pair of men walked in, nodded to the woman at the desk, and continued up the spiral staircase.

Quint followed their progress with his eyes. "You see that bloke, the short dark one?"

The short dark one wore a maroon jacket; a black sash was threaded about his waist. He looked Asiatic, perhaps East Indian.

It turned out he was from Indonesia.

"I saw him this morning going into the OPEC conference, but I certainly didn't expect to see him here."

"What is he?"

"Foreign minister."

The Inverness Courier Service had a far more impressive clientele than Kris had suspected.

It was only now that she became aware of how tight the security was. Idling near the door, by the staircase, and on the balcony were men of imposing size, dressed every bit as elegantly as the clients. They were, however, much more attentive to the movement of people back and forth through the atrium than any client. She liked being here less and less all the time.

At last the woman at the desk received confirmation that Quint and his friend were indeed guests of Monsieur de Forest.

"Would you mind signing the register?"

She indicated a large open leather-bound book. Quint signed his real name, Kris one she made up on the spur of the moment.

"Enjoy yourselves," she said, already losing interest in them.

"That's it? No charge?" Kris asked.

"There's a charge, all right, but Adam gets stuck with the bill."

"I didn't think diplomats made the kind of money that would allow them to entertain themselves this way."

"This diplomat does. Let's say he has other business interests on the side."

That was really what made the world go round, Kris thought: everyone she met had other business interests on the side.

"Where to now?"

"We explore."

Surreptitiously Quint was removing the camera from his pocket, ready to shoot at a moment's warning.

They proceeded up the spiral staircase and began in the direction the music was coming from; it kept growing louder, more propulsive, the farther in they went.

The lights in turn became more subdued, recessed in walls that were variously of moiré and pink taffeta, of brass, and lacquer, and travertine. In one room they found Tiffany lamps and antique chaise longues and love seats; in another everything was high-tech, with the decor all silver and black and white. No matter which way they turned, though, the source of the music always seemed to elude them.

Whereas in the first few rooms through which they traversed there were groups of people, usually men, engaged in conversation, the rooms in back were dominated almost entirely by couples. There was, however, nothing licentious in the atmosphere of these rooms; but with the lighting so low, there was no doubting the erotic nature of the environment.

Bars were everywhere: of various sizes, stocked with an array of liquor from all over the world, they were manned by bartenders who could have doubled as Secret Servicemen, from the looks of them.

There seemed no particular order to the rooms or to the purpose that each one served. A library, paneled in oak, and at this hour, empty save for a solitary reader, would be followed by a game room where Japanese men were playing billiards; a bar, thronged with women who were either Jamaican or Indian, would open onto a swimming pool where several people, some in suits, most without, were floating on their backs while a woman in a floor-length gown strummed a harp in the far corner.

But no matter how glittering the spectacle that greeted him, Quint retained a look of pronounced indifference.

"What's wrong, doesn't any of this impress you?" Kris had noticed that he'd scarcely taken any pictures since they'd arrived.

"This isn't what I'm looking for," he told her.

"Maybe all you heard about unspeakable acts going on here wasn't true."

"It's true, take my word for it. It's just a matter of finding out where they're taking place. There's probably a more exclusive part of the house that not everyone has access to."

"What about your friend de Forest?"

"He doesn't want me to disturb him. That was the deal. Once I got in, I was on my own."

All this while, Kris was keeping her eye out for the woman with the crux ansata, but she was nowhere to be seen.

They finally stumbled on the source of the music that had been reaching them throughout their tour. It was a vast disco, so vast that it was hard for them to figure out how they'd managed to miss it. Mirrors surrounded them on all sides and ran the length of the ceiling, reflecting the dark purple and red neon hues that comprised the color scheme. The couples dancing were periodically cast into high relief by strobes slashing down from lasers overhead.

Tired as Kris was, the noise and lights dazed her. Her only thought was to get away from the dance floor as quickly as possible.

But Quint noticed something that she didn't. "Look there, love. Tell me, what do you see?"

What she saw was a narrow doorway through which a constant stream of people passed, but not before undergoing the scrutiny of a tuxedoed gentleman who was obviously a security guard.

"That must be the entrance to the part of the house we want. That's the doorway to the other world."

The only trouble was that it was hard to pinpoint where exactly this doorway was, for wherever they looked, they could see it. The mirrors were so artfully placed that they bounced reflections back and forth; more than once Kris would gaze into the face of a stranger, only to realize that it was the mirrored image of herself.

The lighting would change too, sometimes subtly, sometimes more dramatically; what you were looking at one moment would be gone the next. Which was how the doorway and the guard who stood by it managed to vanish on them. It was an eerie phenomenon to behold.

"It'll come back if we wait long enough," declared Quint.

Kris wasn't sure she wanted to wait.

But a minute later the lights changed and the doorway materialized again.

"Follow me," Quint said, taking hold of Kris's hand and guiding her across the dance floor.

Somehow he had managed to find the doorway that Kris had begun to think of as a mirage. But she doubted very much that even with his persuasive powers and his acquaintance with Adam de Forest he'd be able to get them into the more exclusive precincts of Inverness.

The guard held a list in his hands, against which he was checking the names of those trying to gain entrance.

Quint confidently gave his name.

The guard scanned the list, flipped over the page, and then curtly nodded. "All right," he said.

"You have a good friend in Mr. de Forest," Kris remarked.

They fell in behind another couple, whose dilated eyes and trancelike expressions evidenced a long night of a lot of drugs. They wove down the passageway, which, in marked contrast to the rooms they'd left behind, were antiseptically white; they could just as well have been in a hospital corridor.

The music blasting from speakers in the disco diminished in volume, muffled perhaps by the dividing walls, though it lost none of its intensity, so that Kris could still register its monotonous vibration through the bottom of her feet. Gradually they began to hear another kind of music, produced by a pianist, which filtered out of one of the rooms just up ahead of them.

In front of them the intoxicated couple was laughing hysterically. The man fell against the woman and she had to prop him up.

"Come on, darling," she said, "we're almost there."

A door was opening, revealing inside a room with walls painted ripe orange, adorned with gold leaf. As many as twenty people of both sexes were gathered in a circle, but it was only by gazing up at the ceiling mirror that Kris could see what had compelled their attention.

A man was coupling with a woman who thrashed beneath him; his haunches rose and fell in rapid succession, and every so often he'd lift his head and emit a bellowing sound that could have as easily been mistaken for a cry of pain as of pleasure. Upside down, the way Kris was viewing him, he looked ludicrous. Of the woman she could see only her limbs, her legs locked about his, her arms carelessly flung about his back.

But if the man in his exertions to come presented an absurd spectacle, his audience made for a sight more grotesque by far. Their faces were flushed with excitement, their mouths hung open, their eyes were gaping, and all the time they kept pressing against one another, attempting to get closer for a better look. There was something incongruous about the sartorial splendor they exhibited, too; sex leveled them, punctured their pretensions.

Kris tried to look away, couldn't. She was as hypnotized as they were. But the sight of this couple on the flat black expanse of the bed provoked in her not lust, only a kind of horrified curiosity, a wonder that otherwise ordinary people would turn themselves into performers like this and would, in addition, pay handsomely for the privilege of doing so. Those who danced topless or engaged in sex onstage for the benefit of a paying public she could understand, but not this.

All at once the man let out a terrible scream and reared up off the woman, sopping wet. Now Kris had a glimpse of his face. It was the man Quint had earlier pointed out to her—the Indonesian foreign minister.

And supine on the bed, her breasts moist with his saliva and sweat, reddened in places where he'd applied too much pressure on her, was the woman Kris had been searching for—the woman with the crux ansata.

It was still there, she saw; it was all she had on.

There was little question in her mind that, like Jackie, this woman was a carrier. Recalling Constable's words about the implications of the OPEC conference, she believed that what she'd just witnessed amounted to an assassination. In three days' time the Indonesian foreign minister would be dead of Heisler's Disease. Among the men of wealth and power gathered here, there was no telling how many were being targeted tonight. For all she knew, murders were going on all around her under the guise of pleasure.

With one performance ended, others were beginning, as if this one sexual act had set off a chain reaction, triggering a surge of erotic energy through the crowd. People were casting off garments with such eagerness that it was questionable whether they'd find them all again. Bellies, constrained by shirts and jackets, came bulging out; breasts, tantalizing in décolleté, drooped suddenly, sadly, on being fully exposed. The smell of flesh in heat pervaded the room so that there was scarcely any air to breathe.

Kris struggled to get to the woman on the bed, hoping to have a word with her, though she had no idea how she'd make her approach. Already she had another man in her embrace.

Kris was seized with the notion of intervening, and somehow, by persuasion or force, tearing the man away from her. If she was mistaken and this woman with the crux ansata posed no danger, then the worst that could happen was that Kris would look like an fool. A small price to pay, she thought.

But then how was she to prevent the woman from taking another lover and another? Why should she believe Kris's story? And if what Kris was witnessing was a series of assassinations, certainly enough planning had gone into them to ensure against the possibility that they'd be easily thwarted.

Nonetheless, she couldn't allow these considerations to deter her. She was certain that Quint would help her, if only because of the urgency with which she intended to make her appeal. He might think her slightly deranged, but she didn't think he'd refuse her.

But when she looked for him, she couldn't figure out where he'd gone. Then she spied him circling around the room, his miniature camera cupped in his hand, not anywhere as well-hidden as it ought to be. He was so preoccupied that he failed to see her signaling him. Nor did he remark upon a fully clothed hulking man coming up behind him.

Kris shouted to him, but he didn't hear her, and in any case, it would have done him no good. The man spun Quint around, angrily gesturing at the camera. Before Quint could respond, the man snatched the camera out of his hand, pried it open, and plucked the film out of it. That done, he proceeded to haul Quint away. Quint protested, but he didn't resist.

For several moments Kris deliberated as to whether she should follow him. But she couldn't see how that would benefit either of them.

Turning her attention back to the bed, she observed that the man had his head buried in her breasts while the woman cradled him gently; her eyes soft and unfocused, she regarded him like a mother would a child.

Only this was a child she would murder.

As Kris started toward the bed, she felt herself grabbed from behind. A hand pressed hard against her breast and squeezed. She cried out, though her cry was only one among many.

She twisted her head in an effort to see who'd locked her in his embrace like this, but she couldn't quite manage it. She tried kicking the man's shin, but there was no strength to the kick and it had little visible effect.

"Get your hands off me, you bastard!" she screamed.

She assumed that, willingly or not, she was going to be compelled to participate in the proceedings. No observers allowed.

The man's grasp tightened. She was being propelled forward, half-stumbling over one entwined couple on the floor. butting into another still upright. Couldn't brake herself, no matter how she struggled.

Another room now. Dark, with flowerless plants climbing up toward the ceiling from vases of pink marble. Her captor released his hold, permitted her to look upon him. She knew him; she didn't know him at all. And while there was nothing different about his face, about the pinched, desolate expression of it, it was as if she were finally able to see it for the first time. See that there was another face beyond this one, that when one mask was stripped away, there'd inevitably be another to take its place.

"Isaac," she breathed his name. "Isaac."

It was no surprise. How could it be? But there was shame, even embarrassment. She had guessed all along; the realization of who he was, of what he was, had penetrated her from the moment she'd first laid eyes on him in Helen's apartment. But she hadn't wanted to acknowledge it. There had been something she wanted from this man, which was why she'd put her trust in him. It was not the story so much. It was knowledge.

There was a gun in his hand. It seemed unreal to her; she could not imagine him using it, but this, she knew, was merely a failure of her imagination. He would use it. Against the background of a hundred people having sex, rasping, moaning, and crying out, the detonation of a gun would seem like nothing.

46

IF THE AUTHORITIES at Heathrow had determined that Barrett ought to be put into quarantine or deported, he wouldn't have blamed them. Haggard and feverish, he'd gotten off the Kuwaiti jet liner and allowed himself to be swept along by the crowd to the appropriate passport station.

Although the inspector had given him a decidedly skeptical glance, he didn't hesitate to stamp his passport. His luggage went unexamined. Had it been, they would have found nearly a hundred pages of documentation stolen from the Melkis Pavilion.

While Barrett had neglected to book a hotel room—he'd had other things on his mind—he nursed the hope that there'd be one available at the Royal Westminster. Actually all he wanted to do was be with Kris. Procuring a room for himself made practically no sense. How many hours did he have before lapsing into a coma? Another twelve? Another twenty-four?

It developed that there was a room at the Royal Westminster, but that was about the only thing that favored him. When he rang Kris's room, no one answered. He went to her door and knocked, but the result was the same.

Returning to his own room, he sat on the bed, thinking that he would first get his bearings and then figure out what he should do next. An instant later he was sound asleep.

When he awoke it was dark. He was unable to see farther than his feet at the end of the bed.

He propped himself up on the pillow and peered into the dimness. It would not come to him at first where the hell he was.

Then he remembered the flight, but in the way he would remember a dream; there was nothing coherent about the memory at all. I am in London, he told himself, though he wasn't quite sure what to make of this information.

It also struck him that he was alive. He was conscious and alive, which came as a pleasant surprise. He put his hand to his brow. He was still warm, but he judged nonetheless that the fever had diminished in his sleep.

Still, when he tried getting off the bed, he realized how weak he was, how wobbly.

I must go very easy, he thought.

All his energy now was directed at turning on the light switch by the door. That meant actually walking over to the door, a laborious enterprise.

The light on, he could see what the hands on the clock by his bed said—11:38.

Obviously it was 11:38 at night. He'd slept for nearly twelve hours. He couldn't recall when he'd had that much sleep, although it was clear to him that he would need a great deal more.

At any rate, he knew from his experience with Heisler's Disease that he should not be feeling even as well as he was. Instead of going into a rapid decline, he felt as if he'd improved, however marginally. His nose was as clogged as before and his skull was still providing a home for a pounding headache, but these things were far better than coma, massive internal hemorrhaging, and severe liver failure.

It might turn out to be an attenuated strain of the virus, a mutant form that manifested different symptoms, and he couldn't rule out the possibility that he still wouldn't make it.

Yet the more he kept on his feet, the more confident he grew that he could continue to function for at least a few hours.

Again he tried Kris. For minutes he listened to the phone ringing in her room. Next he called the *America Now* office, but he wasn't surprised when no one answered; probably everyone had long since gone home. He had no home number for Peter Morris, and the directory he consulted listed six Peter Morrises.

The third Peter Morris he tried turned out to be the right one.

After explaining who he was, and stressing the urgency of the situation, he prevailed on the bureau chief to give him an idea where Kris might be.

"I know she'd set up a meeting with our photographer, Harry Quint," he said. "I'd wager that they went off to the Inverness Courier Service. It's apparently related to her story—"

"I'm familiar with it," Barrett said impatiently. "You're saying she's there now?"

"It's just a guess. I'll give you the address if you'd like, but I want to warn you, they probably won't let you in."

Barrett said he had the address already and thanked him.

It was agony managing to get down to the lobby and going out to find a taxi, but he did it.

Half an hour later he was standing in front of the town house; stretch limos and Rolls-Royces and Mercedes and Alfa Romeos were deployed all along the street. He remembered Morris' words about the difficulty of obtaining admission. He'd discounted them before, thinking that his powers of persuasion would somehow be sufficient. Now he wasn't so sure.

Nevertheless, since he was here, he might as well try.

As he was walking up the steps, a party of four, elegantly coiffed and more elegantly dressed, in black tie and shimmering white gowns, passed by him, leaving in its wake a trace of voluptuous perfume.

Barrett proceeded past them through the open door. No one stopped him.

He thought that he'd actually succeeded in getting in until he spotted the desk with a girl behind it. She gave him a careful smile. "Can I help you, sir?"

He was momentarily distracted by the sight of still more elegantly attired people lining the balcony above the lobby.

He realized that he didn't have a thing to say. He should have thought of something beforehand.

"I'm here as a guest of Mr. Isaac Ninn."

He hoped he sounded confident.

The girl did not appear convinced. She picked up the phone.

"What is your name?"

He figured there was no point in lying.

She spoke briefly into the phone. Hanging up, she said, "I am sorry, sir, Mr. Ninn is not expecting any guest tonight."

Barrett smiled sheepishly. "I must've gotten the date wrong," he said.

About to back away, he noticed that one of the tuxedoed gentlemen who served as security for Inverness was approaching him.

He'd evidently placed himself in some peril by asking for Ninn. Turning, he hastened toward the exit, only to run headlong into yet another guard.

"Excuse me, sir, I'd appreciate it if you could accompany me."

Gripping hold of Barrett's arm, he gave him little choice in the matter. But what struck Barrett especially was just how polite these people were. They might kill you, but they would do so with the best of manners.

47

IN THE BRIGHT ORGIASTIC ATMOSPHERE that prevailed in the rear of the town house, no one noticed the activity of the tall young man with the cropped hair, whose only real distinguishing feature was his unusually long white neck. He seemed not at all interested in the women who paraded about him, half-clad and completely unclothed, nor in the men who tagged along after them.

He was, however, attentive to everything that went on around him; it was his profession to be attentive. In the embassy in which he worked he was assigned a role as a mid-level functionary with a host of uncomplicated routine duties to perform. But it was widely suspected by those on the embassy staff that he worked closely with Johann and Rudy.

About Johann and Rudy's role in the embassy, and indeed in England, there was no doubt whatsoever.

The young man, whose name was Henryk, wore over his shoulder a canvas bag of a kind used to keep an extra set of clothing. There was clothing in it, to be sure, but it only served the purpose of concealing a container of kerosene.

When he was alone in a storage room, he removed the container and went about distributing its contents with a mind to covering the whole floor and most of the shelves.

That much done, he then opened the various cans of solvents and cleaning solutions that were kept in this room, and these, too, he poured out. Now the storage room was filled with a combination of powerfully noxious odors that all but sent Henryk reeling.

He got out quickly, but made certain to leave the door open a crack. He then distributed the last of the kerosene along the floor of the adjoining corridor, an act that took no more than half a minute.

A young Italian woman, wearing a T-shirt and nothing else, her tan legs oiled in sweat, came striding down the corridor. For a moment she stopped, staring at Henryk, her nostrils flaring as she attempted to identify the odor.

Henryk returned the stare. He would kill her if he had to, and perhaps she sensed this, for without a word she wheeled about and hastened back the way she'd come. Henryk viewed the roll of her buttocks with no more interest than he would a moth diving into a lighted bulb.

Completing the task, he deposited the kerosene container inside his canvas bag. One final thing remained to be done.

He placed the bag on the floor, lit a match, dropped it into the oil-soaked clothing stuffed inside it, and ran.

A few moments later flames shot up out of the bag and leaped onto the floor, where they picked up the trail of kerosene and followed it through the open door into the storage room.

There was so much flammable material scattered through the room that it didn't burn. It exploded.

"What the hell was that?"

Ninn turned away from Kris for an instant to regard Johann. Johann's expression hadn't changed at the sound of the detonation, and Ninn consequently assumed that he knew what it was about.

DOUBLE-BLINDED

"It doesn't matter. It means only that it is time to leave."

They were standing in a small library, which Johann had sealed off. He now proceeded to open the door leading to a restricted passageway. A faint trace of smoke was in the air, and it kept getting stronger as the moments passed.

With one hand on his gun, the other clinging to the attaché case with its treasure of a quarter of a million pounds, Ninn had Kris walk ahead of him, following Johann.

He decided that one of Johann's people had set a fire to perpetrate some ingenious deception. By eliminating the role of the Inverness Courier Service in the spread of the virus, they were free to monopolize the girls for themselves. Presumably many of the girls would be thought dead as a result of the fire, their bodies burned beyond all possible recognition, while in the meantime they went on spreading the disease wherever they were ordered to.

Ninn had never suspected that their aims were so grandiose, nor could he have imagined how elegantly they would execute them. But what concerned him most of all was not the destruction of the Inverness operation, but rather his own future well-being.

Having just half an hour ago learned that Barrett was alive and in London, he realized that the virus he'd given Kris hadn't taken, or, more likely, was ineffective.

Kris had all but admitted she'd slept with Barrett. That wasn't in question. Barrett should be dead; he wasn't. Ninn suspected that Heisler had duped him, given him a bogus strain. It would be just like him.

What would happen when he got over to the other side and Johann's people discovered that while they might possess the carriers, they lacked the virus itself as well as the capacity to manufacture it? It was not to be expected that they would forgive him for not fulfilling his agreement.

Somehow he would have to get away and take with him the first installment of his advance.

*   *   *

Kris should've been more terrified. The terror was there, but deep down where she couldn't feel it. The explosion—whatever it meant—changed nothing. The gun Ninn held on her could kill her every bit as thoroughly as a roaring blaze. In some way she was calmer than either Ninn or the man he addressed as Johann. They were both jittery, though Ninn much more so. They were the ones who had to make the decisions, choose when to move—and where. All she had to do was obey.

And while she recognized that they probably intended to kill her, the prospect of death seemed remote. She was powerless to do anything. She was drained to the bottom. No second wind or third remained in her. Heroics were out of the question. She wondered if satori was like this, if it resembled the profound indifference with which she awaited her fate.

"Have you gotten what you wanted, Isaac?"

It was not a question to which she anticipated an answer.

He glared at her, wouldn't reply. Too distraught himself. She suspected that events were not going in his favor.

"What are you planning to do to me?"

The press of the gun against her kidneys was the only response Ninn cared to give her.

"You hate me that much?" she thought she heard herself say, but maybe not. Maybe she kept the words to herself. But of course he hated. It was what he knew best how to do.

The smoke was smarting her eyes, producing tears. If she couldn't cry on her own, she supposed the smoke would have to do the crying for her.

As soon as he heard the explosion, Rudy began shepherding the eight carriers out of the back of the town house. In the ensuing panic, no one wondered at what Rudy was doing here, directing the exodus of the girls and their bewildered clients. It was enough that anyone was sufficiently collected to take charge.

Among those fleeing the fire, which was now eating away the walls, gnawing at the wooden beams that maintained them, were two OPEC ministers. The Indonesian foreign minister, Rudy noted, was naked, more concerned about hiding his genitalia than he was about the flames catching up to him.

Rudy couldn't help but be amused at the Indonesian's predicament. With his body riddled with the virus, all he was doing by escaping the fire was postponing a far more excruciating death forty-eight hours from now.

Nonetheless, it was better this way. Had he perished in the fire, his death, and the death of his fellow minister, would not serve as the warning it was intended to be.

A brick staircase led them out to the rear of the building, close by the garage where the courier service's limousines were kept. There the patrons scattered, disappearing as quickly as they could under the circumstances, not wishing to have their privacy intruded upon by the authorities. Already the dirgelike bellow of sirens signaled the imminent arrival of fire-fighting equipment. Arson investigators and police could be expected to swoop down on the scene in their wake.

Rudy wasn't at all interested in the patrons, though. He and Henryk, who'd just now joined him, were occupied with getting the carriers into the two limousines waiting to spirit them away.

"I count only seven!" Henryk said.

"There should be eight. Count again."

Henryk counted again, but there still were only seven girls.

"Which one is missing?"

One of the girls looked about. "Georgia! She must still be inside!"

Hysterically she cupped her mouth and yelled out Georgia's name.

"Don't be daft," Rudy said. "She can't hear you! No one can."

Henryk started up the stairs in search of her, but all of a sudden half the upper wall collapsed, raining down bricks and mortar and flaming cinders. In the doorway a mass of flames roared up, making it impossible to go back in. Henryk had no choice but to abandon the idea.

"The hell with her," Rudy muttered. "We've got seven out of eight, that's enough."

The smoke took longest to reach the lobby of the town house. It drifted leisurely through the discotheque and down into the atrium, billowing in until it blotted the skylight from view. Many patrons who up until this point had dismissed the threat of the fire, assured by the staff that it had been confined, were now rushing madly in the direction of the entrance.

As brilliant an architectural highlight as the staircase might have been, it was not designed for ensuring the hasty exit of several hundred people. A woman stumbled, fell, and her pink brocaded silk gown, in spreading out over three successive steps, caused others to do the same.

Barrett was in the meantime still sitting in a corner of the lobby under the watchful eye of a security guard.

But as the smoke thickened, the guard bolted for the door himself.

Barrett had no idea what to do. He was gasping for breath, and in another minute or two it would be impossible to stay, but he didn't want to leave without Kris.

Then he spotted her. She was being led out a door to the right of the artificial waterfall by Ninn and another man.

The balcony just above them erupted into flame, and pieces of it began to drop off, igniting the bottom level as well.

Without thinking, Barrett rushed toward Kris. In spite of the smoke and his state of exhaustion, he still had one final store of energy.

Kris didn't hear him until he was nearly upon her. "Matthew!" she screamed, so astounded to see him that she forgot about Ninn and the gun he held on her, and stood there amid the thick whorls of smoke, totally immobilized.

Ninn raised his eyes toward Barrett, straining to make

him out, while Johann turned back, unsure what had happened.

Barrett reached for Kris's hand. An immense distance seemed to separate them for a moment before he felt her fingers catch hold of his.

Johann said something that was unintelligible with so much noise.

"He has a gun!" Kris warned.

Barrett caught sight of the Walther P38 Ninn held, but he failed to see the gun in Johann's hand.

A chunk of wall that ran the length of the balcony broke free and toppled to the floor, drawing Johann's attention away from Barrett—a moment he seized to try to escape.

Still grasping Kris's hand in his, he started in the direction of the door.

Ninn could barely see through the smoke; even so, he didn't hesitate to fire.

Kris heard the shot, but it meant nothing to her until Barrett released his grip on her hand and fell to the tilted floor.

Thinking that he'd tripped, she tried to help him up. Then she saw the blood in his hair.

Distracted, Johann realized Ninn wasn't where he had been a few moments ago. Determined to find him, he plunged back into the smoke.

He finally caught a glimpse of him fighting his way into the panicking crowd, wielding his attaché case to break through, perhaps because in this instance he found it a superior weapon to his Walther.

The man was mad, Johann concluded. To elude him he was racing toward the flames, not away from them. Johann did not share his madness, and so he stopped and watched as the attaché case caught fire and, with the intense heat, suddenly burst open. Thousands of pound notes were set aflame, and, blazing, they flew into the air and in seconds were reduced to charred tatters of paper.

That was the last glimpse Johann had of Ninn. Having

lost all of his money, Ninn had apparently decided to complete the job and throw away his life as well.

Johann was only mildly disappointed. He was in possession of the carriers, after all. He might have lost the virus, but he had not lost the disease.

OPEC CONFERENCE ENDS IN DEADLOCK

London (AP)—Delegates of the oil-producing states meeting here to consider a new benchmark price of oil failed to come to an agreement after five days of acrimonious debate. The breakup of the conference, informed sources say, was partly attributable to the sudden illness of four delegates, including the foreign minister of Indonesia, two representatives from Iran, and one from Nigeria, all of whom had originally favored a lower benchmark price for a barrel of oil in opposition to the Saudi position. That position supported a price within a dollar of its current $30-per-barrel benchmark price. A new conference of OPEC ministers is scheduled for March 11 in Vienna.

48

Leo Heisler lived in opulent solitude on an island off the coast of Florida in a house from which it was possible to view the sun rising and setting over the Gulf of Mexico. These sunrises and sunsets were so monotonously spectacular that he'd grown used to them and in fact no longer took much notice of them.

It had been two months since he'd left Westside Medical Center. For the first month he'd worked in a secret government facility in Fort Myers, trying to develop a vaccine for the disease he'd contrived.

No one had seemed to know whether a vaccine was even necessary until a week ago, when the news came that two technicians working on a U.S. missile installation not far from Frankfurt, Germany, had fallen ill with Heisler's Disease and died.

The news did not come as a complete surprise to Leo. Although one of Parker Grey's intelligence officers had assured him that Ninn had died in the fire that consumed the Maida Vale town house, he'd remained convinced that somehow Ninn had survived and was pursuing his vendetta with the carriers elsewhere in the world. Ninn was as much of a survivor as he'd been in his former incarnation as Colin Thomas.

Yet while the matter of Ninn's fate occasionally intruded on his thoughts, the fact was that it was his own fate which preoccupied him.

Up until a week before, he'd believed that the worst was over, that upon his precipitious departure from Westside, described in a terse press bulletin as "an early retirement," he would be guaranteed both security and anonymity as a result of his association with Parker Grey and army intelligence.

But then a letter had arrived, sent to a special post box maintained for him in Fort Myers. The letter was from Mackenzie Walker, New York senior editor of *America Now*, and it outlined a two-part story that was to run in consecutive issues of the newspaper early next month. The story, he noted unhappily, was written by Kris Erlanger.

The article implicated him as the creator of the disease which bore his name and accused him and his collaborator Isaac Ninn of knowingly spreading the disease by using women based at the Inverness Courier Service. As if that were not enough, he was also to be accused of plagiarism, fraud, and corruption, in view of his habit of squandering grant money in exchange for unusable lab equipment and fabricated biological assays from Torquay Research, Ltd. Furthermore, he was to be implicated in the U.S. government's bacteriological-warfare program at Fort Detrick during the Vietnam war.

Of course, all of it was accurate. It was just that he had never believed that it would come to light like this.

"Dear Dr. Heisler," the letter had said, "please be advised that we have conducted an exhaustive check of the contents of the article by Ms. Erlanger and are satisfied that there is nothing in it that could be construed either as defamation of your character or as grounds for libel."

It added that he was welcome to submit his response to the article, which would be provided him presently in galley form, and that his response would be included in the same issue.

He'd immediately called Washington, using the private line Parker Grey had given him in the event of an emergency.

This, to his mind, was most assuredly an emergency. If the story appeared, he had no doubt that it would create too much controversy to be ignored. Both the federal authorities and Westside Medical Center would be obliged to open investigations. Grand juries would be formed to hand down indictments against him. His wealth would be drained away in ruinous lawyers' fees, and in the end he would most likely still go to jail.

Parker Grey, he was told, was unavailable. The man who answered asked if he could help him. He identified himself as Colonel Jay Haskin, but the name meant nothing to Heisler.

"I need to speak to General Grey personally."

"I'm sorry, Dr. Heisler, that is impossible. I'm authorized to handle anything he did. What is the problem?"

He'd sounded impatient, not an auspicious sign. But there seemed to be nothing else to do but explain his predicament.

"Of course, you will make sure this article is killed," he concluded by saying.

"I regret to say that in this matter our hands are tied," Colonel Haskin told him. "There is nothing we can do to stop publication."

He protested vigorously, he made many more calls, but he knew that he was finished. The government had no intention of protecting him any longer; he was on his own.

And even if he should go public and reveal his association with army intelligence, he realized that he would only be ensuring a darker fate for himself than several years behind bars.

It was ironic that Kris Erlanger had become the instrument of his doom. He should have made certain that Ninn infected her. But it was too late for that. When the opportunity had arisen, his primary objective had been to cut Ninn off, deny him further access to the viral particle. The epidemic had gone far enough, he'd gotten as much as he could reasonably expect from it; there'd been no point in going on.

And that was why he'd given Ninn a counterfeit virus. So that there would at last be an end to it.

But, as it developed, he'd failed to stop Ninn. And now he'd failed to stop Kris Erlanger and her damned story as well.

What he needed at such times was a woman he could depend upon, a woman who would know when to come to him and when to leave him alone, a woman who would not, like Tina, fear for her reputation and rush off at the first inkling of trouble.

He liked to think that he was more favorably disposed toward women then Isaac Ninn had been, but he was also aware that no affair or marriage he had could be expected to last for any length of time. He was too difficult a man to live with, too remote, he supposed. He'd thought that perhaps this prolonged retirement might mellow him, but he had seen no signs of any mellowing setting in.

In the last few weeks he'd befriended a woman who was vacationing a mile or so down the coast in one of those condominiums people put up for rent during the winters. He'd met her at the bar in the golf club, which he repaired to whenever he spent an afternoon on the course. No one at the club knew him as anything but Leo and none connected him with the notorious physician who two months ago was making daily appearances on the six-o'clock news. There were the occasional few who would give him odd looks as though they were trying to place him from somewhere, but that was it.

Few women ever came into the club, which was why one always elicited a certain amount of interest from the regular clientele. Mostly they were guests of club members who'd show up for an afternoon or two and never be seen again.

But one woman continued to turn up often enough to become something of a regular. She was an attractive woman with an easy smile and a loping step that emphasized the sway of her hips and the succulent contours of her buttocks. She said that her name was Carol and that she'd been twice married to the same man in Denver and divorced from him twice. There was a certain bitterness about her that Heisler detected, but she succeeded in hiding it except on those rare instances when she got carried away and had too much to drink.

Heisler's first approaches to her were received politely, but scarcely with any enthusiasm. Nonetheless, there was something about her that appealed to him; he sensed that she had suffered through ordeals of her own and that she was, like him, on the run, desirous of a life of anonymity and the company of strangers.

All she would say about what she was doing on this island was that she was recuperating. "Not necessarily from the divorce," she added. "From other things."

And what, she asked him, was he doing here?

"I live here year-round," he explained. "I am permanently retired."

"You are? Are you very rich?"

"Very."

"And what do you do with all your time?"

"I read and collect shells."

"Shells?" It seemed to surprise her that anyone would collect shells.

"Surely you know that this is one of the best places in the world for it. Why not take advantage of the opportunities that are presented to you?"

For some reason, she thought that this was very funny.

He procured her phone number from her. This could in no way be considered a breakthrough, for she unhesitatingly provided it to anyone who asked for it.

How she would actually respond when he called, he didn't know, but he took the chance. Not very much hinged on this, he thought; it was just that he could do with a woman's company tonight.

It turned out that she had nothing to do, that if all the others she'd given her number to had called, she'd not found them to be worth following up on. Heisler was gratified to learn that she was free, even if she sounded more resigned than excited about spending some hours with him over dinner.

He told his cook to prepare something that would impress her but would not seem so elaborate that her suspicions might become aroused. When the meal, a shrimp-creole dish, was ready, Heisler dismissed the cook for the night.

He expected that Carol would show up in the same kind of casual attire that she generally wore at the club bar, but instead she elected to wear a blouse the color of fine champagne, which, when the sun's last rays struck it, allowed him to see right through it; she had nothing on underneath. Her skirt was white and shorter than he thought was the fashion, but she had such fine long legs that fashion was quite beside the point.

She left him just as the sun was coming up. He didn't mind. She was an ardent lover, but he had not been so enamored of her company that he wanted her around the next day.

He didn't even bother letting her know he was awake. His eyes half-slitted, he watched her as she dressed. He admired the way the first light seemed to ignite her body, turning it so gold that Jason and his Argonauts might be impelled to go in search of her.

But as gold as her body was in the eastern sunlight, it was not so gold as the crux ansata dangling between her breasts.

The first symptoms didn't occur until well on in the day. He thought at first that he might be catching a cold, but it soon became clear that it was something much worse than a cold. While there'd been few new cases of the disease that carried his name in the United States, it was still a long way from being totally eliminated.

Actually he'd been expecting this to happen from the outset. He was disappointed, not surprised.

What interested him, if only as an academic exercise, was who had planned his death. Was it the woman herself, bent on revenge? Was it U.S. army intelligence, looking for a quick and ironic way in which to dispose of him, or was it one of its Communist counterparts?

His suspicion was that it was Isaac Ninn who'd done this. That wherever he was, whatever had become of him, he'd not forgotten the debt that Dr. Leo Heisler owed to Dr. Colin Thomas.

It was unfortunate that he'd not found a cure for the disease they'd created, but he was not anywhere as resentful or furious as he had thought he would be. There seemed to be something entirely appropriate about coming to the conclusion of a life this way.

He telephoned his servants, instructing them not to come by for the next few days; he didn't want people worrying about him and urging him to go to the hospital. No one knew better than he that a hospital was not going to do him any good. He thought of telephoning his lawyer and arranging the formalities to put his life in order. But his life was one of such disorder that he had nothing to gain by attempting to straighten it out with thirty-six hours left to it.

He did try to telephone Carol, though he had no idea what he was going to say. But the number, not unexpectedly, was no longer in service; she'd probably left the island. Well, she was good, she knew what she was doing, he considered. Not once had he ever suspected her.

Twenty-four hours after she'd first walked through his door, he began to experience chills and a burning fever. Though the temperature was in the seventies, he found he could not stay warm. Nonetheless, he refused to take to bed; instead he sat out on the terrace, bundled up in blankets, with a drink in his hand.

He had to drink constantly; his throat was painfully dry all the time. In some part of his mind he was still the scientist, still the physician, dispassionately observing the progression of symptoms in one of his patients. The liver failure had already begun, he was sure, and it should not be too long before the massive hemorrhaging would occur too.

It would be a matter of hours, he knew, before he'd

lapse into a coma; the pain would be worse than ever, but at least he wouldn't be conscious enough to register it.

The Gulf of Mexico was turning a beautiful shade of lavender as the horizon colored with a final burst of sunlight. Through the bushes he could spy elderly couples slowly making their way up the beach in search of seashells just as he was wont to do at this hour of the day if he felt up to it.

His vision was going, which was perhaps the most annoying part, because among the elderly couples there was one person who caught his attention in particular. A woman, and one not so old as all that.

He lifted himself up and leaned over the balcony to get a better look.

The woman had come abreast of his house, and although it was a considerable distance from the beach, she would still have something of a view of it. She'd stopped and was looking in his direction, though whether she could actually see him or not, he couldn't tell.

He had a pair of binonculars, but even if he had had the energy to go in and get them, he wouldn't have. She might be gone by the time he returned. He preferred staying where he was.

It must be Helen. There was something about her stance, the way she stood with her arms akimbo, looking lovely in a white dress that billowed with the wind coming up off the gulf.

It must be Helen come to say good-bye. Maybe it wasn't Ninn at all, but Helen who'd been the instrument of his death. She'd been with him last night. That another woman had had to substitute for her so that he wouldn't catch on to the deception was irrelevant. In a curious way it pleased him to know that things had worked out like this.

When he looked back on the events that had followed upon his plagiarizing Helen's thesis, the one thing he could never understand was why Helen had remained so loyal to him. He might have threatened her with the loss of work, to be sure. But she knew he was bluffing, and yet she never left him. She seemed to believe in him the way someone terminally ill will believe in God. He was somehow necessary for her, the catalyst that made her life work. She needed to hate him.

Well, now she was free.

He thought none the worse of her for what she'd done. On the contrary, he was quite proud of her. She was his star pupil; more than that, his disciple.

Propping himself up against the railing, he waved to her, and he was almost sure she waved back.

And then she turned away and began walking toward the other end of the beach.

His regret was that with his failing vision he would never know for certain that it was Helen. But it pleased him to believe that it was.

The night wore on and the sky had become a theater for thousands of stars, some of which refused to stay in place, but fell all of a sudden in great sweeping arcs into the sea. Heisler hadn't the strength to return inside for more of his iced tea, and so he had to content himself with sucking on what few diminishing chunks of ice remained in the bottom of his glass.

To his surprise, he was still conscious at dawn. But he was very tired and in a great deal of pain. He knew that all he had to do was close his eyes and it would all be gone. But instead he forced himself to watch the sun come into the sky. He half-hoped that Helen, if Helen it was, would be back. He realized he was waiting for her.

But she didn't come. And the sun rose higher. And after a while it made no further sense to wait.

49

WHEN MATTHEW BARRETT WOKE, it was with the extraordinary feeling that he had just come from another world. That world, full of dark forebodings and unexpected violence, seemed so far removed from this one, where each object his eyes rested on glowed with the sun striking it, that he was unsure whether that previous world had ever existed. He would not have been surprised to learn that he'd dreamed up the whole thing.

But if he were uncertain as to the reality of the past—the past that he retained in his memory, at any rate—he was equally perplexed regarding the world into which he'd emerged. It was undoubtedly a hospital room, although from the pervasive scent of flowers surrounding him, he'd opened his eyes expecting to find himself in a garden.

An I.V. pole loomed above his bed; from a bottle attached to it a solution was dripping down into his outstretched arm. He did not immediately know what was the matter with him, why he was in a hospital, but with his free hand he explored his body to see if everything was still there. It was with enormous relief that he found he was intact.

He sat up in bed and blinked at the sun streaming in through the window directly across the room from him. He could see sky, the tips of some trees, very little else. Nothing, in any event, which could tell him where in the world he was.

He decided to use the buzzer at his bedside to summon the nurse, summon somebody anyhow, in hope of enlightenment.

A nurse did appear after a while, a matronly woman in a crisp white uniform, who took one look at him, let out a gasp, and mumbled something so quickly under her breath that he couldn't for the life of him comprehend her.

Then she turned around and ran from the room. He wondered how he'd managed to disconcert her so much. In another minute she was back, this time with a physician, a man in his mid-fifties with heavy pouches under his eyes. He stepped up to Barrett's bed, reaching for his wrist to check his pulse, as if the evidence provided by his own eyes was not nearly enough to confirm the fact that he was alive, at least conscious.

Releasing his wrist, he nodded, but still refrained from speaking.

"Where am I?" Barrett asked.

"London," the doctor replied. "Can you tell me your name?"

Barrett could. He even could state his occupation without any trouble.

"And where do you live, Dr. Barrett?"

Barrett gave him the address.

He proceeded to respond to all of the doctor's questions satisfactorily—up until he was asked about how he'd come to be in London. That part escaped him. He racked his mind, but he could remember only so far as driving madly on the Brooklyn–Queens Expressway to get to Kennedy Airport. Then it all was a blank.

"Have you any idea what day it is, Dr. Barrett?"

It was the sort of question he would've assumed he knew the answer to, so long as it wasn't asked, but now that it was, he realized that he had no idea whatsoever. He again stared out the window, thinking that maybe the shade of the sky or the foliage on the treetops would give him a clue.

It was late in February when he was on his way to Kennedy, the nineteenth or twentieth, he thought, so he presumed that it would be safe to hazard a guess that it was around the twenty-second.

"I'm afraid you're a bit off," the doctor said after exchanging a knowing glance with the nurse. "It is now the fourteenth of April."

"The fourteenth of what?"

Almost two months had vanished and he couldn't conceive how it could have happened.

The doctor repeated the date for him, saying, "You suffered a traumatic wound to the head. You were struck by a bullet that penetrated a couple of centimeters into your skull, just above the hairline."

Barrett reached up and felt the dressing. A traumatic head wound, he thought; it was a wonder he had any memory at all.

How he'd sustained this wound, he supposed, would be a very interesting tale.

"We removed the bullet," the doctor continued, "but we had no way of determining how extensive the damage was. It may still be some time before we find out. However, you are clearly in possession of your faculties, which is indeed fortunate. For that matter, we weren't even certain you would come out of your coma."

Barrett was half-listening. He was still trying to fathom the implications of losing so much time and so much memory. "These flowers," he said. "Who sent them all?"

"Friends, colleagues, but most of them come from a Miss Kris Erlanger."

So, he thought, something wasn't lost in all that time. He hadn't forgotten her, nor had he forgotten that he loved her. He closed his eyes, breathed in very deeply, and was back in the garden again.

*   *   *

Four days later she arrived in London to be with him. She phoned from the airport that she would be at the hospital in two hours' time. Barrett was in therapy and so a nurse took the message for him.

She reached the hospital earlier than she'd expected and failed to find him in his room. A nurse advised her that he was given to exercising in the hallways.

Her search took her no longer than a couple of minutes. She spotted him at the other end of the corridor, making his way along on crutches.

The bullet hadn't impaired his mental state, but it had done some injury to his motor functions.

He didn't see her at first, and when he did, he smiled apologetically and said, "I'm learning to walk again. They say eventually I'll graduate to a cane."

She stepped up to him, and throwing her arms about him, gave him a kiss which practically unbalanced him, propped up as he was by the crutches. His physical unbalance, however, was nothing compared to his emotional unbalance.

"You look lovely," he said, "and different somehow."

And she did. Her hair had been permed and it fell now in artless curls, and it was slightly lighter too, honey-colored. Her pink blouse emphasized the color in her face. It was heartening, and not just a little surprising, to see her when she didn't look tired and drawn. Before, her beauty had had a vulnerability to it, but now it was more defined, with no need to apologize for itself. He suspected that something had happened in the eight weeks he'd been in the hospital.

She walked him back to his room, with one arm supporting him. "You get a lot of sunlight," she observed.

"I get a lot of flowers, too."

"I thought that even if no one could communicate with you, even if you couldn't hear my words or read my letters, at least maybe you could smell these flowers somewhere in your mind. I hoped the scent would reach you and that you'd know they were from me."

There was moisture in her eyes and it moved him enough so that he felt he might soon break down himself.

She brightened, suddenly reaching down into her bag. "Hey, you have to take a look at this, Matthew."

She held out to him two copies of *America Now*, one dated April 8, the second dated the ninth.

"Front page—what do you think of that?"

"Byline in bold Roman type, too," he noted.

"You can read it later. I just wanted to show it to you."

But he'd already begun, and he couldn't stop. As he read, certain details triggered off memories so dim that it would probably be months before they rose to the surface. There was a great deal, he concluded, that he would just as soon forget.

"There are fewer and fewer cases now," Kris said. "Though it seems what's happening is that while Heisler's Disease is subsiding in America, it's becoming more common here and in Western Europe."

"So they never found all the carriers?"

She pointed to the papers he held in his lap. "It says right there. I figured there must be at least a dozen carriers still unidentified, maybe a great many more. I suspect that a number of the girls thought to have been killed in the Inverness fire got away."

"Fire? What fire?"

She was about to tell him, then stopped herself. "I'll explain it all later."

Later? he wondered. Later today? Later a month from now?

"How long will you be able to stay, Kris?"

His doctors had informed him that at least another month of hospitalization would be required, followed by several additional months convalescing at home. A long time to be away from medicine. Maybe he wouldn't go back to it. Maybe he'd take that around-the-world trip he'd always promised himself.

"Oh, I don't know. I'm covering a story for *America Now*, in London, so I should think you'll see me around for a while."

"A big story, I imagine—now that you've achieved a measure of notoriety." His eyes again rested on the headline articles she'd written.

"Oh, it's big, all right. A new spy scandal involving cabinet ministers, East German agents, someone who sits in the House of Lords, and a magnate who dabbles in North Sea oil. Very juicy, very English. My friend Harry Quint's lining up all the people I have to talk to."

Quint? He didn't recognize the name, but he was growing tired and had no inclination to pursue the matter at the moment. He supposed in time he'd find out. "Sounds impressive. You've come a long way from home-decorating hints."

"Did you ever doubt that I would?"

"Not for a minute."

Her smile was a bit too enigmatic for his liking, but he knew better than to inquire what lay behind it.

She was sitting perched on the edge of the bed; there was a distance of five or six feet separating them. With so much to say, for an instant they found themselves out of words.

At last Barrett said, "It seems I have a lot of catching up to do."

And she, taking his hands in hers, maintaining the same enigmatic smile that could have spoken worlds to him if he could've interpreted it correctly, replied, "You do indeed, my darling, but between you and me, I'm sure you'll do just fine."

He believed he would at that.

CODA

IT IS PERHAPS AN APOCRYPHAL STORY and the fact that it is reputed to have originated in so many cities—Rome, Paris, Amsterdam, Copenhagan, Cannes, and Berlin, among others—makes it suspect right away. Yet the story exerts a certain fascination and it is the kind of story that a great many people like to believe because it confirms in their minds their judgment that the very wealthy are also hopelessly decadent. More to the point, they have so much money that they are bored, in need of excitement that even a dangerous sport like skydiving or racing cars cannot satisfy.

If the story does have anything to it, it is likely that it has its origins in Berlin. Berlin, divided down the middle by the wall, like a wound that will never heal, is a city so full of desperation, so claustrophobic, that the pursuit of pleasure has been elevated to an art form. Tour guides are fond of pointing out that if you were to take in just one bar every night, it would require fifteen years before you would get to the last one—and that is just in the west of the city. In the east, another eight years would be necessary.

If it is true that Berlin is the source of this strange story, then it is a reasonable assumption that it can be traced to the bars and clubs in the Kurfürstendamm district. It is even said that bartenders there, for a small sum, will tell you where to find the place, although knowing its address is not the same as gaining admission. That cannot be done without having a considerable amount of money at your disposal. And even money alone will not be enough; you must be recommended by a member if you are to have a hope of entering.

The story holds that it is situated in a run-down-looking building, away from the lights, and that there is nothing about it to suggest that an elegant club exists within.

Members are scrupulously checked and there is a constant fear of police, although this fear may be groundless, since no one would operate a club like this one without making certain the police were paid off.

There is some dispute as to how many members there are, but that they are rich and in many instances titled is something about which there is no dispute. No woman can expect to be admitted; this is not a club where a woman would be comfortable. In fact, it is a club where men come to escape their wives and mistresses.

For most of the evening there is little that would evoke the interest of an outsider; there are card games, chess matches, quiet conversations, reflective and solitary drinking too, if a member wishes to be by himself. The music is always subdued and always pre-twentieth-century; like the interior decoration, the music is designed to recall an earlier era and to maintain the illusion that time has barely nudged forward since 1899.

If there is any tension at all, it is low-key, simmering just below the surface, where only the most sensitive observer could register it.

Precisely at a quarter past eleven the members are alerted by a servant that the time has come to gather in a room that is used for one purpose only. Putting aside whatever they have been engaged in up until this hour, they retire into the elegantly appointed room.

In a ritual lasting no longer than ten minutes, the members are asked to choose lots. The winner is congratulated and led to a chair covered with velvet; it is a chair that a prince would not be embarrassed to occupy.

Then from behind a curtain the women are produced, no fewer than four, no more than six. They have in common only one thing, and that is they are all remarkably beautiful. Otherwise they differ in virtually every respect: they may be Negro or Chinese, redheaded or blond, they may be short or tower well over six feet. From night to night they change. You could come here a hundred nights running and never see the same woman twice. So it is said.

The winner can scrutinize the offering before him for however long he cares to, so long as he eventually selects a woman to take home with him. It is not acceptable behavior for a member to suddenly have second thoughts. That would be a breach of honor and would result in immediate dismissal from the club. Other penalties might also ensue.

It is known in advance that one of the women standing silently before the winner is infected and that to take pleasure with her is to invite certain death. The odds favor the winner, of course, but there are inevitably those who make the wrong choice. Nonetheless, for those who regard Russian roulette as a frivolous pastime that can only result in a stupid death, this form of entertainment has much in their eyes to recommend it.

The hollow click of a revolver can hardly compare to the moment of orgasm which may turn out to be the moment of death.

It is a game that the members of the club, rich and jaded as they may be, never seem to tire of.

The man who maintains this club is said to be tall and angular, with a face that looks somehow misshapen, the way it would be if a sculptor had worked and reworked it, never managing to get it exactly the way he wanted it, and finally, in despair, abandoning it. He has eyes that disclose no feeling whatsoever; to look into them is to see nothing.

The man calls himself Nathan. Whether that is his first or last name is not known. When he walks, it is with a stoop, and there are times when he will cry out as if he's been seized by sudden pain.

He speaks seldom and makes no secret of his contempt for people, even those who regard themselves as his friends.

Night after night he watches the women who come from behind the curtain and exhibit themselves to the winner. Night after night he watches as the winners go home with their choice, never knowing in advance whether they have made a fatal one or not. But there is not the slightest hint in his face as to what he is thinking. He prefers to believe that he is acting no differently from God, maintaining an unshakable silence and letting fate take its course.

ABOUT THE AUTHORS

Leslie Alan Horvitz, a graduate of Brown University and former editor with Fawcett Books, is also the author of THE JERUSALEM CONSPIRACY, THE COMPTON EFFECT, and THE DONORS. He is currently a freelance writer and lives in Manhattan.

H. Harris Gerhard, M.D., is the pseudonym for a New England physician. A graduate of an Ivy League medical school, he did his residency at a New York City hospital. He has contributed to numerous scientific publications and is the co-author of THE COMPTON EFFECT and THE DONORS.

More Bestsellers from SIGNET

More Bestsellers From SIGNET

**Buy them at your local
bookstore or use coupon
on next page for ordering.**

The Best in Fiction from SIGNET